DEATH'S CHARM

ALSO BY THIS AUTHOR

<u>Kenzie Kirsch Medical Thrillers</u>

Unlawful Harvest

Doctored Death

Dosed to Death

Gentle Angel

Rushin' Death

Posed for Death

Death of a Corpse

Endowed with Death

Shattered to Death

Captured in Death

Currying Death

Healed to Death

Death’s Charm

<u>Zachary Goldman Mysteries</u>

Private Investigator

She Wore Mourning

His Hands Were Quiet

She Was Dying Anyway

He Was Walking Alone

They Thought He was Safe

He Was Not There

Her Work Was Everything

She Told a Lie

He Never Forgot

She Was At Risk

He Drowned in Memory

Their Walls Were Empty

They Came for Him

They Sought Vengeance

She Was Their Target

His Fear Was Real

She Was Out of Reach

He Was Deceived

She Once Vanished

AND MORE AT PDWORKMAN.COM

DEATH'S CHARM

A KENZIE KIRSCH MEDICAL THRILLER #13

P.D. Workman

ISBN: 9781774688076 (KDP Paperback)
ISBN: 9781774688083 (KDP Hardcover)
ISBN: 9781774688106 (Lulu Paperback)
ISBN: 9781774688090 (Large Print)
ISBN: 9781774688113 (Digital)
ISBN: 9781774688120 (Auto-narrated audiobook)

To those who refuse

to give up the fight

CHAPTER 1

Kenzie was starting to yawn, a sign she had been up for long enough and it was time to head to bed. She and Zachary had been watching an Unsolved Mysteries marathon, challenging themselves to come up with clues, investigative paths, and possible solutions to the various crimes. They skipped over the ones about UFOs, psychic events, or other paranormal mysteries, sticking to the ones about missing persons, murders, finding long-lost relatives, or exploring family history.

But Kenzie was beat. She was past the age when she could party all night long, or even wanted to. After midnight, she was ready to turn off the TV, put their dishes in the dishwasher, and brush her teeth. Her bed was calling.

Zachary noticed her smothering a yawn and raised his brows knowingly. “Last episode?” he suggested.

Kenzie nodded. “Yeah. Sorry about that. I’d love to watch more, but... my body has other ideas.”

Zachary rubbed his thick five o’clock shadow, bristles rasping. “We’d better solve this one, then; wouldn’t want to go to bed on a failure.”

“Well...” Kenzie covered another yawn. “Since the entire Cincinnati police force was not able to solve it in ten years, I think we can be forgiven for not being able to solve it based on a ten-minute summary and reenactment.”

“So, you don’t think that it was—”

Kenzie’s phone began to ring.

Not just the regular ringtone, but the loud, klaxon blare assigned to the police dispatcher that was designed to wake her from even the deepest sleep. Both of them jumped at the sudden loud alarm.

That meant there was a body to deal with, and Kenzie would not be going to sleep for a couple more hours. She rubbed her eyes and sighed before picking up the phone to get the details.

Zachary waited until she was back off the phone before asking, “You want to watch the end of this one before leaving?”

There were another two or three minutes left, and staying that much longer wouldn’t make any difference to either the police or the woman who had been killed, but Kenzie’s attention was no longer on it.

“You can watch the end of it, or we can rewatch it tomorrow. I’m going to head out.”

Zachary hit the stop button. “No problem. Do you want me to drive you?”

“No. I’ll see you later.”

"You're not too tired to drive?" he persisted.

She had been yawning, so Zachary could be forgiven for pressing the point. Kenzie shook her head, her dark curls bouncing around her face. "No. That alarm got the adrenaline pumping. I couldn't go to sleep now if I wanted to. It's only five minutes away. I won't have time to get drowsy."

He nodded slowly. "Okay. I'll see you when you get back."

She didn't bother telling him to go to sleep without her. He would wait up no matter what she said. And he slept little enough that waiting for her wouldn't make any difference to his schedule. He would watch TV or putter away at a case on his computer until she returned.

Kenzie hated changing out of her comfortable jammies into day clothes, but she wasn't going to show up at an accident scene looking like she'd just rolled out of bed. She changed into a business-professional outfit, reapplied her bright red lipstick, and grabbed her purse. Her small scene-of-crime kit was already in the car, and it didn't sound like she would need anything more specialized for the scene she was going to.

* * *

The accident scene was only a couple of blocks from the police building, which happened to house the medical examiner's office in the basement. They wouldn't have far to transport the body. With a gurney, Kenzie could easily have walked the body to the morgue.

It was a spectacular wreck. Kenzie's stomach clenched when she saw it. She had been at enough accident scenes before that it shouldn't bother her, but the sight of the smashed, upside-down vehicle still affected her.

"Dr. Kirsch." The young cop in charge of the scene probably recognized Kenzie by her red convertible and he didn't require her to show her badge. "Looks like she managed to hit the center median at a pretty good velocity. It acted as a ramp, launching and spinning the car so that it landed on its roof." He indicated both the place that it had hit the barrier, leaving bits of metal and glass behind, and then the car itself, which Kenzie didn't need pointed out.

"Okay, thanks. Paramedics have examined her?" There was an ambulance standing by, red lights flashing. One of the paramedics was in the driver's seat, and the other was leaning against it, smoking. Obviously, there was nothing for them to do; they were just waiting for Kenzie to officially declare the death and send them on their way.

"Yeah. Head injury from being thrown around. Maybe a broken neck. There wasn't anything they could do for her when they got here."

Kenzie signed her name to the log, put on booties and gloves, and walked over to the lone car, upside down like a ladybug in the middle of the street. The streetlights reflected eerily off the road. Firetrucks stood by. There was no smell of gasoline, but the car was pretty wrecked, and they were probably waiting to cut the door free so that the victim could be removed. As it was, Kenzie had access through the shattered driver's side window. She reached in and touched the woman's throat, probing for a pulse.

As expected, there was none. The body was still warm. Not an hour had elapsed since the driver had been speeding down the street toward her doom. Kenzie didn't smell any alcohol, which surprised her. An accident like this was usually the result of drinking and driving.

Kenzie withdrew her hand and surveyed the rest of the vehicle, looking at the damage to the body, the deflated airbag, and the unfortunate woman with a mask of blood.

Kenzie's first reaction to the accident was visceral, a flashback to the accident she and Zachary had been in after their first date. While the cops had initially speculated that it was the result of drunk driving, Zachary had not had anything to drink that night, and rarely did due to possible interactions with his medications. He didn't take his antianxiety prescription or sleep aids every night, but knew that he couldn't combine either of them with alcohol, so he rarely drank in case he would need to take one of them later.

Rather than being the result of drinking and driving, that accident had been caused by someone tampering with Zachary's car. It, too, had landed upside down. Kenzie's memories of getting her seatbelt undone, extricating herself from the wreck, calling for help, and trying to comfort Zachary, who was in and out of consciousness, were astonishingly clear. It had taken a long time, in very cold weather, for the police and firefighters to arrive and cut Zachary free. His injuries had been much more severe than Kenzie's. She had some scrapes and bruises that had been sore for a few weeks, but he'd had a spinal injury and concussion that had made for a couple of scary days before it became clear that the spinal cord had only been bruised and not permanently damaged.

"Everything okay?" the young cop, hovering behind Kenzie asked.

She turned and looked at him, pulling herself away from the flashback and focusing on the present. She looked at his name bar to remind herself who he was. Though she had seen him around the police station or parking garage, they had not worked together. Daniels.

Even while dealing with her emotional reaction to the crash and the memories that forced themselves into her consciousness, she also maintained a sense of the dispassionate, clinical distance that was required to analyze the scene and the woman's body and to start to build a picture of the mechanics of her death.

The victim was a tall, thin, white woman with dark hair pulled back in a bun. She wore a dress and simple jewelry and had probably been out on a date or at an event.

“Yes. Everything is fine. Do you have an ID on the victim? She looks familiar.”

One of the problems with living in a small town was that Kenzie sometimes did know the victims who ended up on her table. She was sure, looking at the limp, bloody figure hanging upside down in the car that she knew this woman. They had met previously, though Kenzie wasn’t sure where. It was sometimes difficult to recognize people in death; faces obscured by blood, facial bones broken, with no animation. She sometimes had to work at it to find the similarities to the person she had known in life or was trying to identify from a picture.

“License plate is registered to a Mariya Markov. Haven’t been able to verify she is the victim, but the picture on her driver’s license looks close enough.”

Mariya Markov.

Kenzie knew the name immediately. They had met more than once at fundraising events for the Kirsch family foundation. Kenzie had attended several galas at the behest of her mother, Lisa Cole Kirsch, and Dr. Markov had been an honored guest.

"Dr. Mariya Markov," Kenzie told Daniels. "She is a preeminent nephrologist." She shook her head. Her mother would be shocked to hear of Dr. Markov's passing.

"A kidney doctor?" Daniels asked tentatively.

Kenzie nodded. "Yes, exactly. She was a great surgeon and researcher, at the forefront of kidney disease research and transplants."

Daniels nodded gravely. "I'm sorry to hear that." He looked over the wreck with fresh eyes, considering. "What do you think it was? Asleep at the wheel?"

That seemed more likely than drinking and driving. Dr. Markov might have been tired after putting in an eighteen-hour day or performing an eight-hour surgery.

“Could be,” she admitted. “We’ll have to see what the accident reconstruction guys and the autopsy show.” She sighed. “This is a great loss to the community.”

CHAPTER 2

Dr. Markov's body was transported to the morgue as soon as it was freed from the vehicle, but Kenzie did not start on the autopsy that night. There was no need to rush into it, and when she had already put in a full day of work, she didn't want to take the chance of making any mistakes due to fatigue. She would do the postmortem when she was fresh and could be sure not to miss anything.

Kenzie arrived at the office an hour later than usual, having intentionally slept in to try to make up for her late night. But it had taken her a while to get settled down for sleep once she was home, and then she had slept fitfully, her mind working away, analyzing the details she already knew about Dr. Markov's accident.

Eventually, there hadn't been any point in trying to sleep any longer. Kenzie would feel more tired from struggling to sleep and dealing with her thoughts, instead of feeling more rested.

She had a couple of cups of coffee to get her motor running and headed in to the office.

Because she was late, Dr. Wiltshire was there ahead of her. Unlike Dr. Cook, who had substituted while Dr. Wiltshire was healing from a broken hand, Dr. Wiltshire usually arrived after Kenzie, allowing her time to get things organized and the morning emails and reports processed before he came in. Dr. Cook had always been there disconcertingly early, making Kenzie feel like she was running behind when she wasn't.

"Morning, Kenzie," Dr. Wiltshire greeted, smiling pleasantly. "How are you doing this lovely morning?"

Kenzie thought back to the weather as she had driven in. It had been a bright, clear, warm day, but she hadn't even noticed it. Her mind had been far away.

"Good," Kenzie told him. "Took a little extra time for sleep this morning, so I'm ready to go."

"Excellent. I'll let you get yourself together, and when you are ready for the autopsy, just let me know."

"Thanks." Kenzie sniffed the air. "You got coffee going?"

"I did remember how to start the machine," he said wryly.

"See, you're polishing up your skills already," Kenzie told him.

Dr. Wiltshire had been doing physiotherapy to rehab his broken hand, but he figured nothing would help him regain his dexterity as quickly as getting back to work.

And the good thing about working on dead patients was that it wasn't nearly as much of a problem if you accidentally nicked an artery during a procedure.

Dr. Wiltshire smiled and shook his head. "I'll be at my desk if you happen to need me for any other complex tasks."

* * *

After processing the daily influx of emails, interoffice mail, and packages she had received, Kenzie finished the last of her coffee and let Dr. Wiltshire know that she was ready to begin the postmortem.

"Did you know Dr. Markov?" Kenzie asked as she gowned up and made the final preparations to begin the postmortem on the body waiting for her.

Dr. Wiltshire shook his head. "We have probably met at some point, but not that I remember. We ran in different circles. She must have been in town for a function, since she operates out of Burlington."

"Yeah, that's what I figured too. I don't remember hearing about anything going on last night, and I usually do if it is related to kidney disease, but there must have been some reason for her to be in Roxboro."

Once they were ready to start, Kenzie tapped the button on the floor to begin recording, then tapped it again to stop and looked at Dr. Wiltshire.

“Sorry, I’m just jumping right in here. You are the senior doctor; you will want to run things.”

He dismissed the idea with a wave.

“Not necessary,” he told her. “Go ahead. I’ll let you run the first few until I’m sure that these old fingers are going to perform the way they are supposed to. If I need a break partway through, it’s better if you are dictating, rather than having to switch partway through.”

“You’re sure? I can take a break anytime you want to, to maintain continuity.”

“Just go ahead, Dr. Kirsch. I’ll run the next one if I feel up to it.”

Kenzie nodded, sure that it was what Dr. Wiltshire wanted and she wasn't stepping on his toes. She tapped the record button again, dictated the date, file number, patient name, and her and Dr. Wiltshire's names. They began with the gross examination of the body, as always.

George had taken swabs of the skin for any trace evidence, being sure to get samples of blood or other bodily fluids or contaminants before washing the body in preparation for the postmortem.

Kenzie noticed again the deformity in Markov's face from broken eye sockets and nose. There was a laceration down the side of her head from where it had hit the window or frame of the car during the rollover. Given that Markov was unresponsive when the first report came in and deceased upon the arrival of first responders, Kenzie would not be surprised to find some severe damage to the neck and spine. Markov had not had time to bleed out, especially not from that head lac, and there were no impalement, amputation, or other serious tissue injuries.

Kenzie dictated the injuries she could see for the recording, taking pictures of each. They would do full X-rays of the head, neck, and torso to see what other fractures had been caused by the accident or the airbag.

“This is odd,” Kenzie said, examining the bruising around Markov’s shoulders and upper arms. “Perimortem bruising. It had a chance to set in before she expired, so it was not from injuries sustained in the accident.”

Dr. Wiltshire leaned in to examine the bruising more closely, then brought the magnifying lens in for further examination. He nodded. “There is inflammation, which would not be the case if it was sustained during the accident. And the location of the bruises is not consistent with a seatbelt or airbag injury.”

“They look like restraint bruises.”

As if someone had been holding her still. Both by grasping her upper arms and by holding or pushing against her shoulders.

“We should check for any other indications of assault.”

Dr. Wiltshire agreed.

There were no other unexpected bruises or injuries apparent on the external examination. Rather than putting on a lead shield, Dr. Wiltshire left the room while Kenzie took a series of X-rays. He returned, and they reviewed the various fractures apparent on the monitors.

“Ribs and wrists from the airbag as well as the nose and orbits,” Dr. Wiltshire observed. “That is all to be expected.”

“And here,” Kenzie pointed to the vertebrae in the neck. “There is damage to the C4 and C5 from the rollover. She must have been going pretty fast. The competing forces from the rollover resulted in cervical spine fracture.”

Dr. Wiltshire agreed. He used the mouse to mark each of the breaks on the X-rays, and they looked for any other fractures that might have occurred during the accident or concurrent with the perimortem bruising. Everything seemed to be straightforward, with no other unexpected injuries.

CHAPTER 3

"Hello, doctors."

Kenzie looked up from her work to the observation room. A black-haired, broad-shouldered cop stood there, his hand on the mic switch so he could speak to them.

"Detective Edwards," she greeted.

"Is this the Markov woman?"

Dr. Wiltshire gave Edwards a stern look. "The Markov woman?"

Edwards cleared his throat. "Er, sorry. Is this Mariya Markov?"

"Yes, it is."

"Anything unexpected so far?"

"A minor point or two," Dr. Wiltshire said cautiously. "We are not finished."

"No, I can see that. Everything consistent with being killed on impact in a motor vehicle accident?"

"Yes. Miss Markov has catastrophic injuries consistent with a high-speed motor vehicle accident, especially a rollover."

Edwards nodded, his shoulders relaxing. "We've pulled some surveillance video taken a few minutes before the accident, which shows her driving very erratically."

Kenzie was surprised and not surprised at the same time. It was not unexpected to hear that the victim of a high-speed motor vehicle accident had been driving erratically before the crash. That was generally the cause of such an accident. But on the other hand, there had been no smell of alcohol from the body, and she could not remember Mariya Markov drinking excessively at any of the functions she had been at. On the contrary, it was unusual to see her drinking at all. If she had a wine glass in her hand at all, it was probably as a social prop. Kenzie didn't think she'd ever actually seen Markov take a sip.

"Define erratically," Dr. Wiltshire encouraged.

Edwards considered. "She was driving at a high rate of speed and unable to stay in one lane. She blew a red light, but luckily, she was the only one going through the intersection at that time of night. I would have pulled her over for impaired driving."

Dr. Wiltshire nodded. "Thank you. We will be sure to run a toxicology panel to see whether she was under the influence of any substance. However, other things can cause erratic driving, as well. Heart attack, stroke, seizure, fever, mental distress, even a mechanical malfunction. It is a starting place rather than conclusive of any one particular cause."

"Yes, I suppose," Edwards agreed. "Though in my experience, when someone is driving like that, it is alcohol rather than a heart attack. Heart attack victims slow down."

Dr. Wiltshire shrugged. “We will keep it in mind,” he agreed. “As I said, we will be sure to do a toxicology panel to check for alcohol and recreational drugs.”

“Seems like a pretty straightforward case,” Edwards posited.

“I suspect so,” Dr. Wiltshire agreed. “Someone who is found dead in the driver’s seat of a crashed vehicle is usually the victim of a motor vehicle accident. Now, whether that person was under the influence of alcohol or had an aneurysm, we don’t know. So we must do our best to find out.”

“Sounds good, doc,” Edwards agreed. He flexed his broad shoulders under the restricting suit. “I look forward to hearing from you.”

“I will let you know of anything unusual and the results of the toxicology screen. It may take a few days.”

Edwards nodded. “Always does,” he agreed.

Dr. Wiltshire watched him walk back out of the observation room. Kenzie went back to the autopsy.

CHAPTER 4

It was clear that Dr. Wiltshire had been away from the autopsy table for a while and did not have his full dexterity back. But he did an adequate job and would only improve from there. Kenzie was glad that he had returned and was on the mend. With the extent of the damage to his hand, she had been worried that he would be forced to retire and she would not be working with him any longer. It was reassuring to know that he could still perform the necessary work, even if his fingers weren't quite as nimble as they had once been.

It was also clear that he was more tired after the postmortem than he would ordinarily be. Kenzie imagined that it had taken a lot more mental energy for him to perform the previously routine tasks, causing him to fatigue more quickly. He had hinted at that when he had said he might need a break.

"You go ahead and relax and check yesterday's reports," Kenzie told him. "I'll clean up in here and check the personal effects."

Dr. Wiltshire didn't protest, but nodded and returned to his office without argument, leaving Kenzie in autopsy to finish with the body, make sure that all of the fluid and tissue samples were properly labeled for the follow-up lab work, and to go through Mariya Markov's personal effects.

Markov had worn a sleek black dress to whatever function she had attended the night before. The evenings were still chilly, so she had wrapped up in a medium-weight long coat before heading home or to whatever hotel she was staying at. The fawn-colored jacket was finely woven, and Kenzie could tell it was high quality before seeing the label. Markov had worn black stilettos and lacy black underwear. Kenzie examined each item closely, photographed it, and rebagged and labeled it. Nothing seemed out of place. No smell of alcohol or vomit. Just the blood on her collars and down into her bra. Kenzie marked the panties for DNA sampling. Though there had been no sign of sexual trauma on the body, the restraint bruises prompted an abundance of caution.

Markov had worn a locket around her neck, an attractive silver watch, and a couple of understated rings. Nothing on the fourth finger of her left hand. No husband or fiancé, if she were to judge from those indicators.

The police had recovered Markov's small clutch purse, which included a minimalist wallet, her phone, and a few other sundries a woman would not be caught without. There was no hotel key, so presumably, Dr. Markov had planned to return home after the event.

* * *

Kenzie was happy to be home at the end of the day. She had not worked as late as she usually did. Not after being short of sleep the night before. Instead, she was out of the office as soon as it hit five o'clock. In a few minutes, she was parking her "baby," a cherry red convertible, in the garage and letting herself into the kitchen.

"Hey, you're home," Zachary observed from the living room where he had been hunched over his computer. Not too immersed in whatever he was working on to notice her presence. "How are you feeling?"

"Sweaty and tired." Like she usually did after a postmortem. Even though she had performed the Markov autopsy early in the day, she needed to wash the sweat and grit of the day from her body before she could be able to relax for the evening.

"Why don't you go shower," Zachary suggested, as she knew he would. "Do you want me to order in? Maybe some Thai?"

"Thai would be okay. Or if you're up for spicy, how about Mexican? We still haven't ordered from that place I was telling you about."

"Uhh..." Zachary hesitated at first, then nodded. "Sure, that sounds good. I like Mexican."

She knew he liked fast-food Mexican, but she wasn't sure how he would feel about the fiery fare at authentic Mama Rosa's. She would soon find out.

"Okay, I'd love to order from there, if you think you can stand it."

"You have the number? You said it was off the beaten path, so I'm not sure if an internet search will find it."

"Yeah, I do." Kenzie pulled out her phone and looked it up for him. "Order whatever you like. I'm sure it is all good."

"Do they have Mexican fries?"

She glared at him. "Mexican fries are not authentic."

He cracked a smile, and she knew he had just been teasing. She gave him a dramatic scowl.

"If I come out here after my shower and find that you've ordered fast food Mexican instead of Mama Rosa's..."

Zachary chuckled. "Not unless I have a death wish. Got it. I'll order from Mama Rosa's. It doesn't matter if it's... chicken feet. You will get your authentic Mexican dinner."

* * *

One of the things Kenzie liked about Zachary was his interest in forensics. They could talk about autopsies over dinner, even look at photos, and it didn't faze him a bit. He quite enjoyed hearing the ins and outs of her latest cases, especially if there were something new or intriguing to learn.

"You did the postmortem for the callout last night?" Zachary asked as they sat down at the table and sorted out the dishes he had ordered. The hearty smell of meat, tomatoes, spices, and garlic filled the air and made Kenzie's stomach rumble.

Kenzie nodded. "Yes. Nothing too interesting, I'm afraid. Single vehicle accident. Detective Edwards thinks that she was impaired based on traffic cam video of her driving erratically a couple of minutes before the accident. We'll have to see what the tox screen says when it comes back."

"You think it could have been something else?"

"We suspend judgment until we see what the tests show. Unless there is evidence on the body to indicate otherwise. If you've got a body with the smell of alcohol pouring off of it, then there is a good chance they were drinking before they died. But Dr. Markov did not smell like she had been drinking."

Kenzie picked up a taco and bit into it. Juices ran down her face and she grabbed one of the plentiful napkins to mop it up before it could drip onto her clothes. An explosion of flavor filled her mouth. It was every bit as good as she remembered. Zachary took the first cautious bite of his own. He smiled and chewed.

“Oh, this is really good. It is spicy, but not as hot as I was afraid it would be.”

Kenzie knew that the heat would take a few bites to develop fully. She just smiled at him.

“That doesn’t mean she hadn’t been drinking,” she cautioned, carrying on with the conversation. “She certainly <u>could</u> have been drinking, or have taken something that impaired her. But we just won’t know that until we get the toxicology report back.”

Zachary nodded. “Right,” he agreed. He took another bite. It was his third or fourth, and Kenzie could see tears beginning to well up in his eyes. He sniffled. He wiped his forehead with the back of his hand. He put down the taco and picked up his soft drink. “Whew... that stuff really is hot. It kind of... grows, doesn’t it?”

"Yeah," Kenzie agreed. Her nose was also beginning to run, but she wasn't sweating like Zachary was. "But it is so good. I just have to keep eating it no matter how hot it is."

Zachary sucked down a few swallows of soda. He held a mouthful in his mouth, swishing it around and trying to quench the fire.

"Milk works better," Kenzie said. "They always say to drink milk. Or sour cream helps to cool it down a bit too."

He scooped up a spoonful of the sour cream in the small plastic tub and spread it over the taco. He swallowed. "I sure hope so." He looked over at the fridge. Kenzie wasn't sure if she had ever seen him drink milk before, but he was obviously considering it now. Anything to put out the inferno in his mouth.

CHAPTER 5

Zachary picked up one of the napkins and blew his nose, crumpling the napkin up and tossing it straight into the garbage. "Sorry…" he apologized. He tried to continue with the discussion. "Dr. Markov? Was she someone you knew?"

"I didn't really <u>know</u> her, but we had met a few times. She was a nephrologist, and you know how much my family has been involved with kidney research."

"Yes, of course." Zachary nodded. "That must have been a shock, seeing it was someone you knew."

"It's not unheard of. Vermont is so small, and Roxboro is a pretty close community. I often end up seeing people I have heard of, or a friend of a friend, maybe an uncle or grandparent. I often have some kind of distant connection with the victims."

"I hadn't thought about that." Zachary nodded slowly. "Does that make it more difficult?"

"I don't know. Not really. It isn't like I am treating someone who is sick and am invested in keeping them alive, worried about disappointing my friends if I fail. They are already dead when I see them, and usually it is natural causes or an accident. Not something that is anyone's fault. Often someone who was old or sick for a long time and the family is not shocked by it."

Kenzie took a sip of her drink. It was good that they would have plenty of time before bed to recover from the spicy meal before trying to sleep.

"Markov. Is that Russian?"

Kenzie stopped, about to take her next bite, freezing at the thought. She'd had too much to do with the Russians lately. The Russian mob had been involved in more than one case. In her father's kidnapping. In Kenzie being kidnapped herself, though she tried to keep that thought far from her and not to feel its full impact.

The Russians were the reason her father had been forced to retire from the lobbyist job he loved. There had been no way to escape the pressure they were putting on him, and the fear that they would again use Kenzie or someone else he loved as leverage to make sure he did whatever they asked him to. Because of the Russians, Walter had pretended to have a stroke that would prevent him from ever going back to work. If he was disabled, he was no good to them. But he hated being retired.

Kenzie cleared her throat and dabbed at her eyes, pretending to be distracted from his question by the spiciness of the meal. “I suppose so,” she said vaguely, and took another big bite of her taco.

Zachary studied Kenzie for a minute, then nodded. He looked through the rest of the food for something to eat that was a little less spicy. He spooned some rice onto a tortilla and wrapped it up with no sauce. Kenzie grinned. The rice itself was spiced. Hopefully, not too much for him. Otherwise, he might be forced to subsist on the plain flour tortillas or to make himself something else from the cupboard. His favorite chicken and stars soup, maybe.

“It’s good stuff, isn’t it?” Kenzie asked him.

“It really is,” Zachary agreed, wiping his eyes. He picked up another napkin and blew his nose again.

“So, what have you been working on today?” Kenzie asked, deciding she had nothing more to share about the postmortem and that she didn’t want to think of the Russians or anything else to do with Dr. Markov for the rest of the night. “Did you pick up a new client today?”

Zachary’s brows went up. He mopped sweat off his forehead with a napkin. “How did you know that?”

He was the private investigator, after all, not Kenzie. He hadn’t told her about the new client or even that he was meeting with someone.

"Well," Kenzie eyed the living room, where Zachary had been working on his computer when she had arrived home. "There is a shirt on the floor beside your laptop desk, and the only time you wear a collared shirt is when you're going to meet with a client or to go to something formal. We didn't have anything, so I assume it was a client meeting. Probably a new client, since you haven't mentioned anything interesting going on with any of your current ones."

"Well, I'm impressed. That's a very good deduction."

Kenzie gazed at him steadily.

"And I will pick the shirt up," Zachary said. "Sorry."

"Also," Kenzie said, dishing up some rice for herself. "It was on your calendar."

Zachary snorted. "Well, that might be a giveaway."

Kenzie laughed. "So, did it work out? Are you doing something for this new company? Green Mountain Genethera Innovations? Medical research, I assume? Gene therapy?"

He nodded. "Yeah. You probably got that from the 'Genethera' in the name."

"You're on to me. So what does Green Mountain need you to do?"

He wasn't likely to tell her very much about it. Client confidentiality. But he sometimes told her what he was working on in general terms. Usually, without revealing the client's name, but this time, he had given it away by writing it out in his calendar, along with the address where he was meeting them.

Zachary shrugged. "Industrial espionage. I can't really say more than that."

He probably figured she could have guessed that much on her own.

“Sounds like it could be lucrative.”

Biotech companies had a lot of money. And they would pay to protect their secrets. Information was currency in those circles.

“Could be,” Zachary agreed neutrally. There was a gleam in his eye. He did a lot of routine investigations. Skip tracing, insurance files, and other stuff that could be pretty boring. He liked it when he got a file he could dig into, especially if it paid well. Who wouldn’t?

Kenzie’s phone rang, and she looked at it to see who was calling. She wasn’t on call tonight, and it was not the klaxon alarm that could not be ignored. She saw her mother’s name on the screen.

Lisa Cole Kirsch.

She grunted and put it down. Zachary's eyes fastened on it. "You can take it if you want."

They had a "no phones at the table" rule, unless it was relevant to their discussion, such as an autopsy report Kenzie wanted to share a tidbit about. But, of course, some callers were exceptions.

"I'll call her back later. I need a chance to unwind first."

"If you're sure."

Kenzie nodded firmly. "I am sure."

CHAPTER 6

After they had finished eating supper, the leftovers put neatly away in the fridge, dishwasher loaded, and surfaces wiped down, Kenzie knew that she couldn't put off calling her mother back any longer.

She had committed to staying in touch with her parents, so she knew what was happening in their lives. And so she could keep up with what was going on in the foundation she was a director of and not be surprised by their funding an organization she had something to do with through the medical examiner's office, or making changes to policies or areas of focus. This had proven to be more important than she had expected in the past.

With Walter home with Lisa at the mansion full-time as part of the charade that he'd suffered a catastrophic stroke—even though the two had been divorced for years—Lisa sometimes needed someone to talk to when Walter's presence and boredom became untenable.

Kenzie had isolated herself from her parents because of the decisions they had made in treating Amanda, her little sister, years before. But they were the only family Kenzie had, and she knew it was important to stay connected with them. No one else could truly understand what she had gone through with Amanda. And how devastating losing Amanda had been for everyone in the family.

"Going to give her a call back?" Zachary questioned, watching Kenzie wipe down every surface of the kitchen once more.

"Yes," Kenzie answered irritably. "I told you I would."

"After you talk to her, you can have a bowl of ice cream."

Kenzie laughed. Ice cream was her suggested treat for going to couple's therapy with Zachary. This positive association helped them both to do something difficult, even if they couldn't always see the intrinsic rewards.

"You know what? You're right. I'll have earned it. After I've had a little chat with Mom, I'll have a bowl of ice cream and chill for the rest of the evening."

"Chill?" Zachary repeated. "I can get you a blanket if you think the ice cream will make you that cold."

She smiled and swatted at him. "Smart mouth. I'll be in the bedroom."

It was better if she had privacy while talking to Lisa. Then she didn't have to worry about explaining anything Zachary overheard or trying to excuse herself if she was more abrupt than she should be. Mothers and daughters needed private space to talk.

She sat on the bed propped with fluffy pillows and made herself as comfortable as she could before calling Lisa—more positive associations—and tapped her name on her favorites list.

Lisa Cole Kirsch answered within a couple of rings.

"Mackenzie? Thank you for calling me back, dear. How are you?"

"I'm fine, Mom. Just tired at the end of the day."

"You must have had a very long day."

"Well..." Kenzie didn't feel like explaining her interrupted evening the night before, her restless sleep, and the autopsy. How she had left work earlier than usual but it had still been a longer day. "Yeah, it felt long."

"I heard... I heard that Mariya Markov was killed in an accident. I assume that went through your office since it happened in Roxboro."

"Oh. You heard about that."

"I was very sorry to hear about it. I've had many discussions with Mariya over the years. She was a lovely woman and a very diligent doctor, scientist, and researcher. She did it all. It was very impressive."

"I didn't know you were that close. I remembered Dr. Markov from some fundraisers but was not as deeply involved as you were."

"No, of course not. We had years to develop a relationship. Kidney research was the foundation's main cause for many years."

Because of Amanda, of course. Lisa had thrown herself into raising funds for kidney research after Amanda's condition was discovered, and especially after things went so wrong with the second transplant. Kidney research had become her sole focus.

But things had shifted recently. The foundation was not putting as much money into kidney research and was putting more into mental health issues, addiction, homelessness, and other important social issues. Walter and Lisa had seen how much Zachary's mental health affected his life, Kenzie's, and their relationship. They had hired Tyrrell, Zachary's younger brother, to help out with office administration, and Tyrrell's fight against alcoholism had inspired them to make addiction one of the causes they championed as well.

"How did Dr. Markov feel about the foundation's change in focus?" Kenzie asked, wondering how it had affected their relationship. It would not be easy to maintain the same level of friendship with someone who decided to defund your project.

"She was disappointed, of course," Lisa admitted. "I have had a number of uncomfortable discussions with the companies and causes that we reduced funding to. But the foundation is a dynamic, growing, and changing entity. If it does not adapt, it stagnates. There are other issues that need our funding too, and mental illness has become so pervasive in our society, we cannot afford to ignore it."

“No. But I don’t imagine that was easy for her to hear.”

“No. Of course not. But we were still on good terms. Mariya understood that our needs changed and fluctuated over the years, and a company like the one she worked for needs to be agile and not just depend on funding from a single source.”

“Yeah. That makes sense. How did you hear about Dr. Markov’s accident? I didn’t think it was that widely known yet.”

“Word spreads quickly. In this day and age, with social media, it is lightning fast. In the past, it might have taken a couple of days for everyone to find out about it, but now, when everything is instant and can be broadcast to millions of viewers with a single click, you can’t keep something like that a secret.”

“What are people saying? Just that she died in an accident in Roxboro?”

"Oh, I don't know. What do you need to know? You will have more information than anyone else. I was hoping... you could keep it from becoming a media circus."

Kenzie gave a bark of laughter. "With 'instant everything'? No. I'm way behind that curve. I don't even know what event she was attending here. I thought I was on all of the kidney fundraiser lists."

"You have probably been removed from a number of them as it became more widely known that the foundation has shifted its funding focus. Invitations need to be targeted at those who will bring you the money. There is no point in keeping a bunch of deadwood on your solicitation list."

"I guess not."

"It was a private fundraiser. Very exclusive list of invitees. Dr. Markov was speaking and her company was going to give a couple of presentations on the promising projects they are currently working on. Gene therapy and transplant innovations, that kind of thing."

Lisa was remarkably well-informed for the director of a foundation that was not putting as much funding into kidney research. But they were still offering a few grants, and maybe Markov's company hoped to snag one of them.

Lisa's comment about gene therapy made Kenzie think about Zachary's new client. Vermont was a very small state, and the number of gene therapy companies had to be a very narrow field.

"What was the name of Dr. Markov's company?"

"Birch Valley Biomed."

"Oh." Kenzie nodded to herself. Not the same company as Zachary was taking on a job for. So she didn't need to worry about the appearance of impropriety. "I don't think I've heard of them before."

"Well, you should be familiar with the name from our financial statements," Lisa informed her with a sniff. "But it is easy to forget one name among many. And they do tend to have similar-sounding names. I guess there are only so many ways to say 'gene therapy' or 'biomedical innovations' in the company name. Birch Valley Biomed is just one division under a much bigger umbrella. A lot of these companies have parent companies or major shareholders in Europe."

Kenzie remembered that a company they had previously encountered experimenting with novel viruses had its major shareholder in Germany. Something in the regulations or economy of that country must make it a favorable environment for those big pharma and biotech companies.

"Maybe I would have recognized the parent company name," Kenzie said, hoping it would give her some excuse for not remembering a name on the foundation's financial statements. She was not sure how many of them she would be able to recognize, though. If Lisa expected her to have them all memorized, Kenzie would have to spend a lot more time than she was on the foundation. Which, of course, was what Lisa had been telling her with regularity over the past couple of years.

“I do hope that you will be able to finish off whatever you have to do on Dr. Markov’s case as quickly as possible,” Lisa told her. “I know that it takes time to wrap up all of the details and close a death investigation, but...”

“We’re doing what we can,” Kenzie assured her. “We’re not stalling or drawing it out any longer than we have to. The autopsy is complete and her next of kin have been notified. They will be able to proceed with the funeral without any delays.”

“That is good to hear,” Lisa approved. “I know you realize how important these things are. These traditions and grieving rituals. It makes people very anxious when there are unexpected delays.”

"Yes, I know that," Kenzie agreed. Probably better than Lisa did. "Believe me, we don't want to delay things or cause the family any extra grief if we can help it."

"Of course," Lisa agreed. "You are very considerate."

"Is that all you called about?" Kenzie asked. "How is Dad?"

"He is fine. You should call him. You know he would love to hear from you. I wish the two of you could get together for lunch or something, but that's out of the question when you are a couple of hours away and he cannot leave the house. But perhaps sometime soon. The... people he is trying to avoid can't keep watching him forever. Sooner or later, they will give up and decide there is no reason to put any pressure on him if he is unable to do the job they want him to."

"I'll give him a call," Kenzie agreed. "And... maybe we can figure something out. I could do a virtual video lunch with him. We both sit down with our own meals and chat while we eat, like we would if we were in the same place."

She could hear the smile in Lisa's voice as she approved this suggestion. "You know, he would love that. His computer skills are growing by leaps and bounds during his imposed quarantine, and he would be tickled to be able to meet with you by video chat."

"We will, then. Thanks for the suggestion, Mom."

"Take care, Mackenzie, and say hello to Zachary for us."

CHAPTER 7

Kenzie earned her ice cream for making the call to Lisa. Not only that, but she also called Walter and touched base with him. As Lisa had predicted, he was tickled at the idea of having lunch with his daughter and even more with using his newly discovered bent for technology by making it a video call.

She spent the rest of the evening being lazy and not doing any of the chores or other tasks that she had planned to do. They would have to wait until a day when she had not been up late, performed a postmortem, and made calls to both of her parents. Zachary was happy to cuddle on the couch and head to bed early with her, though she did not delude herself into thinking he would fall asleep early. He would wait until she was asleep, and then go back to the computer or a late-night movie. Eventually, he would fall asleep, probably on the couch, and then he would be up before she was in the morning.

But that didn't matter, as long as he was willing to spend some time together in bed and help her sleep so she could be fresh for work the next day.

Everything proceeded without complications, and she felt much better as she got ready for work the following day. They had breakfast together and Zachary saw her off to work. She arrived before Dr. Wiltshire as usual and had some quiet time before his arrival to get everything processed and start on her filing, which was slightly backlogged. She logged into her computer, went immediately to her email inbox, and started skimming through the subject lines to see what reports and inquiries had come in while she'd been away from the office.

She paused, frowning, at one subject line with her name and a profanity in it. Obviously some bit of spam that the automatic filters had failed to catch. She clicked to open it, even though she knew better. No good could come of opening spam email. The best thing was just to delete it and continue with her day.

She stared at the vitriol in the email body, stunned. She looked around, feeling suddenly removed from herself. She found herself looking for someone observing her, a hidden camera, something to explain why someone had sent her something so shocking in her email. Obviously, it was just to get her reaction.

But she was by herself in the large, echoing office suite. Dr. Wiltshire would be there soon. The other morgue workers came and went on their own schedules. Not everyone worked regular "office hours" at the medical examiner's office. Kenzie closed the email and got up to go to the breakroom. She refreshed her coffee and sipped it, leaning against the counter, her mind spinning.

There was nothing to be concerned about. Everyone got spam emails. She was sure there wasn't a person using the internet who hadn't received something. It was the nature of the internet. In the early years, before anti-spam laws and good heuristic filters, she'd seen a lot of graphic and shocking things that never should have made it to her inbox.

But even then, she had not received threats and personalized, targeted hate mail like the one she had just received.

Dr. Wiltshire walked into the break room and looked at Kenzie in surprise.

"Already on cup number two?" he asked. "You must have gotten in early today!"

"Uh, no, regular time. I just felt like... I needed to take a break."

He looked at her closely. "Is something wrong?"

"No. I don't know, actually. I guess not. I just... got thrown for a bit of a loop."

Dr. Wiltshire frowned and shook his head. “By what? What happened?”

“I just... I was just processing my email. Checking to see what came in overnight and what needs to be done...”

He nodded encouragingly and put a mug under the spigot of the coffee maker. He pressed the button to fill the cup and looked at her. “You were processing your email, and...”

“Nothing. I just got this one email that is... well, it was disturbing. But it’s nothing. Really, nothing to be concerned about.”

“It doesn’t sound like nothing to me. Disturbing in what way?”

“It’s just spam. One of those auto-generated things. The more AI has access to, the better it gets at generating something that sounds like it was written by a human being...”

"Why don't you show it to me?"

Kenzie's face got hot, and she broke into a sweat. "No, that's okay, Doctor. Really. I'll just delete it. I don't really want anyone else to see it."

He shook his head, brows drawing down. "Who is in charge of this office?" he asked sternly. "Who is responsible for what goes on inside these doors? I want to know what's going on. You need to show it to me."

Kenzie felt herself wilting. She put her coffee mug down and her hands over her eyes. "I don't think that's a good idea... you really don't want to see it."

Dr. Wiltshire picked up his mug of coffee and headed out of the breakroom. For an instant, Kenzie thought she'd won the argument and he was going to his office. But he was not; he was walking back out to her desk. He walked around it to stand in front of the screen and clicked the mouse to wake up the screen. As he read the email, his face drained of color.

Kenzie, following with her second cup of coffee, tried to think of the right thing to say to him to get him to focus on something else and leave the email to her. It was her email, received at her email address and with her name on it. She should be able to deal with it herself.

But she could think of nothing to say, nothing to pull him away from it. Dr. Wiltshire reached for her desk phone and tapped a number into it.

“It’s Dr. Wiltshire.” He explained the situation succinctly and waited for an answer. “Good, thank you.”

He hung up the phone. “Someone will be down to take care of it. Let’s go to my office and review the day.”

“I haven’t had a chance to get everything prepared yet…”

“Let’s go over what we’ve got.”

He led the way to his office and Kenzie followed, leaving her workstation unattended without locking the screen, something she never did. She was in a daze, still feeling removed from herself, and did what Dr. Wiltshire told her.

He steered her into the guest chair she always used in front of his desk and slid into his seat. He sipped his coffee and then started drilling her about the upcoming day.

Kenzie remained distracted for the fifteen or twenty minutes it took to review their open files and other plans. Dr. Wiltshire's phone rang and he picked it up. “Yes?”

He listened for a moment, and then stood up. “We'll be right out.” He hung up and looked at Kenzie. “Let's go have a chat.”

Kenzie followed him back to her desk again. A young man she didn't know was sitting at her computer, tapping away. She was alarmed at first, even though she knew he was someone Dr. Wiltshire had called. She didn't like someone else having access to her computer, with its sensitive files and the filing systems she had set up in a very particular way.

Though she understood that sometimes IT needed access to computers for setup and maintenance, she preferred not to deal with them.

The young man looked up as they approached. He was a millennial, a digital native, with brown hair and eyes, a casual look, and glasses rather than contact lenses. He had the gangly look of a teen who hadn't yet grown into his frame, though she would have put him at twenty-three or four. His eyes flicked over the two of them.

"You must be Dr. Kirsch," he said to Kenzie.

She nodded, her face again burning with embarrassment that he should associate her with the words in the email.

"I'm Elijah. I'm going to work on tracing this to see if we can find out where it came from and whether there has been a breach in the security system that allowed him to get your email address."

He pushed his glasses up to the bridge of his nose and typed, staring at the screen.

"It's easy to figure out my email address if you know how the other addresses on the system are formed," she told him. "You just need to know my name, which used to be on the ME's website and has been in the news in the last couple of months."

Elijah gave a brief nod. "Okay, yeah, that makes sense." He didn't look at her. "You need to file a police report about this email."

"What?" Kenzie looked at Dr. Wiltshire and shook her head. "No, I don't want to do that. I get spam emails all the time. There is no reason to turn this into such a big thing."

"There are death threats," the young man said, not waiting to see what Dr. Wiltshire would say about it. "There are personal details. It is a crime and needs to be reported."

"So he can be charged a $250 fine for cyberstalking?" Kenzie challenged. She had been down this path before when Zachary had been the target of a cyberbully. "What is the point?"

"This is criminal threatening. He has made specific threats. That's a thousand bucks. And you're a public employee and work from a municipal building—that makes it two thousand."

Kenzie shrugged. "Two thousand dollars isn't going to deter anyone. And the police will not want to waste man hours on something with such a light sentence."

"It still needs to be reported," Elijah insisted. "You need to let the police know. Open a file. If there are additional charges, it could end up being something bigger, if they can demonstrate a pattern."

Kenzie sighed and rubbed the center of her forehead, which was aching. "Okay," she said finally, "I'll send a copy to Sergeant Campbell, and he can open a file for me."

"I wouldn't recommend forwarding it by email," he warned. "Doing so could violate cyber laws."

"Me forwarding it to the police could be a crime?"

"Best not to take the chance. Print a hard copy. Put a copy on a USB stick. Take them to the police by hand rather than transmitting them."

Kenzie rolled her eyes. "Since you're on my computer, would you please do that?"

"Of course," he agreed. He hit a few keys to send it to the printer and dug into the soft-sided courier bag he had with him and opened a fresh USB drive from a package, which he inserted into the computer tower. "I'm going to be here for a while if you want to do something else. Or if you want to run this upstairs to the police now, then just give me the file number and I'll submit my report when I'm done. I want to do a full system check, make sure you don't have any viruses or vulnerabilities that need to be patched."

Kenzie looked at Dr. Wiltshire.

"You may as well file the police report now," he told her. "We don't have anything that won't wait. And then you're not standing around waiting to get your computer back again. By the time you're finished, Elijah will probably be done here."

"Do you really think I need to?"

"I think you know you need to. It isn't fun, but it still needs to be done."

"It isn't going to go anywhere. And even if it does, who is going to care about having to pay a fine?"

"There could be jail time too."

"You know there won't be. Jails are overcrowded. It will just be a fine, especially if he is a first-time offender."

Dr. Wiltshire raised his hands in surrender. "Even if it is just a fine, it needs to be done. There needs to be a consequence."

But Kenzie knew there wouldn't be. The police would barely even look at the file.

CHAPTER 8

Kenzie was happy, as she rode the elevator back down to the ME's office, that filing a report with Sergeant Joshua Campbell had been so quick and painless. He didn't seem particularly concerned with it, but agreed with Elijah that the email needed to be reported so that they could follow up on it and have it on record in case they could find a lead or if the same thing happened again. There was no way to tie two incidents of the same thing happening together if one of them was never filed. He had taken the information she had provided him, asked her a few questions about whether she knew who the threat had come from or if it was the first one she had received, gave her the file number for the incident, and sent her on her way.

She was not so happy when she got off of the elevator and saw that Elijah was still sitting at her computer.

"You're still here?" Kenzie asked lightly, trying to make it sound like a joke.

Elijah barely looked up from the screen. “Yeah,” he agreed, “Still here. Just a few more things to check. You get the full ‘Elijah Carter’ treatment. Others might stop at a simple virus scan or checking the most common entry points. But not me. I check <u>everything</u>.”

“Oh... well, you know how much I appreciate that...”

But she didn’t. What Kenzie wanted was to get back to her work and pretend that none of this had happened. She didn’t want Elijah to be digging down into the deepest of her computer settings to make sure she was safe from attack. She wanted to do her actual work. She hadn’t even had a chance to review all her emails.

“Won’t be much longer...” Elijah promised. He rubbed his head, frowning. He had been looking at the screen for far too long and far too intently, as far as Kenzie was concerned. It was no wonder he was getting a headache from it. He should take a break, focusing his eyes on something in the distance. He could even get up and walk around, stretch his legs a little, do some flexibility exercises, have some water, and maybe have some human conversation before getting back into it again.

Kenzie opened her mouth to suggest that Elijah might need a break, even though he said he was nearly done. They always said that they were nearly done. They needed to be reminded of the importance of breaks while they were still young, before they started to see the ill effects of their digital-centric lifestyles.

Elijah's watch trilled. It wasn't one of the common, understated beeps that Kenzie heard from most watches these days. It was no hourly chime or prompt to get up and walk around. It was much more arresting. And Elijah immediately stopped what he was doing and looked at it, rather than dismissing it without even looking at the screen.

"Oh." He grunted. He reached for his bag and rooted around in it, eventually coming out with a roll of flat, round, pastel-colored candies. He popped one in his mouth and went back to what he had been doing on the computer.

“What was that?” Kenzie asked, though she had an inkling of an idea.

He glanced at her. “Oh, it’s nothing. I have a CGM.” He bared his upper arm, giving Kenzie a quick look at the transmitter affixed to his skin. “Continuous Glucose Monitor. It just sent me an alert that my glucose is getting too low, so I took a glucose tablet to bring it back up.”

“That’s cool. When I think about the kids that I went to school with who were diabetic and had to do multiple finger pricks every day...”

“Oh, yeah, this is way better. And the wearables these days can be really personal.” He tapped his watch. “They have fashion watches now that you would never know are smartwatches. They don’t all have to look like big black sports watches. And there are necklaces, bracelets, even rings and earrings. I imagine you're seeing that all the time now as a medical examiner. It isn't just fall alarms and geofencing anklets anymore."

"There are more smart watches now," Kenzie admitted. "It used to be that it was just the sports geeks that had them. Or the early adopter tech geeks. Now they are almost as common as smartphones."

"You're not going to be able to take any jewelry at face value anymore. You're always going to have to examine it, see if it is a transmitter, receiver, or storage device of some kind. Even just an NFC, like the chip in your credit card."

Kenzie thought about the watch and locket she had logged as Markov's personal possessions the day before. She hadn't taken a close look at them. Could they have been electronic devices without her even knowing it?

"How would I be able to tell?"

"If it doesn't have a charge port, interface, or sensor that you can see—and some of them are getting really subtle now—you might need an x-ray to find a chip inside, an RF scanner for radio waves, infrared sensor for the heat that it produces while it operates... It's like we're all spies now, with these miniature monitoring devices."

"Yeah. I hadn't really thought about it. I recognize the major brands of smartwatches but hadn't really thought about more than that."

"Wait until we all have implants," Elijah grinned and tapped the sensor on his arm. "Biotech to monitor all major health measurements, with pumps and pacemakers or ICDs to keep your heart on the right rhythm, NFCs that will let you make purchases or track your movements even without carrying a phone, data vaults you take with you wherever you go. The possibilities are endless. And they are coming, if they aren't already here."

"Pretty amazing," Kenzie murmured. "Are you going to be here for a few more minutes?"

"Yeah. Be done soon, I just have a couple more things to check..."

"Will you stay here even if you finish? I want to show you something."

He cocked his head and flashed a look at her. He shrugged. "Yeah, sure."

"Great. Just stay there."

Kenzie left him working at her desk and went into the morgue to retrieve Dr. Markov's personal items. She went through the package and pulled out the watch and the locket in their clear plastic bags. At a glance, they looked just like a traditional watch and locket, like jewelers had been making for a hundred years, but when the packages touched each other, the two pieces of jewelry clung together, like one or both of them were magnetized. Kenzie returned to her desk and stood by it, hovering over Elijah and waiting for him to look up.

He looked away from her computer screen and leaned in to look at the packages she held before him.

“Oh, sure,” he said, touching the package with the watch in it. “I recognize the brand name on this one. It’s pretty, isn’t it? Not like a sports watch at all.”

“Does it have a screen? How does it display anything?”

“It’s a sensor and can receive alerts. Sound or vibration. You learn to recognize what the different alerts mean. Some of them have voice responses, so you can talk to it and get feedback without a screen.” He looked at the second package. “And if I’m not mistaken, the locket is a digital memory vault. You can store pictures, recordings, documents, sometimes even videos, depending on how much space it has available. Can you take it out?”

"Better if I don't. There's no way to tell without taking it out?"

Elijah considered for a moment, then pulled his phone out. Kenzie thought he was going to take a picture of the locket or search for it online, but he tapped a few buttons on his screen and held it close to the locket, watching his screen. Nothing happened. He tapped the locket with his fingertip a few times.

"Ah-hah," he exclaimed. "There it is!"

He turned around the phone to show her the Bluetooth discovery screen.

Markov2

"Wow. I guess that's it, then. Are you sure that's not the watch?"

He scrolled down the list, and she saw the brand name of the watch farther down. "That's the watch there. Markov2 is the locket, unless you have something else on your desk or person transmitting a Bluetooth pairing signal."

"No. Markov was the owner of the locket."

He nodded smugly. "There you go, then."

Kenzie wondered how many other smart devices had passed through her possession without her realizing it.

"Do you have her phone?" Elijah asked. "You should be able to use it to see what information is stored on the locket."

"So it is a miniature storage device? Like a little hard drive?"

"Exactly."

"Wow. Well, thank you. I never would have thought to check that out."

"Her next of kin might not know it is a digital device either. If that's where her most precious memories are stored, they will need to be told."

"Yes. Definitely. I wouldn't want them to miss out on those after Dr. Markov did so much work to keep them safe and close to her."

CHAPTER 9

It seemed like the whole day had gone by before Kenzie was able to sit at her computer and again try to start her day. Everything was jumbled, since she'd had to jump back and forth to other activities that she would normally have done later in the day, without getting a chance to finish sifting through her emails and the various reports and attachments.

She stood in Dr. Wiltshire's doorway at the end of the workday with a stack of results and reports to go over with him. He hung up his phone call and nodded to her pleasantly.

"Ready to start your day, Doctor?" Kenzie asked.

Dr. Wiltshire chuckled. "I'm sorry it ended up being such a jumbled, disjointed day," he told her. "We like to follow a predictable routine and do everything in order, and then you get a day like today when all of that gets thrown out the window, and you just have to tread water to keep your head about the surface."

Kenzie nodded. “You would think it would be easier to adapt. I never really thought that I was attached to any particular routines. I can be a pretty spontaneous person. I would look at other people in my sphere who like to follow rigid routines”—like Zachary, of course—“and think I am not like them. But a day like this comes along, and I realize how accustomed I have gotten to following a certain routine, day in and day out. It’s kind of like when you look in the mirror and realize that somehow you have aged ten years past that image you had of yourself in your head. You’re not a teenager or twenty-something anymore. You’ve... matured.”

“Don’t remind me,” Dr. Wiltshire laughed. “I’m far beyond twenty-something or even thirty-something. I don’t know if your brain ever catches up to your true age. Maybe for some people it does, and for others it doesn’t.”

Kenzie nodded. She set her stack of reports down on the desk. She looked at the top one. “Mariya Markov’s toxicology report.”

Dr. Wiltshire took it with interest. “Alcohol is nice and low, well below the legal limit. And... nothing else. No common recreational drugs in her system.”

“But Detective Edwards said that she appeared to be driving impaired.”

“So what did we miss? Why was she driving like that?”

Kenzie nodded. Dr. Wiltshire motioned for her to lay it out.

“We didn’t find any evidence of heart attack or stroke. There are no obvious intoxicants. We didn’t find anything else on the body that indicated Dr. Markov was impaired.”

“So what are other options? What should we be looking for?”

Kenzie rubbed her temples, thinking about it. “There is the possibility that she had taken some substance that does not show up on the standard tox screen. Could be a less-common recreational drug, something someone had dosed her with, or just a reaction to a cold medicine or prescription that was unexpected. I can put in a request for mass spectrometry and see if any foreign substance shows up in her blood."

Dr. Wiltshire nodded his agreement. "Definitely. And if it isn't an intoxicant or something that she reacted to? Any other possibilities?"

"Uh, seizure, allergen…" Kenzie paused, thinking of Elijah, "or hypoglycemia. What about lack of sleep or an altered mental state? I haven't been told about any preexisting medical conditions, but that doesn't mean that she didn't have anything."

"The police contacted her family and work; their numbers are on the file. You will need to interview them, see if they were aware of any conditions. Find out who her doctor was or who she might have seen. And find out if any colleagues saw her at the event that night. Was she acting normally, or was something off? Did anything happen that night that might have upset her? Being angry or upset can certainly cause erratic driving."

Kenzie nodded her agreement. She made a few notes for herself for follow-up. She looked at the face of her phone. Unfortunately, with most of the day lost to the email threat and possible computer security problems, there wasn't really time to be making such phone calls.

"The hours slip through our fingers like sand," Dr. Wiltshire observed. "Before you know it, the day is gone."

"You're certainly waxing philosophical," Kenzie observed.

"To be honest, I'm just glad to be back into the regular swing of things. I can assure you—as can Mrs. Wiltshire—that I am not the type who does very well with a lot of idle time. You might think I would have plenty of things on the 'honey-do' list to keep me busy, but with my hand out of commission, I wasn't much good around the house. And all of those books I had planned to read or other things I was going to do when I had some time... if they weren't so darn boring, I might have found the time for them before. As it was, I couldn't sit down and read for more than half an hour, and then there are still another twenty-three hours in the day to deal with."

"And a half."

"And a half," he agreed. "Heaven help us when it is time for me to retire. I understand now why cops die so quickly after retiring. The boredom is excruciating."

Kenzie didn't know whether Dr. Wiltshire had any kids or grandkids. She didn't think he had ever mentioned any. She actually wasn't even sure whether there was a Mrs. Wiltshire or whether Dr. Wiltshire just liked to call upon the mythical wife to explain his actions sometimes.

"Well, we certainly don't want you dying of boredom. I'm glad to have you back, too. And glad that you have gotten so far along in your healing."

"You must miss the handsome and brilliant Dr. Cook." Dr. Wiltshire's eyes twinkled. "You really want to look at this craggy old face after seeing his apple cheeks?"

"Dr. Cook was very capable. He was fine as a substitute. I was certainly grateful to have someone taking on some of the workload so I didn't have to cover everything. But he wasn't you. I'm glad to have you back."

Dr. Wiltshire smiled. "Well, I'm sure Zachary would rather have me as his competition than Dr. Cook."

Luckily, Zachary had not gotten too bent out of shape about Kenzie working for Dr. Cook with his movie star good looks. He had joked about it occasionally, but had not shown any real signs of insecurity.

"Yes, I'm sure he's greatly relieved to have you back too."

CHAPTER 10

Kenzie was not happy to have to talk to Dr. Markov's family about her death. It would be one thing just to convey to them how sorry she was for their loss, but she hated to have to bother them with getting all of the details of Dr. Markov's personal and medical history. They were in mourning and wanted answers, not questions they couldn't answer.

It was Dr. Markov's sister who came in to talk to Kenzie. She had some similarities to Dr. Markov in her build and coloring, but her face was much narrower and sharper, making her look angry and irritated, even though her tone of voice was calm and velvety smooth.

"I am Alina Markov," she told Kenzie when she stopped at her desk at the entrance to the medical examiner's suite. "I am here to see Dr. Kirsch."

"That's me," Kenzie told her, standing and offering her hand to shake. Alina took it in a thin, dry hand and gave it a short squeeze. "I am so sorry for your loss."

Alina nodded and let go of her hand. She looked around. "You wanted to ask me some questions."

"Let me just lock up here, and then we will grab the boardroom." Kenzie quickly forwarded her desk phone to voicemail, secured her workstation, and then led Alina into the boardroom where they could speak in private without danger of being interrupted by inquiries from the public. She offered Alina a beverage, but was turned down.

Kenzie and Alina sat down in two adjacent chairs.

"You and Mariya both have traditional Russian names, but you don't have any accent," Kenzie said. "I don't remember her having an accent either."

"You knew her? Yes, we are natural-born citizens. Our parents left Russia some years before having children."

Kenzie nodded. "I'm very sorry for your loss. Do you have any other siblings?"

Alina waved the question away. "You had questions about Mariya's history. I don't understand what that had to do with anything. She died in a car accident. That is what killed her. Why do you need anything else?"

"She was observed to be driving erratically. Like she was drunk. But there was very little alcohol in her system. So we are looking for any other medical history that could explain why she was driving the way she was."

"Wouldn't you know that from your autopsy?"

"Some things we would be able to tell from the autopsy, and some of them are much more difficult to spot. She didn't have a medical bracelet. Did she have any chronic conditions like epilepsy or blood sugar problems?"

"No. She was very healthy. Nothing like that."

"And would she have told you? Were the two of you close?"

"Yes, we talked all the time. She would have told me if she had been to the doctor and was told that she had a condition like that."

"She had never fainted without any explanation? Had any heart condition?"

"No."

"Did she have any allergies? Reactions to medications?"

"No."

"She might have just been tired after the event she had been at that night. Would she have stayed here in town or gone home?"

"She would not have driven if she was too tired."

Kenzie paused, hesitating before asking the next question. "Did Mariya suffer from any mental health issues? Depression or anxiety?"

"No." Alina bit her lip and frowned.

"Nothing?" Kenzie asked, wondering about her reluctance. "Even if she hadn't been diagnosed, you might have noticed some changes in behavior or things that concerned you?"

"No. Mariya was stressed lately. I did notice, she was distracted sometimes. Or wanted to get away from it all and relax. I think that work was stressful." Alina shrugged. "But that was not odd or unusual... she had a stressful job. Lots of pressure."

"She must have kept very busy with everything she was doing," Kenzie suggested. "Her research and development work, and she was still an active surgeon too, wasn't she?"

“She wasn’t doing a lot of it, but she was still qualified and took on the occasional case. Mostly transplants.” Alina followed the border on the edge of the table with her finger, not looking at Kenzie. “She had been put on a new project at work. I don’t know what it was, but something about it must have stressed her out. She never said exactly what it was. Not that I would have understood it if she had. But she said that... things were not right, and she wasn’t sure what to do.”

Alina drew in a breath and let it out slowly. Her eyes were moist.

“I don’t think I was very sympathetic. I just figured... there wasn’t anything I could do about it. I couldn’t give her any advice. All I could do was nod and tell her it would all work out; she would know what to do.”

“Sometimes we just need a listening ear,” Kenzie assured her. “We’re not looking for someone to solve all of our problems, just to be there for us.”

"But I don't see what this has to do with your job here," Alina asserted. "Being stressed at work didn't have anything to do with Mariya's death."

"It might lead me to a better understanding of what happened. If she was stressed, she may have been on medication without telling you about it. Something that she didn't realize shouldn't be mixed with alcohol, even the very small amount that she'd had to drink. Or, it may have led to sleepless nights, and she didn't realize how sleep-deprived she was and that it wasn't safe to drive. We are all affected in different ways by stress."

Alina shook her head slowly. "Mariya was very careful of her health. I don't think she would ignore sleeping problems or not know the contraindications of a medication."

"And as far as you know, she was not on anything."

"No."

"She had a smartwatch. Did she use that to monitor her health?"

"Yes. Mariya thought everyone should use technology like that. She loved her phone and devices and used them all the time. I didn't want anything to do with it. I'm just fine with my dumb watch. I don't need one that talks to me or monitors my heart rhythm or sleep patterns or how much water I am drinking." She rolled her eyes. "Not only is Big Brother watching, we're feeding him every last little bit of our lives voluntarily. Who knows how that information is being used."

Kenzie nodded. "I don't know. I suppose that's a good question." She knew that she would be looking over Mariya's health information to see if she could detect any worrisome patterns or maybe some notes on her health that might lead to some answers.

“You said that you are releasing the body,” Alina said, her voice cracking a little. “So you are done the autopsy. You are finished.”

“I am not finished my investigation. But I do not need her remains kept here. I took what samples I needed; you can have your funeral home pick up the remains at any time. You do not need to wait until I have closed my file to go on with your grieving process.”

Alina nodded. “Then I do not need to know what you put in your report or do not put in your report. It is irrelevant.”

“Yes, it is. I don’t think it will make any difference to how you proceed. We just like to tie everything up neatly. I’ll need to hang on to her phone and locket for a few days, but once I have finished with those, I can have them delivered wherever you like.”

“Her locket?”

"She was wearing a locket when she... had the accident. It's actually another smart device. I haven't had a chance yet to find out what she stored on it."

Alina picked at her cuticles. "Pictures. Maybe a recording. It was just... sentimental stuff."

"Well, I will be sure to return everything to you undamaged so you can access those special memories."

"Thanks. She said... it was stuff she wanted to keep close."

"Of course. It's amazing what we can do with technology now, how we have repurposed or put a whole new spin on the traditional locket and other jewelry. And other things, of course. Who would ever have guessed when we were kids that we would one day carry powerful computers around in our pockets."

"And use them to watch cat videos," Alina added.

Kenzie laughed. “Yeah. The ultimate in the evolution of technology. Access to cute cats.”

“Mariya loved cute dog or cat videos. She was always sending me one or another that she had seen somewhere. I was watching one this morning, and I could just hear her cackling at it. She always got such a kick out of them.”

CHAPTER 11

Kenzie hoped that she hadn't upset Alina too much with her questions. She had done her best to be gentle and respectful and not stir things up too much. Hopefully, Alina would not make any complaints to her family that got back to the Kirsch family foundation and Kenzie's parents. She didn't need a call from Lisa telling her off for upsetting the child or grandchild of one of their very dear friends.

Or if they complained to the governor. It wouldn't be the first time his authority had been brought to bear on the medical examiner's office.

"I am going to head over to Birch Valley," Kenzie told Dr. Wiltshire before heading out. "The company that Dr. Markov worked for. See if I can find out anything from her coworkers about what might have been happening in her life."

"Any insight from the family?"

"Unfortunately, no. No conditions or medications that her sister knew about. She apparently took good care of herself. She was under stress, but the sister was not aware of any prescriptions. I didn't turn anything up on the computer, either. Nothing in her medical records other than annual physicals and the occasional antibiotic or booster shot."

"Good for her. Doesn't make your job any easier, though."

"No. But maybe I'll find something out at the office. Fingers crossed. From what I know of Dr. Markov, she probably spent most of her time working. So maybe her coworkers will have more answers for me than her family."

"Good luck. Let me know if you need anything from this end."

"Only to confirm who I am if they try to kick me out."

Kenzie turned some music on in the car and headed for Burlington. A couple of blocks away from the police station, she passed the place where Markov had crashed, and frowned to herself. After thinking about it for a few minutes, she used her car's Bluetooth to call Zachary.

It rang a few times and she thought the call would get dropped into voicemail, but Zachary picked up before it did.

“Hey, Kenz,” he greeted, a little out of breath. “How are you doing?”

“Good. Do you have a minute to bounce some ideas around?”

“Sure,” he sounded pleased at the prospect. “What about?”

“Okay. So my car crash victim lives and works in Burlington.”

“Uh-huh.”

It was perfectly natural that a doctor and scientist would work out of Burlington rather than in a little town like Roxboro, so this was unsurprising news.

"But she had come to Roxboro for a fundraising event. She was a guest speaker. The event was held at the Inn."

It was one of the few places in town with conference facilities, so again, this lined up and made logical sense.

"Sure," Zachary agreed.

"But the accident occurred on Main, a couple of blocks north of the police station. The car was traveling south."

"Wait, what?"

"Southbound on Main, a couple of blocks from the police station."

"Are you sure it was southbound? Maybe it spun during the accident. Sometimes cars end up a complete one-eighty from the way they were heading."

"I'm sure. Detective Edwards has traffic cams, so I'll get his confirmation. But even if she had been going north, she was still south of the Inn. If Markov had left the Inn to go home to Burlington, she would have been north of the Inn. She had no reason to go south, deeper into Roxboro. Did she? I mean, I can't think of any reason for her to be in the middle of Roxboro rather than between the Inn and Burlington."

"Well, there might be a reason; you just don't know what it is." She could hear Zachary tapping something into his computer. "Let's bring up the map and have a look at it."

"If she needed gas, it's right there. She doesn't have to go further into Roxboro for that."

"Food?"

"She was just at a banquet. There was food in her stomach, barely digested."

"She had just eaten. So scrap that. It's the middle of the night, so none of these businesses would have been open..."

"What else could it have been?"

“Visiting a friend or family member?”

Kenzie shook her head. “I just talked to the sister. She was the closest family member. She didn’t say that the victim had been visiting anyone.”

“That doesn’t mean she wasn’t. I think it would have to be a personal visit. I don’t see any amenities she would have needed to use that she wouldn’t have been able to find on the outskirts of town.”

“Well, that’s just weird. Going to visit someone in the middle of the night?”

“It is. I’ll keep looking and let you know if I come up with something, but I can’t think of anything offhand that makes any sense.”

“Okay, thanks.”

“You said she was driving erratically.”

"Yes."

"So maybe she was disoriented and had taken a wrong turn."

"Ahh... maybe that's it," Kenzie agreed. The piece fit into place like it was a puzzle. Maybe Markov hadn't intended to go south; she had been turned around. Whatever had caused the crash had also caused her to go in the wrong direction. "Yeah. I'll bet you hit the nail on the head. She never meant to go that way."

"And that might also explain driving erratically. She wasn't sure where she was going, wanted to get turned around, and was in an unfamiliar place at night."

"Yeah. Slowing down, trying to find something and figure out which way to go, speeding up to get to the next off-ramp, swerving lanes as she tried to find the right route—a lot of it could be explained by being turned around and trying to get on track again. Maybe she was in a bit of a panic because she wanted to get home and didn't recognize anything in the area."

Kenzie couldn't see the careful, logical Dr. Markov getting panicked over a wrong turn, but it was still possible. Especially if it was late and she was tired.

"Good thinking," Kenzie told Zachary again. "By the way, I am heading to Burlington now."

"Oh. You going to see your mother?"

"No. Doubt I'll have time. I'm just going to do some interviews and then be back in Roxboro for supper."

"You sure you don't want to surprise her?"

"No, not this time." Kenzie didn't want to get roped into staying for dinner and not getting back to Roxboro until it was far too late. It was one thing to do it with Zachary when she was well-rested. She didn't want to be too tired on the way home herself.

Sometimes the deaths that she dealt with had that impact on her. They stood as warnings for her, portents of things that could go wrong if she made the wrong choice. Other people might have brushed it off and said it wouldn’t happen to them. Kenzie was going to make sure it didn’t.

CHAPTER 12

Birch Valley Biomed was headquartered in a low, unassuming building, white and blue, that could have been anything. A company that supplied water for office coolers. Light industrial. Office temps. There was nothing graphic or showy about it. Only the word "biomed" gave any clue about their actual business.

Kenzie walked into the front lobby, noting the security keypads at the doors. Although they were unlocked at the moment, during business hours, it was clear that the place was locked up tightly at night. The doors between the reception desk and the rest of the office were closed, with red lights glowing to indicate they were locked.

The professional-looking woman with her hair wrapped into a smooth, sleek bun smiled politely at Kenzie.

"Good afternoon. How can I help you?"

"I am here to talk to someone about Dr. Mariya Markov."

"Dr. Markov. She isn't in at the moment."

"She's not going to be," Kenzie pointed out. "She's deceased."

The woman was not shocked, so that fact was already well-known, even if they were not advertising it to members of the public who just happened to walk in off the street.

"I'm afraid so."

"I would like to talk to her coworkers, her boss, anyone who worked closely with her."

"I don't think that will be possible. What station do you work for?"

"I don't work for a TV station. I work at the medical examiner's office in Roxboro. I conducted the postmortem on Dr. Markov and I have some follow-up questions as part of my investigation."

The woman stared at her. "Who are you, exactly?"

"Dr. Kenzie Kirsch. Assistant Medical Examiner."

"I see... I don't know if there is anyone here to talk to you at the moment. Maybe you could make an appointment and come back."

"I just drove all the way from Roxboro. There must be someone in."

The woman rolled her eyes. "Why would you come here without setting it up with someone first? Your failure to make an appointment doesn't make it an emergency for us. You must call ahead of time if you want to be able to talk to someone."

"I see."

Kenzie stood there, allowing the woman to grow more uncomfortable. At first, she seemed triumphant after having put Kenzie in her place, but the expression faded as Kenzie stood there looking at her.

"I'm sorry," she said, "you will have to make an appointment and come back another time."

"You haven't even checked to see if anyone is available."

"I know our employees are busy and do not take unscheduled meetings."

"I think they will today. This is an unusual circumstance. You have lost one of your own. I'm sure people want to help out. They want to do everything they can to find out why Dr. Markov died."

"She was in a car accident."

"Yes. Why?"

The woman shook her head, frowning. "Why what?"

"Why was she in a car accident?"

“Because… I don’t know. Because she hit something.”

“Why did she? Did she normally go around driving into barriers?”

“No.”

“Then why was she driving so erratically? Why did this happen?”

The receptionist shook her head again. “I have no idea.”

“Then let me investigate that. I need to talk to her coworkers. So start making some calls and see who is available to talk to me first.”

“But that’s not my job. I’m supposed to—”

“You’re supposed to be the gatekeeper to make sure that no one gets in and disturbs the scientists. I know. But this is different. Call your boss and ask him who I should talk to first.”

She turned red. “I can’t do that.”

“You’re not allowed to call your boss?”

“I can’t just... decide that you’re allowed to see people.”

Kenzie folded her arms and waited. “I think you have the brains to figure this out.”

The woman finally motioned Kenzie over to a small grouping of chairs. “Would you please sit down so I can make some calls?”

Kenzie sat down. But she wasn’t going to stay there for long. If the woman didn’t start cooperating in another five minutes, she would get up again and hover over her.

Kenzie couldn’t tell what was being said, but she could hear the woman whispering into the phone, trying to explain to someone what was going on and that they were going to have to talk to Kenzie. Before long, she hung up the phone, and a few minutes later, a small man with glasses materialized from beyond one of the sealed doors and approached Kenzie.

"Uh, Miss Kirsch, is it?"

"Dr. Kirsch," Kenzie told him. "Medical examiner's office. Maybe you're familiar with my mother, Lisa Cole Kirsch? Or with the Kirsch family foundation?"

His face seemed to lose a little color at that. Kenzie didn't know if he thought he had lost funding from the foundation because he had taken so long to deal with Kenzie. The fact was, most of their funding of the organization had already been withdrawn. The Kirsch family foundation just wasn't supporting kidney research at the same level as it had been. But let the blowhard think he had just lost them a load of money, if it worked in Kenzie's favor.

"Of course I am familiar with the Kirsches," he immediately gushed, holding his hand out for Kenzie's, and then clasping it between his when she responded. "I'm sorry you were kept waiting. Donors should never have to wait!" He flashed a glance toward the receptionist, who opened her mouth to protest that Kenzie had never said she was a donor.

"I'm not here to talk money," Kenzie told him. "This is a totally different matter, and I don't want you to confuse the two. This is about Dr. Markov and the investigation into her death by the medical examiner's office in Roxboro."

"Roxboro. Of course. I'm sure that it was just a misunderstanding. You know that we will always cooperate fully with the authorities."

Kenzie had stood up to take the man's hand, and she now pulled it back from him.

"Thank you, Doctor..." Kenzie waited for him to introduce himself.

"Shepherd," he told her. "Merle Shepherd."

“Nice to meet you, Dr. Shepherd. Is there a meeting room we could use?”

“Actually, it isn’t doctor. You can just call me Merle, please. My expertise is in administration, not science. And yes, we have a room I’m sure you can use. And you’re actually here to talk to...”

“Dr. Markov’s boss and the people she worked the most closely with.”

“Oh, yes. Of course. Let’s see.”

Merle led her through the previously locked door, patting her arm and murmuring about what a great pleasure it was to see her.

He eventually saw her to a seat in their boardroom, provided her a fresh cup of coffee, and promised to start rounding up the troops to talk to her.

CHAPTER 13

The first few people that Shepherd rounded up were not at all helpful. Kenzie was at a loss as to why he had directed them to her at all. They knew little about Dr. Markov or her work, and were probably just intended to keep Kenzie busy while Shepherd figured out how to get the people that she really needed to talk to.

The third person sent into the boardroom to talk to her was a woman in a bright pink shirt and lab coat who studied Kenzie myopically for a moment before smiling and holding out her hand to shake. "You're a medical examiner?" she asked Kenzie in a deeper voice than Kenzie expected. "You're very young."

"Well, not that young." The woman herself was younger than Kenzie, perhaps in her late twenties. "Just not the old man you were expecting to see."

"Fair enough," she laughed. "You're not a grumpy old man at all."

Kenzie joined in the laughter. "No, I'm not. My boss is an older man. Not grumpy, though. He is quite nice."

"That's good. If you're going to work with dead people all day, you might as well do it with someone who isn't going to bring you down."

Kenzie agreed. "It may be a morgue, but it doesn't have to be funereal."

"I'm Dana Pratt. I worked with Dr. Markov." Dana's eyes were bright with tears. "I can't believe she was killed. I just couldn't believe it when I heard. How does something like that happen?"

"I am endeavoring to find out. But I did need someone who knew Dr. Markov, what she was working on, how she felt about her job here and maybe a personal friend. I really need more than shows up on her curriculum vitae."

"Yes, yes, that's me. We worked closely together. She was like my best friend. I really want to help."

"Come sit down with me, then, and let's put our heads together. I really need to know who Dr. Markov was."

"Can we call her Mariya? We didn't go around calling each other 'doctor' like robots. We were colleagues. And even though she had a ton more experience and training than I do, she treated me like an equal."

"Okay, Mariya, then. How long had you known her?"

"About... three years, I guess. I really liked working with her."

"It sounds like she was friendly. With the Russian name, I kind of expected her to be more reserved and standoffish. It just goes to show you that we are all prejudiced in our own ways." Kenzie didn't say that she had met Dr. Markov a couple of times herself.

"No, she wasn't like that at all. She was a little... shy. She found meeting new people a little difficult. We're scientists, you know, we're all a little socially awkward. So she could come across that way, as reserved. But she was really good at speaking to groups and explaining medical stuff to laypeople in an accessible way. And she wasn't reserved with friends. She was open."

"She was easy to work with?"

"Yeah. She was. You might find that surprising, with her being as smart and revered as she was, but she really didn't care that I was just a junior researcher. She just wanted to get her hands on the science."

Kenzie smiled at the turn of phrase. It made Dr. Markov sound like an eager elementary school student rather than the esteemed researcher and surgeon she was—full of curiosity and delight with her scientific discoveries.

“So, what did you two talk about?”

“Everything under the sun. Everything related back to our work sooner or later. No matter what time we spent talking about personal or family stuff, it all got back to research eventually.”

“So you knew she had a sister? Had you ever met her?”

“Alina. No, never met her in person. But Mariya liked her. She wasn’t into science, but she was a nice person. They grew up doing everything together and were still good friends.”

“Yes. Alina seemed quite nice. Definitely feeling her sister’s loss.”

“Aww.” Dana touched her chest. “I feel bad for her. At least here, I’m surrounded all day long by people who knew Mariya. Alina... I mean, she’s got her parents for support, but that’s not the same as being here... the place Mariya loved the most." Dana swallowed. "I don't know if you've ever lost a work colleague before... you wouldn't think losing someone you work with would be so hard. But it is. I pick up my phone to send her a message and start typing her name before I realize... she's not there to get it anymore."

Kenzie nodded. She had lost people too. People she had thought she would work with for a long time, that she would be able to develop a longer, deeper relationship with, and who were now gone from her life. It was hard for people to believe that losing a work colleague could be just as difficult as a family member. People didn't get the same level of support for losing a colleague. They were expected to get over it and quickly move on.

"How had Mariya been lately? Alina had thought that she might have been more..." Kenzie trailed off, letting Dana fill it in. She didn't want to put something into Dana's head, but at the same time, she wanted her to believe that Alina had also noticed and already told Kenzie about it.

Dana pressed her lips together, thinking. “Well… yeah. You’re right. She had been having some trouble lately. She didn’t want to talk about it, even though I did ask. I wanted her to know that she could trust me, could lean on me.”

“Was it personal, then? Or work-related?”

“It was work. I think this new project Mariya was working on with Morgan. She just seemed like… she had been really thoughtful and worried since she started on the new project.”

“What was it about? Do you know what the project was?”

“I wasn’t in on all of the details. Some transplant research that was really promising. Morgan was moving it down the field. Mariya said that we needed to be careful, not to move too fast, and to make sure that all of the research and testing was done properly. Sometimes, you know, something looks really good and they rush it through testing, and it always goes badly. Something that looked really good at the beginning might have just been… an illusion. Something that didn't actually work the way we thought it did. A correlation that wasn't."

"And that worried Mariya? She was worried that Morgan was rushing his research through?"

"No, not in so many words. She just… I don't know. She kept reminding me there was a way to do things properly and that you couldn't rush things through without proper protocols. People would get hurt. That was what happened when you rushed into medical research that hadn't been properly tested. People getting hurt."

"It sounds like she was pretty worried. Did you notice any physical changes in her? Trouble sleeping? Did she seem down or complain about anything? Brain fog? Not being able to concentrate or remember things?"

Dana gazed at Kenzie as if she knew she had said too much.

"Some of that," Dana admitted eventually. "She had bags under her eyes, so I didn't think she was sleeping well. She'd lost weight and was quite skinny."

"Did she talk to you about it? Say what she was worrying about?"

"She was on her phone a lot, so at first, I thought maybe it was some relationship thing. But we talked a bit... I think it was the possibility of going to human trials. She didn't think they were ready. But Morgan... he said that there was no need to pull back. They had done the research and proven it was safe, and now they wanted to save human lives, not to put it off any longer."

"Who was senior? Who would actually make that decision?"

"Morgan is senior. He has a stake in the business. I don't know all of the details, but he is one of the owners as well as the senior researcher. So basically... what he says, goes."

"Is he here today? I'd like to talk to him."

CHAPTER 14

Morgan Tucker was not someone that Kenzie immediately warmed up to. When Dana Pratt had walked into the room, Kenzie had felt an immediate affinity for her. She was friendly and helpful and had been good friends with Mariya. Kenzie liked her bright clothing and buoyant smile. Despite the tragedy of losing Mariya, a close friend and colleague, she had been helpful and easy to talk to.

Tucker, on the other hand, was the diametric opposite. He clearly was not happy about his work being interrupted to talk to Kenzie about Dr. Markov. He was unsmiling, with closed-off body language that told Kenzie right off the bat that she was going to have a difficult time talking to him. He had already made up his mind about the conversation and was not going to cooperate.

He was a heavyset man with a round, ruddy face. The shirt he wore under his lab coat strained at the buttons, as if he had put on a lot of weight recently and hadn't had a chance to buy properly fitting clothing since then. He sat down in one of the boardroom chairs and tipped it back, making it squeal alarmingly. He looked around the boardroom, his eyes eventually returning to Kenzie.

"I thought this was a police investigation," he said, looking at her. "But you're not a cop. Where are the others? Where is your boss?"

"I'm with the medical examiner's office, not the police. I am working in conjunction with the police in determining what caused Mariya's death and all of the contributing factors."

"You are a medical examiner?"

"Yes."

"You don't have very much experience."

He didn't ask whether she did; he just assumed that she did not, which Kenzie bristled at.

“I have the necessary training and experience. I have been with the medical examiner’s office for several years now. I work with a more senior pathologist as well, and I can assure you that between the two of us, we will cover all of the bases and come to a conclusion about how Mariya was killed.”

“You don’t know her personally, why are you calling her Mariya?”

Kenzie hadn’t realized that she had continued to call the scientist by her first name after the interview with Dana.

“Excuse me. I’m sorry. The last interviewee wanted me to call Dr. Markov by her first name. I didn’t mean to be disrespectful. So…” Kenzie folded her hands on the table in front of her and leaned forward. “I’m sure you don’t want to have to spend any more time on this than you have to. I understand that Dr. Markov had been working on a new project for you recently. Can you tell me about it?”

"She was working with me, yes. Dr. Markov was a very prestigious researcher and surgeon. It was a privilege to have her on my team."

Kenzie was surprised to hear him laud Dr. Markov. She had been expecting the opposite. Some kind of dig about how he was the more senior researcher and she did whatever he told her to.

"I had met her at fundraisers before," Kenzie said. "She seemed very competent and people spoke highly of her."

Dr. Tucker nodded. "She was very experienced and highly skilled. It was a coup for us to entice her over to Birch Valley. And I was delighted to have her on my team."

He still looked sullen and mulish, but maybe that was just his natural expression and did not reflect how he felt.

"Dr. Markov's sister suggested that she had been stressed lately, and she thought it had something to do with the new project that Dr. Markov had been working on. Would that have been your project?"

"It could be stressful work," he admitted. "That would not be unexpected."

"What exactly was she stressed about, do you know? Was there a lot of pressure surrounding this study?"

"A firm like this does not get funding unless it is able to show progress, not just promise. We need to be able to show that we are at the cutting edge of the industry, not just suggest that we have some fresh innovations that investors might be interested in. We have to show it in practice."

Kenzie nodded. "That makes sense. And I can see how you would always be under pressure to perform. Not every theory you have is going to pan out, but you will be judged for the ones that don't."

"Yes. And we are not just talking about theoretical physics or things happening in a solar system across the galaxy from us.

We are talking about people whose lives hang in the balance. We will save them, or they will die. Do you know anything about kidney disease?"

Kenzie raised her brows. "My sister died from complications of kidney disease and a transplant. Have you heard of the Kirsch family foundation?"

His eyes flashed. "You are one of <u>those</u> Kirsches?" His lips tightened, and all the lines in his face pointed downward. "You have the gall to come here to question our success after pulling your funding?"

"No. This has nothing to do with your success or failure. I am here to find out what happened to Dr. Markov. As a medical examiner."

"How do you expect us to succeed without funding? I have to waste my time running around after funding, putting on dog-and-pony shows for potential investors, rather than focusing solely on my project and helping people with kidney disease."

He slapped his palm down on the table. "We could be curing kidney disease, giving them a new life, but instead—" he threw up his hands in surrender. "Instead, we are trying to get the study funded!"

"Can we get back to Dr. Markov? She was feeling the stress of the situation?"

"Of course she was. We were all feeling the pressure. It was time to go to human trials. Putting kidneys inside of patients who had been on dialysis for months or years. Do you know what that would mean for them?"

Kenzie remembered the long hours Amanda had spent in dialysis. What it had meant for her to get Kenzie's donated kidney and suddenly not to be tied to the machines all the time, but to be able to live a normal life, as if the kidney disease had never happened. Except for the cocktail of pills to keep rejection at bay.

"Yes, I remember when Amanda got my kidney."

He considered her for a minute, some of the bullishness falling away. Maybe he was realizing now what she had sacrificed for his cause. Not just funding from the foundation, but a piece of herself.

“You donated a kidney?”

“I would have given her both if I could have. But they wouldn’t let me do that.”

“No.” He gave a humorless chuckle. “Not until we can signal your body to grow a new one.”

“That would be handy. What was the project Dr. Markov was working on with you? It was about transplant technology?”

“Gene editing donated organs so that they can be transplanted without fear of rejection. We have been very successful in animal studies. You see how this would revolutionize the industry? How different it would be to simply transplant an organ and not to have to take anti-rejection medications for the rest of your life?"

"Yeah. That would really be something. If you didn't have to worry about complications and compliance..."

He nodded. "This is something we will be able to do within the next ten years," he declared. "In ten years, there will be no more need for follow-up care. Patients will simply be released from the hospital once they are healed and be able to carry on with their normal lives once more."

"Do you really think we can reach that point?"

"Of course we can. With the right funding, it wouldn't even take ten years." He glared at her but didn't say that they needed the funding from the Kirsch family foundation if they were going to succeed. But Kenzie knew that was what he was thinking.

"Dr. Markov must have been really excited at that prospect."

"Of course. We all are. She knew it would take a lot of work, long hours, many different test subjects and studies, but eventually we will get there."

"Did she have any concerns about it?"

His forehead wrinkled. "What kind of concerns?"

"I was just wondering. If she had any concerns with the protocols or how quickly things were moving. Maybe she had doubts about some of the research that had been done or wanted the human trials handled differently."

"Who told you that?"

"I heard that she had some concerns. I don't know much about what they were. That is why I'm trying to find out."

"Why? If she had concerns with the research, that has nothing to do with why she died." He stared at her.

Kenzie shifted uncomfortably. She looked toward the door, wondering when her next interviewee would show up. Was he there now, waiting for her to finish with Tucker?

“Maybe if Dr. Markov was worried about the protocols and what would happen, she was distracted from the job she was supposed to be doing, which was driving. Maybe she was trying to make a phone call. Maybe she was worrying about what you would say if she suggested making changes to the protocols.”

He scoffed at this. “Dr. Markov was a scientist. She knew how things were run. It was my project. She would not be changing any protocols.”

“So she was only stressed about the funding?”

He nodded, folding his arms across his chest. “Of course. The withdrawal of funding concerned all of us.”

CHAPTER 15

There was a knock at the door. Kenzie let out her breath, happy to have an interruption. Tucker didn't want to talk about Mariya Markov. He wanted to talk about the funding, why the Kirsch family foundation had withdrawn their financing from the company, or at least why they should pony up and fund it again. And despite using her name to get access to the company, that wasn't why Kenzie was there.

She couldn't even have made funding or policy changes if she had wanted to. There was a whole process for that, with filing a recommendation for a change, complete with all of the reasons and foreseeable impacts, and that would go first to the funding committee and then to the entire board. It would need a majority vote to be put through. Then, the management would be tasked with making the change, which might take weeks or months. There was certainly no picking up the phone and having the change made with a single phone call. Tucker seemed to think that Kenzie could just make a change unilaterally.

But she didn't think most scientists understood the process. They were too involved in their own studies to care about someone else's area of expertise.

The door opened slightly, and an older, balding man with a white fringe of hair poked his head in the door.

"Sorry, I'm supposed to come over here to talk to Dr. Kirsch? Am I in the right place?"

Tucker rose to his feet, looking irritated at the interruption.

"Hiram. Good timing, we were just finished."

Kenzie wasn't sure they were finished, but she wasn't sure they were going any further anyway. Whatever Tucker might be able to tell her, it didn't look like he was going to reveal anything about Markov and any particular stress she might have been feeling the night she was killed.

Tucker departed without another word to Kenzie. She watched him go, thinking about his attitude. Hopefully, the new interviewee would be more helpful. He certainly looked friendlier.

"Hi," Kenzie extended her hand. "I'm Dr. Kirsch."

"Ah, lovely to meet you, my dear. Dr. Hayes."

"Come on in, and let's get started." Kenzie motioned to the boardroom table, and they both sat down.

Kenzie laced her fingers together, resting them on the table. "I am very sorry for your loss. It must be really difficult working here this week with such a tragedy on your mind."

"Yes, that's very true," Hayes agreed. "I wish I could tell you how emotional it has been... It is very hard for anyone to get anything done. Human beings are programmed to be social, emotional beings, and a loss like this... has a great impact."

Kenzie nodded her understanding. “Yes. You can’t just turn off your emotions and work as usual. At least, most of us cannot. There are those who can.”

“You are very young—and pretty—to be a medical examiner.”

Female, Kenzie assumed he meant. Very young and female. Not the usual crusty old doctor. A lot of people seemed to be under the mistaken impression that a woman could not do the job, or would not want to.

“So, tell me about your work here,” Kenzie invited, without commenting on his biases about medical examiners. “What are you involved in? I was just talking to Dr. Tucker about his… transplant project.”

“Well, I am working on pre-care and aftercare for transplant patients. Pharmaceutical support can be quite complex and is a minefield just waiting to be set off.”

“So your projects are complementary.”

"We always try to support each other and come at the same problem from different perspectives. We develop synergies and more complete models of care that make a real difference to our future patients. To everyone who will be blessed by the protocol."

"That sounds very positive. I wonder how many breakthroughs have been buried or eclipsed by an existing system that can't be adapted."

He nodded eagerly. "Yes, exactly. No matter how revolutionizing a discovery is, if it cannot be implemented, it's no good. Just like... coming up with a superior phone or other electronics that can't be plugged into the existing wiring in a home or office. Who is going to go through all of the trouble of stripping out the old, outdated technology and completely rewiring the home or office with the new infrastructure? No one. If you can't plug it into your wall, you are not taking it home. It doesn't matter how revolutionary it is."

"So you are... modularizing the care model. Rather than just replacing the transplant with a better transplant method, you're integrating the medication protocols as well."

He nodded, apparently pleased that she was a quick study. Kenzie thought about the possibility of gene editing, as Tucker had said, to alter the organ being transplanted so that it would not be rejected by the host. Essentially making it their own organ. Not only would it mean no rejection and no need for a lifetime of antirejection drugs, but it also meant that there would be no need for tissue typing and matching. Any donor organ could be edited to match any recipient. All of that infrastructure could be thrown out.

Hayes was watching her, apparently reading her thought process in her expression and nodding his agreement. "Imagine the difference. A child needs a transplant. They go to the hospital before they get deathly ill. They receive care that strengthens their immune system, heart, and lungs, and prepares them for the transplant. They go into surgery as soon as their doctor says they are ready and get the new organ. It works perfectly and is a perfect match to their own tissues. No rejection. It fills with blood and starts working. We watch for a day or two for any problems with infection or the incision, and then they go home, strong and healthy."

"That would really be something."

"It will happen. We are going to see it happen within our lifetime. We have the technology. We know how to make it work."

"Your animal studies have been promising, Dr. Tucker said?"

"Yes. We've proven that we can do this, and we are ready to start on human trials."

"That seems really fast."

He shook his head, smiling. "You haven't been involved in this research; you don't know how long it has taken us to get to this point. We have been working on it for years. It isn't out of the blue."

"What did Dr. Markov think? She wasn't worried about it being too fast?"

"Dr. Markov was just as excited as any of us to see this technology coming to fruition. The shift from animal trials to human trials can be scary. It is a big change in our program. But we have to move from one to the other and actually get it working! The whole point of this research is to bring it to the world. Not just to sit on it and talk about how someday we will be able to change the face of organ transplant."

"Did Dr. Markov have any concerns about it?"

"Why would you think that?"

"I have heard that she was feeling the stress and thought that it might be going too fast."

"We are all feeling the stress. But it is a good stress. Excitement. Knowing that all of our work is about to come to fruition."

"She didn't think you were ready for human trials."

"As I said, the shift could be a scary one. We all have our feelings of anxiety over it. But we know we are going to succeed. We know it is time to implement everything we have set up." He smiled at her; then his face slowly fell into a poignant expression. "If only she were here to see it."

Kenzie knew that Dr. Markov was a tireless advocate for organ transplant and kidney disease research. Kenzie had heard her speak passionately about it more than once. She felt that same poignancy at the fact that Dr. Markov was not there to see it.

"Were you there the night of the fundraiser?" she asked Dr. Hayes. "Did you see her that night?"

"Yes, I was there. We both spoke. Trying to drum up the last few dollars needed to proceed to the next research stage."

The "last few dollars" would actually have been tens of thousands of dollars. A fancy dinner, expensive wine, and passionate speakers to inspire the funding bodies and foundations to pull out their wallets and checkbooks and give Birch Valley what they needed to enter this new phase of trials, moving from animal models to actual human beings. She tried to envision the excitement of the potential transplant patients anticipating a new model of care and transplants that did not require tissue matches.

"That's amazing. And so now... I assume you reached the threshold you needed to, and now you're getting ready to begin the human trials?"

Hayes just smiled at her. He could not, of course, break confidentiality to tell her precisely what the company was doing. If it directly impacted a death investigation—if one of their transplant patients had a catastrophic reaction to a transplant, for example—then they would be required to disclose all of the relevant information to Kenzie, confidential or not.

But this investigation was different. It was not an investigation into their transplant technology, but simply into the accidental death of a scientist in their cloisters.

Kenzie sighed and tried to push out all of the information about transplants and everything else to focus on Dr. Markov. She had come to Birch Valley to find out why Dr. Markov had behaved the way that she had the night she died. Was she upset? Was she drunk? Did she have another medical problem? Was she disoriented and that was why she ended up on the road into town instead of out to the highway? If she was disoriented, was it because of a seizure? A medication? A fever?

“How close were you to Dr. Markov?”

"We worked very closely together. I would call her a friend, not just a colleague. I daresay... she would have called me one too."

"And had you noticed any extra stress in her life lately? Had she been acting like something was wrong?"

"No more anxious than any of us. We were on the cusp of something very exciting. Something that was going to change the world. We were all feeling that way. Someone outside the office might not understand what was going on, but believe me, everyone was on pins and needles, including Dr. Markov."

"You didn't notice her being negative about anything?"

"No. Cautious, as she always was."

"And she didn't seem depressed?"

"Depressed? No."

“Was she on any medication? Having any health problems that you were aware of?”

He shook his head slowly. “She seemed very healthy. If she was experiencing any health difficulties, she did not mention them. And I think I would have noticed if she had been away from the lab for a lot of doctor’s appointments. But there was nothing that I saw.” He hesitated. “Did you find something in the autopsy that she should have known about? That would have made her sick? Scientists are not always the most self-aware people. We can be shockingly negligent of our own physical care.”

“Dr. Markov’s sister thought that she might be having health issues. She was not sleeping well, had bags under her eyes…”

“Oh.” Hayes chuckled. “Well, that’s true for all of us. None of us were sleeping well, with deadlines approaching and the possibility of beginning human trials right away.”

"You didn't notice her having any more trouble with it than anyone else?"

"No."

"Did Dr. Markov drink?"

He raised an eyebrow. "You would be able to tell from your autopsy whether she had been drinking or not, wouldn't you?"

"She had only had a taste of alcohol that night. And she did not have an alcoholic's liver."

He shrugged. "I do not think she was a closet drinker," he agreed. "And I don't think I ever saw her drain a glass. Perhaps a sip, but usually just holding it in her hand."

"Any other drugs?"

"As I say, you would know better than I would."

"Prescriptions? Over the counter? Herbal remedies?"

“What are you looking for?”

“Anything that she might have reacted to that night, that would have gotten her turned around or impaired her too much to drive.”

“Ah.” He considered this seriously, but eventually shook his head. “I am afraid I do not know of any condition or anything she might have taken that would have impaired her driving. She seemed like a healthy woman to me.”

CHAPTER 16

Kenzie was heading home later than she had planned. There had been more people to interview at Birch Valley than she had anticipated. She was glad she had not made arrangements to see Lisa as well. She would rather get home, enjoy the evening with Zachary, and worry about family obligations another day.

As she left the parking lot for Birch Valley, she noticed a black SUV with tinted windows behind her. Even though it was not the same profile as the vehicle that had previously been used to kidnap her—a white van with the interior stripped—it still sent her heart pumping hard and fast. It looked like the FBI or kidnapper vehicles in a thriller movie.

But this was real life. And in real life, it was just someone who wanted a roomy, comfortable interior and the sun's glare out of their eyes. At worst, it was a drug dealer who wanted to intimidate his buyers and competition. Someone who didn't know well enough to keep a low profile.

Kenzie kept her eyes on the road ahead and didn't even look in her rearview mirror unless she had to. She was not going to let her imagination get away from her. She wasn't going to let herself have a panic attack over the sight of a truck that was not even like the one that her kidnappers had driven. She was just going to drive home, like she would any other day, and Zachary was going to be there when she got home, and they were going to spend a pleasant evening with one another while they eased into the weekend.

She got onto the highway and drove past the next couple of towns before finally allowing herself to look in the rearview mirror.

And there was nothing suspicious. Nothing at all to worry about. No black SUV with tinted windows. No white van. Just other Vermont commuters, making the trek from one town to the next as they thought about their weekends ahead.

Kenzie let out a long sigh. She had been right. It had just been a random black SUV, no one following her or out to get her for some reason. She was perfectly safe in her car, just as she had been every other time she had driven the highway.

The relief and the fact that she had been holding her breath gave her a head rush, and for a few moments, her vision was blurry, and she felt a little lightheaded, even though she knew she wasn't going to pass out.

For a split second, she thought of Mariya Markov and how she must have felt during that last fateful ride. Had she felt woozy? Blurry? Had she known that something was wrong, or had she thought it was just a normal ride like any other and had crashed without anticipating it? Had she been scared or disoriented for the last few minutes? Did she know the danger she had been in?

Kenzie pecked at the buttons on the stereo. She needed to fill the car with loud, happy tunes to raise her spirits. She wasn't going to think morbid thoughts of Mariya Markov all the way back to Roxboro. She had spent all day thinking of the woman and her mental state before she had died. Now, it was time to put aside all those dark thoughts and focus on other things.

She rocked out, cranking up the stereo and speeding down the highway—though she wasn't technically speeding—she had no desire to get pulled over by the police and have to pay a ticket, or admit to Zachary that she had been speeding when she always told him to stick to the speed limit.

As if conjured by her thoughts, blue flashing light lit up in her rearview mirror, getting closer and closer until the police car finally whipped past her on the left. Kenzie watched it go and glanced into her mirror again to ensure there weren't any others coming.

She caught a glimpse of a black SUV in her mirror and caught her breath. Had it followed her after all? She slowed down, watching to see how it would react. After a few seconds, it signaled left and pulled out to pass her. Kenzie let her breath out again and watched it pass her. No tinted windows. Not the same SUV at all. She was just being paranoid.

Her phone rang, making her jump, but she did not swerve lanes; she just gave a little yelp and looked at the phone in its holder. Zachary. Checking in to see when she would be home.

Kenzie swiped and greeted him. “Hey, Zachary.”

“Looks like you’re on your way back.”

“Yes, I am. How was your day?”

Zachary groaned. She could picture him stretching his arms and shoulders, having been sitting too long in front of the computer. How many times had she seen him do just that? “Been doing research. Stuck in this almost all day.”

“Your new file?”

“Yeah.”

"So, do you think your client is being spied on? His secrets stolen?"

"Well... I would say so. Their physical security needs to be upgraded. Security on the individual computers isn't too bad. But they still have holes in their network. And if someone can get on to the network, then sooner or later, they are going to get their hands on information that they are not supposed to have."

"Makes sense," Kenzie agreed. "So you're going to be able to get it straightened out for them?"

"I'll make recommendations. And I'm going to get Gerry to do a quick audit of the systems to see what I've missed. I know some of the stuff to look for, but he's way beyond my skill level."

"You're a lot more savvy than I am about these things." Kenzie thought of all of the time Elijah had spent on her work computer, closing up those open entry points that Zachary was talking about, tracing where the threatening email had come from. She just used her computer the way she had been shown when she first trained on it, and didn't really explore any of the utilities or how to protect it. Kenzie knew there was an antivirus program on it that would supposedly keep the bad guys off, and it auto-updated regularly to include new definitions as new malware was created by the hackers. But she heard every day about the big companies and government systems getting hacked by predators demanding a ransom to bring them back online again. If those huge companies with fancy IT departments and mega budgets couldn't keep the hackers off, how was a little department like the medical examiner's office supposed to protect itself?

“Do you want me to order something and have it ready when you get here?” Zachary asked. “Or do you want to go out? Or make something?”

"Ordering in sounds good to me. I don't really feel like going out anywhere, since I've already been out most of the day."

Dr. B wanted them to use date night to do things other than just staying home and watching TV. But there were nights when that was all either of them could manage. They hadn't specifically planned to do anything else tonight, and that was just fine with Kenzie.

"Thai good for you? I don't think I'm up for that Mexican this time," Zachary offered.

Kenzie chuckled. She was more in the mood for "comfort food" than burning her sinuses out anyway. "Thai it is," she agreed. "I'll be... about another hour, so don't order quite yet. Set an alarm for yourself."

"I'm not going to do any more work right now, so I shouldn't need an alarm. I'll remember."

"Set an alarm," Kenzie said firmly. She didn't want to arrive home ready to eat, only to find that time had gotten away with him as he checked his social networks and nothing had been ordered.

“Okay, I will,” Zachary sighed. But he didn’t tell her to wait while he did it, and she suspected he would not do it until after she hung up, and maybe not even then. He was stubborn sometimes.

“I’ll get off the phone so you can do it,” Kenzie told him. “See you in an hour.”

He barely had time to say goodbye before she hung up on him. Hopefully, that meant that his mind would still be on setting an alarm to order the food, and he wouldn’t get distracted and forget it.

CHAPTER 17

Kenzie was just pulling off the highway into Roxboro when her phone rang again. She expected it to be Zachary, announcing that dinner had arrived and he would see her in a few minutes, but the name on her caller ID was Lisa's.

Kenzie ignored the call. Had Lisa found out that she had been in Burlington and not stopped by to see her? She didn't want to have to lie about it or give an excuse. Best just not to engage with her at all.

The call went to voicemail. But in a few seconds, it was ringing again. Kenzie scowled. What did Lisa have a bee in her bonnet about this time? Kenzie didn't want to answer it, but then she thought about Walter and what if he'd had a real medical emergency? What would her mother do then? She would call Kenzie repeatedly until she answered.

Kenzie swiped to pick up the call. "Sorry, Mom, I just missed it the first time."

"Mackenzie, there's been some trouble."

Kenzie swallowed, a lump forming in her throat. "Trouble? What kind of trouble?"

"Are you at home? Where are you?"

"I'm... just on my way home right now. What does it matter where I am?"

"There was a break-in at the foundation offices. Some vandalism. I am very upset about it! And so is Hillary, of course. I just... needed to know that you were home safe and sound. I want to know that everything else in my life is... in order."

"Oh, Mom. I'm so sorry." Kenzie felt an immediate wave of guilt wash over her. She had been trying to avoid her mother when Lisa had needed her the most. The foundation offices had been broken into? For what? "What happened? What kind of vandalism? Was it just random violence or... or what?"

"Some stuff smashed up. Nothing important, of course. I don't have anything of great value in the office. And some graffiti scrawl that… well, made it clear that it was not just a random attack."

"What do you mean?"

"Names. Name-calling. Phrases about defunding important programs."

"Kidney research." Kenzie's guts tied in knots. She had just been talking to the researchers at Birch Valley about kidney research and how they were on the cusp of a whole new paradigm. She had admitted that they were no longer funding kidney research like they had and were instead focused on other issues.

Had her comments inflamed one of the researchers enough that they would break into the foundation offices to vandalize them?

"When did they break in?" They must have been there pretty quickly after Hillary had closed up, for Lisa to already know about it. If Hillary had still been there...

A hot lump formed in her throat. She hated to think that their administrative decision might bring violence so close to home. She did not want Hillary to be targeted. The administrative office of the foundation was very small, with Hillary often the only one attending in person. She would be vulnerable if someone came to the offices with violence on their mind.

"It was just about twenty minutes ago. Hillary had closed and gone home. The security alarm went off and apparently scared the vandals away. The security company checked out the scene and called the police, and I've just been dealing with them. Everything is fine here, Mackenzie. I just wanted to be sure that you had not been targeted as well."

"No, not everything is fine. Hillary is okay? She wasn't there?"

Even though Lisa had just said so, Kenzie needed the reassurance of hearing it again.

“Yes, Hillary is fine. A bit mad that she missed it, actually. I think she would have liked to have shown those hooligans what for. They violated her space and she wants someone to pay.”

“Did you get any video? Do you know who it was?”

“The security company will review the footage around the building and see if they got any good shots. But the cameras are obvious and they said that the intruders will probably have worn hats or masks to avoid being identified.”

“Well, let me know if you find out who it was. Will they run fingerprints or any other evidence from the scene?”

“I don’t think the police are too concerned about it for the moment. No one was injured. Nothing valuable was stolen. It was pretty minor stuff, as far as they are concerned.”

Kenzie let out a low growl of frustration. “Well, I might have someone here give them a call to light a fire under them. What about your contacts with the governor or someone else? You know people. You can tell them that you are not going to stand around and let them sweep this under the rug.”

“Well, it is pretty minor when you think about it. I am sure they have much more important crimes to investigate. We don’t really want to put a thumb on the scale, do we? Make people think that we are getting preferential treatment? That won’t help with the bad feelings already being expressed about us.”

“Well... I’m not sure I actually care about that. I want this to be investigated properly.”

“I’m sure it will be.”

“I’ll try to be reasonable about it. But I don’t know if I can be.”

Lisa muffled a laugh. “Well, you’re honest about it. I’m glad to hear your voice. Now I know I don’t need to worry about you. Have a good evening with Zachary. Date night tonight, isn’t it?”

“Yes, but we will probably just stay in. I have been out doing interviews most of the day. I’ll say hello to Zachary for you.”

“Yes, you do that. I will talk to you later. Keep you updated on developments here. Take care.”

“Okay, Mom. Bye. I’m sorry you have to deal with this. People really are stupid sometimes. Do they think that vandalizing the place will get them their funding back?”

“No, dear. They just want to vent their anger. They know it won’t get them what they want.”

CHAPTER 18

It felt like Kenzie had been away from home for a long time. Not that she had just been home that morning, like any other day she went to the office. It had been a slightly longer day than usual, but she felt like it had been a week since she had been home.

She was relieved to drive her car into the garage and park it there, safe and sound where it belonged. She listened to the growl of the garage door motor as it shut the door. She hadn't realized until then how worried she had been that something would happen to her on the way home. The combination of the black SUV with the tinted windows triggering memories of her abduction, her investigation into Dr. Markov's death, and the news of the break-in at the foundation had combined to create a dread that something was going to happen to her on the way home.

When she entered the kitchen through the garage door, Zachary was at the table unpacking the food delivery. The warm, savory smells of their favorite restaurant filled the room. Kenzie's stomach growled in response. She put her hand over it.

"I had no idea how hungry I was," she laughed. "Boy, does that smell good."

"You have perfect timing. The food just got here."

"Nice." Kenzie pulled off her shoes and went over to help him set the food out.

"Sit down, sit down," he insisted, herding her to her usual chair. "I can at least do this."

Kenzie sighed, sat down, and rubbed her toes, happy to have her shoes off. She found that her hands were shaking,

Zachary got out plates and cutlery and distributed them on the table. He set out glasses and the jug of water from the fridge, then nodded. It wasn't a big, fancy meal, but it was just what Kenzie needed, and she appreciated the extra pampering.

Zachary sat down, and they started to dish up the food. Kenzie got up to wash her hands at the sink, and when she sat down caught Zachary's eyes on her, a frown creasing his forehead. She forced a smile.

"What?"

"What's wrong?"

Kenzie opened her mouth to deny that anything was wrong and tell him she was just fine. But that went against everything they had worked on together in couple's therapy. Zachary could see that she was trying to compose an answer, and waited.

"There was a break-in at the foundation," she told him finally. "Lisa called me right after I talked to you."

“A break-in. Why would anyone break in there?” Zachary shook his head. “Was anything stolen?”

“Nothing of value, as far as Mom could tell. They... vandalized it. Graffiti about the foundation taking away funding from kidney research.”

“You’re kidding! Who would do something like that?”

“I would guess someone who works at one of the companies doing research. Maybe someone who has a loved one who is waiting for a transplant or some kind of breakthrough, hoping that they will be able to save them.”

Kenzie swallowed, trying not to think too deeply about Amanda. How hard it had been to wait. How terrible it had been when she got sick again after the transplant, and there was nothing they could do about it. What would she have done if a foundation she had trusted, one of those research companies, had told her that they were no longer going to work on kidney disease but had decided on another focus?

For years after Amanda's death, they had hung on to the vision that they would prevent the same thing from happening to others. The research that they were funding was giving kidney patients like Amanda longer lives, better quality of life, and hope for the future. And the foundation was still putting money into those causes, just not in the same amounts. There were other people who needed help. There were even more people who needed help with mental health concerns, with research and treatment and outreach programs.

She was glad that they were putting money into those issues. She was proud of her parents for seeing the need and realizing how important it was to people like Zachary and his siblings. She was warmed that they wanted to do everything they could for Zachary, Tyrrell, and anyone else going through the same things as they had. For children who had been through abuse and other traumas in their early lives.

"I guess they have reason to be upset," Zachary allowed. "But what good is it going to do to vandalize the foundation?"

"It doesn't do anyone any good. Maybe it makes them feel better to have something to focus their anger on and to think that they have struck a blow for their loved one. Or themselves. Or if it is someone with one of the research companies that lost funding, to get some kind of retribution. You damage my work, I'll damage yours."

"People suck sometimes."

Kenzie chuckled. She poked at her food before taking the first bite. Despite her concerns over the attack on the foundation, she was hungry, and the food was as good as it always was.

"They do," she agreed. "I feel like I'm surrounded by these people right now."

"Surrounded?"

"Yes... between the people Dr. Markov worked with, and the one who sent the email, and now this trouble with the foundation, it feels like they're closing in on every side."

Zachary chewed slowly, looking at her. "What are you talking about?"

CHAPTER 19

“Dr. Markov. The team that she was working with was working on kidney research and transplant. They’re just getting ready to go to human trials. They... expressed their displeasure about the foundation not funding them as much.”

“I didn’t know that.”

“Yeah. And...” Kenzie realized that she hadn’t told Zachary anything about the threatening email and the work they’d had to do on her computer and the network to make it secure. “And then with this attack on the foundation, right after I was talking to Dr. Markov’s colleagues... it’s just a bit disconcerting, that’s all.”

She hoped he would not focus on the item in the list she had missed, but should have known better. As distractible as Zachary was, he wasn’t fooled by her glossing over the email.

“What else?”

Kenzie twirled thin noodles around her fork. “It was just something at work. You know. Someone sent a spam email.”

“What kind of spam email?”

“An email that was… very threatening and explicit. Beyond your usual robo-trash.”

“You didn’t mention this before.”

“Well, it was just one email. I haven’t been getting a deluge of them. It was being dealt with by IT. I didn’t really need any other help, and it’s just… it’s upsetting to even talk about it. I’d rather not. Just chalk it up as a particularly nasty bit of spam, and go on with life.”

Zachary picked up a spring roll and toyed with it before taking a bite.

“This email… it wasn’t just a mass email sent out to millions of accounts.”

“No. It was... targeted. Sent specifically to my email address, with personal information in it.”

He looked around, craning his neck to see out the front window, as if someone might be out there stalking her right now. His jaw muscles tightened, and when he spoke it was through clenched teeth.

“It’s good that you had an IT guy in to look at it and make sure that your systems are secure. But you need to let the police know as well. If there was personal information in it, they could know enough to target you. You don’t know whether it came from someone on the other side of the world or if they could be local, someone who could confront you face-to-face.”

Kenzie sighed. “I did file a police report. It’s all taken care of.”

“You did? And you didn’t tell <u>me</u> about it?” He was upset and angry. She could see that he was struggling valiantly to keep himself under control. All of those protective instincts of his were kicking in and he would want to wall her off, keep her isolated from the rest of the world.

Kenzie kept her own voice casual and light. “I didn’t think I needed to. I did everything I could, and there isn’t anything you could do about my work email.”

“But it must have bothered you. Been on your mind. You <u>said</u> you’re feeling like you are surrounded, so it did affect you. Why didn’t you tell me?”

Kenzie hadn’t considered the consequences of leaving Zachary out of the loop. “I just wanted to leave it at work, not bring it home. I just want this to be a stress-free zone.”

Zachary gave a sour laugh at this, drawing an embarrassed smile to Kenzie’s lips. Given how much Zachary’s anxiety and depression affected him and their relationship, and the break-ins and attacks that they’d experienced during the time they have been living together, it couldn't exactly be regarded as a stress-free zone.

But that was all the more reason <u>not</u> to bring more home with her.

"Okay, maybe I'm being silly. Maybe I should have told you about it the day I got it. But like I say, it was being handled by IT and the police, and I didn't want to bring it home with me."

"But now it is part of a bunch of stress that is piling up. And you're feeling like you're being attacked on all sides."

Kenzie nodded and shrugged. "But I'm not being attacked. I know that. It's just a bunch of stuff that has happened at once, so it feels like that. All unrelated stuff."

"It <u>could</u> be a part of a pattern," Zachary disagreed. He stood up, paced around the room, then went into the living room and looked outside.

“It’s not a pattern,” Kenzie insisted. “You can’t take all of the negative things going on in your life and say they are related.”

“What did the email say?”

“It was just a lot of nasty, threatening stuff.”

“About being the assistant medical examiner?”

Kenzie shook her head slowly. “No, some of it was more personal. About my family.” She swallowed. “My parents are well-known and visible. So it wouldn’t take anyone much time to connect them with me and to see all of the organizations that they were associated with.”

Zachary ran his fingers through his hair. “Did your IT guy manage to trace it? To figure out where he had sent it from?”

“No. I don’t think there was a good address on it, just... whatever you call it. Phishing. Pretending to be someone else.”

"But it still had to come from somewhere."

"I don't know. I'll call Elijah tomorrow. I didn't ask him for any details, because they wouldn't mean anything to me. But if you want to know, he can give you a call."

"Yeah. I want all of the details."

"Okay." Kenzie had another bite of her Pad Thai. She wasn't sure if Zachary was going to eat any more of the food. He was pacing now, his mind on other things. But he could still have leftovers when he settled down. "Can we forget about it for now? What are your plans for the weekend?"

"I don't think we'd better go anywhere. Just stay home and keep our heads down."

"I don't think we have to worry about anyone coming after me. Especially if we go away. How would anyone know?"

Zachary turned back toward Kenzie to look at her. She was a little surprised at the anger in his face. "This is serious. When you came in here, you were shaking. Was that because of the break-in at the foundation?"

Kenzie thought about the black SUV. And all of the other things out there that could still trigger panic, even after a year and a half.

"Yeah, I guess so. It surprised me that someone would bother to break in there. I was relieved that no one was there when it happened. That Hillary wasn't hurt."

"But she could have been. If they didn't wait for her to leave at the end of the day. She couldn't have been gone for long when they broke in. That means they were watching the office. They could have ambushed her. She's working there all alone at the office most of the time."

"But they didn't. That's good. That means they aren't violent. Not even against one lone, middle-aged woman."

Zachary nodded jerkily. "Okay," he agreed. "True."

Kenzie released a breath. Score one for her.

"And same thing with these guys I was interviewing today. They knew my relationship with the foundation and could have been really angry and refused to talk to me. They could have threatened me and run me out of the place or told the police I was trespassing. But they didn't. They didn't like the fact that I was part of the foundation that pulled its funding, but they still cooperated and answered my questions."

"Yeah?" Zachary paused, standing with his hands in his pockets for a few breaths. "So that's good."

Kenzie nodded. "And I only got that one email. Not a whole bunch of them. And no direct threats on the phone or people confronting me on the street. Just some guy spouting off in email. Like you said, if he was local and wanted to find me, he could have. I try to be aware of my surroundings—" She'd been ambushed before, and didn't want it to happen again, "—and everything has been quiet. I really don't think you need to worry that there is a pattern of violence here. Just...

some disquiet. People who are discouraged by the foundation pulling funding."

"Disquiet," Zachary repeated.

Kenzie hesitated, wondering whether he was unfamiliar with the word and needed some explanation, or if it resonated with him.

"Disquiet," she said after a moment. "That's all it is. Nothing that we need to worry about."

"But you were worried when you came in."

"I was hungry and tired. And I'd just gotten the news of the break-in. I hadn't had a chance to process any of my reactions to it yet. And it will still take some time. But I'm okay. I'm not worried that someone is... stalking me or plotting against me."

She said the words with a laugh, keeping it light. They had dealt with angry, scared, and vengeful people before. *This* was not that.

“You still want to go see Mr. Peterson this weekend?” Zachary asked.

“I do. I always enjoy seeing Lorne. And Pat said he was making something special. You *know* how good his cooking is.”

Zachary gave a half-smile. He might still be concerned about the potential for an attack from a stranger, but Lorne Peterson, an ex-foster father with whom he had kept in touch over the decades, and Lorne’s partner Patrick Parker, held a special place in his heart. They were his chosen family. They had been there for him since he had been a lost and struggling teenager, and ever since. “I wouldn’t want to miss something special,” he agreed.

"Then let's not change our plans. We'll drive out tomorrow afternoon, stay overnight, and come home Sunday night."

"Maybe it is safer to be away," Zachary suggested.

"It would be a lot harder to track us down at the Petersons than at home. People would have to know your relationship with them and where they were."

Zachary rubbed his jaw, his short whiskers rasping in a way that always set Kenzie's teeth on edge. "That's true." He went over to the couch and sat down in front of his laptop, out of Kenzie's line of sight.

The conversation was apparently over. Wherever else Zachary's train of thought had taken him, he was gone now. She couldn't help feeling abandoned, sitting at the table with her warm Thai dinner, Zachary's plate only half emptied. While she might have "won" the argument and managed to avoid a paranoid meltdown by Zachary, she didn't feel like anything was resolved. She was still anxious about everything that had happened, and wouldn't be able to talk to him about it without his overreacting.

CHAPTER 20

Kenzie had been worried that Zachary would have a fit about her going in to the office Saturday morning, even though that was something she did with regularity. She wasn't worried that he would think she was overworking herself and that she didn't need to go in to work an extra day to catch up on stuff. She was concerned that it would trigger another discussion about the threat to her safety, maybe heading directly into the meltdown they had avoided the evening before over her not listening to his paranoia and warnings. And Kenzie wouldn't have time to pick up the pieces after that.

But Zachary didn't bring it up. He didn't tell her she needed to be careful or couldn't go to the office where people might be looking for her. Especially on a Saturday when she might be the only one in the office.

Instead, Kenzie worried about it herself. Was she being stupid to go in by herself? Was she making herself a target? There was a security gate to get into the parking garage for the building, with guards patrolling it regularly for any trouble. The elevator was not unlocked for public access on a Saturday. If she didn't want to sit at her desk in the hallway outside the medical examiner's suite, she could use one of the inner offices, knowing that the doors were locked and no one could get in.

There was really nothing to be nervous about. Kenzie couldn't be much safer than she was working in a locked office under the Roxboro police department.

By the time she arrived, she had nearly talked herself out of her nervousness. She was sure that once she had been there for a few minutes, she would forget all about any anxiety and be able to focus on her work for the time she was there.

Rather than focusing on the emails and reports languishing in her email inbox, Kenzie decided to review whatever information the forensic experts had discovered on Markov's electronics.

As was proper protocol, no one used the phone or other electronics directly, which could overwrite or obscure evidence. Instead, the memory was copied to a subfolder on the Markov folder on the network, and she could run an emulator that would allow her to interface with the files just as if she were using the phone. She could also look at the directory structure on the back end, but Kenzie generally left that for the tech geeks and just ran the phone apps on the emulator.

Kenzie searched for and found the folders that had been copied from Markov's locket. They appeared to be the same files as were saved to her photo roll on her phone. Recent videos and photographs like she would find on anyone's phone. She played a few, checking to make sure they were what they said they were, hoping to come across some kind of log or journal of what Mariya Markov had been stressed out about at work. Something that indicated where her thoughts had been in the days before her death.

Markov's phone did not include anything in the built-in notes app, and the were no downloaded notes apps. None? Kenzie had difficulty believing that Markov had never made any notes on her phone. Alina and Dana had said that she had used her phone extensively.

So where had she kept her notes? Had someone deleted them? If the notes had been wiped from her phone before she died, they should still be there somewhere in the memory, shouldn't they? Not accessible, maybe, but something that the tech guys could recover. But they hadn't noted that anything had been deleted in the last days of her life.

Kenzie cycled back to looking at the files on the locket again. She played the videos one at a time. They were mostly funny videos Markov had apparently saved from social media posts. Alina had said that Mariya liked funny cat videos, and Mariya had certainly saved her share of them. But why save them in her locket? Kenzie had expected the locket to contain sentimental memories, not cat videos.

There were also pictures of some of her colleagues at work, perhaps taken at an office party. Merle Shepherd, Dana Pratt, Morgan Tucker, Hiram Hayes, and a few of the other coworkers Kenzie had talked to about Markov's last days on the earth. A few other names she didn't recognize. Kenzie clicked through the pictures, looking for some indication of why Markov had taken the photos. There didn't seem to be any pattern. Again, they didn't seem to be the type of photos that she would have expected Markov to keep in her locket. They didn't seem to be anything special. Kenzie looked in the backgrounds for anything out of the ordinary. Maybe Markov had been trying to document something that was going on without tipping anyone off.

Or maybe there was nothing to see. Kenzie could not assume something sinister was going on at Birch Valley. Just because Alina said that Markov had been stressed recently and not sleeping, that did not mean she had secrets to hide. Tucker and Hayes had said that she had not been particularly stressed out about anything. Anxiously anticipating the human trials, maybe. Excited about being able to take the next step in achieving a revolutionary new paradigm in organ transplantation.

Kenzie heard the chime of the elevator and the doors opening and looked up from her work. She could not hear any footsteps, but there was no reason the elevator would have dinged if no one had come down.

CHAPTER 21

A figure stepped around the corner, silent as a shadow. Kenzie let out her breath when she saw it was Elijah.

"Oh, hey. I wasn't expecting you."

Elijah raised his brows. "You wanted to see me, didn't you?"

Kenzie thought back to the message she had left. "Yes. But I didn't figure you would be in today. I figured I'd see you Monday or sometime later in the week."

He smiled and shrugged. "You're not supposed to be in either, are you? I just took a chance that since you had left the message today, you might be in."

"Well..." Kenzie looked at her computer. "I often play catch-up on Saturday when I don't have as many interruptions and can just work through while it is quiet."

"Sure. Me too. They always have me running around during the week, and it is the only time I can actually sit at my desk and get anything done there. It's great being able to be mobile and move around to wherever I am needed, but sometimes I need to sit down at my own desk."

"And here I am interrupting you on your one day off."

"No worries. What can I help you with?"

"Well, I called to find out if you discovered anything about that email. You know, the threatening one…"

Of course he knew exactly what she was asking about. What other email would she mean?

"It was sent using an anonymizer service, so there isn't much we can tell about where it originated. The police will try to get warrants for the information from the anonymizer service, but most of them are located outside the US, so they don't have to comply with any court orders."

"So it's a dead end."

“Unfortunately,” Elijah agreed. “I checked system logs to see what other attacks had been attempted against your office network, and there was a lot of traffic from Russia.”

Kenzie swallowed, her mouth suddenly dry. “Russia?”

“That doesn’t necessarily mean anything. That’s where a lot of bot attacks originate. Some of it is even state-sponsored. You might not think that the Russian government would care about infiltrating a medical examiner’s office in Vermont, but any little place they can squeeze in and get some leverage...”

“Do you think a Russian sent that email?”

“No,” he said patiently. “There is no way for us to tell. It’s a possibility. There may be no connection at all between Russia and the email. Or you might be the victim of both an email attack and a number of unsuccessful hacks originating in Russia. But really, we don’t know.”

“Oh. Okay.” His words did not reassure Kenzie. Had she been targeted again by the Russians? And if so, was it a coincidence, or was it related to her kidnapping by the Russians? And therefore to her father, who had been the real target of the abduction.

She needed to talk to Walter to make sure he was okay. She had to know that the Russians had not renewed the pressure on him, not believing or not caring that he had supposedly been disabled by a stroke.

"Are you okay?" Elijah asked.

She swallowed and licked dry lips. "Yeah. Yes, I'm fine. I was just hoping for some answers, that's all. But this just seems to have raised more questions."

"Sorry about that." Elijah was looking at her screen. "What are you working on?"

"Oh... I'm just trying to figure out that locket, the one with the digital files on it. The electronic forensic guys made a copy of the phone and locket for me so I could look at them and try to figure them out without actually touching the actual equipment. They don't want me to be able to delete or overwrite anything, you know?"

"Sure, sure, of course," Elijah agreed. He leaned in closer to see what she had been doing. "So, what are you looking at here?"

"I was looking at the photos and videos saved on the locket. These files are stored in the locket. And these over here are on the phone's camera roll. So Markov took them on the phone's camera or downloaded them on the phone, and then transferred them to the locket."

Elijah nodded. "Okay. So..." he shrugged, "is that important? Have you found anything on the locket that shouldn't be there? Or that helps you solve your case?"

"No. Well... no, I haven't <u>really</u> found anything that shouldn't be there. Except... I don't know why it would be."

"What do you mean?"

"Well, you would expect the files on the locket to be the things she treasured, the most important memories. Her family, boyfriend, closest friends, pet, whatever. Right?"

He nodded. "Right. That's what it's for."

"But the stuff that is on the locket seems random. Some cat videos. Some pictures of people she works with. Nothing sentimental at all."

"That's weird."

"Yeah. And Alina—the victim's sister—said she used her phone a lot. She kept everything on there. I expected to find... memory aids, journal entries, passwords, all that kind of thing. All of the random notes that you make on a phone. Right?"

"Not everyone does. A lot of people only know their phone's most basic functions. But if that's what the sister said, yeah, I would expect to find a lot of notes and documents on the phone."

"But there aren't. The notes app is empty. There is no third-party app to replace it. Just nothing. Like Markov never used it to write down a note."

"So she deleted them. Or someone else did."

Kenzie pushed herself back from her computer. "Can you tell? I mean, if she deleted them, you can tell that, right? You can undelete them."

"Maybe. It depends on a lot of things. But yes, being deleted doesn't really mean that it's been wiped off the phone; it means that the entry has been wiped from the directory. Unless they used a special eraser program to overwrite the entries. Or installed something overtop it."

Elijah moved around the desk to the space Kenzie had vacated, bending over the keyboard. “This is an image of the phone’s memory, right? Not just a copy of the files?”

“What’s the difference?”

“An image is a bit-by-bit copy that includes hidden files, system files, <u>and</u> the remnants of deleted files that might still exist in unallocated spaces. A copy of the files would only be the copies of files that were in the directories.”

“Oh. Well... I assume the first, since it’s a forensic copy.”

Kenzie had been using the mouse to manipulate the phone emulator on the screen, just like she would use her fingers to access her own phone. But Elijah opened up a command-line prompt and other tools to look at the data at a level Kenzie couldn’t understand. She watched him type in various codes and commands as he examined what was below the surface.

Elijah shook his head. “The phone’s memory is almost completely filled with photos and videos. If she had been using the notes app or using another app to replace it, then after deleting the data in that app, she overwrote it with photos and videos to obscure what had been on it before."

Kenzie sighed. Of course. That's why there were so many videos downloaded from social media, when most people just looked at them online and didn't download them.

"And I guess the same is true of the locket," she said. "That's why there is weird stuff saved on the locket. Because whatever she had originally saved was deleted and then overwritten with this... garbage."

"It's possible," Elijah admitted, turning his attention to the cloned locket files on Kenzie's computer. "So she probably just copied the files from the phone to the locket... Hmm. No." He ran his fingernail down the directory on the screen to show it to Kenzie. "Actually, these are not the same files. The ones on the phone have the original filenames on them. Auto-generated photo names. Your phone doesn't know what it is taking a picture of or how to label it. It just gives it a date or numeric sequence, or some combination of them."

Kenzie nodded. She looked at the files on the locket. They had been changed to reflect the content of the photo. Pratt, Tucker, Hayes appended with the date and a numeric sequence if necessary to make it a unique file name. The same way she would have organized photos she took at an event once she'd had a chance to look at them all. Elijah clicked through the photos, previewing each one.

"Stop..." Kenzie stopped Elijah. "Go back to the last file."

Elijah did. Kenzie looked at the file name. Tucker and a date. But the photo was not of Tucker. It was of Hiram Hayes.

"Wait a minute. Go to the one before that."

Another file named Tucker, and this one was, in fact, a photo of Tucker. Elijah went to the one before that, which was labeled Tucker but was a picture of Dana Pratt. It made no sense.

“What is it?” Elijah asked.

“The file labels are wrong. They don’t show who is in the picture.”

“They don’t?” He looked at a few of them, then nodded, pursing his lips. “Then... what’s going on here?”

“Maybe they were corrupted?” Kenzie suggested. “Somehow they got mislabeled when she copied them to the locket?”

“No, I don’t think so. Then the names would be garbled, not swapped with other people’s names.”

“Can you find the same file on the phone...?”

“Well, that isn’t going to be easy. But let’s just sort the listing by creation date, and then file size, and then we can preview to make sure it is the same file... Uh... hmm...”

Kenzie watched him sort the files and try to match them up. But the creation date and file sizes were not the same between the two devices.

"So they're not the same files," Kenzie discerned.

Elijah highlighted two files and previewed them, revealing identical photos.

Kenzie frowned. "If they look the same, why aren't they exactly the same? The file size is different. The timestamps don't match."

Elijah nodded slowly. "The image dimensions are the same and the metadata matches. If someone just copied the files straight over, they'd be byte-for-byte identical. The only reason they'd be different is if they were re-saved or edited or..."

They stared at the screen in silence for a moment.

Elijah tapped his fingers once on the keyboard and murmured, "Steganography."

CHAPTER 22

"What is steganography?" Kenzie demanded.

"It is a method of hiding information. You put it 'in plain sight.' By altering the pixels in a photo, for example. You can encode other information in the picture. Embed a document in it. Or if you have a video, you might have another sound file hidden inside it—buried in tiny changes to the audio that would be imperceptible to the human ear. These modified files might have additional information in them that you can only retrieve if you know how to find it."

"Why change the filename?"

Elijah stared at the filenames. "They are all people?" he questioned after thinking about it for a while.

"Yeah. The names of people she worked with." Kenzie couldn't see any labeled with Alina's name or any relationships like Mom or Dad. They were all people she had met at Birch Valley.

"Maybe they are embedded with documents or recordings of that person on that day," Elijah suggested.

Kenzie was nervous and excited at the same time. "That would make sense! How do we get access to them?"

"I don't know."

"But it can't be that hard. If we know what it is, we know what to look for..."

"You'll need a steganography expert who can tell you how to encode and decode the embedded documents or information."

Kenzie had assumed he would just be able to click on the files and extract the additional files once they knew what they were looking for. But it didn't sound like it was going to be that easy.

"So... do you know a steganography expert?"

"You'll need to go back to your digital forensic folks. Explain what you think they're looking for, and they'll have to find an expert. I don't imagine there will be anyone in Roxboro, maybe not even in Burlington. Maybe the FBI can give you someone. They'll need to document everything they do to show chain of custody of the information so it can be used in court."

Kenzie's heart thumped hard. She had not actually expected to be able to find anything on the phone or locket that was related to Markov's death. She was just being thorough in her investigation. But suddenly, she had something that suggested Markov had a secret related to her work.

She had been hiding something. Despite everything that she had been told at Birch Valley about Markov not having any concerns about the project she had been assigned to, she'd had something to hide.

It changed everything. Kenzie called Detective Edwards, unsure whether he would answer his phone on the weekend or think this was important enough to interrupt his family or personal time.

It could, of course, wait until Monday. But Kenzie hated to wait that long. She was impatient for Detective Edwards to know that this was not just a routine accident case, but something that needed further investigation. They had already lost precious days by assuming the only thing to be investigated was what caused Markov's impairment.

The phone rang a few times, and Kenzie was resigned to the fact that it was going to go to voicemail when he finally picked up.

"Edwards here."

"Detective, it's Dr. Kirsch. I hate to call you on the weekend, but do you have a few minutes? I thought you might want to know what I found..."

"Dr. Kirsch? Just a minute."

There was a lot of background noise. People talking, strains of music with a strong beat. A party? Kenzie looked at the clock. It was noon. Maybe a kid's birthday party. She hadn't realized how much time had passed since she started looking at Markov's files. Zachary would be expecting her home.

The noise quieted as Edwards obviously shut himself in a room away from the party.

"Dr. Kirsch. What can I do for you? Is this on the Markov accident?"

"Yes. I'm sorry to disturb you on the weekend. You have something going on."

"No problem. I take it you figured out what Markov took that night?"

"Uh, no. I'm still waiting for mass spectrometry on that. As I told you, Markov was not drunk or under the influence of any of the popular recreational drugs."

"Okay, what is it then? I haven't gotten any report back on the car saying that the brakes had failed or anything like that."

"This is less of an answer and more of... an additional question or avenue of investigation."

"Uh-huh?"

"I was examining the files on her phone and electronic locket."

"We looked at that. Mostly photos and videos. Nothing unusual."

"You didn't think it was odd that she didn't have pictures of her sister and loved ones on the locket? That she would store downloaded cat videos on a memory locket?"

"It might be an odd choice of material, but I've seen people do a lot weirder stuff than that. There wasn't anything suspicious about what she had."

"Are you familiar with steganography?"

"With the principles, yes. With doing it or decoding it myself, no. Please don't tell me it was actually porn."

"No, I don't think it is anything like that. I haven't been able to extract the information embedded in the files; we just figured out that it is there. Or is probably there. It will have to be sent to an expert. I think it was information related to her work."

"It's more likely that she would be using the locket for homework than for cat videos?"

"No. I'm thinking more along the lines of corporate espionage. She was hiding documents or recordings of coworkers."

“What evidence do you have of that?”

“Just the names on the files, so far. She had pictures of her colleagues, but the names on the files don’t match what is shown in the picture. I think the names on the files relate to what is in the embedded documents.”

“Really.” Edwards drew out the word in a way that made Kenzie think he was writing something down at the same time as he was talking. “Okay, well, that is definitely interesting. What makes you think that there is something embedded in the files? Other than just the wrong file names?”

“The file sizes of the pictures on her phone are different from the ones on the locket, but not in a way that makes sense if she’d just compressed them to save space. They haven’t been resized, the metadata’s the same, and the image quality hasn’t changed.”

“Okay. That is interesting,” Edwards agreed. “If there is work information on the locket, encrypted in the photos and video… that would suggest that it was corporate espionage. I wouldn’t go as far as to say that makes her death suspicious. But it does make it… an interesting coincidence. What was she using this information for? Was she selling it? Using it for blackmail? Planning to expose unethical practices?”

He didn’t say it in a way that indicated he expected Kenzie to know the answers or even have an educated guess. He was just exploring his own questions aloud.

“Do you have someone you can send the copies of the phone and locket information to who could extract the files and find out?”

“I’ll have to look into it. It is not something I have done before, but I have a couple of places to start with some inquiries.”

“Great.”

"Thank you for the information, doctor. This is... not quite your area of expertise."

"Meaning you are surprised I'm the one who found it?"

"Well... without sounding offensive, yes. Surprised that you were even looking for it. I wouldn't expect you to be investigating the deceased's personal effects at that deep of a level. Our tech guys didn't look close enough to note the discrepancies."

"No. But they didn't have any reason to believe that there was any information hidden there. We all thought it was just a routine accident investigation. There wasn't any reason to be looking for hidden files."

"But you did. What made you think there might be something significant on the locket?"

"I don't know. I just wanted to know what Markov put on the locket, and when I saw that it wasn't sentimental stuff, I was curious. I interviewed some of her coworkers yesterday when her sister said that she was stressed out about work and not sleeping. But their perceptions were quite different, and they said she wasn't worried about anything."

"They did, did they? What kind of medicine did Dr. Markov practice?"

"She was a surgeon and a researcher in kidney disease and transplant."

"That sounds like it might be an industry ripe for industrial espionage."

"Yes. And if I'm to believe what they told me yesterday about the study Dr. Markov was working on, they are right on the edge of beginning human trials in a gene editing project. That is... revolutionary. I'm sure there is a lot of competition to be the first to get a solution to market first. It will be incredibly profitable, if it works."

"Interesting. I guess I will be talking to her colleagues as well, then. Would you send me your notes?"

"Sure, of course."

Kenzie was glad that she would not be the one following up with Markov's coworkers. She was happy to leave that to Edwards and his people and to stick to the medical findings.

"And you will let me know as soon as you find out whether Dr. Markov was under the influence of any substance you can identify?"

"Yes. I'll let you know as soon as I get the lab report back."

CHAPTER 23

Kenzie luckily arrived home in good time to make the trip to the Petersons'. Zachary was looking slightly stressed, but kept his feelings to himself. She had not promised to be home at a particular time, but he had clearly been starting to worry that she might have forgotten about the trip and might end up working too late for them to go. Kenzie didn't say anything to excuse herself, but just acted as though that had been the time she had been planning to arrive home all along.

No need to make him think that she had lost track of time. She hadn't, really.

Things had just taken a bit longer than she had expected, and then the new investigative channel had appeared, and she had needed to follow up on it before it grew stale. It had been especially important to get Detective Edwards on the case right away if corporate espionage was involved, since Kenzie's questions the day before might have sent up some red flags with anyone who might have been involved or might have been concerned about Dr. Markov's activities.

She didn't have much preparation to do before they hit the road for the Peterson house. They made the trip every few weeks, so both were well-prepared to grab their overnight kits and go. Kenzie had started to leave a few things in the Petersons' guest room closet so she didn't have to take as much back and forth between the two locations. That had worked out very well and reduced the friction of getting ready.

"Pat said that he was making something special," Zachary reminded her, once they were in his car and on their way.

"Pat always makes something special. If he is making something more special... well, you can bet it will knock our socks off," Kenzie contributed. She stretched her legs out as much as she could in the compact car, ready to start the relaxing part of the weekend.

Zachary was at the wheel, which would help polish any rough edges left from his anxiety over whether she would arrive home in time for the trip. He loved highway driving and sometimes she thought it was the only time he was ever fully relaxed while awake. The guy should have been a long-haul truck driver. But then maybe driving professionally would be a stressor, and he would lose that one thing guaranteed to calm his restless brain. She also wasn't sure he would ever be able to be in a job where there wasn't the opportunity to help other people out and find justice for those who had been neglected or abused. Zachary was all about resolving injustices.

"I think I'm going to close my eyes for a while," Kenzie said. "You don't mind, do you?"

She didn't plan to fall asleep, but sometimes as soon as she closed her eyes it would sneak up on her. Zachary's smooth highway driving might just lull her to sleep.

“No, go to sleep,” Zachary assured her.

“You’re not tired?” She didn’t think that he would fall asleep at the wheel—not unless he was very sick and tired, as he had been after they had contracted a novel virus a couple of Thanksgivings before. But normally, she didn’t have to worry about it; he could stay awake and focused on the road for hours at a time and it wasn’t that far to the Petersons’.

“I’m not tired,” Zachary confirmed. He glanced aside at her. “You didn’t sleep very well last night?”

“No, I slept okay. I just want to close my eyes and relax.”

“I’ll wake you up when we get there, then.”

“I’m not going to actually sleep. Just rest my eyes.”

“Okay.”

* * *

The next thing Kenzie knew, Zachary was shaking her gently awake. The engine was no longer running, which meant they weren’t just at a stop light or getting close, but had already arrived at their destination. Kenzie blinked her eyes several times, trying to focus on her surroundings. She had been far more deeply asleep than she could remember having been for a long time.

“Oh, boy. I wasn’t expecting that.”

Zachary grinned at her. “But you weren’t tired.”

“No.” Kenzie stretched. “I didn’t think I was.”’

She opened her door and stood up. Zachary followed her up the sidewalk, bordered on both sides by blooming flowers. Pat’s gardening skills were just as legendary as his cooking. Kenzie didn’t know how he found time for it all.

Lorne Peterson had the door open and was eager to greet them before they reached the doorstep. Zachary and Kenzie both accepted hugs and were ushered inside.

“How have you been?” Lorne asked both of them. Zachary and Kenzie settled down into their accustomed places on the couch, relaxing in the warm, familiar atmosphere. Pat didn’t put in an immediate appearance, so he was probably making a last-minute run to the grocery store or working in the back garden. “It seems like it has been longer than just a couple of weeks since you were here last. Is that all it has been?”

Kenzie had to think back, but she didn’t think it had been longer than usual, although sometimes she did lose track of whether one of their cases or a dinner with Kenzie’s family had kept them away longer than usual.

“I don’t think it has been.” Zachary shook his head. “What have you guys been up to?”

"Well, you know us." Lorne waved the question away. "We're not so busy anymore. Photography, the gardens, going out to a few plays or musicals. It's all pretty low-key."

Kenzie hoped that when she was old enough to retire, she would have a calm, comfortable life like Lorne and Pat, rather than the restlessness and boredom her father was dealing with. The man was not used to sitting still and letting life pass him by. He had always been the type to be in the midst of things, shaking hands, negotiating, and effecting change. For him to no longer be part of that society was torture.

"Hey, I have something to contribute to the photography talk today," she offered, getting surprised looks from both Zachary and Lorne. They were used to her bowing out of the conversation and either talking with Pat or picking up a book when their talk meandered around to their shared hobby and the more technical aspects of subjects and camera settings like f-stops and shutter speeds.

“Yeah?” Zachary asked, “Have you taken up photography recently without me noticing?”

“I got into something very interesting at work today when I was checking out the files on a victim’s devices.”

“Is that something you usually do?” Zachary frowned, puzzled by this development.

“Not generally, no. Usually, if there is anything interesting about electronic devices, the police take point on it. They are the ones with people trained in electronic forensics.”

He nodded. “Then why...?”

“The police had already looked at it, but I wanted to make sure they hadn’t missed anything.”

“Aren’t you risking contaminating evidence if you do that?”

“Who is telling this story, you or me?”

He made a motion back to her with both hands. “Sorry, this is all yours.”

“I was only looking at digital copies of what was on her devices. Not the devices themselves. You can rest assured that I wouldn’t lay a finger on the actual digital files.”

“Ah.” Zachary nodded. “Right. Gerry, my computer guy, he always says to make a clone, never work from the original.”

“Yeah. We want everything to be intact in case it is used as evidence.”

Lorne leaned forward, elbows on his knees. “So, what is this about photography? Was she a professional photographer?”

“No. A surgeon and researcher.”

“Well then?” Zachary prompted. He, too, was intrigued by what Kenzie had to contribute to today’s photography discussion.

"What do you know about steganography?"

"Steganography," Lorne repeated. "Hiding information in pictures."

"Right!" Kenzie pointed at him to confirm this. "Or some other method of hiding it in plain sight. Right under your nose. Or under your eyes."

"I've heard of it," Zachary confirmed. "But I don't really know anything about how it is done or what kind of information you can hide."

"Virtually anything," Lorne said. "Pictures are made up of millions of pixels. You can change a few pixels to hide a short message. Or if you want to hide a longer message, you can change a whole bunch of pixels by a value undetectable by the human eye, but that a computer can find and reverse-engineer to decode the message."

Zachary looked at Kenzie, impressed. "And are you saying that your victim hid a message in the files you were looking at today with steganography?"

"Well, that's what we believe. But it has to be extracted before we know exactly what the message is."

Zachary chuckled "Who is this victim?" he teased, "a Russian spy?"

CHAPTER 24

Russian.

Kenzie considered the possibility as she swallowed hard, struggling to catch her breath. She felt for Zachary's hand, and he took hers in his and squeezed gently.

"I... I..." Kenzie tried to continue the conversation naturally, explaining that she didn't actually know Markov's history and whether she was part of some sort of foreign service. Could she have been spying for the Russians? Sending information back to them buried in seemingly innocuous videos?

And if she was, were the bot attacks on Kenzie's network from Russia related? Or just coincidental? Elijah had said bot attacks from Russia were not unusual. It was something they saw all the time. But what if there was a meaning behind it this time? What if they had been trying to break into her network and her computer specifically to see where her investigation had led her and whether she was on to the fact that Markov was an enemy agent?

“Sorry,” Zachary apologized. “I didn’t mean that—that was a stupid thing to say.” His voice was tight and clipped, angry at himself for letting the words slip out of his mouth before remembering that she had previously been attacked by the Russians, that her father had been involved with them, pulled into their net and his life threatened by them. Even Dr. Wiltshire had been accused of being complicit with the Russian mob. Zachary hadn’t intended to trigger a panic attack with his teasing reference to Russian spies. But the words were out of his mouth, and he couldn’t take them back. Kenzie knew he hadn’t meant the question seriously, but she couldn’t reverse the cascading reaction the words had triggered.

Zachary let go of Kenzie’s hand and went into the kitchen, where she could hear him getting a glass from the cupboard and a jug from the fridge. He sat beside her again a minute later, pressing an icy glass into her hand.

"Here. Have a drink. I'm sorry, Kenzie. I'm sorry."

Kenzie took a few swallows of the frigid water. She pressed the glass against her forehead. She tried to anchor herself to the sensations and other physical sights and sounds in the room.

"It's okay," she assured Zachary. "I'm fine."

"That was really stupid. I didn't mean to upset you."

"I'm not upset. Just..."

Panicked. Anxious. Pulled into a flashback of being kidnapped and thrown into that white van. The white van she had been thinking about again lately for no particular reason. She had thought she was through the flashbacks and had left these symptoms behind.

She had been too quick to assume she was cured.

"It's okay," she told Zachary again. She took a deep breath and let it out again slowly. "The woman *does* actually have a Russian name. So it's kind of funny."

She wasn't laughing. No one was laughing about it. Zachary and Lorne were both looking at Kenzie with concern and didn't crack a smile.

"But she was American born. I'm sure she was *not* a Russian spy." Kenzie laughed weakly.

She patted Zachary's leg to reassure him that she was fine. "But we are wondering about industrial espionage. Don't *you* have a case of industrial espionage that you are looking at right now?"

She wanted him to take control of the conversation for a while to give her time to calm down and relax after the unexpected trigger.

"Yeah." Zachary took up the theme with determination. "I can't reveal the parties' names, of course, but a medical research company asked me to investigate some possible industrial espionage at their company."

"That sounds pretty specialized," Lorne commented. "Is that something you do?"

"I haven't done a lot of this kind of work," Zachary admitted. "But I'm good at digging deep to find the clues that I need. And I've always got people I can call to give me tips on what to look for and where. After that, it's just... tedious grunt work until I find what I'm looking for."

"What if it isn't there?" Kenzie asked, having another sip of the cold water. "What if they were wrong, and there wasn't any attack or theft of property?"

"Then I'll eventually figure that out too." He shrugged. "It might just take longer."

* * *

It wasn't long before Pat was home with several grocery bags full of ingredients hanging from his muscular arms.

"They're here!" He put the grocery bags down in the kitchen and came out to the living room to greet both with open arms. "Nice to see you! How was the drive?"

"It's a beautiful day out today," Kenzie told him. "Perfect driving weather."

Pat gave Zachary a sideways squeeze around the shoulders. "As far as Zachary is concerned, any day is the perfect driving weather," he teased. "Isn't it?"

"Well..." Zachary shrugged and smiled at him, "pretty much."

"Good, I'm glad you had a good trip." Pat looked over them all. Kenzie thought that his gaze might have lingered on her a little longer than on the others. Was it obvious that she'd had a minor panic attack? Kenzie resisted checking her forehead for sweat or patting her hair, giving him what she hoped was a casual, natural smile.

"I am going to make some gnocchi and garlic bread," Pat went on breezily, looking away from Kenzie. "I know, I know, gnocchi is pretty standard fare. I've made it plenty of times before, and I promised you something special. But it is the dessert that is going to be the star of tonight's dinner."

"Gnocchi and garlic bread is fine!" Kenzie told him. "You know we love it."

Which was undoubtedly why he had picked it.

"Well, I seem to remember Zachary liking the garlic bread," Pat chuckled. "Now, Zachary, you'll need to leave some garlic bread for everyone else and leave space for dessert. I don't want you turning down my—turning dessert down because you've already stuffed yourself."

"Noted," Zachary agreed. "I'll leave some space."

"You'd better."

Before long, Pat was cooking up a storm in the kitchen, popping in and out of the conversation as he poured glasses of ice water or wine, making sure everyone was happy while they waited for the meal. Kenzie didn't see Pat making anything that looked like dessert. He must have made it ahead and it was secreted away in the fridge or pantry.

The hearty scents of tomato sauce, garlic, and warm bread filled the house. Eventually, the main course was ready and the gnocchi and garlic bread were placed on the table as they gathered around. Zachary's eyes twinkled as he gazed at the glistening sheen of butter on the bread toasted to golden brown perfection. Kenzie had to admit that she would be happy to pick up the entire loaf in both hands and dive into it herself. But they all waited politely and took turns dishing up, and then were finally able to dig in.

Pat's gnocchi and garlic bread were all just as good as they ever were, if not better, and it was hard for Kenzie not to stuff herself. Eventually, the time came for the main course to be cleared away and the dessert was served.

Pat brought out a tray of four parfait glasses with red and white layers. “This is trifle. Layers of sponge cake mixed with custard and cream, alternating with layers of strawberry and rhubarb compote. The very first of Vermont’s spring fruits. Sweet and rich and refreshing all at the same time.”

He put a parfait glass in front of each of them. The delicate scents of vanilla and berries teased at Kenzie’s nostrils. Each parfait was topped with slices of delicate wild strawberries arranged like a flower.

“Oh, this looks wonderful,” Kenzie gushed. Pat handed out long, thin spoons to each of them.

She was very glad that she had managed to save enough space for the dessert. It was worth every bite.

CHAPTER 25

After saying their goodnights to Pat and Lorne, Kenzie and Zachary retired to the guest room to prepare for bed. Kenzie brushed her teeth and returned to the room to find Zachary sitting on the bed, hunched over his laptop computer, tapping away. Clearly not getting ready for sleep.

He was usually pretty good about not getting the computer out while they were still visiting, and he and Kenzie usually went straight to bed at the Petersons'. Zachary would get his usual two or three hours of sleep and then be on his computer when she woke up. Pat was usually up before Kenzie as well, with her and Lorne competing for last place. Kenzie always felt a little decadent sleeping in after everyone else, but none of them ever made her feel bad about it.

"What are you doing?" Kenzie asked curiously. "You're supposed to be getting ready for bed."

Zachary typed away. He spoke to her after a few minutes without looking up.

“What do you know about your Dr. Markov’s background?” he demanded.

Kenzie sat down on the edge of the bed. “Well, I don’t generally get a very in-depth report. Just vital statistics, maybe a short summary including job and next of kin. It doesn’t really enter into the cause of death investigation. We ask questions about medications and lifestyle if it is appropriate.” Kenzie scratched the back of her neck. “In Dr. Markov’s case, I have met her personally a couple of times. I talked to her sister and went to her work to talk to her colleagues because of some of the unusual aspects of the case and the fact that her sister said she had been quite stressed about work.”

“Single car accident,” Zachary summarized, his eyes still on the screen and the words spilling out rapidly. “Her car was seen racing through town at unsafe speeds. She was swerving lanes and it is thought that she was driving under the influence."

"Was all of that in the news?" Kenzie was surprised they had said anything about her being under the influence. The medical examiner's office would never have released that to the press, and the press was running the risk of being sued for libel if they couldn't prove that it was true.

"Sure. Is any of it wrong?"

"It all sounds pretty accurate."

"Dr. Markov was in Roxboro for an appearance at a function. The Future of Transplant Technology."

"Uh-huh. Zachary, where are you going with this? I didn't ask you to look into Dr. Markov's death. It really isn't appropriate, given my role."

He raised his head and looked at her. "She was Russian. I want to know what that means to us."

"It doesn't mean anything. It has nothing to do with her being killed. It has nothing to do with why she was in Roxboro, or why she spoke, or why she was driving under the influence... of some unknown substance or condition."

"Then it shouldn't make any difference whether I look into it or not."

"It doesn't," Kenzie agreed.

Zachary nodded. He looked down at his computer and continued to do his unauthorized research.

"I need to go to bed," Kenzie told him. "Why don't we sleep now, and you can look at the rest of that in the morning? Nothing will change between now and then. We both need sleep. You'll be fresher if you look at it tomorrow."

"She was born in America, like you said. Her parents are both Russian-born. She has—had—relatives still living in Russia."

"It doesn't matter. I told you that."

"It doesn't matter that you received an email threat after beginning your investigation into her death? An email that originated in Russia?"

"We don't know where the email originated. There was a bot attack from Russia. But it sounds like those happen quite a lot."

Zachary grimaced and nodded. "The bot attack was from Russia," he repeated.

"And that wasn't targeted. They happen all the time. To all different companies. Even those huge ones that they bring down with ransom attacks."

"How is Walter?"

Kenzie gave a little shake of her head and tried to keep up with Zachary's thought processes. His ADHD brain made rapid-fire connections between data sets, sometimes intuiting a connection where there was none.

But of course, she understood the leap from Russians and a ransom demand to Walter. He was the person in their sphere who had been most affected by the Russian mob. It was because of Walter that Kenzie had been targeted and kidnapped, and because he conceded to their demands, she had been released unharmed. Now, Walter had tried again to pull back from the Russians. Having to give up his career as a lobbyist was the steep price he had to pay for having them out of his life.

She swallowed. "The last I heard, Dad is doing just fine. I'm sure Mom would have called me and told me if he was not."

"She didn't call to say that there was anything wrong with him, but she did call about the vandalism at the foundation."

"Right. Which was unrelated."

"Unrelated as far as we know."

"I don't see how it could be related. The vandalism at the foundation had to do with the change in funding direction."

"And Dr. Markov was Russian and a transplant surgeon and researcher."

"Yes," Kenzie admitted.

"There is a nexus."

"No, I don't think so. And Dr. Markov is <u>not</u> Russian. She has Russian parents. A Russian heritage. But that doesn't make her any more Russian than either of us."

Zachary considered that. "Until I can find more information... no."

"And you aren't going to find anything else tonight. I need to go to bed. And that means you are going to bed."

At home, she wouldn't have made such a big deal of it. When he dove down some rabbit hole before bed at home, she didn't try to talk him out of it. Or at least, she didn't try very hard to talk him out of it. When his brain was occupied with researching or investigating an intriguing question, there was little point in trying.

But when they were staying at the Petersons', Kenzie felt it was rude to stay up at all hours rather than trying to operate on a similar sleep schedule to the hosts. It was only sensible that they should try to sleep at the same time, eliminating the need for the hosts to tiptoe around and be quiet because someone was sleeping on a different shift. The hosts should be able to function as they normally did.

"I just want to take another minute on this," Zachary told her.

"One more minute of research is just as likely to be one more hour, and I can't stay up that late. Let's put it away for now. You can look at it tomorrow and during the week."

"I won't keep you awake."

"You will. I'll lie awake waiting for you to come to bed."

Zachary scowled at the screen of his computer. “This is important. It could impact you and your family.”

“It’s a tangent. Dr. Markov having a Russian heritage has nothing to do with her death or my investigation. Or the threatening email or vandalism at the foundation.”

“You don’t know that until I investigate it and tell you that.”

“You can do that tomorrow. Tonight, no one knows where we are. It is perfectly safe.”

He looked at her for a long moment, thinking about it. Kenzie waited. It was easy for him to slip into paranoia, but he had been stable lately, he was on a good med cocktail, and as far as she knew, he had been sleeping well and had not been triggered by any of his big anxiety triggers.

“Did Pat set the burglar alarm?”

Kenzie nodded. “Yes.”

She didn't mention that Zachary had already checked it once as well. Or that she knew he would check it one more time before climbing into bed.

Zachary slowly closed the lid on his laptop, putting all of the demons to bed for the night.

Hopefully.

CHAPTER 26

In the morning, Zachary appeared to have forgotten all about the rabbit trail he had been chasing down the previous night. Kenzie patted herself on the back for being able to stay calm about his repeated reference to the Russians. And Zachary had done well to be able to put the research away and go to sleep.

They had more time to visit with the Petersons and enjoy a late-morning brunch before heading back to Roxboro. Everything was relaxed and pleasant. There was no more mention of the Russians or the need to protect themselves from some unknown threat.

Zachary and Kenzie reached home in the early afternoon. Kenzie would have time to relax, run an errand or two, and maybe read a book, or at least a few chapters.

There was an unfamiliar car parked in front of the house. Kenzie frowned at it as they pulled up behind it. She didn't recognize it as one of the cars that was normally parked in front of a neighbor's house. Maybe it was a friend visiting one of them.

Except that someone was sitting in the driver's seat. Just sitting there, not getting out of the car to go see someone else. Kenzie shifted uncomfortably, watching him.

Zachary seemed unconcerned by the presence of the parked car, and that was backward. He should have been the one who was concerned about it, while Kenzie rolled her eyes and told him it was just someone visiting, checking an address, making a food delivery, or something else innocuous.

Zachary got out of the car and, instead of grabbing his overnight gear, walked up to the strange car and bent down to look at the driver. He talked for a moment, his voice too low for Kenzie to make out. Obviously, it was someone he recognized, even if Kenzie didn't. She got her overnight bag out of the car and left the rest for Zachary to deal with. He straightened and looked at her, lifting the handle on the stranger's car to open the door and let him out.

The driver was tall and broad. In very good shape. An older man. A face that she nearly recognized, but she couldn't quite put her finger on who he was. Zachary walked him toward the house. "Kenzie, you remember Hal?"

Kenzie stared at Hal, trying to put it all together. It helped to have the name, but she had not had much to do with him when Zachary had dealt with him on a case before. An old case, where Hal had helped him to find Robbie Elder, a friend of Tyrrell's who had disappeared years before. And they had succeeded. Zachary had initially been very uncertain of Hal and whether he was really an ally or a threat. Hal was an ex-cop and had been undercover in one of the crime syndicates Zachary had once run afoul of. Zachary hadn't been sure which side of the law Hal had been on for some time.

"Oh, Hal. Good to see you again," Kenzie greeted, wondering what Zachary was up to. Maybe Hal was going to give him a hand on his big new case. Helping him sort out the industrial espionage.

“Give me a minute, I’ll be right with you,” Zachary told Hal. He returned to the car to get out his laptop case and overnight bag. He locked the door, armed the security system, and checked both a couple of times more before he was satisfied and joined Hal and Kenzie on the sidewalk up to the house. Hal was, apparently, going in with them.

Kenzie looked at Zachary, raising an eyebrow. She unlocked the door and disarmed the burglar alarm to let them in. She was surprised that Zachary was working his case on a Sunday, which they usually took off to rest and relax.

“So… what’s this about?” she asked when he didn’t give her any information.

Was he going to work the case the rest of the day and expect her to just relax on her own? Was he expecting her to make supper? For all of them? Had he thought through any of the logistics?

“I asked Hal to help with security arrangements,” Zachary explained.

She blinked. “What security arrangements?”

Zachary swallowed and licked his lips, looking around as if he hoped that someone else would jump in and explain in his place.

“I think this case warrants some additional security,” he said obliquely. “I want to make sure everyone is safe.”

“What case? Your industrial espionage case?”

“Well, not so much that one, as the one you are investigating, and the thing with your family.”

“I told you there was no connection between them.”

“I know. But if you are getting threats from multiple directions, wouldn’t that make it even more important to beef up security?”

“I’m not getting threats from multiple directions. I got one email threat. That’s it.”

“And the bot attack on your network.”

“But that wasn’t anything. Not a threat.”

“Maybe.” He shrugged. “And then there was the break-in at your family foundation.”

“Again, unrelated.”

“An attack from a different direction,” Zachary reframed it. “Threats coming from multiple directions. You said yourself that you were feeling overwhelmed, like they were attacking on all sides.”

"But I didn't mean that it was really anything serious, just that it felt overwhelming... Sometimes, being overwhelmed just means I am tired and need a good sleep."

"Well, Hal is here to make sure that you can get it."

Kenzie studied Hal.

If she was looking for a big, solid man who could handle threats of all kinds, no matter which direction they came from, Hal was a good candidate. He was physically imposing, well-trained, had a professional law enforcement background and had, as Kenzie knew, been undercover in criminal factions. He would have all kinds of connections and experience in personal protection.

And he must cost a fortune.

"Are you telling me that he will be around here, personally keeping guard over us, for an undetermined length of time?"

Zachary's head and shoulders made a slight side-to-side movement. A shrug? A concession that she was right, even if she made it sound like that wasn't what she wanted?

"I'm here to do a threat assessment," Hal said, speaking up for himself for the first time. "We won't know for sure what is needed until I've had a chance to look around and talk to you both about the threats you have faced in the last few weeks."

"There haven't been any threats," Kenzie said. "Not overt ones. Other than that one email. Anything else is just... stuff that has happened."

"Can I get a copy of that email?" Hal asked immediately.

"The police are handling it. It's on my work computer. I don't have it here."

"Can you log in to your email remotely to retrieve it?"

"The police have it. They are already taking care of it. There is no reason to get someone else involved. And I work in the police station. In a suite in the basement. So, I am physically protected by the police and security systems. There is no need to ramp up the security there."

"You were once attacked in your office," Zachary pointed out.

"That was... some time ago. Everything has been secure since then."

"The public has access to you during business hours."

Kenzie looked at Hal. "So you think you're going to send him to work with me? So that he can hover over me while I work and make sure that no one can approach me?"

"I don't need to be visible," Hal said. "I can evaluate the security situation, make suggestions for improvement, and be close by while you work in case something should happen."

Kenzie shook her head. “You are not coming to work with me.” She spoke to Zachary. “I do not need a personal security guard at work. He’s not coming in.”

Zachary shrugged and didn’t argue the point. He had probably already considered her arguments and knew convincing her to take a personal guard to work was a losing proposition.

“He can still assess our security here and how serious the threats are. Wouldn’t you rather be safe than sorry? Your family foundation has been targeted. You were sent an email threat. Isn’t that enough to consider that maybe we need to pump up security until we are sure that neither of those is a real threat?”

“I already know that.”

“Okay... well... don’t mind us, then. We’ll just be going over some stuff.”

Kenzie eyed Hal and Zachary. She could see that she wasn't going to get anywhere in talking them out of it. And if Zachary believed that there was a threat, then wasn't it better that he hire an expert to review the situation than to go all paranoid, locking down the house, thinking that everyone who called on the phone or walked up to the house was trying to track them and blow them up? It was a reasonable response. If Kenzie talked to Dr. Boyle about it, the therapist would agree it was a measured, logical response to the perceived threats. She would tell Kenzie to just go with it. Arguing the point would suggest a distrust in Zachary's mental health and his ability to make decisions for himself.

"Okay," Kenzie said. "If you don't need me for anything, I am just going to go on with my day as if Hal wasn't here. That's probably the best. I'll just stay out of the way and let you guys handle it."

Zachary nodded, looking slightly relieved that she wasn't going to blow up or argue with him over it.

“I’ll still need to ask you a few questions,” Hal told her.

Kenzie braced herself. “What else?”

“Zachary mentioned that your family foundation offices were broken into. Do you know if anything was stolen? Or only vandalized?”

“Nothing was stolen. And no one was hurt. Whoever it was intentionally broke in when there was no one there.”

“Did they get onto the computers?”

“I... don’t know. No one said anything about the computers. I assumed they just spray-painted the walls or used a Sharpie marker on the furniture or something. I don’t think there was any concern about the computers being broken into.”

“It’s not hard to put a key logger on a computer; just plug a USB stick into an open port. Some of these devices even operate wirelessly now.”

"I can ask the office manager to check, but I don't think there is anything to worry about."

"And you believe that this was done by the Russian mob?"

Kenzie looked at Zachary. "No! It was done by some company that we pulled funding from. Because we are concentrating on other areas of research right now."

"Do you know which company?"

"No."

"Can you get me a list of the companies you have reduced or pulled funding from recently?"

"Maybe. But I don't think that any of them are a physical threat."

"If they broke into your office and sabotaged it, they are a physical threat."

Kenzie looked for an argument, but she had to admit that a person or organization that was willing to break the law, physically break into the office, and vandalize it was probably capable of personal violence as well. What was to stop such a person from approaching Hillary, Lisa, or Kenzie herself? None of them was that difficult to find.

“Zachary mentioned that your father has been under considerable pressure from the Russian mob.”

“Yes. But he’s told you all about the fake stroke and forced retirement too, right?”

Hal nodded. “Will you be talking to him today?”

“Uh... I hadn’t made any specific plans, but it would probably be a good idea.”

Zachary nodded his agreement. “It doesn’t have to be anything formal,” he said. “Just touch base with him and see how he is doing. Whether they have tried to reach out to him in one way or another. So we know how much of a threat they are."

"He hasn't said anything to me, so I don't think they are still in contact or have tried to pressure him."

"That's good... but just follow up. You know that he would try to shield you, like he has in the past."

He had a point there. Walter had never been particularly eager to tell Kenzie his troubles, even when they had directly impacted her. He kept it to himself, and even, she suspected, lied to her face to keep it from her.

"He might not tell me."

"Or he might tell you if you ask."

"Okay. I'll check in with Walter today to make sure there is no trouble brewing. And I'll find out how concerned they are about the foundation and the break-in."

Hal and Zachary nodded.

“And you’re not asking any more questions on the Markov file, right?” Zachary asked. “No more interviewing coworkers. You’re just letting the police take over there.”

“Yes. They’re looking at the files that Markov might have hidden information in, and they will talk to her colleagues at work to uncover anything suspicious there.”

“You’re done with the case otherwise? You’ll be issuing your final report?”

“No, not yet. I’ve mostly drafted my preliminary report. But we are still waiting for some tests back.”

“Okay.” Zachary nodded and looked at Hal. “Okay, let’s review the security systems and procedures.”

Kenzie took it as her dismissal and withdrew to the bedroom with her overnight bag.

CHAPTER 27

Kenzie placed a video call to Walter, unsure whether he would answer it. He didn't have a lot to do, so she thought he would take a call from her, but it was harder to reach him on a video call than just a regular phone call. He might be at the other end of the house from his computer, and he preferred to take video calls on the computer rather than his phone, disliking holding it in front of him while he talked.

But he was, in fact, at his computer, and his face appeared on Kenzie's screen, smiling genially at her. His study glowed with the golden light of the afternoon sun.

"Mackenzie, how nice to see you. How are you today? I thought you would be at the Petersons'."

"We just got back. It's been a few days since we talked, and I thought I would touch base and see how you are doing."

"Always a good day when I can see you. Things went well with Zachary's foster father?"

"Yes. We always have a nice time there. Pat made a delicious trifle with strawberry and rhubarb compote. It was so good!"

"She must be a very good cook; you always rave about her cooking."

"His, Dad. Patrick."

"Right, right. I don't know why I forget."

It both charmed and irritated Kenzie that he couldn't seem to remember that Lorne and Pat were a same-sex couple. She was irritated when he would forget and get it wrong, yet at the same time, Walter obviously wasn't prejudiced against them, or he would have remembered from one conversation to the next.

Walter waved his hands, trying to get past the mistake. "Maybe it is just because we have never met," he said. "If we got together as an extended family, I'm sure I wouldn't forget those details. I'd have a face and personality to go with the name."

Kenzie shook her head, not wanting to go there. She was trying to build a better relationship with her parents, but still did not find them easy to get along with, and felt like their relationship was an uncharted minefield, full of hazards and potential pain. As much as she loved her father, his morals were different from hers and his mind worked differently. Lisa was more like Kenzie, but hard to get close to. She seemed to hold herself at a distance.

While Kenzie was sure of both of her parents' love, it was not a comfortable relationship like she had with Lorne and Pat. And she didn't want those two worlds mixing. She wasn't sure what would happen if the two worlds mixed, nor did she want to find out. It could be disastrous, and the very chance that things could go badly prevented her from attempting it.

But she couldn't tell Walter that. It would be unkind to tell him she didn't want him and Lisa to meet Lorne and Pat. He would think she was ashamed of him, and that didn't really convey how she felt.

"Yes, maybe sometime," she demurred. "I'm sure they would love to meet you too."

"Maybe it could be a festive dinner of some kind," Walter suggested. "Fourth of July or Labor Day. Or maybe it could be some other event where it was natural for the two families to celebrate together." He smiled, his voice teasing. "Maybe an event celebrating the two of you as a couple... if only there was something appropriate..."

Kenzie chuckled. "Don't start planning our wedding yet," she warned. "Neither of us is ready for that."

At least, she wasn't ready for such a permanent step. Zachary, she was afraid, would agree in a heartbeat. He had felt the dissolution of his marriage as keenly as the day that his mother had turned him over to child services, refusing to be his parent anymore. And while Zachary had been blamed for this, she had abandoned all of her children that day, not just him. Now the children were back together again as adults, feeling their way through a renewed relationship.

The end of Zachary's relationship with Bridget had been similarly wrenching, coming amid a false pregnancy and the news that she had cancer. She didn't want children and she didn't want him. She had kicked him out at that point. Even though both Bridget and his mother had been abusive, the losses had broken Zachary's heart.

And Kenzie couldn't do that to him. She couldn't commit to Zachary casually and then have to end the marriage a year or two down the line. She had to know for sure that it would be permanent, and she wasn't ready to commit to that right now. Not after witnessing her own parents' ambivalent relationship.

"Oh, you know I wouldn't push you into it," Walter told her softly, leaning slightly toward his webcam. "Don't look so serious all of a sudden."

"I'm not... I mean, no, I didn't take you seriously. It's just that I know how hard it would be on Zachary if things didn't work out. I just... couldn't do that to him."

"But what is going to happen? The two of you get along well; you are living together, and you are doing therapy together. That tells me you are committed more toward each other than married couples."

"And why did you and mother get divorced?"

Walter's gaze turned pensive. He nodded. "Fair point," he admitted. "We are good friends, but that isn't always enough. It is a good beginning... but for us, it couldn't be permanent. We both needed our freedom."

"Even though you both still like each other and are back to living with Mom again."

"We are living in the same house. And with the size of this place, that is more like living on the same block. We can still be independent. As independent as a man can be when he has suffered a catastrophic stroke and is not able to leave the house," he joked.

Kenzie smiled. He said it lightly, but she knew how hard it was for him to be confined to the house day after day, week after week, and now, month after month. She hoped that he would soon be able to get out occasionally. Surely he could begin his public recovery now?

"How are things on… that front?" she asked. This was what Zachary and Hal had wanted her to find out, and she was glad that the subject had come up somewhat naturally. "I assume that the Russians aren't that interested in you anymore, and as long as you stay retired, you can start to... be seen."

Walter gave a little grimace. "I expected them to give up months ago. I didn't think it would take this long. Once you hear that someone has had a stroke, that they have had to retire, you don't assume that they will be able to come back from it, do you?"

"I don't," Kenzie admitted. But maybe that was because of her medical training. She knew how devastating a stroke could be. Other people heard of friends who had suffered minor strokes or miraculously recovered most of their functions, and thought that was normal now. That you had a stroke, and then you got better again and could resume your pre-stroke life. And modern science had made that possible in many more cases. But she had seen how serious and life-altering a stroke could be, even with clot-busting medications. "So... you think they are still waiting for you to get better and go back to lobbying again? Have they contacted you?"

"Well, you know that I have been brushing up on my computer skills, researching legal cases to keep myself occupied..."

Under an assumed name, Kenzie hoped. It wouldn't do for the Russian mob to find out he was working again, just in a slightly different field.

"Yes, you had mentioned that."

"Well, I do occasionally... take a poke around online to see what people are saying about me."

"Oh." Kenzie nodded. "Well, that makes sense."

"There are certain places online where people exchange messages or jobs of a... less-than-legal nature."

Kenzie's stomach clenched. She had known that he was getting internet savvy, but she had not realized he had gone so far. "Dad, you don't mean the dark web, do you?"

"The deep web is more accurate. And... yes. There are still places where my name is mentioned and discussions are held in languages other than English. And they... are not convinced that my career is over. They are still watching and waiting and talking about... my future."

"Oh, no. Really?"

"It is mostly just rumblings. People who would like to see me back in action and helping out their causes. It is less than it once was, and maybe in a few more months... it will all have faded away. But for now, there is still chatter in certain circles, and I cannot give anyone cause to believe that I might still return."

"Oh, I'm sorry, Dad. I thought that by now, people wouldn't be concerned anymore, and you could pursue your hobbies and maybe get out of the house now and then."

"Yes. We all hoped that they would be less persistent. But apparently… the Russians play a long game. They don't mind waiting a few months or a couple of years to see how everything will turn out."

Kenzie hoped that it would not be another couple of years. Walter would go crazy. Or he would drive Lisa crazy, and she might just kill him.

"I'm really sorry. I thought it would work out a lot faster than that."

"Well, we will just continue to do what we are doing to the best of our abilities. I was not expecting to be quarantined for so long, but I am certainly not the only man who has ever had to suffer such a confinement. Helping out with these innocence projects—men who have served decades in prison for something that they did not do—I realize how lucky I am. They have become different people, having to live in those terrible places with the violent, amoral people they are incarcerated with. Or living out their lives in total isolation in the harshest of surroundings. Here I am, in a lovely setting, with everything I could want. I have nothing to complain about."

Kenzie nodded her agreement. His quarantine or confinement could not be compared to those living in maximum security, segregated, or on death row. So he was bored sometimes and couldn't see the friends and business associates he had cultivated over the years, or word would get back to the Russians that he was just shamming being sick. He could still learn new skills, talk to his daughter, and make himself useful in helping out those who were actually in such dire situations.

"And... you don't think they will come after you there? They are willing to just leave you alone until you 'recover'?"

"It has been quiet. No one has breached the security here. A few people talk to your mother occasionally to find out how I am recovering, but she has let it be known that she prefers not to talk about the situation, and they mostly leave her alone."

"And the break-in at the foundation...?"

Walter raised his brows. "Yes, what about it?"

"You don't think that had anything to do with the Russians?"

He shook his head. "Heavens, no. Your mother has been the one to handle the foundation, not me. The Russians know it was never my baby. That was just... people who were unhappy about the decision to defund a number of the projects that we used to support. But it will blow over. Don't you worry about that. People can only shout into the wind for so long. Then they will give up and take their pleas to other foundations who are more likely to help them."

"Do you feel bad? That we're not doing as much for kidney research anymore? Do you think Amanda would be upset about it?"

"No, of course not. We did everything we could for Amanda and many others like her. The technology is maturing, and it will not be long before they can cure many of the kidney diseases that were previously hopeless. She would be very proud of our part in that. And she would be happy that we are reaching out to people like Zachary who need a helping hand, and setting up social programs that will provide a safety net for those who haven't ever had one."

Kenzie was soothed to hear him say it. She had worried, not just since the break-in at the foundation, but before that. Even though she had heard it discussed at the board level, she wanted to know that they were doing the right thing and that Amanda would not have felt betrayed. Kenzie didn't really believe that Amanda was out there somewhere, watching over her and aware of everything she did. But she still wanted to know that Amanda would have approved.

“You look tired,” Walter observed.

Kenzie rubbed her eyes. They were a bit gritty and tired. “I slept pretty good last night. Maybe it’s just the lighting.”

“Well, make sure you are getting enough sleep. We don’t want you getting burned out.”

* * *

Kenzie was loath to tell Zachary and Hal that her dad was, in fact, still under threat from the Russian mob. But if she hid things from Zachary, he would assume he couldn’t trust her to tell him everything, and she would be left out of the loop. And since they were talking about her safety, she really didn’t want to be left out of the conversation.

She would have to tell him.

CHAPTER 28

Hal followed Kenzie to the office. He promised not to get in the way or attract attention to himself unless she were in actual danger. He would stay out of sight, and no one would know she was being followed by a personal bodyguard unless someone tried something.

If Zachary wanted to waste his money paying for a bodyguard when one wasn't needed, that was his own business. After a day or two of this nonsense, he would see that there was no real threat against Kenzie's life, that the Russians and other threats that he saw at every turn were just random occurrences that his brain was mistakenly tying in to a pattern. He would agree that Hal could go back to doing whatever Hal did when he wasn't watching Kenzie.

Hal promised that after escorting her to the police parking garage, he would let her proceed from there on her own and not go inside. The parking garage was blockaded and guarded, the elevator was guarded and was locked during non-public hours, and if she left the medical examiner's office to go somewhere else in the building, she was surrounded by cops. She couldn't get much safer than that.

After glancing at Hal's car in the rearview mirror a couple of times on her way to the office, Kenzie decided to just ignore him. He was supposed to be on covert surveillance and she shouldn't do anything to attract attention to him. She would just let him stay in the background, like Zachary when he was on a surveillance job.

The thought gave her pause for a moment. Where was Zachary? He wasn't going to follow her to make sure that she wasn't bothered by some unknown Mr. X? He was just going to stay home and work on his corporate espionage file as if he weren't worried about her?

She understood that Hal was intended to be a deterrent. Zachary didn't carry a gun, and he wasn't a big man. He didn't lift weights or train as a ninja, or do anything else that would help him to protect her physically. He could watch her, but if she were in danger, he would have to call the police for help or put himself in danger, pitting himself against someone bigger, stronger, and better armed. That was why he had sent Hal with his imposing size, bulging muscles, and police training. He had worked for cops and cartels. He carried and knew how to expertly handle a weapon.

But what was Zachary doing? Sitting outside the police department in his car, watching the triangle that marked Kenzie's location on his tracking app as she moved from one part of the office to another?

Kenzie tried to put Zachary's worries and whatever he planned to do out of her head and focus on doing her work as usual. She followed her usual Monday morning routine. Checking to see what had come in by email or delivery, or had been picked up and logged into the morgue over the weekend. She checked labels and file numbers to ensure everything was cataloged correctly and could not be mixed up.

Dr. Wiltshire got in as Kenzie was reviewing the mass spectrometry results on the Markov file. Kenzie bunched up her eyebrows, looking at the various peaks on the graph. Dr. Wiltshire chuckled. “Don’t let your face freeze like that. What have you got that is making you go cross-eyed?”

“Mass spectrometry on the Markov file. The unknown chemical in her blood.”

“Ah,” Wiltshire drew closer and looked at the graph while she studied it. “I guess from your expression that it did not exactly match any known result.”

“Of course not,” Kenzie agreed. “That would be too easy.”

“What is the molecular ion peak and the base peak?”

Kenzie turned the results toward him, and he muttered the values to himself. She hoped that he had enough experience with mass spec results to be able to tell her something useful about the graph.

Dr. Wiltshire scratched his head. “I’ve got a chemist who might be able to give us some direction. The lab didn’t give you any indication of what they thought it might be? It wasn’t close to a known substance?”

Kenzie flipped through the other pages of the report, but mostly it just seemed to summarize the numbers on the graph, giving the component parts of the chemical without actually telling her anything useful about what it could be.

“No. I’m going to need the number of your chemist friend. I don’t think I can figure this out without him.”

“I can’t say that I’m that much more useful. I can recognize some substances on mass spec, but this is not familiar. If Dirk can’t figure out what it is, we’re going to be looking through a lot of textbooks trying to match the numbers up to something.”

Kenzie really hoped that Dirk would be able to tell her something. She didn’t relish the idea of spending all day going through chemistry textbooks looking for a chart that looked similar to the one in her hands.

* * *

It was several hours before the chemist, Dirk Hassan, called Kenzie back about the mass spec results.

“I’m looking for Dr. Kirsch?” he told her after announcing his name.

“Yes, that’s me. Dr. Wiltshire said you’re the guy to talk to about mass spec. He said that if anyone could identify what is showing up there, it would be you.” Kenzie didn’t worry about laying it on too thick. She needed Dirk to be motivated to help her understand the results.

Dirk chuckled. “Well, glad to know that my skills are appreciated. And the fact is, it is always fun to help out with a coroner’s investigation. It makes it a little more interesting than some of the industrial applications we usually deal with.

Identifying a contaminant or dealing with someone who is trying to figure out a competitor's formula."

"Do you get that a lot? That doesn't sound very ethical."

"Under trade secret laws—no, it is definitely frowned upon. Luckily, I don't have to worry about that when dealing with your office."

"No," Kenzie agreed. "We're not looking to steal anyone's intellectual property. So... given that, what can you tell me about the unknown substance in our subject's blood?"

"Knowing that it was in someone's blood gives us a starting point. Obviously, we can't catalog every chemical substance known to man. Or not yet known to man. Since it was found in someone's blood, and it was not identified as any of the usual recreational drugs or common poisons, the obvious place to go is medications."

"Right."

"We're working on the assumption that your victim didn't generally consume non-food, non-drug substances."

"Like what?"

"Like… dirt, glass, bleach, antifreeze, rubbing alcohol."

"Okay. No, I haven't had any reports of her eating non-food substances."

"It's rare, but not unheard of. So, we start looking for familiar chemical signatures. What is the base peak? What is the molecular ion peak? And finally, what are the other fragments? Do they fall into a familiar pattern?"

"I'm hoping that your answer is yes."

"The closest substance I can find is Propranolol," Dirk revealed. "But it is <u>not</u> Propranolol."

“What is it, then? Something like Propranolol?” Kenzie tried to remember everything she knew about the drug. It was a beta-blocker. It helped to regulate heart rate.

“Yes, close to Propranolol, but with some significant differences. I suspect we are looking at a drug in the developmental stages. If so, I would not expect it to be in human trials. I haven’t heard of any next-generation beta-blockers in development right now, but companies do tend to keep that under the radar if possible.”

“A new beta-blocker.” Kenzie thought about that. “Okay, good. But why would our victim have it in her system? She worked for a research company, but she wouldn’t be taking it herself, would she? That would break all of the protocols.”

“Yeah. Though I can’t say that all companies always follow the laws and ethics surrounding testing protocols for new drugs. There have always been scientists willing to experiment on themselves.”

"That sounds pretty dangerous. Why would they be willing to do that?"

"Some people don't wait for Christmas to open their presents, either," Dirk teased. "Some people just are not very good at waiting. They want answers, and they want them right now. What do you know about your victim and her medical conditions? Was she on beta-blockers?"

"No. From what I understand from her sister and the people she worked with, she was in good health. And nothing showed up on her medical records that I could find about a heart problem or beta-blockers. The heart looked quite healthy on postmortem. Some occlusion in the arteries. No dilation or thickening of the walls."

"She might have participated in some stage 0 testing. It is a conflict of interest for the creator of a drug to test it on herself, but that doesn't mean it never happens. She wouldn't put it into the official testing documentation for the drug, but she might try it unofficially to convince people that it was safe to participate in the trials. Snake oil salesmen commonly imbibed their own products in public demonstrations to show how safe and efficacious they were."

"People are crazy. I can't imagine doing that with the ingredients that were in some of those old patent medicines. Lead, opiates, poisonous herbs."

"I wouldn't recommend it," Dirk agreed. "Microdosing on a beta-blocker is one thing. I don't think I would want to experiment with snake oil."

"With the concentration that was in her blood... I don't think it could be considered microdosing."

"Hmm." Dirk didn't counter Kenzie's suggestion. "That would be for you to determine. It would be... very unusual for a scientist or researcher to overdose on their own newly developed medication. I won't say it could never happen, because some people do incredibly stupid things. Is that the sort of thing your subject might have done?"

Kenzie thought about the very modest amount of alcohol in Dr. Markov's system. "No... I don't think she would. She barely drank. She was healthy. She was..." Kenzie suddenly thought of the documents embedded in the picture files on the locket. Was Markov selling trade secrets? Was she performing her own experiments and keeping records of them hidden in her secret memory vault?

"She was what?" Dirk asked. "Sorry, you cut out."

"I think she was a cautious person, from what I have been able to tell. I don't think she was the type to do something dangerous like that."

"Maybe she ate her lunch in the lab and picked up the wrong beaker to drink from?" Dirk joked. "I really don't see any other way she could inadvertently have taken an experimental beta-blocker."

CHAPTER 29

Kenzie knocked on Dr. Wiltshire's open door before entering his office. She took her usual seat when he motioned to it and put her files on his desk.

"So, have you had some success?" Dr. Wiltshire asked, eyeing the pile of papers.

"Yeah. I think we are moving things forward."

"Good to hear it. Did Dirk have any insight into what the mystery substance in Dr. Markov's blood might have been?"

"He was really helpful. It looks like it was a beta-blocker."

"A beta-blocker?" Dr. Wiltshire's brows went up. "I don't recall seeing anything on her medical records about a heart condition or blood pressure issues."

"No," Kenzie agreed, pulling the copies of medical records she'd managed to get ahold of. "Nothing in her records to indicate any problems. She was very healthy."

"Then why beta-blockers? Am I missing something, and they are being used as recreational drugs now?"

"No. I did a bit of research on any off-label uses, and I guess some people do occasionally use them to reduce the effects of performance anxiety—in precision sports like archery, test anxiety in students, stuff like that."

"You think she took them to calm her down about speaking that night?"

"I guess it's a possibility. The only thing is… what was in her blood was not an approved drug. It was not an exact match for Propranolol or any other beta-blocker on the market. It was likely an experimental drug."

"And why would she have an experimental drug? Was this one that her company was developing?"

"Possibly. It would make sense. Well, to an extent. It still wouldn't explain why it was in her system, but would at least account for her access to it."

"So, maybe to enhance her performance that night. Take the edge off her nerves."

"That's a possibility. But it doesn't sound like her. I mean, she has been speaking at functions for years. Was she taking beta-blockers that whole time? And no one ever noticed? She never had any problems driving before this? And if she just started taking it, then why?"

"You said that she had been stressed lately. That would tie in."

Kenzie nodded. "Her sister said she was stressed out, but her coworkers said she wasn't. That maybe she was excited about beginning human trials, but not upset."

"What human trials were they starting?"

"A new organ transplant protocol. Gene editing to eliminate rejection."

Dr. Wiltshire sat back in his chair, looking shocked. "Organ transplants? They were ready to go to human trials with a new organ transplant protocol? Without antirejection drugs?"

Kenzie nodded. "I believe the word they used was 'revolutionary.'"

"No kidding." Dr. Wiltshire rubbed his forehead, still thinking through the implications of this news. "The most common failing of organ transplants is rejection or patients not taking their medications. They feel fine, and they don't like taking a whole pharmacy of drugs for the rest of their lives. Maybe they don't like the side effects of the antirejection drugs, and they start to miss doses. They don't notice any ill effects after missing doses, so they dial it back even more, until eventually, it catches up with them, and they blame the transplant failure on the organ itself."

"I've read that as many as fifty percent of patients are non-compliant with post-transplant medications."

Dr. Wiltshire nodded. "It is the leading cause of transplant failure. If we could eliminate the need for antirejection drugs, the long-term success of organ transplants would likely double. Maybe even more, if you factor in the cases where the organ is immediately rejected despite the presence of immunosuppressants."

"That's incredible," Kenzie murmured. She remembered the number of drugs that Amanda had been required to take after her transplant. Even though they were sisters and the organ was a good match, Amanda had needed to take immunosuppressants for the rest of her life. She rarely complained except to joke that she took so many pills she rattled when she walked, but Kenzie knew that Amanda suffered a lot of side effects. But the headaches and nausea and the chance of developing diabetes or osteoporosis were nothing compared to the effects of kidney disease, long sessions of dialysis, and the predicted survival rate.

"So what does this have to do with beta-blockers?" Dr. Wiltshire asked. "If they were working on gene editing for organ transplants, why would they also be experimenting with beta-blockers?"

"Well… I don't know, exactly. But they were a research company, so it would make sense that they would have more than just one project on the go. You can't rely on just one technology or drug, in case it doesn't work. The company would go bankrupt. Dr. Hayes talked about strengthening the patient's immune system, heart, and lungs before transplant surgery to increase the odds of success, so maybe the beta-blocker was a part of that protocol. Or maybe it was completely unrelated."

"Regardless of the reason they were pioneering a new beta-blocker, it still leaves us with the question of why it was in Dr. Markov's system. Did she take it just to steady her nerves?"

Dr. Wiltshire stared off into space. "We doctors can be a stubborn bunch, refusing to admit our own weaknesses and human failings. Maybe she did take it to help her with her speech. It was on hand, and they needed to test its safety anyway..."

Kenzie didn't believe that was what had happened, but she shrugged. "Maybe."

"The 'why' may be something we will never know."

"Yeah. It's possible. I'm going to give Detective Edwards a call and fill him in. Maybe he will discover something in his interviews."

Dr. Wiltshire nodded. "At any rate, he will be happy to hear that we can give him a reason for Dr. Markov's impaired driving. Combining a beta-blocker with alcohol, even a modest amount, could definitely result in slow reaction time, inability to recognize how fast she was going, disorientation, and misjudging distances."

"The perfect storm. And Markov must not have taken it before driving before, or she would have a record of DUID or negligent driving offenses."

"Well… she hadn't been caught. Or she hadn't taken it before driving. She might have made alternate arrangements for transportation before, or had been able to clear the beta-blocker from her system before driving."

"Or taken a different beta-blocker. And she didn't know she would react differently to this one."

Dr. Wiltshire nodded. "All possibilities," he agreed. "Let Detective Edwards know, and… I think we can move toward issuing a ruling of accidental death."

CHAPTER 30

"Dr. Kirsch," Edwards greeted when he answered the phone. "I suppose you are calling to find out where we are on decrypting the information on Dr. Markov's locket."

"Oh. Actually, no. Though I would definitely be interested in knowing if you have made any progress."

"Well, a fine detective I am. As to our progress... we have taken several steps forward. As far as I understand from what the techies have told me."

"Great. So there were hidden files?"

"Yes. There were files embedded within the pictures and videos. That was a good call. I'm guessing you are a lot more computer literate than I am."

"No, I just happened to have someone on hand who was. I can't claim to be the one who made the breakthrough."

"We'll still give you the credit. The techs were able to extract files from those pictures. But there was a second level of encryption. They were not just hidden inside the graphics. They were also password protected. Don't ask me for details on the level of encryption and how long it would take them to figure it out with brute force. Suffice it to say that it will be some time before we can understand exactly what is in those files. Unless you happen to have the password or encryption key for me."

"No... not yet. Maybe it's on her phone?"

"It's possible. But if it is, it is hidden as well. Maybe it is disguised as a personal note, journal entry, or a shopping list, or another picture. They are doing everything they can to track it down and decode the file. If you happen to have any suggestions, feel free to email me, and I'll pass them on to the techies."

"Okay. You might try her sister Alina's name or birth date. They seem to be quite close."

"All right. I can pass those on. But that wasn't what you called about?"

"What about the file names on the locket? Could they include the password?"

"They already tried that. Any form of the filename or dates. But no luck. When you look at them together, though, they do form a pattern. Not a pattern that points at the encryption key, but maybe a clue to why Dr. Markov was collecting and encrypting the data she was."

"Do you think... it was industrial espionage?"

"That is always one of the considerations when you are looking at hidden files for a high-tech company like this. Industrial espionage is a real risk, and the companies do a lot to ensure employees can't walk out the door with secrets. But I think she had them fooled with the locket. It doesn't look like an electronic storage device, so chances are she could walk right through security wearing it, without risking detection."

"Yeah. I don't know how companies are going to stay on top of security when anything like that could have a chip embedded in it. Almost anything could be a storage device."

"From the names on the files, Dr. Markov was recording conversations or copying documents from a limited circle of people within the company. We are trying to discover in our conversations with the employees whether those people were working on one particular project together."

"Has there been any indication that the company knew she was gathering or sharing information?"

"Not yet. But of course, they would keep it very quiet if they suspected something. Especially when we are talking about a death investigation. They don't want to have to disclose knowledge of trade secrets being sold. That would impact their ability to fund or sell their products."

"I might have one piece of information that could help. It is possible that Dr. Markov was involved in the development of a new beta-blocker. That's a drug that helps to regulate heartbeat and blood pressure."

Edwards grunted. "I'm familiar with beta-blockers."

Kenzie wondered whether he was on one himself. There was no way to tell by looking at someone whether they had a problem with an irregular heartbeat. She might be able to guess that an overweight patient had high cholesterol or occluded arteries, but an irregular rhythm could afflict a child or someone who was apparently slim and healthy just as easily as it could someone who was grossly overweight.

"The drug that Markov was under the influence of was an experimental beta-blocker. Or it appears to have a similar profile to known beta-blockers. A beta-blocker mixed with alcohol could certainly have impaired her driving."

"Ah, filling in a missing piece of the puzzle. Thank you, Dr. Kirsch. And you think that this beta-blocker is something Dr. Markov was involved in the development of?"

"That would be my guess, yes. It is not on the market yet; Dr. Wiltshire and I are uncertain as to why she would have the drug in her system. Unless she took it to reduce anxiety over speaking that night. It is possible that she was testing its safety on herself, but that is not typically done. It would be quite reckless and might screw up her drug trials if someone found out about it. So if she did take it, she probably would not have kept any official records of the fact."

"Would you be able to tell by looking at her that she had taken it?"

Kenzie considered what she knew about beta-blockers, and shook her head slowly. "No. Probably not. Is there a video of her speech? If she was acting slowed-down or clumsy, that might be a clue."

"We have been gathering photos and video taken that night. I'll send you a link to the gallery, and you can see whether you can spot any possible indicators. But I understand that you probably won't be able to tell."

"Yeah." Kenzie was curious, though. "I'll look and see if I can tell you anything."

CHAPTER 31

Kenzie was ready to go home at the end of the day. She was glad to have been able to move the Markov case forward. Perhaps, as Dr. Wiltshire had said, it was time to issue her final report on the matter, closing it as an accidental death. That was what it was, after all. Regardless of why Dr. Markov had taken the experimental beta-blocker or if she had been stealing files from the company, it was still an accident that had resulted from the interaction of alcohol and the experimental drug.

She liked it when everything lined up and she could issue her findings and close the file at the same time as the police finished their investigation, with everything wrapped up and neatly aligned. But it might be some time before the police finished their investigation not only into Markov's death, but also the possible theft of trade secrets.

As Kenzie stood by her car, fitting the key into the lock, she heard the staccato click of approaching heels, and turned her head to see who else was there. She recognized most of the other people who had reserved parking spaces close to hers. And very few women wore high heels, which were not practical in law enforcement or other positions requiring them to be on their feet for long periods. But some women had positions that regularly put them in the public eye, so they had heels with them, even if they didn't wear them all day.

She did not recognize the woman who approached her, a brightly lipsticked smile on her face. Kenzie paused as the woman approached her. Maybe she was lost and wanted to ask Kenzie for directions to the public parking lot. People did sometimes walk into the private parking by mistake. Security would walk her out, if she were discovered.

“Dr. Kirsch?” the woman questioned.

Kenzie raised her brows. “Yes?”

"I'm glad I managed to catch you," the woman said brightly. "Rilla Vale, from Channel Eight News."

Kenzie pulled back from her. "This is a secure area," she told Vale. "You need to leave."

"I wanted to talk to you. Wouldn't you rather I did it privately than approached you in a public area? Or your home?"

"I don't have any reason to talk to you. Sorry. If you need a statement from the medical examiner's office, you need to reach out to the public relations department."

"I understand you are the one who has been working on the Mariya Markov file."

"Call PR."

"Is it true that you have found evidence that Markov was poisoned?"

Kenzie's jaw dropped. She almost answered, then caught herself and just closed her mouth. Rilla Vale could float whatever wild theories she wanted to. Kenzie was not going to speculate or ask her what she was talking about and where she got her information. Kenzie unlocked her door and lifted the door handle. She turned and slid into the seat.

"Is it true that Dr. Markov was involved in illegal experiments?" Vale persisted. "Industrial espionage?"

Kenzie pulled her door shut with a slam. She locked the doors immediately so that Vale could not open them. Vale tapped on the window with her phone, her smile broad. "Are you being pressured by Birch Valley Biomed to declare Dr. Markov's death an accident to shut down speculation on their R&D program?"

Kenzie started the engine. It mostly drowned Vale out, but the woman raised her voice so that Kenzie would be able to hear her still over the engine and through the closed window. "Are the police investigating Markov's death as a homicide?"

Kenzie backed out of her parking space, ignoring Vale other than to make sure she didn't back over her toes. Such a tragedy might result in litigation, which Kenzie would prefer to avoid.

Her baby's tires squealed as Kenzie pulled forward again and swerved into the exit lane. As she navigated the ramp to the street level, she saw one of the security guards, his face curious as he turned toward her to see who was leaving in such a hurry. Kenzie pulled to a stop and motioned to him, rolling down her window.

"Dr. Kirsch," Nathaniel's brows drew down and he reached for his radio. "Is something wrong?"

"A reporter by my parking spot. Rilla Vale from Channel Eight News."

"Oh, good grief." He pulled his radio out of its holster and pressed the side button as he called the other guards to let them know what was happening. “Thanks, doctor. We’ll get rid of her. Sorry about that.”

Kenzie nodded. She knew it was impossible to keep the parking garage completely secure. There was a barrier arm rather than a garage door, so people could walk around or duck under it. Even if there were a garage door, it wouldn’t stop people from darting in while the door was up to admit a legitimate parking pass holder. Security did the best they could to make sure that people were not bothered by intruders.

Nathaniel gave her a nod and a little salute, and Kenzie continued on the ramp to street level and let herself out.

She had only gone a block or two when she realized there was a car close behind her, apparently shadowing her. Darn Channel Eight News. They weren’t going to give up that easily.

Kenzie hit her brakes, and the car was brought up short behind her, nearly hitting her bumper. She should be more careful; she didn't want to end up having to repair her car because someone had been following too closely.

She stared at the driver in her rearview mirror for a few seconds before she recognized the big man. Hal. She'd completely forgotten about his being there to tail her back home.

He raised his hand to wave at her. With a sigh of relief, Kenzie released the brake and started moving again. She drove directly home and into the garage. Zachary was on the couch when she walked in through the garage door, and she ignored his greeting and went to the front door to open it for Hal, who looked at her questioningly. "Is something wrong?"

Kenzie motioned for Hal to enter, and armed the security alarm behind him. They both went into the living room, where

Zachary was sitting up and looking around, wondering the same thing.

“There was a reporter in the parking garage,” she told them. “She approached me at my car asking me questions.”

“What?” Zachary squawked. He looked at Hal. “Didn’t you see her? She should never have gotten in.”

“I couldn’t be at all entrances,” Hal pointed out. “I was keeping an eye out for anyone suspicious and for Dr. Kirsch to leave the building. I can’t vet everyone who walks in every entrance. That’s why they have their own security.”

“Did you tell the building security?” Zachary demanded. “They need to keep a better lookout. They need to know there is a problem.”

“Yes, I stopped and talked to one of the guards and he was going to take care of it. I’m sure they’ll be on the lookout for her tomorrow.”

"Why was she there to try to talk to you? Was it for this case? The Markov case?"

"Yes. That's what she was asking about. She had… all kinds of questions. Obviously, word is out that there is more to it than just an accident."

"You think it was more than just an accident?" Zachary asked, brows drawn down.

"There was a drug in her bloodstream. Something called a beta-blocker." Kenzie looked around. She wanted something to do with her hands. She didn't want to just stand there telling them everything. There would be more questions and she wanted to feel comfortable in her own home, not like she was being interrogated. She retreated to the kitchen and started banging through the cupboards, looking for something simple to make for supper.

"Did she know that?" Zachary asked. "The reporter?"

"She asked whether Markov had been poisoned. So, yes, I guess they got word that she had something in her system. How she found that out so quickly, I don't know. We just got the lab tests back this morning."

"A leak at the lab? Or in your office?"

"I don't like the idea of either one. But we've had information leaked before, so I can't say it is impossible. There is a leak somewhere in our office or the police department. There are a lot more people in the police department than the medical examiner's office, so if I had to pick one over the other, that's where I would guess the leak is."

"What else did she say?"

"She wanted to know if it was a homicide. If there were illegal experiments going on. If there was industrial espionage."

"So they know a lot." Zachary frowned, thinking about that. He looked at Hal, who was standing by listening to the conversation without comment. He had been undercover as a security guard in a cartel. He had lots of experience listening and gathering information without inserting himself into the conversation.

"Is it being investigated as a homicide?" Hal asked.

Kenzie shook her head slowly. She pulled out a loaf of bread and started laying out slices of bread on the counter like a card shark dealing cards. "It is being investigated as... more than just an accident. I wouldn't say it was a homicide, but the circumstances surrounding her death are... unusual. The drug in her system, the possibility of her stealing trade secrets... no one aside from the police has that information. And if Channel Eight News releases it... that could cause the police significant difficulties in their investigation. It is much harder to get information from people who think they are under suspicion or there was something illegal going on in the company than if they thought it was just a routine inquiry."

“Yeah,” Zachary agreed. “It will make things much more difficult for them if that leaks out.”

“Poisoned,” Kenzie murmured to herself. She went to the fridge and started pulling out condiments and sandwich fixings. “Who would poison her with a beta-blocker? It would stop her heart if she was given enough. But that couldn’t have been the intention... if it is a beta-blocker they are developing, they wouldn’t want to use it to commit murder. They wouldn’t want to risk someone tracing it back to them...”

“Do you think she was poisoned?”

“No. She wasn’t killed by it. And there was no guarantee that she would have been. I don’t know how much her body had metabolized, but it would have been a risk to use it as a weapon. Especially if it could be traced back to them... like I said.”

She kept herself busy, slathering butter and mayonnaise on each of the slices of bread.

"Are sandwiches okay?" she asked Hal belatedly. "Do you have any special dietary needs?"

"Sandwiches are fine," he said, looking amused.

Zachary started stacking meat and cheese on every second slice, working alongside Kenzie. Kenzie motioned to the lettuce. "Lettuce, too, and I'll slice the tomatoes."

If she let him slice the ripe tomatoes, the slices would be half an inch thick.

Kenzie shook her head, wishing she knew where Rilla Vale had gotten her information.

CHAPTER 32

"We need more information about Dr. Markov," Zachary said, speaking around a mouthful of sandwich.

Kenzie looked at him, waiting for him to finish what he was chewing and clarify his point.

"What information?" she prompted when he didn't offer more. "And why 'we'? You already looked into her background, and I thought we were letting the police do the investigating."

"I want to know how she is connected with everything. What was she working on? If she was poisoned, then who poisoned her? Who had a motive? Was she stealing trade secrets from her company? What was the company name?"

"Birch Valley Biomed."

Zachary stopped, his mouth open as he was about to take a bite of the sandwich. He froze and looked at her.

“What?” Kenzie demanded.

“Birch Valley Biomed,” he repeated.

“Yes. You knew that. You just looked her up yesterday or Saturday night when we were at the Petersons. You knew what company she worked for.”

“I didn’t remember the name. I didn’t really think about it at the time.”

“Think about what?”

“Birch Valley Biomed. That’s part of the Ural Genetika AO group of companies, right?”

Kenzie shook her head. “Uh, I have no idea. Is it? I don’t know who or what owns Birch Valley.”

“Ural Genetika,” Zachary confirmed. He looked at Hal as if he, too, should understand the significance of this, then back at Kenzie again. "I know that because of the work that I've been doing."

Kenzie frowned. "The work you've been doing? You mean the data breach that you were investigating? You said it was a biomed company... I didn't remember its name, though. It wasn't Birch Valley."

"My company is Green Mountain Genethera Innovations."

"Right. Gene therapy. It seems like all of these players are into gene editing. That must be the next big thing."

"It is. Cutting edge. That's where everyone wants to be right now, and the competition is fierce. There is a ton of corporate espionage going on. They all want to know what their competitors are up to, so they are inserting moles into each other's companies. They are doing background checks, but they are not thorough enough to catch the spies. Their backstories are too good. Their true affiliations are buried too deep."

"And... what? You think that Markov must have been one of these moles?" Kenzie shook her head. "Dr. Markov has been widely admired for years. She is a public figure. She was one of the country's preeminent transplant surgeons and kidney disease experts. You can't take someone that prominent and expect them to operate as a mole. She can't be undercover."

Zachary was frowning as he concentrated on her words, nodding along to what she said. "That would make her harder to recruit," he agreed.

"Harder to recruit! Who would approach her? Like I said, you couldn't hide her. She couldn't be low-profile."

"People wouldn't suspect her," Zachary said with a nod.

"You really think she could be recruited to spy for a company? Who? You think that she was working at Birch Valley but she was actually working for another company? She was stealing information from Birch Valley for someone else?"

"Well, isn't that what you are saying? You believe she was hiding information and walking out with it. Walking out where? Taking it home to study during her time off? She had to be passing it on to someone."

"Well... yes, I suppose so," Kenzie admitted. She hadn't really thought about who Markov was passing the information on to. Maybe she was passing the information on to the people who needed it more. Or she was trying to speed up the process of developing new technologies that would benefit everyone. Kenzie hadn't thought about it being for money. About Markov working for one company while she pretended to be working for the other. Going behind their backs to give the information to someone who didn't need it more, but was simply willing to pay for it.

Zachary was looking at Kenzie, waiting for her to catch up and agree that they were on the same page. She nodded. "Okay... yes. She was passing that information on to someone else for some reason. I don't know why, but I guess it could have just been a case of selling out to the higher bidder."

"So we need to know more about her. What was her financial situation? Was she a gambler? In debt? Trying to bail out someone else in her family? When did they recruit her? Before she started at Birch Valley or after?"

"All good questions," Kenzie agreed. "To pass on to Detective Edwards."

Zachary rolled his eyes and looked at Hal, making sure that the other man was in agreement with their investigating it rather than just leaving it to the police and hoping that they came up with something.

"Is she working for the Russian mob? Just because she was born in America, that doesn't mean she couldn't be pressured into helping them, just like Walter. What if they threatened her aging parents? Her sister? Maybe a little niece or nephew? Or maybe they had some other kind of leverage on her. Maybe one of her parents, or both of them, are Russian spies. Sleepers for decades. It happens. Then, when their daughter becomes such a preeminent doctor, they activate them."

"That sounds like some cheesy spy movie," Kenzie said, shaking her head. "Not like something that happens in true life."

"It does, though. Sure, they use that kind of thing in movies, but that doesn't mean it doesn't happen in real life. We're not talking about a radioactive spider turning some guy into a superhero. We're talking about spycraft and leverage. Those things are real. Just ask your dad."

Kenzie rubbed her head. She thought she might be on the edge of getting a migraine. Maybe she should have made something healthier for supper, rather than relying on luncheon meats full of nitrates and preservatives, and who-knew-what-else that might trigger a migraine.

"How are you going to find those things out?" she demanded. "Because it isn't something that I'm going to be able to figure out from what I already have. And I'm not the one going back to Birch Valley to do the interviews. That's all up to Detective Edwards and the police. They are the experts, and they'll be conducting interviews to find out if someone in the company had it in for Dr. Markov or had reason to suspect her of stealing company secrets."

"I can do some of the initial research on the computer. I already know Birch Valley is stealing information from Green Mountain Genethera," Zachary told her.

Kenzie stared at him, shocked. "How would you know that?"

As soon as Kenzie said the words, she knew. Because that was what Zachary had been investigating. That was why he knew Birch Valley Biomed was a subsidiary of Ural Genetika AO.

Zachary nodded, seeing the understanding in Kenzie's eyes. "I can't say much about my client," he said. "You know I have to keep anything I find in the investigation confidential. But there have been some major data breaches. These companies are cutthroat."

And Dr. Markov, somehow caught in the middle of it all, had ended up dead.

"What do you know about the files hidden on Dr. Markov's locket?" Zachary asked.

"Not much," Kenzie said, glad she didn't have any information she would be required to keep from him. "They have extracted the files from the pictures and videos, but they are encrypted. The police have to find out how to decrypt them before they can read them and find out what they were all about."

"And you don't know the passkey."

"No." Kenzie cocked her head. "You wouldn't happen to have it, would you?"

Zachary laughed. "That would be handy, wouldn't it? No, I don't have that information. They apparently don't give all of their moles the same encryption passkey and keep a copy of it on their server in case anyone else should need it."

"They're just getting too big for their own britches," Kenzie teased.

Zachary nodded his agreement. He looked at Hal, and at the sandwiches that remained on the plate. "Help yourself. You still look hungry."

"I've had more than my share."

Zachary shook his head, waving this away. "I can't eat anything else. I don't have that much space to stuff it into."

"Are you calling me fat?"

Zachary looked Hal over. “I’m calling you big. And you’ve got even bigger muscles. And muscles burn calories faster, right Doctor?”

Kenzie was surprised that Zachary knew this bit of trivia. She nodded. “I’m not going to have any more, and neither is Zachary, so you might as well either eat them now or take them home with you.” She looked sideways at Zachary. “He is going home, right?”

“I figured he could stay in the guest room for a day or two.”

“Seriously?” Kenzie shook her head. “Do you really think we need a bodyguard inside the house?”

“You were threatened. Your dad is still being threatened. You’re investigating a possible Russian spy. You were already waylaid once today by someone who snuck into the parking garage.” He folded his arms and let Kenzie think about it.

Just the previous night, Kenzie had argued that these things were not connected. She still believed that. Didn’t she? The more she learned about the theft of secrets and other secret operations around the biotech companies, the less inclined she was to scoff at the possible connections.

Would having Hal around for a couple of days hurt that much? He was a large, capable man who could intervene if someone broke into the house despite their security measures. It would take the security company several minutes to get to the house, and a lot could happen even in two or three minutes. Hal would be right there.

“Fine,” she agreed curtly. “But I’m not entertaining. It’s been a long day, and I need to take a break. If you two want to watch a game or something...”

Hal shook his head. “I’m going to nap from now until the two of you go to bed. I need time off the clock, and then I can keep an eye on things after you go to bed.”

“You’ll need more than a few hours...”

"I'll get enough. And I can take a few more when you're at work again tomorrow, as long as you're in a secure area."

"Well," Kenzie stood up. She motioned to the sandwiches. "You'd better have those, so you're not going to bed hungry. And Zachary can clear and start the dishwasher. I'm going to have a warm bath and put on my jammies."

CHAPTER 33

Kenzie and Zachary did not watch the news on TV that night, which turned out to be a mistake. They both just wanted to relax and put the real world on hold for the rest of the night. Network news was always negative, and Kenzie preferred to keep it to small doses that she got over social media or news feeds she monitored. And Zachary's evening could easily be undone by watching something on the news that made him anxious. They needed relaxation and entertainment in the evening before bed. An escape from the real world, not being plunged into the tragedies and troubles of reality.

And there were no phones or social media allowed at the breakfast table. Just pleasant conversation, coffee, and a gentle ramp-up into the day. It was stressful enough to have an extra person hanging around, especially when that extra person was a constant reminder that they could be in danger from one of the threats that they had identified. Kenzie was regretting her agreement to let Hal stick around for a few days to make sure that they were safe from any outside forces.

Although she had slept pretty well, knowing that they had the double protections of the state-of-the-art security monitoring and the imposing physical presence of Hal Delaney. She had thought she would be on edge, tuned in to his movements while she was supposed to be asleep, but she had not been. He was quiet, and she didn't hear him watching TV or creeping around the house. His calm presence reassured her that it was safe to turn off her brain and just go to sleep.

"How did you sleep?" she asked Zachary. He was the one who had the most sleep issues. Kenzie could go for a night or two, sleeping restlessly and not getting the amount of sleep she needed without too many ill effects. Zachary slept little at the best of times, so a night or two of zero sleep because of anxiety or the distraction of knowing that Hal was there could really derail his health.

"Not bad." He shrugged. "Still got a few hours in, nothing out of the ordinary. And Hal and I played cribbage this morning while you were sleeping."

The mental image of Zachary and Hal bent over a cribbage board, intent on their game in the wee hours of the morning, made her laugh. Somehow, she couldn't see either one of them being able to maintain their focus on a game while they thought there might be a physical threat. They might have talked as the hours ticked by before the sun came up, but Kenzie doubted they'd had a "guy's night" while she slept.

"No threats?" she asked Hal, who remained silent while consuming a stack of toast with peanut butter and jam.

"All quiet," he agreed. "No one crossed the perimeter. No surveillance that I could spot. No suspicious activity in neighboring houses."

Kenzie pondered this as she took another bite of her toast with marmalade, trying to imagine all of the things that Hal had been doing to keep them safe during the night. What activity by the neighbors would have triggered his attention? Taking out the garbage at odd hours? Lights left on overnight? A loud argument? And what would that have meant for her and Zachary?

“Good,” she approved, for lack of something else to say.

Zachary nodded his agreement. “You slept okay?” he asked Kenzie. “You seemed to be pretty deep when I left.”

“I didn’t hear you, so I must have been.” Her body had grown used to Zachary’s nocturnal movements, and it was rare that his getting up and leaving the bedroom during the night or early morning would wake her anymore.

“That’s good. I was worried that you would be too anxious.”

“Not me. Slept like a baby. And now,” Kenzie glanced at the clock. “I’d better be getting on my way. The office awaits.”

“They’re dying to see you,” Zachary intoned.

Kenzie laughed. "Yes, they are," she agreed. A message she had received from Dr. Wiltshire overnight advised that he had been called out to a scene of death, so they had another guest to deal with once she had checked her email and other inboxes for anything of importance. He hadn't indicated there was any urgency or anything unusual about the scene, so she assumed it would be pretty routine. Perhaps a heart attack in the home or something equally mundane.

If they had watched the TV news the night before, she would have been forewarned that Rilla Vale had gone ahead with her report on Dr. Mariya Markov's death and the eddies of intrigue that swirled around it. She would have been prepared for the reporters and rubberneckers who were congregated outside of the parking garage entrance, waiting for a glimpse of her and hoping for the opportunity to talk about Dr. Markov and her suspicious death.

The security staff was obviously aware of the small crowd awaiting Kenzie's arrival. Still, there wasn't anything they could do about it until someone crossed the line, trespassing on the property or accosting Kenzie or one of the other staff members.

“What the heck is this?” Kenzie murmured as she pulled up to the entrance to the parking structure and saw the group jockeying for position, excited to see her, even though she had no idea who they were. There were a couple of homemade placards. Justice for Dr. Markov and Stop Xenotransplants with a picture of a brown kidney. Enough to give Kenzie an idea of what was going on.

Xenotransplants? Kenzie supposed gene editing could pave the way for transplants of animal organs into humans without the fear of rejection just as easily as human organs that were not perfect tissue matches. The the human genome and that of a pig were remarkably similar, sharing 98% of genetic material, and most of their organs were similar enough structurally to facilitate cross-species transplants. But there were other dangers and ethical challenges to be navigated in connection with cross-species transplants. People were far more likely to object to the use of animals being raised for organ transplants than for the dinner table.

One of the eager beavers banged into the side of Kenzie's car, making her grimace. He'd better not have scratched the paintwork on her baby.

That contact was enough to allow the security staff to take action, and they surged forward, herding the small gathering back from Kenzie's car and the entrance to the parking garage. One of them bent down to address Kenzie, which meant she had to pause to roll down her window to hear him.

"Sorry, Dr. Kirsch," he apologized. "We'll keep an eye on things here, and you shouldn't have to worry about any security issues inside. Someone will walk you from your car to the elevator."

Kenzie nodded. "Okay, sounds good."

He stepped back to allow her room to get into the building. He waved his badge in front of the scanner to raise the security gate, so Kenzie didn't have to use hers. He waved her through, which was unnecessary, considering that Kenzie was already halfway through the gate.

There was a guard hanging around near her reserved parking space. In case Kenzie hadn't already guessed it, this confirmed that she was the target of all of the interest, whether people really were concerned about justice for Dr. Markov or fighting against a medical practice that wasn't likely to mature in the near future. If transplanting non-matched organs through the use of gene editing was ten years away, cross-species transplant and raising animals for transplantation was probably another decade beyond that.

"Morning, doctor," Franklin, the security guard greeted as Kenzie climbed out of her car. "I guess you're aware of the disruption today."

Kenzie sighed and nodded. “It would have been nice to have a heads-up before I arrived. I could have had Zachary drop me off at the front of the building.”

“Uh… yes, ma’am. Maybe someone should have contacted you.”

Kenzie walked with him from her car to the elevator, and he pressed the elevator call button for her.

“We’ll keep public access closed today,” he advised. “If you are expecting anyone, just let us know and we will make sure that they are allowed through. We’ll route any routine inquiries or requests through the security desk upstairs.”

CHAPTER 34

Kenzie was disgruntled when she got to her desk and logged in to her computer. It wasn't that security had mishandled anything, just that she didn't like being ambushed. Especially two days in a row—yesterday by Rilla Vale and today by the small mob outside the building. It threw everything off.

She tried to put her bad mood aside and just focus on the work to be done. She needed to get through the usual processing of her email inbox and other reports that had come in overnight, check the evidence that had been logged with the body that had come in, and prepare it for postmortem. Dr. Wiltshire might have slept in because of the previous night's callout, but he might have also been in early if he had been unable to get back to sleep after the call.

The desk phone rang as soon as Kenzie took it out of night mode. She rolled her eyes and groaned, and sat down to answer it.

“Medical examiner’s office.”

“You ought to mind your own business,” the caller growled. “Why are you digging into stuff that is none of your business? Just file your findings and close the file.”

“I’m sorry, who is calling?” Kenzie challenged.

She expected him to hang up immediately. People like that didn’t want to have a discussion. They just wanted to vent their feelings and feel like they had done something to make a difference. They didn’t want real answers, and they certainly didn’t want to be identified.

“There isn’t anything going on at Birch Valley Biomed,” the caller snarled at her. “Why don’t you just keep your nose out of it?”

“There’s nothing going on at Birch Valley?” Kenzie repeated. It was an odd thing to say if there really was nothing going on. Why would anyone be concerned about it? There would be no need to worry about being discovered. They would continue their research and development as if nothing had happened. There would be a transition to navigate, with Dr. Markov no longer working there, but her work would be taken up by someone else and everything else would go on just as it had before.

“You don’t know anything about it,” the caller growled. Kenzie tried to analyze whether it was one of the scientists she had talked to before, but couldn’t identify the voice. She had not spoken to any of them for long enough to have a clear memory of their voice.

“I didn’t catch your name,” Kenzie said, again challenging him to identify himself.

The man exploded into rage. He swore viciously at Kenzie and began to berate her, employing foul names and the frequent use of f-bombs. Kenzie tuned the details out the best she could and tapped out a message to Detective Edwards on her cell phone.

Since the medical examiner's office was not open to the public today and she wouldn't have any innocent parties coming along to overhear the vitriol, Kenzie toggled the call to speakerphone, and started the voice recording app on her cell phone.

The caller stopped to take a breath, and Kenzie wondered whether he would hang up. "Are you the same person as sent me an email previously?" she asked. Did the language of his verbal threats align with the language in the threatening email she had received? She thought it might be, but couldn't be sure. She hadn't analyzed it carefully. She had closed it quickly and had not wanted to look at it again.

The man called her a couple more names and hung up abruptly.

Kenzie took a deep breath and stopped the recording on her phone. The ding of the elevator rang down the hall, and she watched to make sure that the new arrival was Dr. Wiltshire or someone else who belonged there. She wasn't going to make any assumptions today. Things were obviously not "business as usual."

It was Dr. Wiltshire. Kenzie gave him a weak smile as he came into view and walked up to the desk, shaking his head in dismay at the increased security or what had been on the Channel Eight News the night before. Kenzie was beginning to regret that she had not kept up with the news. At least she wouldn't have walked into everything without a clue as to what was going on.

"Kenzie. How is everything going down here? Holding down the fort?"

"Well... Yes, I guess so. We're all locked down, so it shouldn't be too hard."

He studied her expression, looking concerned.

"Is something wrong, Kenzie? I can assure you that I don't think you were the one who talked to that woman reporter."

Kenzie hadn't even thought about that. She and Dr. Wiltshire had worked together for long enough that she thought he trusted her with communications. There had been a couple of glitches in the past, but they had worked through those, and she was pretty secure in her belief that he wouldn't accuse her of anything like that without quite a bit of evidence.

"No, no," Kenzie agreed. "It's just that... things are a little disrupted. The people downstairs trying to get in. This guy that just called to... I don't really know why he called, but he said he wanted us to stop poking around at Birch Valley, that there is nothing going on there, and he was... offensive."

At Dr. Wiltshire's questioning look, she played back the brief recording she had made on her phone. He rolled his eyes and sighed.

"More threats. I think you are right to connect him with that email last week. I think it could be the same person. We'll need to call Detective Edwards, see if he can pull the call logs and see where it came from."

"It was blocked on my end. I couldn't tell who was calling."

"Police might still be able to identify it. Do you want me to deal with it?"

"I already texted him. I was hoping he could trace it while it was still live."

"Okay, we'll see if he comes up with anything. In the meantime... I suggest you not go out for lunch, but stick around here. You can have something delivered, or I can go out and do a pickup for you."

"I would think you are in just as much danger as I am," Kenzie objected. "If people want us to close the Markov case, you'll need to sign off on it too."

"Well, of course, but these people don't know procedure. They only know what they read in the paper or see on the news. And those sources have said that you are the medical examiner on the case."

Kenzie had to concede that part was true.

"Aside from the fact that women are naturally more vulnerable to attack, you are the one who has been threatened. First by email and now on the phone. This man may be escalating, and you are the one he is focused on."

"You don't think he would come here, do you?"

"The email made it clear that he knows who you are, personal things about you, and where to find you. I don't take that lightly."

"No," Kenzie admitted. "I actually hope it isn't the same guy..."

"Is it worse to have two angry enemies or one who is really deranged?" Dr. Wiltshire asked. He pondered. "I'm not sure which I would choose."

CHAPTER 35

Kenzie ran her fingers through her curls. "It seems like two different enemies would be better," she said. "A force that is split in two different directions... But who am I to judge? Maybe with just one, finding and determining whether he is actually a danger would be easier."

Her cell phone started to vibrate. "That's Detective Edwards."

"I'll leave you to it." He gave a little wave and stepped away from her desk. "Can I bring you a coffee refill?"

Kenzie nodded vigorously in response as she answered the phone.

"Detective Edwards," she greeted.

"Doctor. You had a call you were concerned about?"

"I didn't know whether you would be able to trace it..."

"I've got someone on it. How long did he stay on the phone?"

“Just a few minutes. I have a recording of part of it for you. I didn’t know whether you could analyze it to see if it was the same guy as sent the threatening email last week.”

“The email? Oh, I heard about that. Sergeant Campbell has that file. I’m not sure it matters whether it is the same guy or not. Either way, if he was making threats against a government employee, he’s running up a number of charges. We’ll do our best to track him down.”

“I don’t think that will be too hard. He wanted me to stop poking my nose into Birch Valley Biomed.”

Edwards gave a rumbling laugh. “Well, nothing like making it easy for us. I probably don’t need to trace the call then. It will undoubtedly trace either to Birch Valley’s exchange or an unidentified cell phone number.”

“Have you... been able to find anything out? About whether anyone knew Markov was stealing secrets and if they were pioneering a new beta-blocker?”

“Haven’t made much headway yet. I sent you some of the photographs from the event that night. Have you had a chance to dig through it yet?”

“No. I just got here, and... have been kept busy with other things. I’ll be sure to take a look before we start on the next autopsy.”

“Anything to be concerned about?”

“What? Oh, the new body? I don’t think so. A man who died in his sleep. It will probably not even be a full autopsy.”

“Let me know if there is anything you are concerned about. And we should talk about security when you leave here today. I understand there was a security breach last night—”

“Rilla Vale.”

“I guess she decided she didn’t need your input before running with her story.”

"Apparently."

"And there are already people demonstrating and trying to get past security today. Not a promising start. So, as I say, we should discuss security. Getting you out of here and safely home. Unfortunately, Roxboro is a small town, and that means it would be fairly easy to tail you from here to your house."

"I have a..." Kenzie tried to figure out how to explain the situation. "I have a security detail who will be following when I leave today. He's not in the parking garage, but he'll be with me once I get out."

"You should have him in the garage."

"Okay... then I need a pass for him and for security to let him in and show him to my parking space."

"I'll arrange it. What is his name? Have him come in and ask for me. If you're going to pay someone to watch your back, you should keep him as close as you can. He can watch your car while you're working, something our security doesn't have the manpower to do."

"Hal is his name. Hal Delaney."

"Hal Delaney," Edwards repeated thoughtfully. "Is he an ex-cop?"

"Yes. Not from here. He was on the force in Clintock, I think." Kenzie tried to remember the details. But obviously, Edwards already knew more than she did.

"Yeah. I've heard his name before. You sure you want him watching your back?"

"Why not? Have you heard something that would indicate he isn't a good choice?"

"There was a big mess when he left the force. I don't know. I get the feeling he didn't leave on good terms. That doesn't necessarily mean he was a dirty cop, but you've got to wonder."

Kenzie was more inclined to trust Zachary and his investigations than unfounded rumors. Hal may well have left his last employer under less-than-favorable circumstances, but that didn't mean he had done anything wrong. Considering the corruption within some police forces, he might even have left because he wasn't dirty.

"Zachary's checked him out," she told Edwards. "So I'm not worried."

"Okay. Have Delaney come see me, and I'll get him a parking and security pass."

"Thanks."

"No problem, Dr. Kirsch. I'd rather know that you were being looked after. The publicity on the TV and these ongoing threats... We don't want to look the other way and pretend there is nothing to worry about. You're secure down there when it is closed to public access, but we all know that even the most secure locations can be breached. Best to have as many layers of security as possible."

Kenzie wasn't sure, as she hung up the phone, whether she was encouraged by his approval of her security arrangements or worried by the suggestion that even the best security could be breached.

CHAPTER 36

The photos of the event Dr. Markov had attended were entrancing.

Kenzie studied the women in their beautiful dresses and the dapper men in their black tuxedos. She had been to plenty of fundraising and medical events in her time, so none of it was surprising, but it was always interesting to see what people wore. The little black dress was a popular choice, but it varied from woman to woman and from season to season. Others wore gorgeous, colorful creations, almost always clinging to their bodies like a second skin. Some women who were older or farther away from society's standard wore well-cut dresses of other fashions that were more flattering to their figures or that they considered more appropriate to their age.

The men didn't have the same range of choices, but there were a number of different styles of tuxes on display, with colorful accents of ties, cummerbunds, and pocket squares. Some showed off expensive cuff links or Rolexes to firmly establish their societal status. A few men used canes, exquisitely carved.

The police had collected all of the photos and videos that they could from the photographer who had been hired, employees, and guests in attendance. Reviewing it all was a daunting task, and not actually Kenzie's job. But she had to see it, to learn as much as she could about what had happened to Dr. Markov that night.

Kenzie found herself evaluating the dinner that had been served to the guests, the decoration of the tables and the hall, all of those little details her mother fussed about when she put on a fundraiser or other event. The catering, the flowers, the music, the arrangement of the room, and where each guest was to sit. Lisa had done it all, time and time again, and was an expert in every tiny detail.

The event put on by Birch Valley had been well done. Not the event of the year for anyone, but a perfectly acceptable dinner and presentation. It would, Kenzie was sure, bring in some of the money that they needed to cover the shortfall left by the Kirsch family foundation. But probably not all of it. It would take a few generous donors to make up for it.

Kenzie blinked, rubbed her eyes, and forced herself to look at the pictures for more than just what people had been wearing and whether the event had been carried out to Lisa's exacting standards.

She looked for Markov in each of the pictures, as well as the other members of the staff that she had seen when she had attended at Birch Valley's offices: Merle Shepherd, Dana Pratt, Morgan Tucker, and Hiram Hayes in particular. They were all there. There were a number of other people who were probably employees, judging by the way they stood grouped together.

She recognized some of the other figures in the kidney research and organ donation communities. Donors, researchers, experts, and scientists she had run into over the years at other events. The same people tended to attend all of the events around kidney disease and transplants. They were a close-knit community.

Dr. Markov looked cool and professional, her little black dress modest and conservative compared to some of the others at the event. She had worn her locket and watch for the event.

Markov didn't appear to be nervous in the pictures taken as she was talking to a variety of attendees as cocktails were served. Shaking hands. Making a good impression on people. Telling them how important the research was and how they were making progress in curing kidney disease, improving transplant technology, extending lifespans, and improving quality of life.

There were pictures of Markov at the podium giving her speech, smiling confidently, appearing personable and professional. And pictures of her eating dinner as she courted the largest donors. But she had disappeared during the dessert course. Where had she gone? Perhaps to take a private meeting, standing for a photo op, or receiving a significant check from a donor.

There was a dance after the dessert and coffee. Some guests would stay for it and some would leave, peeling off a few at a time until things wrapped up at midnight. By that time, Markov had been dead.

There were a couple of pictures that caught profile views of Markov in the background, but it would appear that after the dinner had concluded, she had been ready to leave. She wasn't at the center of any more pictures, only at the fringes. Then she was gone.

Kenzie watched the videos of the event, listening to Markov speak in perfect English without a trace of a Russian accent. She had, after all, been born and educated in the USA. She had not learned Russian-accented English from her parents, but the English that her teachers and classmates spoke. Her voice was low in tone, pleasant to listen to. She had a good cadence during her presentation, and people had not been nodding off as if she had droned away like an old professor.

But the last footage that caught Dr. Markov after dinner and before she left for the night was different. She was moving more slowly. A couple of times, she jerked like she had suddenly been caught off-balance. She leaned on the valet counter as she waited for her car to be brought around. She was not just touching it or leaning a hip against it casually, but clearly using it to keep herself on her feet.

The valet gave Dr. Markov her keys, something Kenzie would not have done. She was obviously impaired and should not have been driving herself.

Markov was nevertheless able to walk from the counter to her car without falling or swerving too far off target. She climbed into her car and drove away, initiating the trip that would take her to her final destination.

With a feeling of deep regret, Kenzie watched her drive away. It could have been prevented.

Her death could have been prevented if someone had just recognized that she was too impaired to drive.

CHAPTER 37

"Everything okay, Kenzie?" Dr. Wiltshire asked, catching Kenzie thinking of the Markov postmortem instead of the body in front of her.

She needed to pay attention to the man who had been brought in the night before. It was just as important to do a thorough job on his postmortem as it was to sort out the final details of the Markov report. She could figure out the final wording for Mariya Markov's report later, when she could give it her full attention. She needed to focus on the duties before her.

"Yes. I'm sorry. I was just watching footage of Dr. Markov before she died and it was... it's just distracting me a little. I'll pay attention."

"We need to give our attention to this patient too."

"I know. I'm here. I'm focused. Let's begin. You attended at the scene last night when the victim's body was discovered."

"Yes."

Kenzie looked at the monitor, which included Dr. Wiltshire's narrative of the body in situ. "The deceased was in bed. He had retired for a nap after dinner, experiencing indigestion."

Indigestion is often reported by patients experiencing heart attacks. They either mistook the pain of a heart attack for heartburn or other digestive discomfort, or they had indigestion in concert with a cardiac event.

"When his wife later went to bed, she found the sixty-five-year-old unresponsive and called 9-1-1. The paramedics reported that he was deceased, and you attended at the scene to declare him and to ensure you had no concerns about the scene."

Dr. Wiltshire nodded. "No signs of violence. The deceased was not under the care of a physician and was thought to be in good health. His wife did not know the last time he'd had a physical or seen his doctor."

"Well, that's not a bad way to go," Kenzie observed. "I wouldn't mind just dying peacefully in my sleep. Just go to bed one night and not wake up again in the morning."

"I think most people would agree with you wholeheartedly."

Kenzie looked at the preliminary work that had been done. The victim's medical records had been pulled, but they were sparse. He had obviously not been the type to go to his doctor with every little complaint.

There were no major illnesses, no broken bones since childhood. A few infections or viruses, a few doctor's notes written for work absences, all for apparently minor illnesses.

"Okay." Kenzie laced her fingers together and turned them outward to warm them up and stretch them. "Let's get started, then. Beginning the gross examination of Mr. Cory Smythe."

Kenzie pulled down the drape that had been placed over the body, revealing Mr. Smythe's face. She studied it clinically for any signs that would point toward a heart attack or something other than a heart attack.

His face was clear, with no petechial hemorrhaging, hives, or bruising. There were no marks around the throat. Kenzie folded down the drape a few more inches. Mr. Smythe was overweight with a slight paunch, but not an excessive amount of adipose tissues. He had kept in pretty good shape for his age.

Kenzie examined the body for any signs of violence or pathology. “X-rays?” she suggested.

Dr. Wiltshire nodded. “Sure. What are you thinking?”

“Nothing specific. Just being thorough. Look for any blockages, maybe a broken bone, in case he had fallen or had an accident without telling anyone about it. I don’t see any indication of anything. It’s just nice to be able to reassure the widow.”

She arranged for a series of X-rays, and this time, Dr. Wiltshire donned a lead apron and stayed in the room while Kenzie performed a short series and then examined the X-ray images on the monitor.

“No broken bones. It does not appear that CPR was performed; sternum and ribs all intact. No apparent head injury.”

She looked at the deceased’s face to make a comment and had a sudden lightning flash of memory. Dr. Wiltshire raised his brows. “What is it?”

“This man...”

“Mr. Cory Smythe,” he reminded her gently.

“Where...? I’ve seen him before.”

“That’s entirely possible.”

“But... where? It was just recently.”

"Yes?" Wiltshire did not immediately jump in and start to make suggestions. He knew better than to implant a memory through the power of suggestion. Memory was a remarkably suggestible thing. People didn't realize how much their "real" memories were supplemented with or replaced by details they themselves or other people had implanted. Actual recorded facts were much more reliable evidence than memories recalled later.

"I just... I just saw him recently." Kenzie concentrated, trying to pin it down. The memory floated in front of her, and she tried to anchor it in the appropriate setting.

Then, in another lightning flash, it came to her.

"He was at the same fundraising event as Dr. Markov."

Dr. Wiltshire's brows went way up. "Are you sure of that?"

"I was just looking at photos and videos of the event to see how Dr. Markov had been behaving before her accident. And <u>he</u> was on the video. I'm sure of it."

Dr. Wiltshire started to remove his gloves. "Let's verify that before going any further. We want to be sure that we are not operating under any false assumptions."

"Uh, yeah." Kenzie followed suit, removing her gloves and other protective clothing as well. They returned to Kenzie's computer, where she had been viewing the recordings of the fundraiser only minutes earlier. Kenzie clicked through the files until she found the one she was remembering.

Dr. Markov was getting ready to leave the event. As Kenzie had noticed, she was slower and clumsier than she had been earlier in the evening.

A man stood at her elbow, steadying her when she lurched suddenly. It was Mr. Smythe. He bent over, picked up the small clutch purse Dr. Markov had dropped, and pressed it back into her hand. He kept a hand near her as he guided her toward the valet counter. He made sure she was steady, leaning on the counter as Kenzie had previously noted. The valet gave Markov her keys, and she walked out to her car and drove away. Smythe walked beside her most of the way to the car, watched her drive away, then walked out of the frame.

"Well," Dr. Wiltshire nodded, his brows drawn down. "That's rather disturbing, isn't it?"

"You can see that she was impaired. He knew it. The valet must have known it too. But they just herded her to her car and saw her off."

"It does appear to be Mr. Smythe on the video. And that means..." He looked at her, not finishing his sentence.

"That means," Kenzie continued, "that both Dr. Markov and Mr. Smythe died within a week of attending that event. Coincidence?"

"I cannot say. It is possible that there is a logical connection we cannot yet see. It may be that it was just a coincidence. But we must consider the possibility their deaths could be connected to each other or to that event."

"We already know that Dr. Markov's was partially connected to the event. She drank at the dinner. At some point—maybe during the dessert, when she was not on camera—she took a beta-blocker, which from the evidence... impaired her driving to the extent that she died in an accident minutes later."

"But Mr. Smythe did not die at the event or shortly after it, but a week later."

"Of a heart attack," Kenzie said slowly.

"Possibly. Other suggestions?"

Kenzie was silent, considering the possibilities. "What if he also tested the beta-blocker to make sure it was safe? And maybe it wasn't."

"We need to find out whether he was involved in any drug trials. And whether he also has the unknown beta-blocker in his bloodstream."

CHAPTER 38

Kenzie's phone interrupted dinner, and despite the "no phones at the table" policy, she pulled it out to see who was calling in case it was a break in the case. They had too many questions outstanding, and she needed to know something for sure. She needed at least one answer.

"Sorry, I have to take this," she told Zachary. She walked away from the table so that she would have some privacy. She swiped Detective Edwards's name and put the phone to her ear as she walked into the bedroom and shut the door.

"Kenzie here."

"Dr. Kirsch. I'm sorry to be calling you after hours. This could have waited until tomorrow, but I thought you would want to be kept in the loop."

"No, that's okay. I'd like to know where we are. I need to know that we are progressing somehow."

He chuckled. "I feel that," he agreed. "In some cases, the questions just keep mounting, and you start to think that nothing will ever be answered."

"Exactly. I feel very off-balance. I know it isn't my job to answer all of the questions surrounding Dr. Markov's death, but I feel like... she needs me to bring her some justice."

"I'm sure she would be pleased with the amount of effort you put into this case and how you have poured your heart into it. Even though the encrypted files stored in the locket suggest she was selling company secrets."

Kenzie sighed. "Yeah," she agreed. "But even someone who was involved in something illegal deserves some answers. The way things are right now... I just need those answers. Whatever happened, happened, but I need to know for my report and... because Markov's family and friends deserve some answers."

"I agree. So we were right that the threatening phone call you got today was from Birch Valley. It was traced back to their exchange."

"I figured as much. It's hard to believe that someone who works there, a scientist or a researcher, would be so stupid as to say that's where they were calling from. I wouldn't have known if he hadn't told me. He at least had the chance that you wouldn't be able to immediately trace it back to Birch Valley."

"Criminals can be stupid. That's how we catch them. And smart people can be driven by emotion to say and do stupid things. Even though they would know better if they allowed themselves time to think it through logically."

Kenzie was not immune to being driven by emotion herself, so she couldn't disagree. "I suppose so. I just would have thought that they would have better control."

"Or maybe they knew that we wouldn't be able to trace it any further than the main switchboard at Birch Valley, so they didn't care."

"That's as far as you could get? I would guess it was someone who had been working closely with Dr. Markov. Maybe he was even involved in the espionage himself, since he was insistent that I not look at Birch Valley and that nothing was going on there."

"Or maybe things are not as they appeared," Edwards teased.

"What do you mean?"

"Maybe Dr. Markov was <u>not</u> involved in industrial espionage."

"But the files..." Kenzie caught her breath. "You managed to decrypt them?"

"Not yet. We're still looking for the key to decipher them. But I made some further inquiries at the company today to try to track down our caller."

"And you found..." Kenzie wished that he would just come out and tell her. But at the same time, she was enjoying the buildup of suspense, just like if she were reading a thriller or watching a movie. That delicious sense of anticipation as Edwards skillfully teased her that he'd found the answers they sought.

"Maybe she wasn't a spy. Maybe she was a whistleblower."

"Oh!" Kenzie breathed out the breath she had been holding in a puff. "A whistleblower."

That one answer fell into place and, acting like a key, instantly transformed several of the other clues.

<u>There is nothing going on at Birch Valley.</u>

But there was. They all knew that there was. That much had been obvious from the first moment. Markov was killed in an accident following the fundraiser. Her voice had been silenced. She had been carrying information about the company on her person, a secret close to her heart that she would never reveal.

<u>The bruises around her throat.</u>

Someone had tried to get the information out of her. Had not only threatened her, but had physically assaulted her, trying to squeeze the information out of her. He'd had his hands around her throat, around the chain of the locket. It had dug into Markov's skin. The evidence had been right there under his fingertips, if he had only known how to access it.

But Markov had gone to the grave with her secrets. She had not told him where she had saved the files or turned the locket over.

He had literally held the answer in his hands and not known it.

And what had happened? Rather than killing her, he had let her go, or she had somehow escaped him? Maybe interrupted by someone else at the fundraiser? Dr. Markov had disappeared during the dessert, which was when she had to have acquired those bruises. They had been fresh. They had not yet developed in the pictures Kenzie had viewed of her at the event before she had gotten behind the wheel of her car and raced to her death. She had been flushed and the bruising around her neck had not yet been visible.

She had escaped or been released, but she had taken the beta-blocker, and it had impaired her ability to act. She had crashed on her way home before she'd had a chance to tell anyone what had happened.

CHAPTER 39

"She wasn't driving home," Kenzie said, startling herself and Edwards with the revelation.

"What?" He tried to follow her train of thought. "Markov wasn't?"

"No! She wasn't going home. She wasn't traveling toward Burlington. She was going in the other direction. Because she <u>wasn't</u> going home."

"And where do you think she was going? Was she supposed to meet with someone else?"

"She was on her way to the police station. She was killed just a couple of blocks away. That's why she was going the wrong way. Not because she got disoriented, but because she wanted to talk to the police. To report to them what she knew or what had just happened. She'd been assaulted. They were trying to get the information out of her. She was carrying the files with her. She could have turned them over to the police and revealed whatever was going on at Birch Valley that she had been gathering information on."

"Ahh." Edwards drew out the syllable, a purr of satisfaction. "Yes. That makes sense. That explains why she was going the direction she was."

"And she almost made it. But then..." Kenzie's eyes burned. She wasn't going to tear up. She wasn't going to get emotional about one of her patients. She couldn't allow herself to get so close to the situation. This job would destroy her if she let herself think of every person and what they had gone through before they had died. She needed to maintain professional distance. She swallowed and cleared her throat and didn't try to finish the sentence.

"But she was too impaired to make it," Edwards finished in a flat voice, his professionalism firmly in place. "Do you think she realized when she took the beta-blocker that she would react to it that way? That she would have such a strong reaction to the little bit of alcohol that she had consumed?"

Kenzie was forced to stop and take a step back to examine the beta-blocker from all angles.

"As far as we know, she didn't have a heart condition. So she did not take it that night because she was having palpitations or an irregular rhythm."

Kenzie thought suddenly about the smartwatch. Had it been monitoring Dr. Markov's heart rhythm? They had used a smartwatch heartbeat trace once before to unravel the mystery of a victim's death. Why hadn't Kenzie thought to look at it this time when she knew that Markov had taken a beta-blocker?

"She was taking it to help calm herself down," Edwards said. "To calm her anxiety enough to talk to the police and turn over the files."

It could be, but Kenzie couldn't make it fit the facts. The Mariya Markov she knew would not have taken an experimental drug to calm herself down. Especially knowing that she had already consumed a depressant and that the beta-blocker and alcohol could cause exactly the reaction they had.

"No. I don't think Markov took it. I think... she was given it." Kenzie felt the answer fit into place, like the piece of the puzzle that Edwards had already given her. "I think they probably gave it to her to get her to talk. Or to do what it did —impair her so badly that she couldn't report what had happened. That she would not be able to drive safely. Or so that what happened to Smythe would happen to her—that it would make her heart slow down so much that it would stop, and no one would know why."

"Do you have the test results back on Smythe?" Edwards asked.

"No, not yet. But… I'm pretty certain we'll find out he had the same beta-blocker in his blood. He didn't have a history of heart disease. He'd never had any angina or reported irregular rhythms to a doctor. And he'd had contact with Dr. Markov at the event. I have to believe he was targeted because of what he knew."

"Let me know when you get confirmation."

"I will." Kenzie sighed and reviewed it all in her mind, trying to see if she could figure out any more answers. "Who told you that Markov was a whistleblower? Who knew she was collecting information to expose Birch Valley?"

"Dana Pratt."

Mariya Markov's best friend at the company. Of course she was the one who had known. Or the one who had talked about it. Obviously, others had known that she was up to something. But they had been against her, had tried to get the information out of her or to kill her, and had succeeded only in the second.

"Does Dana know what Markov was trying to expose? Does she have information she can pass on to us?"

"I suspect that woman knows more than she lets on. Right now, she would like us to think that she didn't really know anything, but she had to. We'll need to drill down to get it, but at the moment, she is refusing to answer more than the most basic questions. That Markov wasn't a spy. She was trying to blow the whistle on unethical or illegal practices."

"What practices?"

Edwards blew out his breath. "That is one of the things that she won't talk about. I suspect she knows it will reflect badly on her that she knew what was happening inside the company and didn't report it herself. Even if you've signed a confidentiality agreement, you still have an obligation to report illegal actions."

"Do you think she would talk to me? Or to someone else connected to Markov? If it was someone who came across as sympathetic rather than judgmental?"

"It's possible, but you can't talk to her by yourself. I will need to be with you."

"And she still might not talk with you there."

"That's a distinct possibility." There was amusement in his voice.

"I thought that maybe if Alina talked to her... maybe she would talk if Alina appealed to her for the truth."

"Might be a good idea. We'll see how things progress tomorrow. For tonight, I'm done. We'll let Pratt stew overnight. She might have changed her mind by the morning."

"I hope so... I'd really like to know what's going on over there. Did they intentionally kill Markov? What was important enough to kill over?"

"You can bet that it is something pretty major. You know more about the projects and technology they are working on from your discussions with her colleagues than I do. What do you think it is?"

Kenzie shook her head slowly as she thought about it. "Gene editing, transplant technology, beta-blockers... I don't know. There is some pretty scary stuff that goes on in gray market transplants and illegal organ trade." She remembered some of the horrific practices she had discovered when she had investigated what happened with Amanda's second kidney transplant. The one that her parents had not even told Kenzie about. It made her sick to even think about it.

Would a technology like gene editing improve the transplant situation around the world? Or would it just make it more likely that the rich would get the organs they could pay for and the poor would be preyed upon for those they could provide?

Edwards grunted. “I’ve heard that most of that stuff about illegal transplants and kidnapping and such is just urban legend.”

“No. It’s not,” Kenzie told him flatly.

There was an awkward silence while Edwards considered this. Kenzie waited to see if he would argue the point. Sometimes people were prepared to take a very firm stand on “what they had heard” rather than listening to someone who had the facts.

“Well, if that is true,” Edwards said, “we could be looking at some pretty dangerous secrets.”

“When we were working on the Night Doctor case, there were rumors that he might be involved in illegal transplants. That there were people who had disappeared and never resurfaced."

"There are always open missing person cases. I haven't noticed an increase in frequency."

"Yeah, but you don't take a lot of missing person reports on street people. If they don't have a permanent address, you just assume they've moved on, unless you have proof that they are not voluntarily missing."

"How would anyone know whether some homeless person was a match for their recipient? Wouldn't it look suspicious if you went out and started randomly testing street people to see whether they were tissue matches?"

"If they have taken gene editing to the point where they can prevent rejection without a tissue match, then that doesn't matter anymore. They can use anyone's organs, as long as they are in reasonably good shape. And if they degrade, they can just go get another donor."

Edwards sighed heavily. “We’ll talk to Pratt again tomorrow. Maybe she’ll be ready to spill by that point.”

“I hope so. Let me know if you think she would be more likely to talk if I was there. Or her sister, of course. I’m sure Alina would be willing to help if it meant discovering exactly what Mariya was mixed up in.”

CHAPTER 40

They had put a rush on the toxicology tests for Mr. Smythe. If they were using the beta-blocker to kill people, that was something that they needed to know sooner rather than later. It wouldn't do not to find out about it for days or weeks. Not when there could be a killer out there. Markov's cause of death might be a car accident, but if she had been administered the beta-blocker in an attempt to put her into a potentially fatal situation, then it was still homicide.

Wednesday morning, they had the toxicology and mass spec results. Nothing had shown up in the standard tox panel. But the peaks on the mass spec results were identical to those that showed up on Mariya Markov's. He had been administered the same drug. And the blood test results suggested that it was significantly more concentrated. Smythe had not been given a microdose for safety screening or a single dose for therapeutic reasons. He had been given a massive dose of an unqualified drug that had a direct effect on the rhythm of the heart.

After advising Hal that she was going out, Kenzie departed for the home of the widow, Becca Smythe.

The Smythes lived in a hamlet north of Roxboro, but still within the jurisdiction of the Roxboro medical examiner's office, even though it was probably more than halfway to Burlington.

There were few parking spots left on the street, and when Kenzie walked up to the door, she could see that the living room was filled with visitors, there to comfort the family. It wasn't the best time for the medical examiner to show up asking questions.

Kenzie took a deep breath and knocked on the door. A woman came to the door. She smiled a greeting at first, but then frowned, studying Kenzie and trying to place her. She obviously was not a recognized and beloved family friend.

Kenzie wished she had a hat to take off in respect or a plate of cookies to hand over. She felt like an intruder standing there, wanting to ask Mrs. Smythe questions.

“I’m sorry, my name is Dr. Kirsch. I came over to talk to Mrs. Smythe.”

“Dr. Kirsch?” The woman looked at the couch, where a group of women sat, comforting each other.

“I’m with the medical examiner’s office,” Kenzie explained awkwardly. She had asked Mrs. Smythe whether she could come over, but she didn’t appear to be expected.

“Yes, yes, of course,” the woman in the middle said, dabbing her nose with a tissue and standing up. “I’m sorry, I forgot you were coming.”

Kenzie didn’t want to offer to come back another time. Not when it was apparent there was a killer out there. They wanted to get ahead of this, not to be picking up the victims when it was too late. She nodded and looked at the woman who had answered the door to see if she would be allowed in. The gatekeeper stepped back and allowed her to enter.

Becca Smythe was a sixty-something woman with hair either untouched by gray or dyed. Her face was mostly unwrinkled. She did have dark bags under her eyes that showed she had not slept much since finding her husband dead in the bed. She sniffled and motioned Kenzie toward the back hallway. “Let’s just go into the bedroom. That would be the best.”

Kenzie was relieved not to have to conduct her inquiry in front of all the friends and family assembled in the living room. She followed Mrs. Smythe to the bedroom, where the blinds were still closed and there were clothes on the floor and an unmade bed. Mrs. Smythe looked dully around and sat on the end of the bed. Kenzie wondered if it had all been left that way after Mr. Smythe had been discovered dead, and his widow had slept in another room—or not slept at all—after that.

Kenzie flicked on the overhead light and closed the door for privacy. She didn't sit down, as there were no chairs, and she didn't feel like casually sitting on Mr. Smythe's deathbed would be appropriate.

"I'm so sorry to invade your home and to bother you during such a difficult time, Mrs. Smythe."

"Becca. Becca is fine. Don't worry about it. There really isn't... a good time right now."

"I know. And I would wait, if this wasn't an urgent matter."

Becca's eyes seemed to ask how it could possibly be urgent when her husband was already dead. That was not going to change. They couldn't do anything to turn back time and save him.

"Mrs. Smythe... your husband didn't have any known health issues, is that right? You weren't aware of any problems, and he hadn't seen a doctor to discuss any heart problems."

"No. Cory had always been healthy. He'd barely missed a day of work in all the years that we were married."

"He wasn't on any medications?"

"No."

"And he hadn't been complaining about any issues that night... breathing, chest pain?"

"No. He just said he had indigestion. He wanted to lie down for a while and let things settle."

"Did he work at Birch Valley Biomed in Burlington?"

"He had been doing some contract work for them, yes." Mrs. Smythe lifted her eyes to look at Kenzie's face. "Do you think he got into something there? That he was contaminated or something? I always worried about what they might be testing over there and if something might get out. You hear about viruses and other sicknesses escaping from labs all the time. They aren't as safe as they would like you to think."

"I don't know yet how he was exposed. I wonder... how he felt in the week or two before he passed. Do you know if anything was bothering him?"

Mrs. Smythe frowned. "With his health, you mean?"

"Well, of course, if he had any unusual symptoms physically. But I was thinking about mentally. Whether he seemed like he was worried about anything. Maybe you thought something was going on at work that was bothering him? Maybe his moods were strange, or he couldn't sleep? Maybe he was irritated or away from home more than usual?" Kenzie shook her head. "Really, anything that was different from usual."

"He had been stressed lately. And since the fundraiser... I don't know. I asked him what was going on, but he wouldn't say anything. He just said not to worry. But how could I not? I felt like... the wheels were falling off the bus. He was snapping at me over things that should have been nothing."

She sniffled and wiped her nose.

"He was anxious, pacing at night. I was glad when he laid down because he hadn't been sleeping much. That's why I wasn't worried when he didn't get up after his nap. I thought he was just catching up after having such problems sleeping over the last week. It was bound to catch up to him sooner or later."

CHAPTER 41

Kenzie nodded slowly. “Did he talk to you about work at all? Did he tell you about anything that was going on there? Particularly anything that he was worried about?”

“No, he really didn’t talk about work. When he would do work for these medical companies, he was always under a confidentiality agreement, so I knew that he wouldn’t talk about it. I was used to that.”

“What exactly did he do?”

Becca wiped her nose with the frayed tissue in her hand. “He was a security guard. Evening security. It was nice for us, because we had time together during the day. The commute was a bear, of course, but living in these parts... You know you’re going to have to commute to work. We’re used to it.”

“Security. He attended the fundraiser, but he wasn’t in uniform...?” Kenzie realized that Mrs. Smythe might wonder how she knew that. “I saw some photos of the fundraiser after Dr. Markov’s death.”

“Oh, yes.” Looking troubled, Becca shook her head. “He was so upset about that. He said he should have done something, but how was he supposed to know something was wrong? That she was going to have an accident on the way home? I kept telling him that it wasn’t his fault, he couldn’t have done anything about it, but it didn’t seem to help.

He just kept saying that he had failed her.”

She rubbed her eyes and looked at Kenzie.

“You’re right, he wasn’t wearing a uniform. He didn’t usually wear a uniform for these medical places. They like the security staff to be more discreet. So for day-to-day stuff, they dress casually, like everyone else. He wore a lanyard and had to keep his equipment out of sight. At big events like the fundraiser, he often had to wear a tux. He didn’t have his own.” She sniffled. “We just rented one.”

"He talked with you about Dr. Markov's death?"

"Well... he was upset about it. He said that she was a nice lady and didn't deserve to die like that. I said it was just fate... there was nothing he could have done to prevent it. But he still blamed himself."

"Did he see Dr. Markov a lot? I don't know how this all works." Kenzie thought about the security staff that she saw on a regular basis. "He would know her name if he saw her regularly, but he wouldn't know much about what she did, would he?"

"No. Not a lot. But he knew she was a nice lady and that she was very smart. He would walk her out to her car when she worked late and make sure she got on her way safely. He would do that for most of the staff, but the men usually didn't want to be walked out. It's not a good look for men, I guess. Worrying about personal safety. It just isn't something they do."

"And did she talk to him about what she did? You said he signed a confidentiality agreement, so he must have seen information about products or research now and then. Or talked to the scientists about it."

"I don't know. A little, probably. Just passing time, you know how people are. They tell you when they have done something cool or are facing a particular challenge. Even if you know the other person won't understand all of the intricacies of what you are doing, you still want to talk about it, and sometimes it helps just to say it out loud. You get a sudden brainstorm about what to do about it. Just like when you're in the shower."

Becca gave a little laugh. She folded her arms and hugged herself tightly, trying to keep it together. "So... I don't know how any of this helps you, doctor. I can't see what any of this has to do with Cory's heart attack."

"I just needed a little bit of background to sort things out. Did he... do you know what your husband had for supper that day? Or for his last meal, which I guess was..."

"He had supper with me. He didn't when he was working, but it was his night off. Usually, lunchtime was our big meal, and then supper was something light. They say that's the best way to eat anyway, but I don't know if that's true when you combine it with night shift and aren't going to bed after supper. But it works—worked—for us."

"You both ate the same thing? What did you have?"

"Burgers. But not greasy, fast-food burgers. Homemade, with lean beef and oats, not fried in oil. They were delicious, and it was very healthy. I tried to take good care of him. I wanted... I wanted us to be together for a long time."

"And it was after that he got the indigestion. Did he have that a lot?"

"I know what you're thinking. You're thinking that Cory had heart disease, and we didn't even know it. They say that some people have heart attacks and don't even know they have had. But it wasn't like that. Sometimes, particular foods would give him digestive problems. But it wasn't heart. It wasn't angina."

Kenzie nodded. "Okay. I just thought I would check. Do you know what food triggered his digestive upset that night? Onions, maybe?" she guessed at what she figured was the most likely offender.

"No, it was probably that licorice."

"Oh?"

"He loved licorice. The real stuff, not the flavored candy that passes as licorice. I can't abide the stuff. It's bad enough that it tastes awful. Like eating tires, some of it is so tough. And then I get a belly ache. It's no wonder he felt sick afterward. I told him he shouldn't eat too much of the stuff. I saw an article on the internet, that licorice has a compound in it that can affect your blood pressure, especially if you eat large amounts of it. You should only have a little licorice at a time."

Becca covered her mouth suddenly. "Oh, no! It wasn't the licorice, was it? I could never forgive myself if it was the licorice that killed him!"

"No, no," Kenzie hurried to assure her. Though she wondered about the effect of the glycyrrhizin in the licorice combined with the beta-blocker. Had he taken the beta-blocker when he was at home? If he had been doing a test for Birch Valley, it would seem far more likely for him to take it at the office. It shouldn't have affected him more than twelve hours after taking his dose. "There was another compound in his blood that I am trying to track down. Did he ever participate in drug trials at the medical companies he worked at? Maybe for a little extra money on the side?"

"No. He didn't like to take anything, not even aspirin. I tried to get him to take baby aspirin. It's supposed to be good for your heart, taking a very low dose each day, but he said no. He didn't need to take anything."

"And you bought him the licorice?"

"Me? No. I couldn't even stand smelling it on his breath. He never did understand why I disliked it so much. He couldn't believe that I could still smell it on him an hour after he ate it." She shuddered. "No, he brought that home from work. Someone knew how much he loved the stuff, and they brought him a bag of that double-salted Dutch licorice. He had a few pieces after supper, and that is what triggered his tummy trouble. I told him to go lie down for a while. And he fell asleep, and... he never got up."

Becca turned and looked at the bed, still mussed, where her husband had lain. She shook her head and wiped the corners of her eyes.

"Are you married?" she asked Kenzie.

Kenzie swallowed. "No. I am living with my boyfriend. Or he is living with me. We are very happy together, but we are not married. Maybe someday."

"Don't put it off too long. Don't think it will last forever, even if you are happy together."

Kenzie nodded. "No, ma'am," she agreed. "I won't."

But she didn't know when she would be able to commit to that. She didn't want to promise Zachary something she couldn't give him. They were working hard on their relationship, but could she ever assure him it would be "forever"?

"Do you have any licorice left?" she asked.

"Do you like it? It wouldn't hurt my feelings to get it out of the house. I can't stand even the smell of the stuff, but I can't bring myself to throw it out. Cory loved it so much and was so pleased to get it."

"Who gave it to him?"

"I don't know..." Mrs. Smythe said vaguely. "There was a name on it."

She led Kenzie back out to the kitchen, where she looked through the cupboards for a moment before she found it. Someone had probably cleaned up for her and had put things away in unfamiliar places. She handed the little bag of double-salted Dutch licorice to Kenzie. It had a little ribbon and gift tag tied around it and taped down. Kenzie turned it to look at the gift tag.

To Cory, From Morgan

Thank you for all that you do

CHAPTER 42

Kenzie delivered the package of licorice to Detective Edwards and repeated Mrs. Smythe's story. She filled out a chain of evidence log showing its transfer to him.

"You'll need to have it tested to see if it contains any residue of the beta-blocker. I'm thinking that it was probably laced with the drug. Licorice has a very strong taste. A lot of people don't like it, especially this double-salted stuff. The flavor probably covered up any bitterness of the drug."

Edwards looked at the gift tag. "From Morgan."

"Morgan Tucker, I guess. I talked to him at Birch Valley. You probably did, too."

"Yes. Not the most helpful or friendliest guy. He seemed like a good suspect, but there was no way to tie him to Dr. Markov's death, which I'm still waiting for the medical examiner to classify as an accident or homicide," he said pointedly and raised his brows, waiting for her response.

“I think I’m going to have to say homicide,” Kenzie admitted. “I wasn’t sure I could until now, because it was a car accident. But if she and Smythe both died as a result of the administration of the same drug, and Smythe was deliberately poisoned, then we have to assume that she was too.”

“Good.” Edwards nodded briskly. “There is only so much I can do if it is classified as an accident. If it is homicide, that opens up my investigative channels further. Especially if we’ve got two bodies from one killer.”

“Are you going to question Morgan Tucker?”

Kenzie already knew the answer, of course. There was no question in her mind that he would question Tucker.

“Does he seem to you like the type to give out random gifts to the staff?” Edwards asked. “Especially blue-collar contract workers?”

"Uh... no. He didn't seem like the jolly old St. Nick of the office. He would have to have a reason..."

"No," Edwards agreed. "What I am thinking of doing is talking to Dr. Pratt again. With a little help. Of course, we'll put a man on Dr. Tucker to ensure he doesn't disappear when we show up at the office again. Hopefully, we'll be able to get some more out of Dr. Pratt."

"You want me to come along this time?"

"You or Miss Alina Markov. Or both of you."

"Great idea."

He smiled. "I thought so."

* * *

Dana was wearing a bright yellow shirt this time. Kenzie liked her choice of bright, bold colors. They stood out in the lab full of people who generally wore understated, business casual clothing under their lab jackets. Her outfit provided a cheerful splash of color. It perfectly suited Dana's bubbly attitude, even when dealing with the death of her friend and yet another visit from the police and the medical examiner's office.

She probably wasn't too happy about Detective Edwards visiting her at Birch Valley after she had refused to tell him any more when she had been at the police station the previous day. But she put on a brave face and didn't challenge them or get angry about them possibly outing her as being in league with the whistleblower.

Dana looked at Alina, and Kenzie wondered if she knew Alina for who she was or was wondering why they had brought yet another new person for her to talk to.

"You know me, and you have met with Dr. Kirsch previously," Edwards introduced them gravely as they sat at the boardroom table. "I don't know if you have met Alina Markov before."

"Oh," Dana knew her immediately. "You are Mariya's sister!"

"Yes," Alina nodded. "I was hoping you could tell us more about what Mariya was involved in here. It seems... that all was not as it appeared. I knew she was worried and stressed out about work lately. But I didn't know why. I thought it was just... normal job pressures."

Dana looked at Edwards, her brows coming down in a frown. "I really can't... talk about it. I wasn't involved. I just know that Mariya was worried. She had some concerns. She was... I guess she was trying to gather evidence that she could present to the authorities if it ever came to that. Gathering information that might have... been detrimental to the company or the management."

"But you claim that you don't know any of this information or what in particular was bothering Mariya," Edwards suggested.

"That's right. We didn't work on the same files. I wasn't involved in anything questionable. I just figured... they were eager to get to the next stage of trials. It was exciting technology. I never thought that... anyone would do anything to hurt Mariya. And I don't think they did. I just think something went wrong that night. She wasn't feeling well when she left the fundraiser. Maybe... she was coming down with something. Or she was exhausted after the event. It was stressful and she wasn't sleeping very well."

"No," Kenzie shook her head. "The toxicology testing on Dr. Markov shows that she had taken an unknown drug. It appears to be a beta-blocker." She studied Dana. "Do you know how beta-blockers work? How they might interact with the alcohol Mariya already had in her system?"

Alina covered her mouth and didn't make a sound. It was the first time that she had heard that her sister might have been poisoned, rather than just having an accident because she was stressed or overtired.

Dana frowned and ran her fingers through her hair. “A beta-blocker? How do you know that?”

“Because we had a chemist check the mass spectrometer profile to see what he could match it up to. And the closest composition matches were beta-blockers like Propranolol. I assume you know Birch Valley was working on a new beta-blocker?”

Dana shook her head. “I can’t tell you what they are or are not working on. It is all confidential. You would have to go up the food chain to someone higher than me. I’m not involved in all projects. The company segregates information so I only know what I am working on, not what everybody else is working on. There is so much industrial espionage, you know. They don’t want people to have access to more than their own projects. The supervisors and management would be able to tell you about projects that are outside of my sphere. I’m under a confidentiality agreement, so even if it is something I’m working on, I can’t tell you about it.”

"But you understand what the beta-blocker mixed with alcohol would do to Dr. Markov. You understand that she would be impaired. She was impaired. I've seen video of her before she left the fundraiser. She was having difficulty walking."

Kenzie was sorry they hadn't briefed Alina more completely about their discoveries before bringing her into this meeting. Alina's face was as white as a sheet. She kept her mouth covered and didn't say anything. Her eyes were wide and shiny with tears.

Dana put her hand over Alina's other hand on the table to comfort her. "No. I don't know anything about that."

"Did you go to the fundraiser?"

"I'm really not invited to those big to-dos. I'm not a big name doctor or researcher like Dr. Markov. I just do my little bit and, hopefully, get some more experience so that someday I can have the kind of reputation Dr. Markov does. Did."

"So you weren't at it? You didn't see her?"

"I..." Dana hesitated. "I was there for a while, but I didn't get much of a chance to talk to her, and I didn't see her go. I thought she was too tired or something had gone wrong with her car. I didn't think it was anything to do with... anything like that. Why would she have taken a beta-blocker? She would know that it could react with the alcohol."

"We don't think she took it willingly," Edwards advised in a low, gravelly voice.

Dana shook her head. "That doesn't make any sense."

"Maybe not. But if she was worried about something the company was doing wrong and felt that it needed to be addressed, she might become the target of the people involved in that activity."

"The target?" Dana looked at him, shaking her head. "That's... that's pretty dramatic, isn't it? Things like that don't happen in real life. You make it sound like some TV thriller. If she knew something…" Dana clasped her hands and wrung them nervously. "There are laws to protect whistleblowers, right? They couldn't do anything to her."

"Had you and Mariya talked about what she was doing? Was she planning to go to the medical board? The police? The Inspector General?"

"I don't know. She was just getting the information she would need to prove what was going on. It wasn't anything to do with me. I don't have access to highly classified materials. My security clearance isn't that high."

"Mariya might still have given you the information to backstop her," Kenzie suggested. "She could have made a copy for you, in case she was found out."

"No. Mariya never gave me anything. I don't know what I would have done. I wasn't involved. I just knew that she was worried."

"She was storing the information she had on her locket. Maybe she gave you one too."

"Her locket?" Dana shook her head. "What, like on microfilm or something? Inside the locket?"

"It was an electronic storage vault. For cherished memories. Or... proof of what was going on here."

"I didn't know. I thought... it was just a locket."

"She never gave you something to hold on to for her?" Edwards asked. "A USB drive? A different phone from the one that she used for work?"

"No." Dana shook her head. "She never gave me anything. I wouldn't have been able to get it out of here anyway. Everything is checked before we leave. Devices, X-ray, metal detector. I couldn't have taken any information out with me."

"Dr. Markov got it out."

"She didn't give me anything," Dana repeated flatly. Kenzie didn't see any deception. Dana had liked Mariya Markov. They had been friends. Markov might not have told her everything, but she had told her a little bit about her worries and her possible intention of blowing the whistle on unethical practices.

Kenzie looked at Alina. "Did she ever give you anything like that? A locket or some electronic device?"

"No." Alina shook her head definitely. "The only thing Mariya ever sent me were cat videos."

Edwards opened his mouth to ask a question, then froze, looking at Kenzie. Alina had talked about them sharing funny videos before. Kenzie hadn't thought anything about it. Everybody shared funny videos and memes. But there had been videos on the locket, too, and those files had held hidden data.

CHAPTER 43

"Mariya sent you videos."

"Yes." Alina shrugged. "We liked to share things with each other. We're sisters. It's how we kept in touch."

"Did she send you links or files?"

"Well… usually links, I guess. Sometimes videos Mariya had downloaded to watch later. On some platforms, it's hard to mark your favorite videos or to share them later, like for a special occasion. So you download them to your phone, and then you can send them later."

Kenzie had done it herself a few times. Especially if a friend didn't have an account for that particular service, which could make it harder to share items of interest.

"Is that significant?" Edwards asked Kenzie.

"It could be. Or it might be nothing. But we've been looking for an encryption key. A series of characters that will decrypt the files she had saved to the locket."

"And a video could relate to that?" Edwards considered. "Like maybe the title of the video?"

"It could be anywhere. The title of the video or a comment or caption. Or it could be like the files embedded in the photos and the videos on the locket. Steganography. There could be a decryption key buried in a video that Mariya had sent to her sister, and then deleted from her phone so no one else could find it."

Alina pulled her phone out of her pocket. "On here? You think there was a hidden message?"

Edwards had his notebook open and was flipping through it. "Dr. Markov put in a call to the Department of Health and Human Services the day she died. I haven't been able to find out who she talked to there, but it seems clear that if she was going to blow the whistle on something happening at Birch Valley, she was getting ready to do so. And somehow someone here knew it, and they took action."

Morgan Tucker?

Kenzie didn't know how Morgan or another unknown Mr. X had found out Dr. Markov was getting ready to reveal the information she had managed to compile, but somehow, he had. Maybe they had a phone call logger that had told him Mariya had reached out to the organization.

Alina looked at her phone.

"So... you think that the last video she sent... it might be important...?"

Kenzie hoped she hadn't deleted it.

"Did she send you something that day?" Edwards asked. "Maybe around noon?"

Alina nodded. Her face was pale and pinched. “What’s your number? I’ll send it to you.”

Edwards gave it to her slowly. Alina tapped the number into her phone, and in a moment, Edwards’s phone dinged, and he picked it up. Kenzie watched him tap the play triangle on a video, and she looked on as it played a short video sequence of a cat playing with a baby. It was cute, a video that Kenzie hadn’t seen before. But not something she would have guessed held the key to unlocking Dr. Markov’s encrypted files.

“We’ll give that to our tech guys. Hopefully... there is something in it they can use.”

Dana pressed her fingers to the bony ridges over her eyes, rubbing them tenderly. “This is all... so hard to believe. I don’t know what the company could be doing that upset Mariya so much. I mean... if they were rushing a drug to market... a lot of companies do that. Even going too quickly into human trials... I know she said that they were using it on humans when they weren't supposed to, but that kind of thing is usually kept pretty quiet. With some careful microdosing, you can usually find out if there are problems with product safety. It's rare for a drug that has gone through animal testing successfully to suddenly show really negative effects in humans..."

Kenzie found it hard to believe that all that Markov had been worried about was how quickly a new drug was being tested. That seemed like the kind of thing Markov had probably seen happen many times before and would not have been so shocked and concerned about.

"I guess we'll find out," Kenzie told her. "At least, I hope we will."

Dana swallowed and looked down. "I hope you will too."

Alina stood up. "And I need some air. Are we finished here?"

"We at least have a next step," Edwards said, also rising to his feet. "Thank you for coming and for sending me a copy of that video. I hope Dr. Kirsch is correct and it will contain the information we need to unlock the files your sister had preserved."

* * *

"Are you going to talk to Morgan Tucker today?" Kenzie asked as they stood at the door, watching Alina walk back to her car.

"The question is more likely will Morgan Tucker talk to me. I'll do my best."

"If he is the person who poisoned Mr. Smythe, then he is probably the person who poisoned Dr. Markov as well."

"We will need more evidence before we can connect him to the licorice. Evidence that the licorice was contaminated, for one thing. And then hopefully, Tucker's fingerprints on the packaging and gift tag, a handwriting match... all of those things that will help convict him. If it was him."

Kenzie nodded. Just having a suspicion that he had poisoned Smythe was not enough. They needed all of the evidence to back it up. This was how cases were developed. Not by rushing into things, but by building the case one piece at a time until they had a solid case.

"I don't suppose you want to sit in on the interview with Mr. Tucker," Edwards asked dryly.

"Uh, no. I think I'm okay to sit that one out. I don't need more threats."

"Okay. I'll get that video over to the forensic tech guys so they can get a head start on finding the decryption key and opening up those files, if you are right about it being embedded or incorporated into that video. It's a good hypothesis. I'll let you know as soon as we hear anything back."

Kenzie looked across the parking lot to where her red convertible awaited her. "I'll be back at the office, then."

There was a shout near her car. Surprised, Kenzie saw Hal sprinting across the parking lot in pursuit of a figure in a gray hoodie. She was sure that Hal was faster and would catch his quarry, but as they watched, the hooded figure managed to put on an extra burst of speed and was pulling away from Hal, putting space between them. Edwards looked as though he would join in the chase, but then he relaxed and didn't move from Kenzie's side. It was obvious that the runner was too far away. Hal was closer, and he was going to fail in capturing his prey. Edwards would have been a very distant third. He shook his head.

"What was that about?"

"I guess we're going to find out."

Hal slowed to a jog to return to the parking lot and then spotted Kenzie and Edwards standing there. He changed his path and walked toward them.

"What happened?" Kenzie asked.

"Guy was trying to mess with your car. I had just gone inside to use the facilities." He motioned to a convenience store. "And he moved in while I was occupied." He shook his head angrily. "I didn't see what he was doing, but he was reaching under the front. Let's go have a look; we'll see if he left us with a tracker or another present."

"Why would he mess with my car?" Kenzie asked angrily. Her car was her baby. It was off-limits. Emailing or phoning her with threats was one thing. Messing with her baby was a different league altogether.

Edwards looked amused at her reaction. He trailed them over to the little red car.

Hal was a big guy, and Kenzie would not have predicted that he would have the flexibility to get down to look under the car as he did, feeling around for anything the hooded figure might have planted on it. He stood up again, brushing off his hands.

"I think I interrupted him before he was able to do anything. Let me just get some equipment from my car."

Edwards and Kenzie stood by, waiting.

"I'm guessing someone around here does not appreciate the medical examiner's office being involved with this case," Edwards offered.

"Yeah, you think? Why didn't they mess with your car?"

"I'll have to check it to be sure he didn't. I don't think Hal was keeping an eye on it for me."

"What exactly are these guys doing that they are so afraid of us finding out? We would be a lot less focused on Birch Valley if they didn't keep drawing our attention to it. Why all of the threats? Why bug my car or track it or whatever they were going to do?"

She remembered Zachary discovering his car had been wired with an explosive device. How freaked out he had been when he thought someone might have tampered with it. And she remembered the package bomb that had gone off in their kitchen, the pictures of the scene before it had been cleaned up. Zachary had been lucky to sustain only minor injuries from a homemade bomb that should have been much more powerful.

“Do you think they were going to hook a bomb up to it? They threatened my life. They’ve killed two other people. Do you think they really want to... eliminate me?”

He pursed his lips. “I don’t know what good that would do. You’ve already done your part in uncovering these crimes, and eliminating you would not change anything.”

“But it feels... personal. They didn’t threaten Dr. Wiltshire, and he is the medical examiner. I am only the assistant medical examiner. Why wouldn’t they go after him first, or at least with equal fervor?”

"You were the one who came out here to talk to them. It's probably no more than that. And you have a really sweet car. People get jealous, you know."

The car was Kenzie's one indulgence. She lived in a modest home. She had only the dresses and jewelry needed when attending events for the Kirsch family foundation. She didn't go on exotic vacations, and held a job that had taken years of education, not just a titular role in the foundation, which her parents would happily have given her.

Edwards was right. People did get jealous. The hooded guy might have been doing nothing more than having an up-close look at a sweet ride. Maybe Hal was wrong, and he hadn't reached underneath.

Hal returned, pulling out a long extendable rod, with a mirror on the end of it. He slid the mirror under the car and walked around the front of the car with it, getting a better view of the underside to see if he could find a tracker or device that had been lodged there.

He stopped and held the mirror in position. “You should arrange for alternate transportation.”

“What?” Kenzie squawked.

“I don’t know what that is, but it isn’t a tracker.” Hal nodded to Edwards. “You want to get someone out to look at it? I can take the doctor back…” He raised his brows at her questioningly. “To the office or home?”

“I’m not off yet. I still have more to get done today.”

“Back to the office, then.”

Edwards got closer to Hal to look into the mirror at the device now affixed to Kenzie’s car, and he nodded. “I’ll call for assistance. We’d better set up a perimeter. Dr. Kirsch, I’m sorry, but we’ll be a few hours taking care of this. You’ll have to do without your ‘baby’ for a while.”

“You think it’s an explosive?” Kenzie demanded. “Do you mean to say that someone just stuck a bomb to my car?”

“I can’t tell you for sure what it is,” Hal said with a shrug. “It might just be intended to scare you. Maybe I was supposed to see him, just for the drama. Make you see that they are serious about you staying away from Birch Valley.”

“Well, I don’t think I will be coming back here again any time soon, so I guess they have succeeded.”

Hal nodded philosophically.

CHAPTER 44

Concentrating on her work after returning to the medical examiner's office was not easy. Kenzie had a difficult time keeping her mind off of her car and what was happening with it. Of course, the police would make sure that the device was safely removed and that her car was okay. They would look for the hoodie guy, though it was likely too late to find him. Once he got far enough away, he would strip off the hoodie and dump it in the trash somewhere, and no one would have any way to identify him. Kenzie knew how it worked.

She worked methodically through her inbox and to-do list to keep herself on track, but wondered how much of the work she would have to redo again later because she was too distracted.

Midafternoon, she got a call from one of the forensic tech guys, who reported that they had, in fact, been able to find the encryption key in Alina's cat video and it had worked to decrypt most of the files that Markov had saved on the locket.

"I will send you copies of what we have decrypted for your records. You can follow up with the detective in charge of the case, which is Detective..."

"Edwards," Kenzie supplied. "Thanks, I have his number."

After hanging up, she navigated immediately to her email inbox to look for the email, but it was a few minutes before it arrived. Sometimes, emails didn't appear instantly, especially if they had multiple large attachments.

Luckily, the mail server was configured to allow large email attachments, since Kenzie often received imaging files or large documents. She preferred to download them from the email instead of following a link to a cloud drive somewhere, undoubtedly dealing with passwords and two-factor authentication before finally being able to download the files.

The tech had zipped all of the attachments into a single compressed file. Kenzie unzipped it and saw that they had been arranged in a branching directory structure. The filenames were still the same as they had been when they were on the locket, only now the names made sense and matched up with the contents of the files. Pictures of various Birch Valley employees were labeled with the correct name. Documents were labeled by the date and either who had written them or who they had been addressed to.

Kenzie wasn't sure what all the photos were intended to document, but hopefully, she would after reading the documents.

She selected a memorandum regarding case studies and opened it up. It was a large document that summarized half a dozen case studies. Kenzie skimmed through the first case, eager to know what it was about.

It was the unusual case of a middle-aged man with a Wilms tumor. Wilms was a kidney tumor that was remarkable in how quickly it grew. In those who were known to be at risk, if scans for the tumor were taken at intervals of six weeks, they could generally find the cancer and treat the patient in time to save them. But for those who let their appointments slip to longer intervals of eight to twelve weeks, they were sometimes not able to successfully treat it. It was tragic to lose a child because the parents had not taken the strict six-week scan interval seriously or had believed a doctor who told them that feeling their child's belly for tumors was good enough.

And it was always children. The risk of Wilms tumor dropped away at eight years old, and it was almost unheard of for an adult to get it. But here was a unique case of a man who had developed the very rare, very fast-growing cancer and it had not been discovered until it was too late for successful treatment.

Kenzie went on to the next case. A patient who had developed diabetes and hyperlipidemia after a surgical procedure. Developing both at the same time seemed bizarrely coincidental, especially immediately after surgery. Had they damaged the liver? Had the patient had an adverse reaction to a medication?

He had quickly developed fatty liver and they had been unsuccessful in getting his disease under control, resulting in the patient's death.

Two apparently unrelated cases. Kenzie wasn't sure why they had been presented side by side. She went on to the next.

In the third case study, the patient had experienced a significant mental decline and seizures. The cause was unclear, but both changes had appeared at the same time. It was not possible to tell whether the seizures had caused the decline, as was sometimes the case, or whether both had some unknown cause. He was only in his forties, very young for dementia.

They had ruled out Huntington's, a stroke, or a tumor. They had done cognitive tests, but he had declined so quickly that his doctors had barely had time to slap a label of atypical Alzheimer's on it before he died. Kenzie shook her head. That was very quick. She knew that early-onset Alzheimer's could progress very quickly, but it did not seem likely that the patient could have died that quickly from Alzheimer's. She thought about the novel virus she had seen a couple of years before that had caused the rapid onset of dementia, with death in days rather than months or years. But that particular virus had been isolated and destroyed before it could spread far. It could not be the same thing.

She closed her eyes to rest them and thought through the three seemingly unrelated cases. What could they all have in common? They had been presented together, so they must have been caused by the same thing. A drug side effect did not seem likely. A drug didn't trigger Wilms tumor. There were several known genetic mutations that predisposed children to it, but she knew of nothing that would cause it in an adult.

While many factors could cause diabetes, its sudden onset alongside hyperlipidemia was something she hadn't encountered before. Could something similar have caused the cognitive decline noted in the third case? Some kind of metabolic disorder could cause dementia, and if the cause was not identified pretty quickly, could lead to rapid decline and death.

She read through the remaining cases. Another cancer, this time in the liver. A case of late-onset schizophrenia. And another surprise case of diabetes.

Kenzie read through the introduction and conclusion, trying to determine what the vaguely worded procedure was. The writer of the memorandum had intended to compartmentalize the information on the side effects of the treatment they were testing. The treatment was only referred to by a project number, so someone reading the memorandum, as Kenzie was, had no way of knowing what the project was without insider information. It was precisely the situation they had intended to protect themselves from.

It was clear that it was a surgical procedure. Several of the case studies referred to a lack of post-surgical complications, though the metabolic problems were thought to be caused by the surgical procedures, even though the doctors couldn't find a reason for such a reaction.

Surgery, then. Surgery resulting in a wide variety of unusual side effects, most of them leading to death.

And the only kind of surgery that Kenzie had heard spoken of in relation to Birch Valley since Dr. Markov's death was transplant surgery.

Could all of those side effects logically be attributed to transplant surgery?

Kenzie wasn't sure how. Metabolic problems could have resulted from a liver transplant. Could the Wilms tumor be somehow caused by a kidney transplant? She had never heard of cancer being triggered by a transplant. Transplanted organs were always examined carefully before transplant to make sure they were free of tumors or other issues. At least, <u>properly authorized transplanted organs</u> within the USA were.

There was no telling what the protocol was outside of the USA, where testing was often conducted. In secret, black market or gray market transplants, who knew how well the organs being transplanted were actually vetted? Amanda had contracted malaria from her second kidney transplant. From what Kenzie had learned of the conditions on the island where Amanda's transplant had taken place and in various third-world countries around the world, the transplants were often performed in unsanitary conditions with little screening done of the transplanted organs.

A child's kidney would not normally be transplanted into an adult, but if it had been, and a Wilms tumor had begun to form, that would be one way for an adult to contract the rapidly developing cancer. And no one would think to screen an adult for Wilms until it was too late.

But the other cases... dementia, seizures, and schizophrenia, were puzzling. They would not have received a transplant of brain matter. So, how could an organ transplant have affected the brain?

CHAPTER 45

It was a few hours before Edwards returned to the building and advised Kenzie that her car was fine and would be in her parking space as usual when she was ready to go home. Hal, who had been hanging out at the office and wandering the halls to keep an eye out for anything suspicious, drew closer to listen in on the conversation.

"Was it... an explosive?" Kenzie asked tentatively. She wasn't sure she wanted to know. She didn't want to hear that she had been in any danger. But she also didn't want to think that they had all overreacted over what had actually been a tracking device.

Edwards frowned and hesitated before answering. "Well, that's a more complicated question than you might think," he said slowly.

"It doesn't seem that complicated to me," Kenzie shook her head. "Either it was explosive, or it wasn't."

"It did integrate some explosives in its design, but only a small amount. Its primary function was not to explode and injure or kill you."

Kenzie tried to unpack this. "Okay... what were the explosives for, then, and why was it on my car?"

"From what the tech team has told me, it is a small computer. Its purpose was... to control the electronic interfaces of your car."

"What? Why would anyone try to do that?" But she knew even as she asked it. Why would anyone want to mess with her car? Because they'd wanted her to have an accident. Just like Markov. They couldn't get to her with their beta-blocker, so they'd tried to interfere with her car instead.

"Luckily, because your car is... a <u>classic</u>, it doesn't have all the computer-controlled stuff of most cars on the road today."

"In other words, it's a good thing I have an old car. Or they could have messed with my brake or accelerator or something."

"That's the general idea."

"Then why did it have explosives in it?" Kenzie tried to picture the device and what they had planned to do with it. Blow her brake line apart when she reached a certain speed? Cause some kind of minor malfunction that would result in her crashing the car?

"The explosives were to prevent it being removed from your car intact. A way to try to keep us from being able to examine the device properly."

"It would self-destruct."

"Essentially, yes."

Kenzie shook her head. She looked at Hal. "Have you ever heard of something like that?"

"Heard of it, yes. Seen it with my own eyes... no, this is the first."

"You've heard of something like this before?"

"Like the detective says, it is more effective on a computerized car. The higher the tech, the better. There is only so much it can do on a car without all the electronic modules. It was probably more of a warning than a real threat."

"So you were meant to see the guy planting it."

"Possibly," he agreed with a curt nod.

"No wonder he was so fast."

Hal chuckled. "It makes me feel a bit better if he was picked for his speed. He left me in the dust, and that doesn't usually happen to me."

"So... I guess the bomb squad can't actually examine the thing like they do on TV, finding the bomb maker's signature style and then tracking him down. Or his apprentice, since on TV, it seems like the original bomb maker is always in prison, and their skills have been passed on to some younger acolyte."

"Our bomb squad is pretty smart," Detective Edwards contributed. "An electromagnetic pulse was used to disable the electronics and prevent the device from being able to trigger an explosion. And then, they used a hardening foam to make sure that a motion trigger couldn't move when they removed it from the car. And presto! They could look at it and remove the explosives to completely neutralize it."

"Well, good. So they can figure out who made it?"

"Maybe. We'll leave that part of the investigation to them and see what they come back with. The good news is that your baby is safe and sound."

Kenzie smiled in appreciation. "And this EMP... it didn't wreck anything in my car?"

"Well... you've got an aftermarket stereo system that will need to be replaced. There shouldn't be anything else to worry about. One of the boys drove it back here, so you know it's in drivable condition."

"One of the boys?" Kenzie repeated.

"They were playing 'rock, paper, scissors' to see who would get to drive it."

Kenzie smiled. At least they respected the car. She took a deep breath and blew it out. "Well, thank you for looking after all of that. I'm glad that it didn't put anyone in real danger. And that they got it off without any damage. Or only to the satellite radio."

"Glad to be of service. We don't usually get to see anything quite so exciting. It wasn't exactly the Hollywood 'which wire do we cut?' while the timer counts down, but it was still very interesting to see the equipment and how they neutralized it."

Kenzie was glad there hadn't been a countdown timer. Those things always freaked her out on TV.

"And I understand you've been studying the decrypted files. You were right about the sister's video containing the key. Great call."

Kenzie nodded. "Well... I'm still piecing things together, but let me tell you what I've sorted out so far."

CHAPTER 46

Kenzie was still home in pretty good time, despite her busy day. She drove extra carefully, operating each control in the car with silky-smooth precision. There were no tell-tale clicks, no strange smells, no odd resistance. She had to move her seat back in place after the longer-legged bomb tech had driven it, but aside from that and adjusting the mirrors, everything seemed to be operating properly.

She pulled into the garage and shut off the engine, then sat in the garage breathing and listening to the engine tick as it cooled for a few minutes before getting out and entering the house.

It wasn't until she walked into the kitchen to the smell of freshly baked pizza that she thought about how she would tell Zachary about the day's events and the fact that she had not kept him up to date.

Had Hal told him? Kept him updated without telling Kenzie what he was doing? Kenzie didn't think so. Zachary would have called her to make sure that she was okay, even after assurances from Hal.

Hal had come in the front door while Kenzie had been sitting in the garage gathering her thoughts. He and Zachary both turned toward Kenzie as she came in the garage door. Zachary's expression was almost comically confused and concerned. He looked at her wide-eyed.

"*Everything turned out just fine*?" he said to Kenzie, obviously repeating what Hal had just said to him.

"Uh... yeah," Kenzie agreed, her smile feeling unnaturally rigid. "Everything is good."

"What, exactly, is good? What happened?"

Kenzie grimaced. She shifted uncomfortably. At the end of the day, she just wanted to relax and eat the delicious-smelling pizza, not to have to explain to Zachary what she had been through that day. But she couldn't very well tell him that nothing had happened or that she didn't want to talk about it right now.

According to the rules they had laid down in couple's therapy, she was allowed to say that she didn't want to discuss something yet when it was too traumatic for her to process. But that wasn't the case. She had not been deeply traumatized by the experience. Both Edwards and Hal had been there to help her get through the experience, and it had turned out to be more of a scare tactic than anything else.

She didn't want to talk about it because she didn't want Zachary to freak out and didn't want to have to explain it to him, especially in front of Hal. She didn't need a witness to how she had withheld information she should have passed on to Zachary immediately. It should have been her first instinct. What kind of partner was she that she didn't even think about telling him what was going on when she might have been targeted by an angry bomber?

"We should probably sit down," Kenzie suggested. "And that pizza smells wonderful. Thank you for ordering it."

Zachary just looked at her and didn't move to sit down. Hal looked from one to the other, brows raised with interest. He could have at least excused himself to disappear into another room for a few minutes. Go to the guest room or freshen up in the bathroom. Just to give her a few minutes to sort this out with Zachary without an audience. But Hal didn't move, and Kenzie couldn't very well tell him to leave. Zachary had ordered pizza so Kenzie wouldn't have to cook for company, and Kenzie had just said to sit down.

Kenzie pulled a big slice of pizza onto a plate. "Help yourself," she invited.

Hal stepped forward and took a few slices. He looked at them. "You mind if I check the news?" he suggested.

"Uh, yeah. Sure. Why don't you do that?" Kenzie agreed. Though she looked at the clock to check the time. She didn't want him to turn on the local news and have the police investigation into a possible bombing be the current story. But it looked like the local news would be finished, and they would be on to national news by now.

Hal removed himself and turned on the TV. Politics. Nothing Kenzie had to worry about.

"So, what happened?" Zachary prompted, his voice flat and his jaw clenched. He didn't take a piece of pizza.

Everything had turned out okay. But that wasn't what Zachary was going to hear. He was going to hear about an attempted bombing of his partner's car, and it would bring back all of the stuff he had gone through when the package bomb exploded, and maybe the fire in his childhood, and the whole evening would be shot to heck. Possibly with Kenzie sleeping alone because Zachary was too upset to be with her. Or else buried under his own blankets, shut down and uncommunicative.

They would have plenty to talk about with Dr. B in couple's therapy on Thursday. A good thing it was their week for couple's rather than individual therapy.

"Can you sit down?" she requested.

Zachary didn't. He folded his arms and waited.

"Look, I should have called you. But I was so caught up in what was happening that I didn't even think of it. Think about when you were dealing with that hostage-taking. You didn't call me. You even shut off your location tracking, so I wouldn't know where you were. You could have called me to tell me what was happening so I wouldn't be so worried about you and blindsided by it. But you were in the moment. You were dealing with the police and that situation and couldn't be distracted by other things. And today... that was me. I was dealing with other things, and the police were dealing with this situation. I was safe, and I just kept my head down and kept working so that we can solve this case before anyone else gets hurt."

"So tell me."

Kenzie rubbed her forehead. She didn't touch the pizza on her plate.

"Okay. Hal was keeping an eye on things while I was at Birch Valley with Detective Edwards. I had two people looking out for me. Hal caught someone trying to tamper with my car. Well, he didn't <u>catch</u> them because they were too fast and got away, but Hal had seen that they were up to something. So he checked my car out very carefully, just like you would have, and he found that they had attached something to the bottom, under the engine."

Zachary's brow knotted. He nodded, encouraging her to go on.

“Well, that’s really the whole story,” Kenzie said with a shrug. “Hal took me back to the office to keep working while Detective Edwards had the police deal with the device.”

“What was it? A tracker?”

“No. It was kind of funny... turns out it was pretty harmless. It wouldn’t have been able to do much of anything to my car other than change the station on the radio.”

CHAPTER 47

"What? What does that mean?"

This was not going the way Kenzie would have wanted. She wished Zachary were the kind of guy who could just shrug it off and not have to know all the details. Kenzie was safe. That was what mattered, right?

"It was a little... computer. Designed to take over the onboard electronic systems in a car. But my car doesn't have all those fancy electronics, because it is too old."

"To control the electronics in a car... you mean it was designed to do things like run you off the road or make your brakes fail?"

"I would assume so."

"And you want me to think this wasn't a big deal."

"Well, it wasn't. Because the only thing in that car with a computer chip is the stereo system. It was either a scare tactic or a really stupid criminal who didn't know how his own devices work."

"If you had been driving my car, you would have been in serious trouble."

"Only I wouldn't have been. Because Hal was watching the car and saw the guy tampering with it. And he found the device right away. I never drove the car, never turned it on while the device was attached. The bomb squad fixed everything up and drove it to the station for me afterward. It was no more than a minor inconvenience for me while they took care of it."

"Not if Hal hadn't been with you," Zachary's voice was loud. Kenzie looked toward the living room, not wanting Hal to hear their raised voices.

"But Hal was with me. So you should be happy. You're the one who thought that I needed some extra security for a while, and you were right. It all turned out okay, because you recognized the need and took care of it."

Zachary looked frustrated. He shook his head. "And you are still not taking this seriously."

"I am. What else do you expect me to do about it?"

He slapped his hand down on the counter. "I expect you to tell me about it."

"I admit I should have called you right away. That was an oversight on my part. I should have kept you in the loop so you knew what was going on at the time. But on the other hand, I'm glad that I didn't, because you would have been here alone, panicking about it."

Although she could have gone home. Hal had even offered to take her home rather than to the office. She could have been there with him while she told him and he would know she was safe and not worry about her safety.

Kenzie sighed.

"I'm sorry. I should have thought it through better. Sometimes, when I am in the middle of a crisis situation... I don't do my best thinking. Not about things like relationships. I am just working on getting to the next step."

He gave a curt nod.

"I really am sorry that you feel left out of the loop. That you <u>were</u> left out of the loop."

Zachary was actually taking it pretty well. She had been worried about a lot more emotion. A temper tantrum or meltdown.

"The bomb squad?" Zachary said.

Kenzie looked at him questioningly. "What?"

"You said that the bomb squad took care of the device."

"Uh... yes."

"Why would the bomb squad be there?"

"To make sure that it wasn't dangerous."

"Was it a bomb?"

"No, it was a computer controlling device." Kenzie couldn't lie to him about it. "With a small amount of explosives to make it difficult to remove without damaging the components."

Zachary stared at her, all of the color draining from his face.

"Sit down," Kenzie urged. "Before you pass out."

"If it had an explosive charge, it was a bomb."

"Zachary, please." Kenzie reached across the table toward him. "Please sit down with me."

He continued to stand there looking at her; then he finally moved, sat down in his chair, and took her hand. Kenzie squeezed it.

"I know that scares you," Kenzie told him. "It was kind of scary for me at first too. But it wasn't going to blow me up. That wasn't what it was intended to do. It was just someone trying to scare me."

"Who?" he demanded.

"Uh... well, I guess it was someone at Birch Valley. Someone who didn't like me asking questions about Dr. Markov's death. That's my job. I wasn't doing anything I wasn't supposed to. And I was there with Detective Edwards, not by myself. He invited me along to help with the investigation. I wasn't talking to anyone dangerous. Just a friend of Dr. Markov's who we knew might have some important information."

"A device like that?" Hal spoke to them from the doorway. He had obviously still been able to hear their conversation, even with the TV on. "That's Russian mob."

Kenzie's stomach knotted. She looked at Hal and then at Zachary. "No. This wasn't Russian mob. It was something to do with Birch Valley Biomed."

"Then Birch Valley Biomed is in bed with the mob."

"No." Kenzie didn't have a coherent argument against the possibility. But she was sure that they could not be connected.

"I *told* you from the start," Zachary insisted. "I told you that it was all connected. I told you Russian organized crime was mixed up in this. You've fought me the whole way, but I *knew* it."

And maybe that was why Hal had said it. Why not agree with his client's theory? It couldn't do him any harm to agree with Zachary's theory, even if it was paranoia.

"This is another threat. Another attempt by the Russians to get to your dad."

“My dad?” Kenzie repeated. “How does this have anything to do with my dad?”

“If they never intended to kill you and they knew that the device wouldn’t work on your car, then why attach it? Because they wanted to scare you. Because they know that the police will trace it back to the Russians, and then you will know that they are still watching you. Your dad will find out they are still threatening you and do what they want. You can’t ignore the connection.”

“I’m not ignoring it... I just think you’re making more of it than there is. So we run into possible Russian involvement again. They are operating here. We already know that. So, any time we get involved in a case that might have organized crime connections, we can expect the Russians to be involved somehow. It’s just logical.”

“Have they been trying to get ahold of Walter again? Has he had any contact?”

"He said… that he knows they are still watching him or trying to get in contact with him. But he hasn't talked to them. He's not going to do anything that will make them realize he isn't disabled like he is supposed to be. He's just going to keep under the radar until they give up."

"And what about the threats against you? If they are escalating…"

"They aren't…"

Kenzie had been about to retort that they were not escalating. Then her eyes went to Hal. He knew about the phone call. The phone call was an escalation after the email. If they were both the same person. But the email and phone threat had been about Birch Valley, not about her father refusing to cooperate with the Russian mob. Kenzie rubbed her head, trying to get it all straight in her mind.

Zachary's hand, still touching hers, withdrew. His expression softened. "You need to eat," he said, motioning to the untouched pizza on her plate. "You've had a long, stressful day, and you need to get some food in you."

"I really do," Kenzie agreed. Her stomach was twisting with stress and anxiety, but she was hungry too. The last thing she wanted to do was wolf down the food because she was so hungry and it smelled so good, and then to be sick for the rest of the night because of her anxiety and because she had eaten it too quickly. She picked up the slice and nibbled the point. Just a little at a time. If she ate slowly, she would know if it bothered her stomach, and she would stop. If she introduced the food slowly, then her stomach should adapt. And the anxiety would be partly assuaged by a boost in her blood sugar. If her anxiety were still too high, she could take one of the anxiety pills that Dr. B had prescribed for her to deal with the anxiety following her abduction.

She still didn't like to take them, didn't like to admit that she had a problem, especially in front of Zachary. Which was the silliest thing, because with his crippling anxiety, he was the one person who could understand that it wasn't something she could control, it wasn't something that she had chosen, it wasn't because she was weak. It was just because of the trauma she had been through at the hands of the Russians. Of course, she would remember it and be triggered when someone suggested that the Russians were still there, watching her, pressuring her father, and making threats.

But there it was. Kenzie did feel like taking the anxiety meds was a show of weakness, a moral failing. She felt like she had given in.

"Eat more," Zachary advised, watching her.

"I will. I just don't want to eat too fast."

Zachary motioned Hal from the doorway to the kitchen table, and after a glance at Kenzie, Hal moved forward and sat down. Zachary finally conceded that he needed to eat too, and took a slice of pizza for himself, though he didn't start eating; he just left it cooling on his plate.

CHAPTER 48

“Tell me what’s been going on,” he told Kenzie. He looked from her to Hal and back again. “I thought everything was fine since the email and since we had Hal sign on.”

“It *is* fine,” Kenzie said. “No one has been hurt.”

Zachary scowled. “*No one has been hurt* is not the same as *nothing has happened*. I thought everything was quiet, other than that reporter showing up in your building. I thought that since then, we had everything locked down.”

Kenzie didn’t look at Hal, not wanting to give away how much they had not told Zachary. She picked at the toppings of her pizza before taking another bite. Zachary watched her, not saying anything, trying to draw her out to fill the silence. A PI interview technique. He knew how best to get people talking, and he knew more about how to get her to talk than Kenzie liked to admit. They were supposed to tell each other things.

"There have been some other things going on," Kenzie said in a calm, even tone. "Things that have to do with this case. I'm sure they will settle down again when I've finished my report and am no longer closely involved with the investigation."

"What else?"

"You already know about the reporter showing up in the parking garage. And that she issued her report that night."

"With a lot of information that should not have been available to the public. She has a deep source somewhere."

"Somewhere," Kenzie agreed, "but we don't know for sure where. Someone in the police department, as far as I can tell."

"Okay. And what happened after that?" Zachary shook his head. "It feels like it was a week ago instead of just a couple of days ago."

"I know," Kenzie agreed. She drew a deep breath. "So because of her report, there were… people at the police department parking garage entrance the next day." Kenzie didn't know whether to call them supporters or protesters. Probably a mix of both.

"People?" Zachary pressed.

"People with placards, or just shouting and demanding attention. They want Markov's death investigation to be resolved, or they want someone arrested. Or Birch Valley's work stopped. Just a bunch of people making a ruckus and making it hard to get inside."

"Weren't the security guards there?"

"Yes, and they helped out. But they can't do anything until the people cross the line, so they waited until someone banged into the car before they could push them all back farther…"

Zachary nodded slowly, a deliberately measured response. Showing her that he could take the news calmly. That she could tell him about these things without his blowing his top or having a meltdown. And sometimes she could. She couldn't predict when he would be calm and when it would push him over the edge.

"Okay. Sounds like that was handled. And it was probably just civilians, not anyone actually involved with the Russians."

"Right. It was just annoying. But it was a security issue, and you wanted to know about security issues."

Zachary nodded in agreement. Perfectly reasonable.

"Then later that morning... I did get a threatening phone call."

His face tightened. For a moment, he scowled, but then it was gone, and his facial expressions were carefully monitored and controlled.

"What kind of a threatening call? Did you know the voice? Did the caller have an accent?"

“No. No accent. And the caller was from Birch Valley, not the Russian mob.”

“How do you know that?”

“Because he told me there was nothing going on at Birch Valley.” Kenzie grinned at Zachary. “So you know there is, of course. Like when the kid you’re babysitting tells you he didn’t do anything.”

Zachary chuckled. “He actually told you there was nothing going on at Birch Valley?”

“Yeah, he did. So naturally, his number traced back to Birch Valley. Detective Edwards was back there today to interview the main suspect.”

“And so were you,” Zachary said darkly.

“No. I was there to talk to Dr. Markov’s friend and her sister. Detective Edwards talked to anyone else by himself. After I left.”

"But after being threatened and told there was nothing going on at Birch Valley, you went over there."

"Well, yes." Kenzie couldn't very well deny it.

"Do you think it was the same person who sent the email?"

"I think so. The forensic guys are comparing the language to see what they think."

"You didn't recognize the person's voice?"

"No, but there wasn't really anything distinctive about any of the people I talked to at the company. I don't have a clear recollection of anything about the voice or speech patterns of any of them."

"So, is that everything?"

"Uh..." Kenzie considered what else had happened during the last couple of days. She didn't want to be accused of holding anything back. "No other threats. The next development was the postmortem we did yesterday. It wasn't anything special, not at first. We thought it was just a man who had died in his sleep. It does happen sometimes, you know?"

"So I've heard."

"And because he wasn't under the care of a physician at the time, it comes through the medical examiner's office for review."

Zachary nodded. "And I'm guessing he didn't just die in his sleep. What happened?"

"Well... as it turns out, he was poisoned. He was a contract security guard at Birch Valley. One of the last people to see Dr. Markov alive. He helped her to her car before she died."

Zachary's eyes became unfocused, and Kenzie knew he was thinking through the various possibilities. Envisioning what might have happened and how the guard might be involved.

"How did they poison him?"

"Someone left him a package of double-salted Dutch licorice as a thank-you for all he does at the company."

Zachary made a face. "Double-salted Dutch licorice? That sounds terrible. I like licorice candy, but not the black licorice, and not the real licorice."

"I know. I'm not big on it either. I have no idea if I would like the stuff Smythe was eating. But I guess someone at the company knows that he likes it. And the best thing about it is that its strong taste will cover up any... contaminants."

"Like poison. What was he given?"

"A beta-blocker. The same one Dr. Markov was given."

"Only he didn't have a car accident. He died in his sleep. Is it strong enough to do that?"

Kenzie nodded. "It can stop your heart."

"And that's the end of the line for the guard. I don't suppose you know what they wanted to keep quiet."

"I guess he must have known something about what happened to Dr. Markov that night. Who she was talking to before she left. She disappeared during dessert, and when she showed back up on video... it was obvious she'd been given something."

"And he knew who it was."

"I would guess so. If he knew something, that would be my first guess."

"But why would the guard take a treat from that same person? I don't think I would have taken it. Or I would have taken it so he didn't know I didn't trust him, and then I wouldn't eat it. But obviously, the guard went ahead and ate it."

"If it was in the licorice. That is our theory, but it hasn't been proven yet."

"Doesn't make sense."

"No," Kenzie paused, thinking about it. "It doesn't."

CHAPTER 49

Kenzie ate a couple more bites of the pizza. Her stomach was starting to unclench now that she had told Zachary the most critical points. He was still holding it together, and so was she. Hal remained quiet, listening to them as he ate his pizza.

“Were you able to get any more information from the encrypted files you found?” Zachary asked, finally taking his first bite of the pizza.

Hal helped himself to a couple more pieces.

“Actually, we found the encryption key today!” Kenzie told Zachary, knowing this was something he would find just as fascinating as she did. “She had sent her sister a cat video with the encryption key embedded in it like the other steganography files we found. It unlocked most of the files, but not all of them. So, I don’t know if there is another encryption key out there somewhere. Maybe another friend with another cat video? Or something else?"

"In a cat video." Zachary chuckled. "I love it. What a great idea. Who figured it out?"

Kenzie pretended to be modest about it, turning her face away and shrugging with a smile.

"You did? Good work, Dr. Kirsch! They're going to want you in cryptography now."

"No way, I'm not leaving the morgue. But it has been kind of fun to figure out how Dr. Markov hid this information. It was all quite... elaborate."

"No kidding. And what was in the files? I hope it wasn't just sudoku puzzles."

"No! I haven't read everything yet, but she blows the whistle on what they were doing at Birch Valley." Kenzie shook her head. "It's going to take a while to go through everything and figure out all of what was going on. She had to be selective about what files she copied. She only had so much space on the locket, especially when she was hiding large documents in long videos or splitting them across multiple image files. The locket wasn't designed to hold that much media. And with all of the encoding and encrypting she was doing, that would have also taken time and effort. All while trying to be covert..."

Zachary nodded. "Somehow, they found out anyway. She probably left a trail on the server. They might have put a key logger on her computer. Or just have done an audit of activity and found out she was copying stuff she shouldn't have been or documents she shouldn't even have access to."

"Is that what you're doing for Green Mountain?"

Zachary shrugged. "There are a lot of anti-spy tools available, if you know to look for them. Most companies don't, and they can give spies access to valuable information."

It occurred to Kenzie that the medical examiner's office and police department should probably invest in some anti-spy technology too. They knew they had at least one leak, possibly more. It might be someone who had legitimate access to files and information, but it might just as easily be someone who had access when they weren't supposed to.

"So, what have you had a chance to figure out so far?" Zachary asked.

Kenzie considered her answer carefully. "Well... I have been reading some case studies involving organ transplants."

Zachary nodded. "That's something you've been interested in for a long time. Which is natural, given that you gave Amanda a kidney when you were just eighteen."

"And I would have done it earlier than that if my parents had let me. I never did understand why they wouldn't let me do it while I was a minor. I knew the risks. There wasn't any reason to make Amanda wait for so long. Maybe if I could have donated earlier, it would have extended her life. If she hadn't declined so much before receiving the transplant..."

"She still survived a number of years after that, didn't she? And a year on the second transplant?"

Kenzie hadn't realized that he'd paid such close attention to her story. "Yeah. Eight years with mine, one with the second. But maybe if she hadn't been so sick, hadn't had to wait for so long, she would have been stronger for longer."

Zachary was silent.

Kenzie shrugged. "Anyway, that's not what we were talking about. I was talking about the case studies. I was reading about these strange patient outcomes following transplants."

"Right." Zachary spoke as he took a large bite of pizza, talking around the food. "So... were these outcomes because of a special drug or procedure that was used?"

"They were testing a new protocol. It wasn't specified in the document, but I know from talking to one of Dr. Markov's associates that there is a new transplant technology on the horizon."

"Not a new drug?" Zachary questioned. Kenzie knew he was probably thinking of the beta-blocker. But this wasn't about the beta-blocker.

"No. They are hoping to someday be able to perfect gene editing to the extent that they will be able to genetically alter donated organs to match the recipient's tissues so that there is no rejection. No need for antirejection cocktails, which can be very complex and cause a lot of very serious side effects themselves. Patients give up on taking them and end up rejecting the transplanted organ."

"I've heard that they can be really hard on the liver, kidneys, or heart," Zachary offered. "Which is... kind of ironic. Get a transplant and then destroy either the transplanted organ or another one altogether with the medications."

Kenzie grimaced and nodded. "Well, this new protocol, gene editing, would mean that patients wouldn't have to take those antirejection meds. Ever. It would be just like they'd been given an organ from their own body."

"That would really be something."

Kenzie nodded. "That's the vision... you would never have to worry about finding a match. You wouldn't have to take drugs that destroyed your body or your quality of life. You would just have a new, fully functional organ virtually indistinguishable from your own organs."

"Amazing."

"Then I came across these case studies in one of the first documents on Dr. Markov's locket. It would seem that there have been some human trials of gene editing."

Zachary's eyes widened. "Oh, boy. How much trouble would they—how much trouble would the doctors who did that be in? Since this is not a proven, accepted technology yet?"

"You can't just test things willy-nilly. You think about some of the things they have done in the past to test certain procedures or medications, injuring or killing people with unproven techniques, testing on prisoners or psychiatric patients, all kinds of things being tested without informing the people what they are actually testing."

"They could lose their licenses."

"They could lose their licenses. They could be charged with malpractice, assault, or gross bodily harm. Criminal negligence, maybe even homicide."

"They would have good reason for not wanting anyone to find out about it," Zachary suggested.

"Yeah."

"It's hard to believe anyone would be willing to risk all of that."

"Some scientists are willing to risk almost anything for a breakthrough like this. If they were sure it would work… some doctors have huge egos. They can't imagine it going wrong. Especially when they've already done animal studies where it has appeared to work."

"For fame and fortune? Or because they are driven to find a cure?"

"I'm afraid that for the doctors I know who would risk such a thing… it is the money or recognition. I'm sure there are those with higher motives, but I think most of the ones who cross the lines, it isn't because they want to save everyone in the world who is suffering from the malady." Kenzie tried to suppress her grimace of disgust.

Hal pushed himself back from the table. He looked at the sports watch on his wrist. “I’m going to sleep for a few hours. Enjoy yourselves.”

Kenzie and Zachary both nodded and said goodbye and watched him walk away.

CHAPTER 50

"I don't know how he could leave in the middle of this conversation," Zachary said, shaking his head. "I mean... how can he not want to know about the outcomes of these case studies?"

Kenzie would have thought that Zachary was being facetious, but she could see the gleam in his eyes and knew how much he enjoyed a good medical mystery or new nugget of knowledge.

"I know, right?" she agreed.

"So I guess the case studies didn't say 'everything worked and everyone went home happy.'"

Kenzie chuckled. "No, they did not. They were all cases of serious or fatal outcomes. Fast-growing tumors, metabolic disorders, dementia or mental illness..."

"Ooh." Zachary winced. "Not good. And do you think these were all caused by the gene editing?"

"I researched the possible unintended consequences of gene editing, and it isn't all roses. In fact, it's pretty scary."

"How much do we really know about the human genome?" Zachary asked. "I mean… I know they've mapped it, but that doesn't mean they actually know how everything works, right? And there are large portions of our chromosomes that they think are just junk?"

"They think now that maybe they aren't just junk," Kenzie said, raising her brows. "They recognize that a lot of it does have functions we just didn't understand."

"So we're taking the code of life and playing around with it when we only understand one percent of how it works?"

Kenzie shrugged. "More or less."

Zachary nodded. “Did these patients have any idea what they were getting into? Did they know that gene editing was being used and did they know the risks?”

“I don’t have the disclosure statements they were given, so I don’t know. Maybe that is in the documents that I don’t have access to. Maybe it is only available on the servers of Birch Valley. Or maybe the patients weren’t told anything at all. I don’t know yet. But even if they were given full disclosure... did they really understand what they were getting into? Probably not.”

“Did the doctors and researchers understand?”

“I think from what I read in the case studies... they really didn’t have any idea. They thought that the animal studies had been fully successful. They thought that our technology was good enough to be able to edit only the area of the genome we want to and not affect any other area, and that none of the changes that we make would have any other effects. But genes are not simple on-off switches, and we don't know all of the complex ways that they interact."

"The animal studies were not successful?" Zachary's brows drew down.

"Well... I've had to extrapolate because I don't have all the documentation. But from what it says in the case studies, the animal studies were not... long term."

"And what does that mean?"

"They performed necropsies on the animals that received the organ transplants a couple of days after the transplant, to confirm that there were no signs of organ rejection."

"A couple of days."

Kenzie nodded.

"And how long was it before the human subjects started showing ill effects?"

"Some of them almost immediately. Others took a few weeks or months to develop fully."

"And it wasn't organ rejection. It was other stuff."

"Yeah. I don't know whether the animals they experimented on would ever have shown the same negative consequences as the people in these case studies. I have to assume that some of them would have."

"What percentage of the subjects had these consequences?"

Kenzie shook her head. "I have no idea. I don't know how many of these transplants they have done. The case studies document brings forward six cases where there were problems. Nothing in the document says what percentage that is or how many people they trialed the procedure on. It could be six out of six or six out of six hundred."

"You think they could have done six hundred transplants without people finding out about it? Someone would have let the details slip."

"I don't think they had the resources to do gene edits on six hundred organs. It takes time and patience. And I don't think they've been doing it long enough to have done six hundred procedures. I got the feeling that they had barely started on human trials. The memorandum on the case studies is only a few weeks old."

"So let's say it was somewhere between… ten and sixty transplants."

"Seems reasonable," Kenzie agreed. "Maybe even on the high side."

"With unintended consequences in… ten to sixty percent of cases. That's really high."

Kenzie nodded her agreement.

“No wonder someone wanted to put a stop to it.”

“Dr. Markov knew what was going on. I don’t know how much she knew, but it was obvious from her access to these files that she figured it out. I don’t know what part she was supposed to play in the project, but I guess she decided that things had gone far enough, and the others on the team were not willing to abandon the project.”

“I can’t imagine anyone pushing through with those kinds of results.”

“People are desperate for transplants. Do you know how many people die while waiting for a suitable match? Meanwhile, there are people out there willing to make live donations, and there are organs that are not being used because there is not a match that they can get the organ to in time to use it. These people are willing to risk anything to get an organ that will allow them to survive. The alternative is not very attractive.”

"No," Zachary agreed with a rueful smile. "I guess I get that. I just don't know how the doctors can think they are doing the right thing by putting people through what they are. If half the people you give a transplant to end up with one of these fatal conditions, or with a brain condition that is going to last them the rest of their lives, how can they continue to push it as the solution?"

"Because it may still be the solution," Kenzie pointed out. "When they have perfected it. And in the meantime, those people would have died. If you know someone is going to die tomorrow, do you perform a procedure today that has a fifty percent success rate?"

"Well... yeah, I guess so," Zachary admitted. "As long as... they understand it could cause unnecessary suffering. I mean, would they choose to die tomorrow or to suffer for a few weeks or months?"

Kenzie had to admit that was a good question. It all hinged on informed consent. Did everyone understand what they were getting into? Were they willing to gamble their lives? Were they willing to take the chance of untreatable cancer, seizures, or schizophrenia in exchange for their lives?

It was worth it for the doctors. They had to keep working on the technology if it were going to succeed. They had to keep experimenting until they got it right.

"But they could go back to animal trials," she pointed out to Zachary. "If they realized that the failure of the animal trials was that they didn't look for anything but rejection, and not the unintended, long-term consequences of the gene editing, then they should go back to the animal trials and observe what happened after a few days, weeks, or months. And after they get that under control, they could go back to human trials."

"And in the meantime, more people would have died waiting for organs."

"Yes."

Zachary nodded slowly. “I’m glad I didn’t have to make that choice.”

CHAPTER 51

Kenzie was determined that the next day would be a normal day. She would just go in and do her regular work, and there would be no threats, no car bombs, and no talk of gene editing and ethical dilemmas.

As she reviewed her schedule to ensure she wasn't forgetting anything, she realized it was couple's therapy day.

That might be a good idea after their marathon discussion of what had been going on at work, the Markov case, the danger from the Russians, and everything else they had discussed the evening before. But after all the emotions, Kenzie wasn't up to it. She needed just to be able to have a normal, routine day.

"I don't think I'm going to be able to get there for couple's counseling today," she told Zachary. "Do you mind doing a single session instead? Maybe that's even better, if there is anything you want to talk to Dr. B about after yesterday. Maybe there is some stuff that you want to discuss privately."

He was sure to have a beef with how Kenzie kept things from him. He could surely spend an hour going over whether Kenzie had really forgotten to keep him updated or whether she had some darker motive or deep distrust of him. Dr. Boyle could give him some tips on keeping communications open and expressing his feelings clearly, and Kenzie would do her best to cooperate with their new plan, and then they could discuss it after working on it for a week.

"Sure," Zachary agreed, nodding as he put bread into the toaster for Kenzie's toast. "That's not a problem. We talked a lot last night. You're probably all talked out."

"I am, at that," Kenzie admitted. "I could use some time just to let everything percolate for a while."

"Speaking of percolating..." Zachary poured Kenzie a cup of coffee and presented it to her with a flourish.

"Thanks. I really appreciate it. The coffee and the extra week. You really don't mind?"

"No." Zachary made a motion as if to wave this away. "I prefer knowing ahead of time."

Then he didn't have to worry the whole morning that she would forget and not show up for couple's therapy. It had only happened <u>one time</u>, but he couldn't stop obsessing over it every time they were scheduled for couple's therapy, believing that it would happen again.

"I'll see you after work, then, and you can tell me all about it. Or tell me whatever you want to, I mean. If there's anything that I should know."

Zachary nodded his agreement and put the marmalade on the table.

* * *

When Kenzie picked up her voicemails at work, there was one from Detective Edwards.

"It turns out that Dr. Tucker's fingerprints are <u>not</u> on the packaging for the licorice," he told her. "I also have samples of his handwriting from independent sources, and it does not look anything like the handwriting on the gift tag. I'm no expert on handwriting, of course, and we'll get confirmation from our expert, but it would appear that he was <u>not</u> the one who left the gift for Mr. Smythe. Whoever did it was smart enough to cover their tracks."

Kenzie swore irritably. Of course it would have been too easy for the killer to simply have signed his own name. Of course it had been left by someone else and the guard had been misled. If he knew who had poisoned Markov, he wouldn't have been stupid enough to accept food from the guy.

A lab test result in her email inbox confirmed that the licorice had been tainted with the same chemical as had been found in the blood of both Dr. Markov and Mr. Smythe. As they had suspected, the beta-blocker had been in the licorice, its bitterness disguised by the overwhelming flavor of the double-salted Dutch licorice.

Kenzie watched the video of Markov leaving the fundraiser again. She watched the guard help Markov by picking up what she had dropped and guiding her to get her key from the valet and navigate safely to her car. Then he stood there and watched her go.

Markov had apparently been drugged at some point between her talk, when she appeared to be functioning normally, and when she had reappeared in the video to get her car to go home. Or to go to the police department, as it had turned out.

But at what time had she actually been drugged? Who had taken the opportunity? Was it someone who Markov trusted, or was it done covertly?

Kenzie sat with her eyes closed, rubbing her temples, thinking about it. She knew the general window of time. She knew an oral beta-blocker generally took about an hour to take effect. That was in tablet form. If it had been powdered or dissolved in something, it would take considerably less time to act. Kenzie was sure it had not been introduced intravenously; there had been no injection marks found during the autopsy. Could she narrow down the timing of the introduction of the drug any closer than that?

Kenzie reviewed what else she might have that would also show her the timeline of when Markov had been out of sight of the cameras.

It wasn't until then that she thought about Markov's watch. Even though it did not look like a sports watch, it monitored several health indicators and relayed that information to the health app on Markov's phone.

Kenzie still had access to the phone memory and emulator. With a few mouse clicks, she found the health app and narrowed her focus to Markov's heartbeat and blood pressure. Both had dropped precipitously partway through the evening. That was the point at which the beta-blocker had taken effect on Markov. The drug would have been administered during the hour before that, possibly half an hour if it had been crushed or dissolved, as Kenzie had to believe it was. It didn't seem likely that Markov would swallow a pill someone gave to her. She hadn't been taking any regular prescriptions, and if she had needed a painkiller for a headache or something of that nature, she would have known by the pill's shape and color if it wasn't what she expected it to be.

Half an hour before the time Markov's heart rate had dropped, she had still been eating dinner. So it had to be in the food. Kenzie rewound the video of the event and tried to keep her eyes on Dr. Markov and who had been close enough to her to have poisoned her food. It had to have been done at the table, unless Markov had ordered a special meal that someone could have recognized and dosed in the kitchen.

Kenzie watched the video intently. Markov conversed with various people at her table as she ate. She seemed relaxed but engaged. Kenzie watched each of the people who were within reach of her plate.

The camera didn't stay on Markov constantly, but returned to her frequently since she had been the special guest speaker. Each time it panned away, Kenzie feared that she would miss whatever had happened.

Then she saw a hand near Markov's coffee cup. It hovered over the coffee for a brief moment. The video was not clear enough for her to determine whether the person had actually dropped a powder or liquid into the cup, but the timing was right, and why had the hand been there, over Markov's cup, otherwise?

The person who had sat next to Markov, who had chatted with her throughout the evening and used a distracted moment to pass her hand over Markov's cup, had been Dana Pratt.

CHAPTER 52

Kenzie stared at the screen in disbelief. Dana Pratt? The one who had professed to be Mariya Markov's best friend? Who had sat across the table from Kenzie and Alina and said how sad she was to have lost such a good friend?

Kenzie couldn't believe it.

She knew she must be seeing something that wasn't there. Assigning blame to Pratt for something she hadn't done. There was no way that pleasant young lady had poisoned Markov's drink.

Maybe she had done it without understanding the consequences. Someone had pressured her into doing it, and she had been told that it would have a different effect. Maybe Markov didn't think that the beta-blocker should be approved, but someone else did and wanted to prove how safe it was by administering it to Markov. <u>You see, it was so safe you didn't even know you took it!</u>

Or maybe Markov herself had asked her to get something for her. A painkiller or stomach remedy. And someone had tampered with it so that Pratt unintentionally gave her the wrong thing.

Just because Pratt had been the one to administer the poison, that didn't necessarily mean that she had intended for Markov to die, did it?

Kenzie knew that the scenarios she was considering were unbelievable. She just wanted to reassure herself that it wasn't the vibrant young woman who had said Markov was her friend. She just didn't want it to be true.

She reviewed the other photos and video recordings of the evening, looking for Markov and Pratt in each of them. She looked at their body language. Looked for anything that indicated one was upset with the other or there was any bad blood between them. But they looked like good friends. They seemed happy and relaxed with each other.

Kenzie couldn't believe that Pratt could have administered the drug that had caused Markov's death. She was mistaking what she had seen on the video. Mistaking an innocent movement for something that it wasn't. Someone else had been responsible. The waiter. Someone else at the table with them. Someone in the kitchen. Or she had miscalculated the time when she was most likely to have been dosed with the beta-blocker, and it had been a different time altogether. An hour earlier. Fifteen minutes later. It was not an exact science. Different beta-blockers took different amounts of time to take effect. And it depended on how they were administered. While she knew that it hadn't been given intravenously, she didn't know whether it was given as a pill or a powder or liquid. Each one would be absorbed at a different rate, and it was ridiculous for her to estimate something so impossible to pin down.

She also didn't know whether Markov was sensitive to beta-blockers or not, or whether she was taking another drug that might block the action of the beta-blocker or make her more sensitive. There were too many variables. It could have been given to Markov at any time that night, on camera or off.

Kenzie finished watching all of the other footage of the event. The last video on the list was the traffic cam that had captured part of Markov's drive from the event toward the police station, which she would never reach. She tried to watch the video dispassionately, to look for anything that any of them might have missed. Had she called anyone while she was driving? Had she swerved between lanes because she was distracted by something she had seen? Did she have any difficulty with the car they hadn't recognized before? Kenzie thought of the device that had been attached to her car. The computer that couldn't do much to disrupt a classic old car like Kenzie's, but could easily have taken over the onboard computer chips of a modern vehicle like Markov's and changed the car's speed, steering, or brakes.

Cars with antilock braking systems, cruise control, lane assist, and automatic parallel parking had multiple systems that could be controlled by such a device. People worried about self-driving cars going rogue, but Kenzie was already seeing cases of cars causing accidents when one of the built-in safety features took over from the human driver. Cars that slammed on their brakes at a mirage, pulled the vehicle into another lane when it misread a previous lane marking that was supposed to have been blacked out, accelerators that stuck on or turned off because of a glitch in the system. They didn't need to wait for robocars. The future was now.

But Kenzie didn't see anything on the video that suggested Markov's car had been controlled by someone or something else. She didn't appear to be fighting it. And Detective Edwards would have had the mechanics check the car for any sabotage or mechanical problems. There hadn't been an electronic hacking device attached to it like the one that had been installed on Kenzie's baby. They would have seen that.

It wasn't until Kenzie watched the traffic cam video yet again that she saw the other vehicle.

She leaned in and watched it again. Could it be? She found Detective Edwards's phone number on her phone and tapped it. It rang a couple of times and then was answered.

"Edwards. Oh, hi, Dr. Kirsch."

"Did you notice the other vehicle on the traffic cam video of Dr. Markov?" Kenzie demanded without preamble. She didn't need any small talk to lead up to it. Detective Edwards would want the meat of the conversation immediately.

"Another vehicle?" Edwards repeated. "No. Wait while I pull it up."

Kenzie waited. "Tell me when you are pressing play," she told him. "I'll start mine at the same time."

"Okay. Three, two, one..."

Kenzie pressed play on hers. "Now watch as Markov's car goes under the traffic light, and then a second or two later..."

Kenzie marked the second vehicle. “Now.”

“Black SUV,” Edwards observed. “Tinted windows. Okay, what about it?”

“Can you get a license plate?”

“Should be able to. They are scanned a couple of times on that road. Why? You think it had something to do with the accident? Or just that it might have been a witness?”

“There was a vehicle like that following me a few days ago. When I came back from talking with Dana Pratt. Oh, and Dana Pratt…? I think she is the one who gave Markov the beta-blocker.”

“Dana Pratt?” Edwards was surprised. “Really? I wouldn’t have pegged her.”

“Me either. I thought… they were friends. I thought she wanted to be helpful. As much as she could be. Why else would she tell us that Markov was a whistleblower?”

"Do you think the SUV is registered to her?"

"I... no. I don't think so. I think it is probably registered to someone else at Birch Valley... but I don't know. I can't imagine her chasing after Dr. Markov. But it looks like it was going pretty fast. It could have been chasing her. That would explain her going too fast. Trying to get away from it. Trying to get to the police station before they could catch her."

"They?"

"Whoever was involved in this. Whether it was Pratt or someone else. Maybe I'm wrong about who poisoned Dr. Markov. I can't quite believe it myself. But if the driver of that SUV is involved..."

"I'll check the registration. Don't worry about that. We'll track both vehicles back as far as possible and see if it was harassing or chasing her. See whether it came from the event as well."

"Thank you."

"And tell me why you think Pratt gave her the beta-blocker."

Kenzie gave him the file name of the video she had seen of Pratt possibly dosing Markov's drink and found the time code to give him.

"I tried to calculate from Dr. Markov's sports watch what time she was given the beta-blocker," she explained, "and then watched the video from around that time. It's only a guess, not one hundred percent, and there were not cameras on Dr. Markov the whole time, so we might have missed something much more obvious. But take a look and see if you think she puts something in Dr. Markov's drink there."

Edwards was silent as he watched the video. Kenzie thought he probably watched it a few times, walking through it at regular speed and slowed down, frame-by-frame, to try to catch the details of Dana Pratt putting something into Markov's cup. Eventually, he spoke.

“I see what you mean,” he agreed. “I think you might have something there, but it isn’t a slam dunk. Certainly enough to ask her about it. Confront her and see if she breaks down when she realizes we saw something.”

“Good. I have a tough time accepting that Dana might have done that to her friend. But... I can’t talk myself out of it. It really does look like she might have tampered with her ‘friend’s’ drink. I just can’t understand her motive. Unless someone else coerced her into it.”

“Well, the good thing is, we don’t need to know her motive. I know that’s the big thing in detective novels and on TV. That you always need a motive. But in real life, you don’t need a motive. You need evidence. Follow the evidence and build a case, and that will get you a heck of a lot farther than speculating about motives.”

"Just like a postmortem," Kenzie said. "You can't let your biases dictate what you follow and what you don't. You have to stay objective and see what story the body has to tell you."

"Exactly," Edwards agreed. "We are not going to eliminate Pratt as a suspect just because we don't understand the why. We will bring her in for questioning this time. Get her on our turf. And maybe she'll tell us the why as well as the how."

"There were bruises around Markov's throat. If it was Dana Pratt... do you think they were lovers? Do you think Pratt would have the strength to do that? It takes a lot of force."

"Whatever happened took place behind closed doors. Markov disappears from the video. Whatever happened during that time... I don't think we're going to find out unless someone who was there tells us what happened. You didn't get any fingerprints or DNA from her neck?"

"No, unfortunately not. That's pretty hard to do, even if you are looking for it. Prints smear in a struggle, and touch DNA is difficult to find and process. She didn't have any skin under her nails, so she wasn't able to scratch whoever it was that throttled her."

Kenzie thought about the bright yellow dress Dana Pratt had worn at the event. It had not covered a lot. She couldn't imagine how Pratt could have strangled Markov and not sustained any scratches on her bare arms, throat, face, or chest. If Markov had struggled with someone, she had not been able to scratch them. And there was plenty of opportunity to scratch a woman in an evening dress. Scratching a man in a tux and tie was not so easy. The only thing that was bare on the men was hands and face. The thought made her feel a little better. It was far more likely that Markov had been throttled by a man—bigger and stronger and protected by layers of clothing—than a woman.

"You'll let me know what you find out?"

“Of course, doctor,” Edwards agreed. “Thanks for letting me know what you found. Have you issued your preliminary reports on Markov and Smythe?”

“Yes, Dr. Wiltshire has them on his desk. I’ll officially release them as soon as he approves them.”

“Homicide on both?”

“Yes.”

“Good. I’ll talk to you later.”

CHAPTER 53

Kenzie locked her computer screen and her desk drawers. It was time to stretch her legs. She had been sitting for long enough. She had some samples to process and send to the lab. She needed to check with Dr. Wiltshire about where he was on the preliminary reports Edwards had mentioned. She expected him to approve them without any questions. They had already discussed most of the findings. There wasn't anything in there that should have been a surprise to him.

And she needed to get some lunch. She knew she wasn't supposed to go out alone to get lunch after everything that had happened. She needed to be wise and protect herself.

Kenzie started with a trip to the ladies room. One of the perks of being a female medical examiner was that pretty much everyone else in the office was male, so she generally had the restroom to herself. She had privacy and it stayed clean between the twice-weekly sanitizing by the janitorial staff.

So it was a surprise to enter and realize someone else was in the second cubicle.

"Oh—hi! You startled me," she told the unseen occupant.

There was no answer from the other woman. Kenzie didn't want to make anyone feel awkward, so she left it at that and didn't try to carry on a conversation.

She quickly used the facilities and left the cubicle, heading for the sinks. The other cubicle door opened behind her, and she heard the light skim of sneakers on the floor rather than the tap of heels. Someone who was used to being on her feet. Maybe one of the delivery or transport people who were in and out of the medical examiner's suite regularly as bodies were transported and various samples made their way in and out of the office. There was more activity than outsiders would think. It was not "dead," as Zachary often joked.

Just as she looked at the reflection in the mirror to see who was behind her, she was hit from behind. Kenzie let out a cry, whirling around and trying to protect herself as she assessed the situation.

It was Dana Pratt.

Kenzie swore to herself. This was not just some random attack. It was planned and prepared for. It was someone who wanted to eliminate her as a threat. Kenzie had figured out too much, and Pratt realized it. She had taken the time to figure out exactly where the medical examiner's office was in Roxboro. She had learned the public hours, planned how to get inside, and worked out how to sneak into the restroom and wait there—possibly for hours. After a two-hour commute from Burlington.

She had killed or helped to kill Dr. Markov, who she claimed was a friend. And she was going to do the same to Kenzie if she could.

“Stop!” Kenzie shouted, using her hands to block any further blows. “What are you doing? Get out of here!”

Dana shrieked with rage. “What am I doing? I warned you! I told you it was none of your business. I told you what would happen if you didn’t back off. But did you?”

Dana brought the heavy object in her hand down again, grazing Kenzie’s head and shoulder.

“What?” Kenzie demanded. “What are you talking about?”

“I hate you and your company and everything you stand for. Do you realize what you have done? Do you know how many lives you have ruined?”

“My company? I work for the medical examiner’s office. The lives I deal with are already ruined. Either people whose lives are over or who are dealing with the loss of those lives.”

“Not that company,” Dana snapped, swinging at Kenzie and trying to get close enough to strike another blow, while Kenzie kept trying to get away from her, to stay just out of reach. She wanted to get to the door, but so far, Dana had blocked her from making a break in that direction. "Your charity. Your family foundation. That company."

Kenzie stared at Dana, not moving. "What? The Kirsch family foundation?"

"Yes."

"What has the foundation done to hurt anyone?"

But just before Dana answered, Kenzie knew what she was going to say.

"Because you withdrew our funding. What do you think happens when you take money away from kidney research? People die! Think of all of the people that you took that money away from when you pulled funding from Birch Valley. That's your fault. Yours!"

Dana raised her arm high above her head. Kenzie looked at her hand to identify the bludgeon she was using. It looked like some sort of trophy or commemorative award, pieces of rock cemented together into a shape Kenzie couldn't make out. Kenzie cringed and shrank back, afraid that Dana was going to throw it this time rather than trying to get close enough to hit her.

"You're the one who made the threats?" Kenzie asked. "You?"

She had been sure that the voice on the phone had been male, and it had been nothing like Dana's pleasant tones. She must have used a voice-changing device to make the call. That possibility had never even occurred to her.

"You should know better," Dana growled at her. "For years, your family has been funding the research and helping to move things forward, and then you come along and disrupt everything and tell them to give their money to other causes."

It hadn't been Kenzie's choice. It was because of her that the family had decided to turn more of their funding toward mental health. But the entire board had voted on it, and it wasn't something that Kenzie had suggested. It was just her parents, trying to keep the family foundation doing something meaningful to all of them. And to stay on top of the changing times, during which mental health had become a much more prominent issue.

The door of the restroom crashed open, making both of them jump and look at it. Hal stood framed in the doorway, his face tight with anger, eyes immediately focused on the threat. He pulled a gun and pointed it at Dana. “Drop it. Now!”

Dana’s jaw dropped. “What? Who are you?”

“Drop your weapon and put your hands behind your head.”

“You can’t come in here,” Dana pointed out, as if the fact that it was the ladies room should keep Hal from entering.

“Drop it now, lady!”

Dana finally seemed to become aware of the danger she was in. She dropped the rock sculpture to the ground with a crash. She put her hands behind her head and looked at

Kenzie as if this were just another in the long list of injustices that Kenzie had perpetrated on her.

Once she had her hands behind her head, Hal moved in, slapping a pair of handcuffs over her wrists. Then he turned to Kenzie.

"You know this woman?"

"This is Dana Pratt. She's an employee of Birch Valley. She's..." Kenzie hesitated. If she said, "She's the one who poisoned Dr. Markov," she could just hear the protests that Dana would make. And anything she said should be recorded. Kenzie didn't want to mess things up for the police. "She's someone Detective Edwards needs to talk to."

"Give him a call," Hal told her. "We'll just hold her until someone gets down here to arrest her."

Kenzie nodded, feeling dazed and a little removed from the situation.

"Are you okay, by the way, Doctor?" Hal asked.

Kenzie swallowed and ran her fingers through her hair. "You should call me Kenzie. Yes. I'm fine. I don't think..." She ran her fingers over the bruises on the back of her head where Dana had initially hit her. A lump was swelling up already, and the skin had split, as Kenzie discovered when she pulled her fingers back sticky with blood. "Well, I guess she did get me pretty good."

Hal gave Dana's shoulder a shove, like a parent silently reprimanding a child for something she knew she shouldn't do.

"I can call Edwards if you like."

"I've got his number right here." Kenzie pulled out her phone and found the detective's number on her call log. She tapped it and listened to it ring before connecting.

"Dr. Kirsch. If you're calling for an update, I haven't yet been able to track down Pratt. She didn't show up for work today.

I've asked Burlington to send a couple of officers to her house to look for her."

"She's here."

"In Roxboro?"

"In the ladies room."

"In the ladies room... downstairs?"

Kenzie gave a little nod of confirmation. "Yeah. Down here in the medical examiner's office."

"Are you okay, Dr. Kirsch? You sound funny. Dana Pratt is down there? In the medical examiner's office?"

"Yes."

"Okay, I'll be right down."

It didn't take him very long to get there. He stepped tentatively into the bathroom and looked around.

"Does somebody want to tell me exactly what happened here?" he demanded. He looked at Dana, who gave him a wide-eyed look of innocence. Edwards looked at Hal and then met Kenzie's gaze. "Explain."

"She was hiding in one of the stalls. When I came out to wash my hands, she attacked me. She says..." Kenzie looked at Dana, wondering if she would deny it now, "She says she was the one who made the threatening email and phone call."

"Is that true?" Edwards demanded, looking back at Dana.

She nodded. "Yes."

"What did you do, use a voice changer for the phone call?"

"Yes."

"Those things are the bane of my existence," Edwards muttered to no one in particular. Kenzie couldn't imagine that he ran into them <u>that</u> often during his investigations. He shook his head. "And you admit that you attacked Dr. Kirsch?"

"Yes."

"We need to go upstairs and have a little chat. You understand that you're in trouble, don't you?"

Dana shrugged. "I know that you think I did the wrong thing. But I didn't. If that gets me in trouble… I'll have to take my medicine."

"You don't think there is anything wrong with threatening and attacking Dr. Kirsch?"

"After what she did to us? I think… someone had to show her how she had hurt everyone else."

Edwards cocked his head and looked at Kenzie. "Do you know what she is talking about?"

"She's talking about the Kirsch family foundation taking funding away from Birch Valley."

"Oh, I see. So Dr. Kirsch had to be punished for that?" Edwards asked.

Dana nodded. "She has pronounced a death sentence on those who have kidney disease. In order to cure it, we need that money. People are dying while we scramble to get money to replace the Kirsch family's funding."

"I'm sure they are," Edwards agreed. He rolled his eyes at Kenzie, turning Dana so that she faced the door. "Let's go upstairs and have that chat. While you're at it, you can tell me about Dr. Markov and why she deserved to be punished."

"Mariya?" Dana asked, looking shocked. "She didn't deserve to be punished! What are you talking about?"

"We'll get a tape rolling first, and then discuss it."

Edwards paused in the doorway as he escorted Dana out. “You should see a doctor, Doctor. I’ll send someone down for that thing and to take pictures of your injuries. Then maybe have someone patch you up.”

“I’d like to hear…” Kenzie nodded to Dana. She wanted to hear what Dana had to say about why she had done what she had. She didn’t need to be part of the interrogation, but she wanted to understand why.

Detective Edwards looked at his watch. “You want to come up in half an hour? We’ll get her booked for the assault and the threats first. Maybe you can have Dr. Wiltshire fix you up. How is his hand? Is he still able to do stitches?”

“Yes, of course. He wouldn’t be back here if he couldn’t do that much.”

Of course, his stitches were not as small and neat as they had once been. He would need a lot more practice to get completely rehabilitated. Assuming he could get full functionality back.

“I don’t think it will need stitches,” she said, prodding the split skin on the back of her head. “It’s not that bad.”

“Have him look at it. After we get some pictures. I’ll take at least half an hour to get Miss Pratt processed, and then you can come up and listen in.”

“Thanks.” Kenzie brushed her forehead with the back of her hand. “I think I’m going to need a Tylenol.”

CHAPTER 54

"I'm sorry," Hal apologized after Detective Edwards had taken Dana Pratt away. "I should have been here sooner. I was not aware of the threat, and I should have been. I should have been closer, maybe even checked out the room before you entered."

Kenzie shook her head. "It isn't your fault. You were close by. I had no idea that Dana was here or that she would attack me. It came out of the blue."

"Apparently not, if she is the one who has been threatening you. We should have realized it sooner."

"There may have been signs… but I didn't catch any of them. I thought Dana was Dr. Markov's best friend. She never said anything that led me to believe that she had been part of the plot that killed her, or that she was any kind of a threat to me." Kenzie shook her head. "And I was a lot closer to her than you were. You weren't part of any of those interviews."

Hal shook his head, obviously still not happy with himself. Kenzie didn't know what he could have done any better. He was acting as her bodyguard; he wasn't expected to solve the case. How could he have known that Dana was becoming unglued?

She had seemed perfectly logical and reasonable when Kenzie had talked to her. How could either of them have known that she was the person behind the threats? She had kept that part of herself concealed, even revealing to Detective Edwards that Markov had been a whistleblower.

"You couldn't have known," Kenzie assured Hal again.

"I'm going to need to report this to Zachary."

"He's not going to get on your case for not being in the bathroom with me," Kenzie insisted. Then, at Hal's look, she realized he wasn't saying that because he was embarrassed at having missed the signs that Dana Pratt was a direct threat to Kenzie's safety.

He was pointing out that he needed to report the attack to Zachary, as his security detail. But if Hal broke the news to Zachary rather than Kenzie, there could be negative consequences. Namely, Zachary would be ticked that Kenzie again failed to tell him what was happening in her life and that she had been in danger.

“Oh, dang. I’ll call him.”

Hal nodded. “I’ll wait until you’re finished talking.”

“Yeah, thanks.”

Hal left the ladies room. Kenzie paced across the floor in front of the sinks, putting her phone to her ear and trying to figure out how to break the news to Zachary without upsetting him.

He was going to be upset. There was no way around that. But she wanted to minimize the shock as much as possible.

“Kenzie,” Zachary’s tone was casual and unworried. They often touched base over lunchtime, so her call coming in now was not out of the ordinary. “How was your morning?”

“Well,” Kenzie said, thinking about her script. “It was challenging.”

“Oh? Things didn’t go well?”

“I was able to make some progress on the case. Managed to catch a couple of things on video that we didn’t see the first time.”

“Well, that sounds good. Good for you.”

“Yeah. The thing is, the person that we identified was not someone who was initially on our radar. In fact, we had talked to her a couple of times, and she had given us information that we hadn’t already had. So, it never occurred to us that she was part of the plot. She said she wasn’t on the project, but she was lying about that.”

“Have the police had a chance to question her yet?”

“Not yet. Detective Edwards just took her upstairs.”

“He just took her upstairs,” Zachary repeated slowly. “You mean she was there? At your office?”

“Yeah. She came to... have a discussion with me.”

“What?” His tone was immediately laced with concern. “Are you okay? What happened?”

“She was the one who sent the threats. The email and the phone call. That was her.”

“But everything is okay? You said that Edwards was taking her upstairs to question her. What happened? Where is Hal?”

“He’ll be calling you to report after you and I get off the phone. He wanted to give me a chance to talk to you first.”

She heard Zachary take a couple of deep breaths. She could picture him trying to stay in control. He had to be experiencing a flood of emotions right now: fear, anger, relief, maybe dread for what might happen to them next.

“You’re talking to me, and you don’t sound like you are hurt. Unless I’m talking to a ghost. And I don’t think they can operate phones.”

Kenzie appreciated his attempt at humor. She chuckled. “I’m just fine. I got a little bump on the head, but that is all. I’m going to go upstairs to watch the interview in a few minutes. They’re going to book her for assault.”

“How did she get in there? Did she attack you at your desk?”

“Hid in the ladies room. I’m sure Hal will give you all the details. Go easy on him; he’s beating himself up for letting it happen. And I don’t think there was much he could have done to stop her. She was pretty determined, and she doesn’t look or act like a threat. No one would have thought that she was dangerous.”

Zachary grunted. “We’ll have a debrief.”

“Okay. I’ll talk to you later. I just didn’t want you to worry. Or to be taken off-guard and think I was trying to hide it from you. I really am okay.”

“You’ll have someone look at that bump?”

“I’m going to have Dr. Wiltshire take a look at it after the evidence techs get a couple of pictures.”

“You do realize that all of Dr. Wiltshire’s other patients are dead.”

Kenzie laughed. “Mmm-hm. I’ll have to be the exception. I don’t feel like waiting in some emergency room or clinic somewhere. It’s just a bump and it isn’t worth wasting my whole day to get it cleaned up and be told to put an ice pack on it.”

“If you’re sure. You have to be careful of head injuries.”

“Tell me you would go to the hospital for a little knock on the head.”

“Well... no. Probably not.”

“Definitely not. I know you. You’d have to be knocked unconscious to even consider it, and even then...”

“You might be right,” he admitted.

“I am,” Kenzie told him firmly. “I’ll see you tonight. Don’t worry about me. I’m not leaving the building.”

CHAPTER 55

Once Dr. Wiltshire had seen to Kenzie's injury and assured her that it didn't seem to be anything to worry about, she went upstairs to the police offices. Edwards situated her, as he had before, in a room where she could watch the interview on camera, out of the way where Dana would not be able to see her and Kenzie could not participate in the conversation. Kenzie sipped her fresh coffee and waited for them to begin.

After a few minutes of playing on her phone to stave off boredom, Kenzie saw Edwards and Dana appear on the screen. They sat down at the table. Dana was not handcuffed. Her body language suggested that she was comfortable and unworried about the interview. As if she were just there as a witness with information to report.

Edwards began by announcing the date, time, and parties present. He gave the Miranda warning, and Dana waived her right to counsel.

"Let's start at the beginning," Edwards suggested. "You told us before that you were not involved in the same projects as Dr. Markov."

"That's right," Dana agreed.

"But you have been on <u>some</u> projects together, haven't you?"

"Yes. But not all of them."

"And that's why you said you were not involved in the same projects."

"Right," Dana agreed. "Some I was involved in, some Mariya was involved in, and some we were both involved in. They weren't the same."

"Uh-huh. So you knew about things like the experimental beta-blocker, gene editing, and human trials of new organ transplant procedures."

Dana considered this carefully before agreeing. "Yes."

"And you knew that Dr. Markov objected to them."

"No, she didn't object to the projects. She just thought they were going too quickly to human trials."

"On which thing?"

"The gene-edited organ transplants. All of it was about the gene-edited organ transplants."

"Even the beta-blockers?"

"Yes. It is important to control heart rhythm and blood pressure and ensure the circulation is as good as possible. You can't have healthy organs without good oxygen circulation. And if the blood pressure is too high, it damages the brain and can result in a stroke. It damages the heart, the kidneys, and peripheral blood vessels. If you want long-term health and fully functioning organs, you need to control the circulation."

"I see. So it was all about a protocol to protect the health of transplant recipients as much as possible."

Dana nodded. "Yes. We wanted to give them every advantage."

"And the current beta-blockers on the market just wouldn't cut it? What was wrong with them?"

"Well… there's nothing wrong with them… but with a new product, we might be able to manage side effects better, tailor treatment, overcome drug resistance…"

"Not to mention being able to patent new products and profit from your own line of drugs."

"A company like ours can't continue without money," Dana pointed out. "We need that research money. All of this testing and development takes money. A <u>lot</u> of money. I'm not in management, so it isn't my job to worry about that stuff, but really… it's everybody's business, isn't it?"

Edwards smiled. “I suppose it is. Everyone needs to contribute somehow.”

Dana nodded her agreement.

“Why did Dr. Markov think you were going to human trials too soon?”

“There were… some glitches. Side effects. Unexpected consequences. She thought we were pushing it too fast and needed to do some long-term animal trials.”

“Why didn’t everyone else agree with that? It seems like it would only be logical.”

“Humans and animals are not the same. And why perform all of your testing on healthy animals when there were people who needed those organs? People were dying while we were doing animal trials that didn’t really matter. It makes more sense to develop the technology for the species you are actually going to use it on.” Dana’s eyes were bright. The evangelical light of the converted. She knew all the right things to say, but Kenzie sensed she was repeating someone else's words. Somewhere else in the company's chain of command was the prophet who taught these principles. Who believed that animal testing was pointless.

"Were you involved in that decision?" Edwards asked, his thoughts following the same lines as Kenzie's.

"No. I'm just a researcher. I don't get to perform the surgery or make the management decisions. But maybe someday..."

Kenzie doubted Dana would be moving very far up the ranks at Birch Valley. She was too undisciplined. She had told the police too much already, had sent emails and voicemails that could potentially be traced back to the company, and had attacked Kenzie physically.

Not only that, but she had administered poison to one of the company's top people. And maybe to another person as well. She was not a disciplined team member, but a rogue player, a cowboy.

"Was Dr. Markov blocking the proper development of the gene editing? Is that why you poisoned her?"

"Poisoned her?" Dana sat back in her chair. "I didn't poison her!"

"You administered the beta-blocker to Dr. Markov's drink. And that caused her to have an accident. She was too impaired to keep the car on the road."

"That wasn't what was supposed to happen. He said that she would be more pliant... Mariya would tell him where she had saved the files she had stolen. Where all of the copies were. It wasn't meant to hurt her."

He. They were getting closer to the answers.

CHAPTER 56

Edwards nodded and leaned forward. "So you believed that by giving Mariya the drug, you would be helping her. You would be protecting her from coming to harm by fighting him."

Dana nodded eagerly. "Yes! I didn't want Mariya getting hurt because she was trying to inform on the company. Especially when we weren't doing anything wrong. I know she thought she was doing what was right, but she didn't realize that shortcutting the animal studies was the best possible choice. She didn't see how denying people these early transplants was harmful. She was a scientist and didn't think about the human cost."

"And you wanted to help move them forward without harming the company."

"Of course. These technologies need to be developed. We can't sit here where we are, with transplant recipients having to take complex cocktails of drugs—for the rest of their lives

—that end up damaging their other organs! And people not being able to get transplants because there are no matches. Do you know how many people die on a waiting list?"

Edwards nodded. "I had a niece..."

"Everybody has someone. There are so many people out there who will not survive unless this technology is perfected. And the only way to do that is by trying and refining it, over and over again."

"But Dr. Markov couldn't see that."

"She knew it needed to happen, but she thought... she thought we needed to do more work on the earlier stages. She didn't understand that we are there; we are right on the cusp of success." Dana jabbed her finger into the table, thumping it down to make her point. "We are ready to bring this to fruition. We will be the first ones to show the world that it can be done. Can you imagine the recognition she would receive for her contribution? She could get a Nobel prize!"

"Did you tell her that? What about the other doctors on the project? Were they all in? Was there disagreement between Dr. Markov and the others about their direction or how the testing should be done?"

"People can be so shortsighted," Dana lamented. "If you were on a waiting list, you would want this technology, wouldn't you? You would give anything for it. The other doctors saw that. They saw how vital it was for the testing to proceed, despite the challenges."

"So all of the others were on board? It was only Dr. Markov who was being difficult about it?"

"The senior staff were all on board. Anyone lower down in the organization could be let go if they disagreed with the direction the company was going. Or someone could explain to them why it had to be done that way."

"But Dr. Markov was too senior to fire her or transfer her to a different project."

Dana nodded. "I didn't want her to leave anyway. I enjoyed working with her. She was a really great person, you know? I'm sorry you didn't get to meet her and see what kind of a person she was."

"It sounds like she had a highly developed sense of ethics."

Dana showed irritation for the first time. "Mariya was stubborn. She shouldn't have copied those files. If she didn't want to be a part of this, she should have just left. Gone to another company where they would appreciate her contribution and not want to do anything she disagreed with."

"Instead of fighting a losing battle against the other principals in the company."

"Yeah."

"They must have still thought a lot of her. She was the guest speaker at that fundraising event."

"She knew how to get donations. She knew how to talk to people. And she actually enjoyed doing it. She wasn't afraid to get up in front of people."

"That's an admirable quality. Did you know that she had put in a call to the Department of Health? It looks like she was ready to give them the information she had been... collecting."

Dana's lips pressed into a thin line. "I know. She told me."

"She didn't know you would pass that information on to the others?"

"I told her not to do it. I told her it was not the right thing to do, but she was convinced. She said what the company was doing was wrong and was against the law. But we weren't doing anything against the law."

Judging by the information that Markov had collected, that was doubtful. What they were doing was at least unethical, if not outright illegal. And having seen the dark side of transplant tourism in the past, Kenzie was sure that a lot more was probably being done behind the scenes that amounted to assault and murder. They wouldn't have let Markov see that part. Dana probably had no idea it existed. But those who were in charge were undoubtedly complicit.

"Who told you to put the beta-blocker in Dr. Markov's drink?"

Dana looked away from Detective Edwards. "I don't remember. We talked about it a few times. I didn't want to, but like you say, Mariya had already made the initial phone call. We had to do something about it. They said that the drug would act like a truth serum. It would make it easier for them to get the information they needed from her."

Kenzie noticed the switch from "he" to "they." She had admitted that other staff members knew what was going on. How many people knew that what they were doing was illegal and that Markov was going to take it to the authorities, and had decided to kill her? How many people would have taken it that far? Kenzie pictured the other people she had seen at Birch Valley and envisioned how they would have felt about it.

“Who was it that questioned Dr. Markov that night? Who was it that put their hands around her neck and tried to squeeze that information out of her?” Edwards demanded, his voice louder and more aggressive. His manner made Dana shrink back from him. She held up her hands.

“I don’t know what you’re talking about.”

“You were there when they questioned her. You drugged her so that they could; you were part of that whole operation. Was it you?” He stared pointedly at the hands Dana was holding up.

She pulled them back in horror and hugged herself, hiding her palms from sight.

“I would never do anything to hurt Mariya. What are you talking about?”

“I’m talking about the bruises around her neck.” Edwards opened his file and pulled out autopsy photos showing the bruising. “You and Dr. Markov were two of the people who disappeared for a while that evening. Where did you go? Were you the one who tried to get that information out of her?”

“No! I had already tried. I had tried to ask her about it as a friend. As someone who cared about her. But she wouldn’t tell me. She just said she kept it close to her heart.”

Kenzie nodded to herself. That had certainly been true. Dana hadn’t known how accurate Mariya had been about the files stored on the heart locket.

“So Mariya didn’t know that you were working against her. That you were informing against her even as she was trying to inform against the company. You let her think that you were her friend."

"I was her friend. I didn't want her to get hurt. No one had ever planned for her to get killed."

"No? Really?" Edwards stabbed a finger toward the photos. "You think they were just playing games? I want you to watch something." Edwards opened up an iPad and tapped on a video. "Look at her. You tell me whether she was in any shape to drive after you dosed her."

He played the video of Markov's wobbling walk toward the front door, of her dropping her clutch purse and Smythe picking it up for her, making sure that she got her keys and made it to her car.

"Does she look like she was okay to drive after you drugged her?"

"No. But... that wasn't what was supposed to happen."

"What was supposed to happen? She was supposed to just give up the location of the files, and then... what? They would take her home and put her to bed? The only reason they needed her alive was for her to tell them where the files were and who she had talked to, to make sure that she hadn't left any clues behind. You didn't seriously think they would let her keep working for the company after that?"

Dana shook her head. "I didn't think about it. I didn't think about what would happen next."

"Once they got the information they wanted, they were going to kill her anyway, weren't they?"

"Nobody killed her. That wasn't the plan."

"Do you even know what the plan was? Was this the plan?"

Edwards selected another video and played it. He pointed to make sure that Dana didn't miss what he wanted her to see. "She was never going to get home. It was better that she should suffer an accident on the way home than to be found choked to death at the party, so they let her leave. And then they chased her. They pursued her, terrified her, while she was impaired by the drug you gave her. Until she made a fatal mistake and flipped the car. And then they drove on happily home. You and Morgan Tucker and Hiram Hayes and —"

"No! I was not a part of anything like that!" Dana insisted. She stared at the vehicle on the screen where Edwards had paused it. "I wouldn't do something like that!"

"Whose vehicle is that?"

She shook her head. "It doesn't belong to anyone at Birch Valley."

"Come on. It was seen there not even a week ago."

"It doesn't belong there. It wasn't anyone that works at Birch Valley."

"Then who?"

Dana looked terrified. She looked at Edwards for a fraction of a second and then away again. She looked at the iPad screen even though it was no longer playing and the screen had dimmed, ready to shut off.

“The man in the SUV…” Dana looked at his face again, hesitating. Kenzie held her breath. She did know something. And she needed just a little more encouragement to say who it was.

“Who was it? Which of the men did you work with?”

“No. It wasn’t anyone who worked at Birch Valley. I saw him there once… maybe twice. I don’t know his name. I just know what they called him… a weird name. I can’t think of it right now. He was this blond guy. Pale skin. He was tall and thin. He had an accent, like Eastern or something. Short hair. He was… like his suit was really expensive. You could tell that. I’m no fashion expert, but his clothes were really expensive.”

Kenzie swallowed. She replayed the description in her mind and could not help flashing back to the man she had seen at the hotel, one day a year and a half before. The man who was in charge of the Russian mob in Vermont.

She tapped a quick text to Edwards.

The Oligarch.

CHAPTER 57

Kenzie saw Edwards pause as he considered the vibration of his phone. He hesitated for a moment before sliding it out to glance at the lock screen messages, then put it back away.

"The Oligarch?" he said to Dana.

She nodded, eyes lighting up. "Yes! That's what they called him. I couldn't remember. Such a weird word."

"Russian mob," Edwards suggested.

Dana cocked her head. "Uh... he sounds Russian, yeah. But..." She shook her head quickly. "Mob? I don't know anything about that."

"He is known to us."

"Well then... maybe he is. But I don't know anything about it. Why would some Russian mob guy care about what we are doing? Unless he needs a transplant, and he doesn't look like he needs a transplant. I think he's in pretty good health."

"There is only one reason for an oligarch to get involved in any business."

"What's that?"

"Because he figures it will make him a lot of money. If Birch Valley is poised to make millions, it makes perfect sense that he would be in the middle of things."

"Millions?" Dana blinked and scratched her head. "I guess it could. I mean, pharmaceuticals make a lot of money. Organ transplant... I don't know. I've seen a couple of things saying how much they can cost... but I always thought of them more as charitable. You know, the person giving the organ doesn't get anything; they're probably already dead. And living donors, I don't think they're allowed to take any payment for their organs. There are lots of rules to try to keep people from being taken advantage of."

"You're assuming he is only interested in legal transplants," Edwards pointed out. "Why would he care about following the rules? He hasn't made his money by only investing in legal ventures. He is the boss of a criminal enterprise. Don't you think there are probably more ways for him to make money in transplants by <u>not</u> following the rules?"

Dana looked a little green at this suggestion. She straightened her shirt, pulling on the collar as if it were choking her. She looked again at the picture on the table, the bruises on Markov's throat. Her one-time friend.

"You create a bidding system," Edwards suggested. "Whoever can pay the most gets the organ he wants. You folks are talking about being able to tailor-make the perfect match for him with gene editing, so it doesn't matter what the origin of the next heart or liver that comes in is. It doesn't matter what blood type or tissue type it is. You'll just edit it for compatibility. He can get to the top of the list for an organ by paying the right people. Or he provides his own organ from an unknown source."

"But that's not..."

"It doesn't matter if it is legal," Edwards told her patiently. "He's Russian mob. He does what he wants. And if that means he runs down a pedestrian on the way to the hospital and demands that you transplant her healthy organs into his dying uncle, you do it. He pays you a million or two to assuage your guilt. And the next week he brings you his favorite tyotya."

Kenzie was trying to stay focused on the conversation, even though her stomach was doing flips over the thought of the Oligarch being involved in Dr. Markov's death. Had he been the one giving the orders? From what Dana had said, it certainly sounded like a possibility.

Zachary had been worried about all of the Russian connections. Kenzie had not believed that any of them had anything to do with the Russians who had been pressuring Walter and been involved in Kenzie's abduction. And now she found the Oligarch right at the center of everything again.

Was that the reason Markov had not wanted to be involved in what the other principals in the company were suggesting? If her family had known about the Oligarch and who he was or how he was involved in the venture, then Markov's extreme measures to keep her evidence from falling into the wrong hands made sense. She thought she had been safe talking to Dana Pratt, but she had put her trust in the wrong person.

"Was the Oligarch the person who talked to Markov at the fundraiser?" Edwards asked. "Was he the one who threatened to choke her?"

Dana shook her head. "I don't know," she insisted. "There were lots of people there. Lots of people talked to Mariya. She was very popular. I don't know where she was all the time or who did that to her. And I never would have agreed to anything like that. I would have... I would have told someone."

"You would have told the police if you thought that someone was going to harm Dr. Markov?" Edwards asked skeptically.

"Yes! I wouldn't have let them hurt or kill her. I didn't know what they were planning. They lied to me about everything. I thought it was just... they would pressure her. You know, verbally. There wasn't supposed to be any physical violence. I would never have gone along with something like that."

"But you would poison her."

"It wasn't supposed to harm her. It was just... so that she would be more susceptible to pressure. She would agree to do what they said and turn over the documents she was going to leak."

"But it didn't work out that way. Why didn't you tell us what happened when you realized it?"

"What? I just thought it was an accident."

"After you drugged her. You must have seen how she was wobbling around the fundraiser an hour later."

"No. I didn't know it would affect her driving or that she would have an accident."

Edwards sat back, looking at her skeptically.

"Who was it that told you to give her the beta-blocker? Was it the Oligarch?"

"No, it was Dr.— it was someone else."

CHAPTER 58

Kenzie had known when Edwards booked Dana for assault that she would not be in custody for long. So, she was not surprised when Edwards called her to apologize for the fact that Dana had been released.

"There just isn't enough space to hold people until trial," he explained. "Unless someone is an obvious threat to the public or herself, we can't hold her until trial. This is Dana Pratt's first involvement with the police. She has no record, no history of violence of any kind. She has ties in the community and has no reputation for violence or anger issues."

Kenzie found it hard to believe it was the first time Dana hurt anyone. Most people who had been nonviolent their whole lives did not find it easy to make the shift and physically harm someone, even if they were angry. And Dana had been pretty determined to hurt Kenzie.

She blew out her breath and told Edwards she understood. "It's outside your control; I get that. If she is released on her own recognizance or on bail, there isn't anything you can do about it."

"No. I did get conditions attached to her bail that she cannot have any contact with you, but that's as much as I could do. You can apply for a restraining order as well."

"Yeah. I've seen how well those work." Kenzie had seen enough women come into the morgue whose exes had broken restraining orders repeatedly to assault and eventually kill them. She knew that the police did what they could to enforce such orders, but there was nothing they could do until they were broken, and then it was too late.

Edwards sighed. "She seems reasonable enough; maybe she'll be smart and obey the conditions. But these guys really seem to have her brainwashed about the righteousness of what they are doing. And as long as they are getting informed consent for legitimate medical procedures performed within the confines of the law, there isn't much I can do about it. Even knowing the Oligarch is involved... I need to catch him or his people breaking the law. I can't just break up their operation because I think they're ruthless Russian vultures."

"We just have to do the best we can," Kenzie agreed. It wasn't the first time she'd had to deal with the turmoil caused by the Oligarch and his minions. It probably wouldn't be the last. One day someone would take him down, whether it were law enforcement or a bigger fish. "Thanks for doing what you could."

"Take care of yourself. You've got Delaney taking care of you for a while?"

"For a bit," Kenzie agreed. She didn't know how long Zachary would insist on her having protection. But at least she'd had someone there when she had been attacked. Who knew how badly she might have been hurt by Dana if Hal hadn't been close at hand?

* * *

Hal was standing by as Kenzie prepared to go home.

“How are you feeling?” he inquired. “If you are at all dizzy or lightheaded, I can drive, and your car will be safe here until tomorrow.”

“No, I’m not having any concussion symptoms. Just a little bit of a bump on the noggin. Not anything to worry about.”

“Swelling on the outside is better than swelling on the inside, or so I’ve been told.”

“Definitely,” Kenzie agreed. She stretched and rolled her shoulders. “I’m ready for a quiet night tonight.”

Hal nodded. “Let me just scout ahead,” he told her. Kenzie waited while he walked the route to the elevator, locked the elevator so that it could not be called to another floor, and then returned to escort her.

When they reached Kenzie's level in the parking garage, Hal insisted on doing the same thing again, leaving her there with a security guard while he scouted the route to Kenzie's parking space.

Kenzie heard him shout when he was out of sight. The sound went through her like an electric shock, jolting her stiff. Her heart pumped hard, and she stepped forward, wanting to help him. But there was nothing she could do for him. He was the one with a weapon and the proper training. She would only be in the way. But she reached for her phone. She could call for more help in case the situation called for more hands on deck.

But as she reached for her phone, the security guard touched her arm, stopping her. He held his radio to his mouth. "Assistance needed for Dr. Kirsch," he barked.

A racing engine sounded almost immediately. Kenzie turned toward the noise, looking for one of the white security vehicles. Instead, it was a black SUV. Kenzie stared, frozen, unsure what to do.

The guard put his hand on her shoulder, holding her still. She didn't move, afraid of being caught between the guard and the Russian mob during a firestorm.

The SUV pulled up close. Kenzie stared at her white face reflected in the tinted windows, her mouth opened in a surprised O.

One of the doors flew open.

The security guard grabbed Kenzie and shoved her into the vehicle, into the arms of another man inside the car.

Kenzie resisted too late, shocked by the push from behind. She tried to escape the hands that grasped her and held her in place. The security guard hopped agilely into the vehicle and pulled the door shut.

The SUV immediately took off with a screech of tires. It was crowded with the three of them in one row, struggling as the SUV spun around the ramp, headed for the exit.

Kenzie protested and swore and tried to escape their grasps, but it was hopeless. They did not throw her to the floor or put a bag over her head, as they had the first time she had been abducted, and Kenzie didn't know whether that was better or worse. If they let her see their faces, it meant they intended to kill her, didn't it?

She couldn't help turning on the security guard, furious that he had let this happen or been a part of it. He just grinned back at her. Not one of the guards that she knew. She had seen the unfamiliar face when she and Hal had stepped out of the elevator, but she had not understood the danger she was in.

He was not a real security guard, but someone standing in to help facilitate the abduction. Had they hurt the regular guards? Killed them? Or just thrown them tied up in a service area or storeroom?

“Who are you, and why are you doing this?” Kenzie demanded.

She seethed, angry that she had let this happen again. That they had fooled her. That they might have hurt the men who were there every day to protect her. That they were going to put her through this nightmare again, and her family, and Zachary. And what about Hal? Had they hurt or killed him just for being there to keep Kenzie safe?

She was furious that they could just walk in and do what they liked. The Oligarch used violence or his money to get everything he wanted. Why did that have to involve her? Why did he care that she was investigating Markov’s death or that she had been asking questions at Birch Valley? Did it really affect him? Cost him money? Why not just ignore her investigation?

CHAPTER 59

The guard just ignored her. The man on her other side said something in Russian that made him laugh. They both smirked. The guard hadn't shown any weapon, but the other man had a handgun in a holster close to his hand. The man who was driving didn't say anything to anyone else. He apparently already knew where he was going, and there was no discussion of what to do next now that they had Kenzie.

Kenzie nursed her anger. She wasn't going to shut down. She wasn't going to let them push her around. The first time she had been abducted, she had succumbed to the shock and the violence, not to mention the blow to her head, and her body and brain had shut down, making her the perfect victim, determined to please her captors, to survive by compliance.

But that wasn't what had saved her. Walter had stepped in and negotiated for her release. He had buckled to the pressure they had put on him to help lobby against a bill before the Senate. They had succeeded in winning his compliance by using Kenzie as leverage.

This time, they were not using her against Walter. They just wanted to shut her up. Kenzie's compliance would just lead to a grave somewhere in the Vermont wilderness, and the best she could hope for was a beautiful, peaceful location.

Only by keeping her wits about her and by fighting back did she have any chance of escaping them.

She fought back against the logical part of her mind that wanted to know how she expected to escape from three capable Russian mobsters, at least one of whom was armed and sitting only inches away from her. But she shut this part of her mind down, compartmentalized it, and would not let it speak. She would find a way to escape. She was smart. She was resourceful. And she had other people on her side.

It wasn't just her against the men. Hal would raise the alarm. If they hadn't silenced him, Zachary would know something was wrong within ten minutes. He knew the police. He knew Campbell, and he knew Edwards was on the case. She had the full force of the law, Zachary's private investigator mind, Hal's insight into organized crime, and her father's experience with the Russians. She was not alone, even if it felt like it.

"You need to let me go," Kenzie told the men, her voice strong. "The police will be on to you in minutes. You won't get away with this. You'll just end up in prison. You should just let me go if you want to avoid trouble. Tell the Oligarch," she paused to emphasize the fact that she knew who their boss was, "that his plan failed, and if he wants to keep his transplant business a secret, he's too late. The cops have already figured it out, and they are going to shut him down."

"That's funny," the phony security guard said, but he didn't laugh at her words. "The little woman thinking she can order around someone like the Oligarch."

"I've beaten him before."

He failed to disguise his surprise at this remark.

"Yeah, he didn't tell you that, huh? I forced him to move his operations. To shut things down. But apparently, that wasn't enough. Maybe this time, he'll get arrested. How do you think he'll like that?"

"What will you do?" He showed her his teeth in the threatening smile of a shark. "You can't even get out of this seat. You can't do anything."

"You'd be surprised." Kenzie forced herself to smile back and look confident. They couldn't tell how scared she was. She wouldn't allow the fear to crack her veneer. She would only let them see her anger and determination. "I don't need a gun, because I have knowledge. I know what he is doing. And he can't afford that. He thought he would shut down the leak by killing Dr. Markov. But he was wrong. That didn't stop anything. She still got us her files. We still learned all about his plans and got proof of what he had been doing. Because she was smarter than he was. He thought that he could bully and threaten his way through. He thought that he could silence her. But he was wrong. She still managed to pass on the files she had copied."

The guard looked at the other man. He shrugged. "I don't know anything about any of the files. I do know that the suka is dead."

"Killing will not get him what he wants. My people already know everything. They know about the transplants. They know about the files. Dana Pratt has told them what she knows. It's over. Tell him he may as well shut his business down, because the police will not let him continue now."

The two Russians spoke with each other. They must have known that she couldn't understand them and they could talk openly. Or maybe it didn't matter whether she could understand them or not, since they didn't intend for her ever to be able to talk to anyone else about it.

They didn't call anyone or need to get any new instructions. They were not concerned about the police showing up and breaking up the party.

The security guard grabbed Kenzie and pulled on her arm, jerking her halfway to her feet. Kenzie was so startled that she didn't even resist. Not that resisting would have done her any good. It was obvious that either man was stronger than she was and could have taken control of her with little effort. Together, they were an overwhelming force, even without the second man's gun or the third man driving.

He had lifted Kenzie up for one reason, which became immediately apparent. He forced the cell phone out of her pocket, and in a second, had opened the SUV door and thrown it out. Kenzie's heart was pounding hard. She couldn't stop to mourn the phone. A phone could be replaced. Their actions told her that they were worried about being tracked.

They didn't want anyone to know where they were taking Kenzie.

So they weren't going to kill her right away. If they were, there would be no need to worry about the police tracking her location. They could quickly stab or shoot her, toss her out of the car, and be gone before anyone could stop them. The police would be welcome to track her phone and find her body, and she would make her way back to the morgue through the loading dock rather than her usual route.

But there was not going to be a body for Dr. Wiltshire to autopsy, or to recuse himself and have another pathologist in to autopsy. Because Kenzie was going to outwit them. The police knew about the Russians' involvement. They would be able to find her. They would shut down the Oligarch's little organ trafficking ring. He would be forced to move his business again, to reorganize. Maybe they would even have enough to arrest him and put him behind bars. Kidnapping a government employee was not a smart move.

Kenzie lifted her chin and looked at them boldly, committing everything she could to memory. Not just their faces, but also the things that were not quick fixes. Ears were as unique as fingerprints. The men could not change the shape of their heads and their hands. They wouldn't bother to change the pattern of the freckles on their hands. A disguise or some quick plastic surgery might change their faces and tattoos, but she would still be able to recognize them by other features. By the size and shape of their bodies, the way they moved, their voices as they spoke to each other in their clipped, guttural mother tongue.

"You'd better call him and tell him to shut things down before the police arrive," Kenzie told the security guard. "He's going to need to go underground."

They paid her no mind. They didn't talk to the driver. He didn't appear to be worried about what their kidnappee had to say. Maybe he didn't even understand English. They were going to continue as previously planned, unconcerned about the possibility that the police could disrupt any of the Oligarch's plans.

While one part of her mind worried that they were taking her to some remote location with a handy lake or ravine, she stayed in control of her emotions. She couldn't stop the wild beating of her heart, but she didn't have to show them how scared she was. They were not going to kill her right away. They had already shown her that.

They were out of Roxboro in a few minutes but stayed on the main highway. They didn't immediately wander off into the wilds to find a nice remote dump location. She again tried to push the thought out of her mind.

She didn't have to count the turns or listen for clues as to where they were taking her. She was not blindfolded. She just watched the highway and the road signs and waited to see where they would turn. She knew that meant they never meant to let her go or to talk to anyone outside the organization again, but she focused on her anger. Focused on the fact that they wanted something from her, or they wouldn't be bothering to keep her alive. A dead prisoner was much easier to control than a living one. She might not be actively trying to escape, but she would be watching for an opportunity, and they had to know that she could try to signal passing motorists or do something to attract attention.

They wanted her alive, and that meant that she would have opportunities. Sometime along the way, she would get the chance to escape, negotiate, or signal. Time meant opportunities.

The same exit Kenzie had taken when she had gone to talk to Cora Smythe about her husband's death. About halfway between Roxboro and Burlington. Had there been another connection between Birch Valley and the security guard? Or was it just coincidental? Smythe had not been Russian. Or at least, Kenzie had not seen any obvious Russian connections. No Russian name, no Slavic features, no Russian prison ink or dental work. His wife had not had an accent and had not given any indication of a Russian connection. She had talked about medical companies. Smythe had worked for more than one of them.

Before long, they were pulling to a stop behind a large brick building. Kenzie was not familiar enough with the town to know for sure what it was. A research building? An old factory?

The guard opened his door and grabbed Kenzie by the arm. “Out you get.”

She tried to jerk back from him, but he kept an iron grip on her arm. “Don’t be silly. You’ll just get hurt.”

“Let go of me, and I’ll come with you.”

He snorted. He obviously wasn’t going to give her the opportunity to dart away from him. He had no reason to believe she would stick to the promise to come with him.

"You're hurting me," she complained, hoping he would at least loosen his grip.

"Too bad."

He said something to the other man, who came with them, drawing his gun out of its holster. The driver did not get out of the SUV, but drove away as soon as they were out. The two Russians escorted Kenzie into the white corridors of the building.

CHAPTER 60

"What is this place?" Kenzie asked, looking around.

It was obviously a clinical setting. Some kind of hospital, research lab, or private clinic. She remembered the private psychiatric clinic that Zachary had been held at, but it wasn't the same place. She knew all the major hospitals in northern Vermont, but this was not one of them.

"Why don't you shut up now?" the guard suggested.

Kenzie was watching for the opportunity to shout out to someone for help. But the few people she saw as she was escorted through the corridors apparently did not think there was anything surprising about a woman being escorted through the halls at gunpoint and were therefore not likely to do anything to help her. They looked back down at their clipboards or straight ahead at their next destination and did not question the Russians' right to be there or what they were doing with a gun.

"You're not going to get away with this," Kenzie warned, aware that she was talking like some TV character. Empty threats. The Russians knew that they were just empty threats. Kenzie couldn't do anything to hurt them. The police had no way to track her location. They might have enough information to zero in on the Oligarch and make some trouble for him. Still, unless Kenzie was in the same location as the Russian mobster, there was no way for them to find her, and she doubted he was at the hospital unless he needed a transplant himself.

"You want to go to prison?" she demanded.

The Russian with the gun made a comment. The security guard looked at Kenzie. "American prisons," he scoffed. "Club fed."

"Have you ever been there?" She scanned his exposed skin for prison ink, but did not see any. "You might not find it as easy as you think."

“Not a problem,” he assured her.

They escorted her without saying much. Kenzie looked around, keeping alert, trying to take in everything she saw in case it afforded her more information on their operation, a tool, or way to escape. She needed to be smart and not let herself shut down. She could have a good cry about it later, tell Zachary and Dr. B about the experience. Until then, she needed to hold it together.

“In here.” The guard motioned to a closed door. There was a lock on the door requiring a key. If it was a secure unit, she would not be able to open the door from the inside without a key. There was no swipe card or electronic access, just a good, old-fashioned key, which the guard supplied, unlocking the room. He stepped back and motioned for Kenzie to enter the room.

Kenzie turned the handle and pushed the door open. It was a small patient room. A bed, bedside table built into the wall, and little else. No curtain on a track around the bed. They had the usual outlets and oxygen access on the wall, a call button, and a night-time light over the head of the bed for patient use. There was no IV pole or equipment. There was no door to a bathroom. A secure room, with limited ways for a patient to hurt herself or someone else.

"Sit on the bed," the man with the gun told her. Kenzie took her time obeying. She didn't overtly oppose him. Didn't tell him no, try to fight back, or to run. But she thought about all of her options, considered whether there was any way to get out or signal for help. She hoped that she would be able to put her medical knowledge to use to escape from the room or attract the attention of someone who would be sympathetic to her plight.

The man motioned with his gun, and Kenzie walked over and sat on the bed.

"Good." He looked at the guard and said something in Russian. They both just looked at her for a moment.

"You will be our guest for a while," the guard told her eventually. "You be a good guest and don't cause us any trouble. Maybe then... you will survive. If you are going to cause trouble..." He shook his head. "That will be too bad."

"What, you will make me the next donor?" Kenzie asked. She watched their eyes carefully to see if they understood what she was talking about. They exchanged a glance, but didn't say anything to her about the transplants.

"What about a bathroom?" Kenzie asked. "I don't see any facilities."

"You do not need anything right now. You will wait." The guard approached her, and Kenzie drew back warily. The man with the gun kept it trained on her, clearly indicating that she was to stay still.

Kenzie knew what was coming before the guard touched her. He grabbed her arm and held it still while he put a hard restraint handcuff around it. Kenzie pulled against it, her body rebelling at being tied. “Hey!”

“Sit or lie down so I can put the other side on.”

“No. One restraint will keep me here. I don’t want any others. I want to be able to move around the bed, not to be forced to stay in one position.”

“Did I ask you what you wanted?”

“Please,” Kenzie said reasonably. She pulled on the restraint, demonstrating how secure it was. “I’m not getting out of this. The only reason you need to put a patient into restraints on both sides is so that they can’t harm themselves. I’m not going to harm myself. You just want to keep me in place.”

He looked at the other man, who shrugged as if he didn’t care. After another moment of consideration, the guard decided that was enough and didn’t force her to lie in the bed so he could secure her other wrist. Or even worse, the ankle restraints as well. She had no idea how she would get out, but she had a better chance if she only had one limb restrained than all four.

Animals managed to get out of snares and traps. But animals chewed off their legs. Kenzie wasn't planning to go to that extreme. She would find another way.

There was a reason handcuffs were only considered by the police to be temporary restraints, or that patients in restraints were supposed to be checked every fifteen minutes.

The two men left the room and shut the door behind them. Kenzie did not hear a key turn in the lock, but it was possible that the door would lock as soon as it was shut without needing to be manually locked.

Kenzie sat on the bed and looked around the room, searching for any way to escape her wrist restraint and from the room.

CHAPTER 61

Kenzie heard voices come and go. She imagined various scenarios as footsteps echoed past her door. People who knew she was being held there and why. People who didn't know what kind of a facility it was or that anyone was being held there against her will. Doctors and security guards, nurses and interns. Would the doctors do rounds like they would at a regular hospital? If so, would they assume that her room was empty or would someone come in and ask her what was going on?

Was this where they did the surgical procedures to transplant the genetically edited organs? Was it where they did the editing? A recovery facility, a place that was only used to observe the transplant patients for any sign that they were negatively reacting to the foreign organ?

It sounded like one of the voices in the hall had stopped directly outside her door. Kenzie held her breath and considered her options. Should she yell to attract attention?

Keep quiet? Hide on the other side of the bed so she wasn't visible when he came in the door? She couldn't exactly get to the other side of the bed with one wrist chained to the rail. She had experimented with the length of the chain to see how far she could move around the room still on the chain. It wasn't far.

There was the sound of a key in the lock. She couldn't hold her breath anymore, but let it out and stood up, looking around the room for some means of escape. She felt safer on her feet, but it was an illusion.

The door opened, and an older, balding man with a narrow fringe of short white hair slipped into the room and pulled the door shut behind him.

It took Kenzie several long seconds to process. She opened her mouth, shocked.

"Dr. Hayes! Am I glad to see you!"

He stared at her, smiling politely. They had only met once before; clearly he didn't remember her.

"It's Dr. Kirsch," Kenzie reminded him. "From the medical examiner's office."

"Yes?"

"I'm..." Kenzie fumbled, trying to find the words. "I'm being held prisoner here. Thank goodness you came along. Would you unlock me, and then we can call for help..."

His expression did not change. Was he in the early stages of dementia? If he were, it would have been easy to take advantage of him for the project. Dr. Tucker and the others could convince him to do whatever they wanted. She should have noticed the warning signs when they had spoken before. But dementia patients had good days and bad days. Some days, they seemed normal, until they hit a particularly challenging or stressful incident, and then the deficits became more apparent. Dr. Hayes hadn't expected to find her there, and his brain was struggling to fill the gaps and come up with an explanation. Kenzie tried to bring him up to speed before his brain could manufacture an explanation that would not serve her.

“There is… a very bad man—a gangster—who is holding me here. He is involved in a lot of criminal activities. He’s trying to use your clinic for his own purposes. We need to call the police and get this taken care of right away. Before he can hurt anyone else or figure out that we know who he is and what he is doing.”

“Is that so?”

“Yes!” Kenzie was getting desperate. She pulled on the restraint. “Do you have the key to open one of these? I need to get out.”

He drew a few steps closer to her. “Now, why would I do that?” he asked gently. “After I went to all the trouble to have you brought here?”

Kenzie shivered with a sudden chill. Goosebumps raced over her from head to toe.

No.

No, no, no.

Kenzie brought her hands up to her face, one hand pulled short by the restraints, and she tried to force her brain to process this and come up with a suggestion. But she was stunned. Frozen. All of the willpower she had been using to hold herself together dissolved.

Not Hayes.

Not that nice old doctor who had been so pleasant and polite with her. He was, she was sure, the same with everyone. Just a nice, old gentleman who wanted to help people. The healer.

Why did she always fall for the nice old man?

"It's all right," Dr. Hayes told her. "You weren't supposed to know. No one else would have guessed it either."

He walked farther into the room and sat at the end of the bed. As if he were a friend there to comfort her. "I don't have the size and strength of the young people today. They are taller with every generation, and I was never a jock in my day. I was much more interested in books and science than in the playing field. And as I have aged, I have only become more..." He smiled beatifically, "More adorable. More trustworthy. More harmless."

"You had me brought here? You are the one who is... in charge of all of this? The transplant program? What happened to Dr. Markov? You?"

"I know. You can hardly believe it, can you?"

Kenzie was speechless.

"But why?"

She expected him to tell her what she had heard from Dana, his acolyte. How many people out there were suffering and would die on the transplant waiting list. How her withdrawal of the foundation's money from Birch Valley had crippled them so that they were no longer able to proceed with the work they had planned. And so they had made a lateral move. A project that would bring in enough money from wealthy patients to be self-sustaining.

"Because it is profitable," he told her with a shrug. "Because I like money and all the comforts it can bring me. I should be comfortable in my old age, shouldn't I? Why shouldn't I be able to do what I want to, and to do it in style?" He shifted, getting more comfortable in his seat at the end of the bed. "I love what I do. I love the research and the practical application of years of study. But I don't want to sit around in a drafty apartment with nothing but a stray cat to keep me company." His eyes sparkled. "I want all of the comforts money can buy."

He reached over to pat her knee, playing the part of the pleasant old gentleman to the hilt.

Kenzie grabbed his wrist. She had been furious ever since the guard had forced her into the SUV, but had not been able to fight back. Not against three grown men bigger and stronger than she was, against firearms, against locks and keys. But she did not have to let this old man paw at her. She grabbed him, twisted his arm, and held him tightly, pulling him closer so they were eye-to-eye.

His face registered shock. He was politely surprised that Kenzie would grab him and that she was so angry.

“Unlock me,” Kenzie ordered.

He tried to draw back from her. Kenzie kept a tight grip on him. She glanced toward the door, worried that a guard would peek in to see how everything was going. She remembered which pocket Dr. Hayes had put his keys into. She pulled him closer so she would be able to reach them.

"Unlock me now."

He gave another little shake to make her let him go, but she didn't.

"Miss Kirsch, you don't want to do this."

"Dr. Kirsch," she corrected.

He nodded. "Dr. Kirsch. Of course. I am so sorry, but that is not possible. You need to let me go. I am not alone here. You can't get away with this. Now, let's not do something you are going to regret..."

"What I would regret is not taking any chance I get," Kenzie told him. "Now reach into your pocket and get out your keys, and nothing else. I want this unlocked."

"What makes you think I have the key for that? I wasn't the one who locked it."

"I think you're the kind of guy who comes prepared."

He tried one more time to pull out of her grasp. She didn't loosen her grip. With one more disappointed look, Dr. Hayes reached into his pocket and daintily pulled out a ring of keys. Of course if he had the room key he also had the restraint cuff key. Kenzie transferred her grip on Dr. Hayes's wrist to her handcuffed hand, and used the free one to take the keys from him, sort out the handcuff key, and unlock herself. After a second of consideration, she pulled the cuff around Hayes's wrist and locked it up. He pulled against it in anger, his eyes flashing.

He lost all of the cheery old guy persona. "You get this off of me right now!" he ordered in a steely voice. He jerked hard on the handcuff as if it might just snap if he willed it to. Kenzie walked around to the other side of the bed to grab the other wrist cuff. He avoided her grasp as she tried to catch his other arm.

"Stop this right now!" He raised his voice to a shout. "Someone, some help in here!" His voice echoed in the bare room with all of its hard surfaces. But there was no response from the hall. Whoever he had been talking with just a minute earlier had obviously gone on to do something else and was out of earshot. But Kenzie was sure that other people would be coming by to check on her all too soon. The clinic was not empty. It was not bustling like a public hospital, but there was enough staff around that she was not going to be able to get away with much without anyone noticing her escape.

She slapped Hayes on the thigh. A loud, ringing slap that made her hand sting and provoked a yelp and a reflex reaction from him as he reached for the spot with his free hand to rub the injury and protect it from further assault. Kenzie grabbed the hand and slapped the other cuff around it. While Hayes whooped and hollered in a voice that was high enough to be a woman's, Kenzie shortened the tether on each cuff so that Hayes didn't have any play, each arm stretched out to the side railing.

With both of his hands out of the way, Kenzie went through his pockets. He spat and swore and tried to bite her, but Kenzie had dealt with enough combative patients during her residency not to be concerned about his straining and threatening her. He didn't have much that Kenzie could use. She had the keys already. She took his phone. He had a nice silver-plated, inscribed pen. Some paper clips bent into random shapes. A money clip with a big wad of money folded into it. His slim, minimalist wallet with his ID and a black credit card.

Kenzie wasn't a thief by nature, but she thought it best to relieve him of these items for now, in case they might come in handy for her, or alternatively if Hayes got free, she could prevent him from using any of them for the first few minutes, maybe giving her a bit more time in her bid to escape. So she pocketed them all despite Hayes's bitter protests. Kenzie considered leaving him with the pen. It was, after all, a personal item, and she didn't need it. But she didn't want him to be able to use the sharply-pointed pen as a weapon or to disassemble it and use the cartridge to unlock the handcuffs.

He could have the pen back after he was arrested.

Kenzie went to the door and inserted the key into the lock. She pressed her ear against the door, listening for anything happening in the hall nearby. Straining her ears, she could not hear a sound. She knew the door couldn't be soundproof, or she wouldn't have been able to hear Hayes talking before he entered. She turned the handle slowly and opened the door just a crack, watching and listening. It wouldn't make sense for them to leave her alone there without some kind of guard. She had been handcuffed and locked in the room, but things could still happen. Anyone who worked in a hospital knew that. One sneaky psych patient could wreak havoc.

Today, <u>she</u> would be that sneaky psych patient.

There was no sound from the hallway, so Kenzie slipped out the door and pulled the door shut with a quiet click. She tried the handle to make sure it was engaged. Hayes started to shout again, but his tenor voice was close enough to Kenzie's that the Russians might not immediately realize it was Hayes calling out for help rather than Kenzie.

She walked down the hallway, forcing herself to go slowly and not attract attention to herself from anyone who might enter the hallway for some errand. She walked close to the wall. She lowered her head and looked down at Hayes's phone. It had not occurred to her to unlock the phone before leaving him behind in the room. She wasn't going to go back there to hold it in front of his face to unlock it. She tried 1-2-3-4 and a couple of other passcodes that she knew from her work as a medical examiner were very common. It didn't unlock. She swiped to the Emergency Call screen and swore under her breath when she couldn't get a signal. No bars. She couldn't do much with the phone other than use it as a prop, walking down the hall looking at it so that she looked like any intern or other Gen Z with her phone always in her hands and her head down.

There was laughter somewhere close, making Kenzie jump and look around for the source. She could hear only snatches of conversation as they laughed about the woman screaming her head off when no one had done anything to hurt her yet. She shook off another chill. She was free for the moment, but she wouldn't stay that way if she let her focus be distracted and didn't stay aware of everything going on around her.

Let them laugh. Let them mock. They wouldn't be doing so once the police showed up or they discovered it was Hayes chained to that bed.

Kenzie reached the end of the hallway and opened the door to the stairwell. Signs warned that the fire exits were alarmed, but Kenzie was unconcerned. If alarms were triggered, they were triggered. If she were lucky, fire and other first responders would be called to the building and would evacuate it while they checked to see if there actually was a fire. They probably wouldn't evacuate. They would just walk around looking for what had set the alarm off. And then Kenzie would be able to grab them and get help. Or they might find Dr. Hayes chained to the bed and demand an explanation that would be difficult for him to give.

CHAPTER 62

Zachary saw Hal's name on the caller ID and swiped to answer the call.

"Hal? I thought you were on your way. Is she holding you up?" he teased. Maybe a fresh body had come in, and Kenzie was stuck logging it in along with any evidence before she could leave. It had sounded like they were on their way out the door, but sometimes things didn't work out as expected. Especially if he was talking about Kenzie coming home from work at the end of the day. The woman liked her job.

"Zachary… there's been trouble," Hal's voice was a deep rumble, triggering all kinds of worries about what might have happened.

Zachary gripped the phone more tightly. "What? What happened?"

"There was an ambush. They… got Kenzie."

"What?" It was a good thing he was already sitting down, or he probably would have collapsed. "What do you mean they got her? That was what you were hired to prevent!"

"I know," Hal sounded miserable. "It was all set up... a diversion for me to investigate, only to be ambushed. I left Kenzie with the security guard. But... he was a decoy. As soon as I was out of the way, they swooped in and snatched her."

She must have been terrified. Zachary remembered the tears and panic when she had finally told him about the first abduction, months after it had happened. How even saying the word "kidnapped" was nearly impossible for her. And now it was all happening again. She must be paralyzed with fear.

"We have to find her, get her back," he said urgently. "Call the police and let them know what you saw and heard. We have to get her."

"Cops are already here. They're pulling all the video they can. Parking garage, traffic cams, whatever they can get from retail or doorbell cams. We'll find out everything we can."

"What about her phone?"

"They'll contact her provider and see where it is pinging. With any luck, it will lead us right to her."

Zachary wasn't expecting that kind of luck. If the Russians were involved, as Kenzie now conceded, they wouldn't make the mistake of letting her phone be tracked right to her. But they'd follow it as far as it led.

"She shares her location with me," he told Hal. "Hang on while I check what it says."

Hal wasn't one of those people who kept talking when Zachary said to wait while he checked another app on his phone. Hal actually stopped and waited, not trying to tell Zachary anything else or ask any questions while he was waiting for the friends app to pop up Kenzie's last known location.

"It's still showing up in Roxboro," Zachary said, disappointed that it wasn't farther away. If it was still in Roxboro, they had disposed of it almost immediately. "Looks like they headed north. I'll track it down and then join you at the police station."

"Okay," Hal agreed.

"Anything else I should know?"

He didn't think that they would know much yet. Best to let them get all the information they could first, and then try to put it all together in a way that would lead them directly to Kenzie.

"She was taken in the black SUV that chased Dr. Markov down the day she died. The vehicle that a witness said belongs to the Oligarch."

He knew it was the Russians.

Zachary swore, a tight knot of fear in his stomach. That was all he needed. The Russian kingpin himself being involved in the abduction. What did they want? What were they going to do? Kenzie didn't have anything they wanted. The last time, they had used her as leverage against her father, but as far as they were concerned now, Walter had suffered a stroke and was no longer able to provide the services they had wanted from him. So why did they want Kenzie this time? Other than to get her out of the way.

He couldn't remember later how he had ended the phone call with Hal. Whether he had just hung up, said nothing, or carried on a conversation with one part of his brain while the other part tried to sort it all out and devise a plan to find and rescue Kenzie.

He followed the signal on his phone to find Kenzie's, screen cracked, lying on the sidewalk where it had been tossed. He put on a glove before picking it up and slid it immediately into a bag for protection. He looked down the road in the direction they had gone, as if he might be able to see all the way to where they were holding her or figure out their plan just by seeing the direction they had gone.

He headed immediately to the police station, where he met with Hal, Sergeant Campbell, and Detective Edwards. He handed Campbell Kenzie's phone. "You might get lucky and pull prints from that, if he wasn't wearing gloves."

Campbell nodded. "We'll have a look."

He didn't say, "Highly unlikely," which was what Zachary was thinking.

"I know it hasn't been very long," he said, "but what do you have so far, other than that they went north?"

"It's slow work. Highway cams confirm that they were going north, but we don't know yet how far, which exit they took.

We'll keep searching. How much do you know about the situation?"

"I know she was investigating two connected deaths. That it was something to do with the Russian mob. I know she's been threatened lately, but I thought you got the person responsible for that?"

"And had to release her again, yes," Edwards confirmed. "Bail conditions that she couldn't get anywhere near Dr. Kirsch. But we both know a piece of paper doesn't give her any actual protection. It doesn't look like the woman who made the threats had anything to do with the abduction. She was already gone by the time that happened. She didn't hang around the police station, talk to the guys that did this."

"Do you know who was in the van? Was this Russian in the van?"

"Just thugs, from what we can tell. Windows are tinted, so it is hard to get a camera angle that shows anything, but they don't appear to match the reported appearance of the Oligarch."

"What do they want her for? Why did they take her?"

Detective Edwards shook his head slowly. "Dr. Kirsch is very good at what she does. Not only did she figure out that Dr. Markov's accident was actually murder, but she was also the one who discovered the hidden files and the encryption code needed to read them. This whole operation with the company going around the established procedures for transplants and using experimental methods on whoever is desperate enough to afford their prices..."

"How could that be going on without anyone knowing about it?"

Detective Edwards shook his head, lips pressed tightly together. "It couldn't. Not really. They could do it without the authorities finding out about it and fining them for unethical human experimentation, and apparently have, but they couldn't do it without anyone knowing. They had to have researchers, lab technicians, doctors, nurses, anesthetists, a facility with staff, cleaners, security guards... and of course, the patients he's performing procedures on and their families."

Zachary rubbed his bristly chin. "That's a lot of people. You're right. A lot of people know what he was doing, and where."

"Even if they were only doing it on a small scale... they either need their own facility or access to an operating theater."

Zachary's brain was going in a dozen different directions at once, testing theories, running through possibilities, trying to figure out the most efficient method of investigation. Kenzie was in danger, and the longer it took to find her, the more likely it was that she would be harmed. He knew how terrified she must be and was desperate to end the nightmare for her as quickly as possible.

CHAPTER 63

They had data, plenty of data, and Zachary needed to find a way to process it all and form a plan.

“The patients…” he said slowly. “You know some details about them. Because of the case studies. Have you been able to identify who any of them are? Are their names ever mentioned in any of the documents?”

Detective Edwards shook his head grimly. “We haven’t had much time, or maybe I would have more for you. But the fact is, their family members don’t want them to be identified. The doctors who operated on them and other people involved in their care don’t want them to be identified.”

“What about when they died? Can Dr. Wiltshire match the descriptions of their illnesses or complications up with patients he did autopsies on?”

“Generally speaking, patients under a doctor’s care do not come through the medical examiner’s office. Unless the doctor or the family requests it. And in this case, they want to keep it quiet, because they know what they are doing is illegal or unethical."

"Are we sure that none of them were ever reviewed by the medical examiner's office? What about a son or daughter who thought something weird went on with Mom or Dad's medical care and wanted to know what it was? Maybe they ask for a review, not knowing the parent would have wanted it kept quiet."

"Well... that's a possibility, I suppose. We'll have Dr. Wiltshire review the case studies with an eye toward identifying if any of those bodies came through the medical examiner's office."

Zachary rubbed his head. "And maybe Dr. Cook too. Because Dr. Wiltshire hasn't been doing the autopsies for the last six months. Dr. Cook might remember something that Dr. Wiltshire wasn't around for."

"Dr. Cook isn't exactly in our good books right now. He might refuse to cooperate."

"Refuse? When Kenzie's been kidnapped?" Zachary knew his voice was raised in outrage, but couldn't tone it down. "If he does, you let me know, and *I'll* talk to him."

Edwards gave him a small grin. "All right, Zachary. I'll do that. Now, unfortunately, there is not much that you can do right now except wait to see if our investigation turns something up or we hear from the kidnappers."

"She wasn't taken for ransom. The kidnappers are not going to call you. Or me. Or anyone. It isn't about ransom."

The whole scheme had been about money. Zachary was pretty sure of that. But Kenzie's kidnapping wasn't an attempt to get more money. It was about protecting themselves and their operation.

And that did not bode well for Kenzie.

Zachary refused to think about what the chances were she was still alive and would be when they found her. The Russians were ruthless. They would not hesitate to murder to achieve their goals.

“Her family has money, don’t they?” Edwards pointed out. “That woman scientist was really upset about their funding being pulled. Wanted Kenzie to give it back. If her family offered to fund Birch Valley again at the levels that they were before...”

“That woman was just a small fish,” Zachary disagreed. “She thinks that people are going to die because the family foundation pulled the money. But they’re not. The patients that the Russians are catering to are not indigent. They don’t need any outside funding. They are the people who can afford to pay hundreds of thousands of dollars for a black-market organ.”

Campbell nodded his agreement.

Edwards shrugged. “Then why did they take her? If it wasn’t for ransom, then why snatch her?”

“I’m trying to work that out. If they wanted to stop her, it would have been easier to shoot her than to kidnap her. So why didn’t they? Why didn’t they just drive by in that black SUV and mow her down instead of going to all of the trouble to set up a diversion and a fake security guard?”

“They wanted to get her cleanly away for some reason.”

Zachary’s brain raced in all directions, trying to gather all the information.

The mention of Kenzie’s parents and the possibility of ransom stuck in his head. The Russians didn’t want money from them. But they had been trying to get Walter back in the game for months. What if the kidnapping had nothing to do with the organ transplants, but just as with the last time, they hoped to use her as leverage to force Walter to do what they wanted? It had, after all, worked once before.

"I should call her parents," he said slowly. "Let them know what is going on, and to call me if they hear anything from the Russians."

Campbell nodded his head. "A good idea," he agreed. "I was going to have them called on the off chance that there was a ransom call." He paused. "I'd rather you broke the news to them than me."

Zachary grimaced and nodded. It was not going to be an easy call. But he knew he couldn't put it off just because it was unpleasant. He couldn't let anything stop him or slow him down right now. He needed to stay focused on the job at hand. Getting Kenzie back. He would do everything he could to track her down and get her back. If he were going to have a breakdown, he could do that afterward. Right now, he needed to press forward through everything, no matter how difficult or even impossible it seemed.

"I'll give them a call. Can I get a room?"

"Of course. Do you want to send techs to their house to monitor and trace their calls?"

"Uh… I'll let you know after I talk to them."

Campbell agreed. He directed Zachary to one of the interview rooms. Zachary looked at the surveillance camera bubble and said nothing. It would be an insult to Campbell to tell him not to listen in on the conversation. Zachary didn't think that he would. But if he was going to, it didn't really matter what Zachary said. He would do it anyway. And having an argument about civil liberties and everything else would only sour the relationship between them.

"Just come find me when you're done," Campbell told him. "Let me know if they need anything from us or have any helpful suggestions."

He didn't sound hopeful that they would have any.

Zachary waited until the door was closed and he was alone in the room with the surveillance equipment before dialing Walter's number.

Walter had been helping Zachary with some of his investigations as a way to keep himself from being too bored during his forced convalescence, so he had the number in his contact list.

"Zachary," Walter's voice came over the line. "How did you know?"

CHAPTER 64

“How did I know?” Zachary repeated, baffled.

“Of course you know,” Walter muttered. “It’s Kenzie. She’s been taken.”

“Yes,” Zachary confirmed. “She was snatched from the police parking garage.”

“I was hoping it wasn’t true,” Walter’s voice was tired and defeated. “How could this happen again? After all we have done to make them believe I can’t do anything for them anymore. What was the point?”

“What did they say? Did you talk to them?” Zachary couldn’t believe that Walter would just talk to them when they said they had Kenzie. Kenzie would be furious if he broke his cover story.

"No. They don't have this number. They talked to Lisa. And she held to the story that I'm unable to do anything. So they want <u>her</u> to..."

Zachary made an encouraging noise when Walter trailed off.

"I should let you talk to her. But I don't know if she's in any shape to do that right now. They want Lisa to convince Kenzie to give them all of the information that Dr. Markov had and to destroy everything. I don't understand—isn't Markov the woman who died in that terrible accident? We knew her through the foundation. She was a fine doctor."

"Yes. She's the one."

"I don't understand. What information would Kenzie have that the Russians care about? And how could they expect her to... destroy evidence?"

"They want you to talk to Kenzie? When? How?"

"They said they would call back. That Lisa has to answer the phone, and she will be able to talk to Kenzie, to convince her to do the right thing and... protect the mob."

"So that's why they've kept her alive. That's why a kidnapping rather than murder. They want to know what information Kenzie and the police have, and they want it destroyed." Zachary shook his head. "But how would she destroy it even if she wanted to? It is on the police computers and in their evidence room. Kenzie doesn't have access to that."

They were both silent for a few seconds, considering it. It was Walter who spoke first.

"Kenzie could destroy what the medical examiner's office has. They must have someone else who can destroy what the police have."

A mole within the police department. Kenzie had worried before about a leak in the police department or medical examiner's office. Or someone who worked with both of them.

There were several contract workers who bounced back and forth between the offices as they were needed. Julie, the girl who sometimes covered Kenzie's phones and reception desk. Some of the transport people. Zachary didn't know who else. Even someone like a custodian might have access to sensitive information if any computers or filing cabinets were not locked up overnight.

"That can't be our concern," Zachary said slowly. "The police will have to look after their own concerns. But they'll need to put a trace on Lisa's phone in case the Russians call back again. Especially if they want Lisa to talk to Kenzie. That call will lead us directly to wherever she is being held."

"Is that safe for us to do? It won't trigger... negative consequences for Kenzie?"

"If they want Lisa to talk to Kenzie, they'll have to call. They'll know it's a risk. They'll do what they can to obscure where they are calling from."

"Okay," Walter agreed. "They called Lisa on her private house line." He recited the phone number for Zachary. "I assume that's the one they'll call her back on."

"The police will probably come by," Zachary told him. "They can do tracing and recording remotely, but Lisa might need help handling the caller and knowing what to say to them."

In his mind's eye, Zachary could see Walter's grave nod of agreement. They all knew how strong Lisa was, but in the face of a call from the kidnappers, she would need some help. Civilians were not trained in how to handle kidnapping calls and negotiations. The excitement of what happened in TV dramas was far different from what Lisa would experience when the Russians called her to demand that she talk her daughter into cooperating with them.

"Of course. I'm sure that would be helpful," Walter agreed. "I'm not sure what else I can do for her right now. I never felt so useless."

He couldn't deal with the kidnappers. He couldn't threaten any kind of political leverage. All he could do was stand by and watch his ex-wife deal with the kidnappers. Both of them were dealing with the same pain and panic that Zachary was, trying to hold it together for each other.

"Walter... in the work you have been doing to monitor the Russians' activities, have you come across a medical facility? A clinic or something that might be used as a hospital, operating theater, care home...?"

"I'm not sure," Walter said slowly. "I can poke around, review my notes, and do a few searches on some of the messaging boards they use to see if anything pops up. You think... that might be where Kenzie is being held?"

"I don't know. We know that they have to have access to a place like that, and it's possible that is where they would take her. But it's just as likely they would take her to a cabin in the woods somewhere. I'm grasping at straws."

"I'll see what I can find." Walter's voice was hopeful for the first time, happy to have something he could do. "I'll let you know if I find anything."

"They were heading north on the highway," Zachary advised him. "I doubt it is as far as Burlington, though it could be, since that's where the research facility and lab are. But I wouldn't expect it to be any farther than that."

"That's a start. I'll see what I can find."

The lump in Zachary's stomach had not abated when he hung up the call with Walter. If anything, it was bigger, the dread more overwhelming than ever.

But he couldn't let himself feel it. He tried to compartmentalize it and push it away.

He could do that. He had spent his entire childhood and teen years learning how to seal off the pain and fear and to act as if they weren't there at all.

CHAPTER 65

Zachary returned to the bustling incident room, where everyone was working hard to gather information and coordinate the effort to find and recover Kenzie. The whiteboards were filling up with details and lists of actions to be completed. Campbell motioned Zachary over to him after he finished talking to a couple of younger LEOs. Zachary didn't recognize them and didn't know whether they were patrolmen or detectives, or operating in some other capacity.

"How did it go?" Campbell inquired.

"They received a call from the kidnappers." Zachary set out the details as quickly and succinctly as he could. Bare and bald. There was no covering up the implication that the Russians had someone in the department who would cover up and destroy evidence.

"We'll coordinate with Burlington and get someone experienced over there to help," Campbell promised. "And get an immediate trap and trace on that phone number."

Zachary turned this over in his mind uneasily. "And any other phone lines going into the house," he advised. "And I'll give you Lisa's and Walter's cells. They might decide to call back on a different line. Lisa's private number would not be easy to get. I didn't even know about it. If the Russians have that number... they have all of their numbers."

"Got it," Campbell agreed. "All numbers going into the house plus both cells. Do either of them have a second cell phone?"

"Not that I know of."

"Okay, thanks."

Zachary pulled out his laptop and placed it on the closest desk. He didn't know whose it was, but no one was hovering over it, so he would commandeer it.

"I've been working on a private investigation," he told Campbell, as he booted it up and started typing. "I was hired to look into some industrial espionage that involved the group of companies that Markov was working with."

"You were hired by Birch Valley?"

"No. A competitor. But the espionage included intrusion by Birch Valley. Or related companies."

Campbell leaned on the desk, his eyes sharp. "Really. And this was just coincidental?"

"I got the initial call from the client before Dr. Markov's death. I don't think it had anything to do with Kenzie's investigation."

"Hmm." Campbell didn't immediately accept this as gospel, but he nodded. He watched Zachary's search for the information he had saved. "And what did your investigation reveal about Birch Valley?"

“I have IP addresses for the intrusions. That’s how I back-traced the attack to them.”

“They didn’t use a proxy or anonymizer?”

“The service subscriber is a holding company owned by the Russian parent. No direct connection to Birch Valley. But I know both are owned by Ural Genetika AO through different intermediaries. Maybe they didn’t think they needed to obscure it any more than that. There is no proof that Birch Valley had anything to do with the attack by the sister company.”

“We need some kind of evidence if we are going to get a subpoena for location information from the internet service provider.”

Zachary nodded his agreement. He found his records showing the IP addresses that had been associated with the attack.

"*You* need proof for a subpoena. But I don't need one to check the public ownership databases, and I don't need evidence or a subpoena to check commercial geolocation services."

The corner of Campbell's mouth twitched. "I can't argue with that," he agreed.

Zachary had previously only used the ownership and general geographical information available to the public. Now he needed more. He entered his credit card information into one of the more trustworthy commercial sites, and once he was in, he plugged in each IP address. He watched the map as it zoomed in stage by stage, and eventually was presented with a range of addresses and a two-block radius on the map.

"I don't know if this is where they took Kenzie... she could be anywhere. But this is where the cyberattack came from, and it was targeting the same type of medical research that Kenzie was talking about. There were probes for documents or directories on gene editing, organ transplants, animal studies, protocols for human trials. The target company has not been doing human trials—at least not that they told me—but the Ural holding company was looking for any plans they might have to do them. The attack was unsuccessful, but they left their footprints all over the place. It was clear what they were looking for."

"They were competitors, following parallel paths?"

"Yeah. I didn't look to see exactly what data was targeted until after I realized that Kenzie's investigation was into a related company. They are both following similar trajectories. But the Russians don't have any qualms about jumping straight into human trials, whether the technology has been proven safe or not." Zachary paused, considering his statement. "I don't mean <u>all</u> Russians," he clarified. "Just these ones. The ones controlled by Ural or associated with the oligarch."

"An interesting point. Can you tie Ural to the oligarch? Is it his company? Or is he employed by it?"

"I don't have any direct connections. Just that the oligarch is somehow involved in this Markov situation, and so is Birch Valley, a sub of Ural. And Birch Valley and the subsidiary that targeted my client are both subs of Ural."

His brow knitted, Campbell copied down the information that the IP search had produced. "It's in the general area that the black SUV was last seen. We'll get the staties to scout it out and see if they can find the SUV or see anything suspicious. Or anything that looks like a hospital or clinic."

Zachary let out his breath in a long stream, struggling to keep his anxiety at bay. He wanted everything to happen instantly. He didn't want to have to wait for the situation to unfold. Every second that Kenzie was tortured was an agony for him. He couldn't stop the images that flew through his mind. He drilled a knuckle into the knotted muscles in his forehead, trying to release the tension and relieve the pulsing headache.

Campbell stepped away, already tapping his phone screen to initiate a call. He went into his office and shut the door. Zachary could still see him through the narrow window beside the door as he made one phone call after another, pacing back and forth across his office. Zachary looked away and studied the whiteboards arranged around the room, looking for new information and trying to figure out how it all fit together and how he could help advance the investigation further. He had never actually been in the incident room while they were running a case like this before. As a private investigator, it wasn't his place. Luckily, he had a history with Campbell and was familiar with Edwards, who had worked with Kenzie on a few death investigation cases recently.

A female detective hurried over to Campbell's door and hammered on it loudly. Through the narrow window, Zachary could see the thunderous expression that came over

Campbell's face, a mixture of irritation and fury over being interrupted so disrespectfully. He walked over and opened the door, his phone still to his ear. He raised his brows at the woman, waiting for her explanation. The incident room had gone almost silent in response to the loud knock and the sight of this woman interrupting Campbell.

"Sir." She held up a wireless phone handset. "A call came in through 9-1-1. It is her. It's Dr. Kirsch."

Campbell snatched the phone from her, handing her his cell phone in exchange.

"Dr. Kirsch?" He listened for a few seconds. Looking across the room, he saw Zachary watching and motioned him over. Zachary didn't need a second invitation. He fairly sprinted across the room. He followed Campbell back into his office and shut the door as Campbell put the phone into speaker mode and set it on his desk. Kenzie's voice was broadcast mid-sentence.

"—I pulled the fire alarm, so there should be a call out to the fire department right now and they'll have the address."

"Okay," Campbell nodded briskly. "We'll dial in with them and get it. You're okay? Zachary is here with me."

"I'm okay," Kenzie assured him. "So far. As long as I can avoid getting caught before the cops get here. It's pure luck that I managed to get away." She breathed heavily. "I'm okay, Zachary."

"Good." Zachary could barely get the word out, his throat closing up.

"I'm going to have to go," Kenzie said. "I can't stay here. I had to come out in the open to get a phone signal. I don't know if they have a jammer or if it's just these concrete walls."

"Kenzie," Zachary tried to find the words to tell her to keep herself safe and that the police would be there soon.

There was a yelp from Kenzie, and the call was cut off. The line went dead. Campbell hit the hangup button.

“What happened? Are you going to call her back?” Zachary demanded.

Campbell shook his head slowly. “If she is trying to hide or escape and I call her back, it could give away her location and put her in danger. She knows how to get ahold of me again, the same way she did the first time. The staties are tracing her location by the new phone, and they’ll get us the details as soon as they have them. We should know where the fire alarm was ringing by now. Let’s find out.”

He opened his door and they returned to an incident room buzzing with even more activity than before. A number of people were gearing up to go out. The woman who had knocked on Campbell’s door handed him back his cell phone.

"They've got the address," she told him. "It's going out to everyone. Are you going to stay here?" Her eyes flicked to Zachary, "Or going out?"

"I think I'd better go. Make sure everything is handled professionally and that civilians don't get in the way of the operation." He winked at Zachary.

Zachary understood the upshift in the mood of everyone there. They hadn't known exactly where to find Kenzie, and now they had an address and were shifting into action.

But they didn't know she was okay. She had been okay when she called, but something had happened that had resulted in her getting cut off or having to hang up the call. She had been startled or scared and had not even had time to say goodbye.

Two minutes ago, she had been alive and unharmed.

But now?

CHAPTER 66

Kenzie stood in the stairwell, just outside the second-floor door. While it seemed like the best place to hide while still retaining her ability to escape to another part of the building or outside, she had put her hiding place in peril by pulling the fire alarm. About half of the building's residents and employees seemed to have evacuated, and of course, they had to go through the stairwell to do so. Kenzie kept her head down, looking at her phone, pretending to message her friends like anyone else to tell them about what was going on, traveling within the herd so that she wouldn't stand out, but then as they exited the building, she needed to find her way inside again before they locked the place down.

Not everyone had evacuated. There were still patients in some of the rooms. Gurneys were lined up outside the elevator to be taken down to the main floor one at a time. Each patient had to be evaluated to ensure it was safe to move and take them out of the building.

It was obvious that there was no fire, so people were in no great hurry to get out of the building or to do the work of moving all of the patients. Kenzie kept her ears pricked for trouble, which she knew would find her sooner or later. One of the other negative consequences of pulling the fire alarm was that each patient room would be checked, and sooner rather than later, they would find that Kenzie had escaped and chained Hayes to the bed in her place.

There were sirens as the fire engines pulled up to the building, and Kenzie could hear the high-pitched wail of police cars in the distance. They were coming. Soon, the police would be there, and she could turn herself over to them and be safe. As long as they were not corrupt and in the pay of the Russian mob. She would have to trust that not enough of them were corrupt for them to act openly against her.

“Search every room!”

Kenzie looked up at the shout. It was starting. There was a lot of swearing, cursing, and muttering about people being properly restrained.

She looked around for somewhere to hide that would not be searched. A men's room? A supply cupboard or boiler access? There were likely maintenance rooms and tunnels in the basement. What about roof access? She always hated it when suspects fled to the roof in TV shows. Why go up? There was no escape from a roof but risking death. Hollywood did it just to amp up the tension. In real life, the quarry would go down. They would go to the ground floor where there was the best access to multiple escape routes.

If they had her picture or description—and Kenzie had to assume they did—they would know her when they saw her. Her dark hair, in bouncing coils around her face, was far too distinctive. She needed to do something about that. She needed to blend in better and not look like herself. Take a page from Zachary's PI book of tricks and find a way to become invisible.

In short order, she had done her best to transform herself into one of the nurses. It was a dangerous ploy, because in such a small hospital, the nurses were bound to know each other. But would they immediately realize she was who she was rather than assuming she was a new staff member they hadn't met yet? Or could she gain the few minutes she needed to stay out of the hands of the Russians or anyone controlled by them and get to one of the police officers arriving at the scene?

A surgical cap hid the recognizable curls. Kenzie wore baggy nursing scrubs over her own shirt and pants. She had picked up a pair of reading glasses from one of the nursing desks—luckily not too strong a prescription—and had scrubbed off her bright red lipstick. To her own eyes, she looked quite different, but would it be enough to stay one step ahead of the criminals for the next few minutes?

“Hey!” a man shouted down the hall as Kenzie closed the door of the room she had just changed in. She froze and looked at him. He stared back, not recognizing her as a staff member.

“Did you check that room?” Kenzie demanded, pointing to the one to the right. “I’ve done the other side, but you need to check these ones!”

He looked momentarily confused, but he nodded acquiescence and opened the door she had pointed to. Kenzie went into the next room and banged the door loudly as she went in to “search” it. She and the man worked their way down the hall, getting closer to each other one room at a time.

Too close. As Kenzie came out of the next room, she held Hayes’s phone to her ear, covering up as much of her face as possible from her “coworker’s” view.

"What?" she demanded, "How could she get up to the roof?" She waved at the man to get his attention, as if he wasn't standing just a few feet away from her, and she pointed to the nearest stairwell. "Up there!"

He dashed to the stairwell and started up the stairs, taking them two at a time.

Kenzie waited a few seconds and then started down the stairs, keeping her feet as quiet as possible and hoping the man's pounding steps and focus would keep him from hearing her or realizing what she had done.

She headed toward the door at the bottom, ignoring the yellow, red, and black warnings that it was alarmed, and looked around cautiously.

Kenzie took a deep breath and pushed through the door. It wasn't like she would set off any more alarms, and people had been exiting through that door since she first pulled the fire alarm.

She hit the crash bar, pushed the door open, and stepped out into the evening dimness and cooling air. Employees stood in small clusters chatting with each other, some of them taking the opportunity for a smoke break. Directly in front of Kenzie was a knot of men in suits or uniforms involved in an animated discussion. They stopped, looking at her with mouths open. The one with his back to Kenzie turned around, and she saw it was the fake security guard who had snatched her from the police parking lot.

Kenzie moved faster than any of them. She was motivated. They stood there frozen, and she hoped they stayed that way for a few more seconds, trying to figure out what to do about her. They couldn't chase her with the police starting to show up, could they? They couldn't be that obvious about it.

She hoped.

She dashed back up the stairs, mentally reviewing her options. She had sent the other man up to the roof. By this time, he would have figured out that was a wild goose chase, but would he realize that she was the woman they were looking for, or just assume that someone had been mistaken?

There were only so many rooms that she could be hiding in. They had already searched most of them and would, she assumed, continue to search the rooms that they had not yet searched. They would not recheck the rooms they had already searched.

Not yet.

Hopefully.

They were coming up the stairs behind her now. At least two separate voices and sets of pounding feet.

She had told the other man that all the rooms on the other side of the unit had already been checked. She didn't know whether they really had been or not, but hopefully, they would not have time to re-search every room before the police locked the building down and started to look for her.

She could hear the man coming down from the roof. He, the guard, and the men from outside would stop to consult, figure out what direction Kenzie had gone, and split up to search the rooms on that floor.

Kenzie followed her instinct and dashed across the unit to the other side. There was no guarantee that wasn't exactly where they would start, or one of them, anyway. There was a serious lack of ways to defend herself against a physical attack. She needed to hide, yet there was nowhere in the bare rooms to hide. The rooms in this unit had curtains around the beds, but they didn't go all the way to the floor and it would not take long to peek around a curtain to reveal anyone hiding anyway.

There was a door labeled "Office" instead of the dual slots for patient names. Kenzie took that chance that it would be unlocked and there might be more places to hide in an office than in an empty hospital room, and she tried the door.

The handle turned in her hand, and she dashed into the room, turning to press the door shut faster than the hydraulic door closer would do it alone, turning the handle to prevent the snick of the door catch slipping into place. With any luck, her pursuers would not see or hear the door shut. There was a thumb-turn lock inside the door handle, and Kenzie turned it to lock the door. They would skip over a locked door, at least initially, assuming that Kenzie had not been able to get in.

She turned to look around the room and pick out a suitable hiding place.

It wasn’t until then that she realized she was not alone in the room.

CHAPTER 67

Kenzie had assumed that the room had been evacuated just like the patient rooms. It had not occurred to her that it would be occupied. Instead of locking out her pursuers, she had locked herself into a room with an enemy.

The man sitting at the desk, watching her with evident surprise, was Dr. Morgan Tucker.

Kenzie's knees went weak. Tucker, who from day one had made it clear that he did not like her and had no use for her investigation. One of the men who had spearheaded the project editing the genes of donated organs and implanting them into patients who were willing to pay top dollar for an experimental treatment.

Kenzie leaned back against the door, staring at him, aghast. There was nowhere to go. There were men in hot pursuit on the other side of the door. She could hear their shouts and footsteps.

Doors opened and closed. A hand tried the door handle of the office and found it locked, rattled it a few times, and then went on to the next room. But less than thirty seconds later, he was back, rechecking, retesting. He hammered on the door with his fist.

“Anyone in there?” he demanded. And to his compatriots, “Who has a key?”

Kenzie was trapped. There was no way out of this.

Morgan Tucker rolled his office chair back. He made a motion to Kenzie.

“Here,” he said in a low voice. “Get under.”

Kenzie stared at him blankly. Morgan widened his eyes and thrust his head forward. “Dr. Kirsch. Come here.”

She followed his gesture. Under the desk. In the kneehole.

The space on the other side of the kneehole was covered by the single piece of wood that ran the length and height of the front of the desk. No gap between it and the floor. Kenzie dashed forward and slithered around Morgan in his chair, into the kneehole, and made herself as small as possible. Morgan slid his chair forward until his feet and shins were against her.

He had barely rolled back into place when a key was inserted into the door lock and Kenzie heard the door swing open. There was little movement by Morgan. A startled exclamation from the man who had unlocked it.

"Oh! Sorry, Doctor, I thought this room was unoccupied."

"It is not," Morgan snapped.

"No. Sorry. We were looking for... you heard the alarm, didn't you? The building is supposed to be evacuated."

"Then what are you doing here?"

“Well...” the searcher fumbled for what to say. “We were looking for the woman. The one who escaped. It’s just... I’m sorry, I didn’t realize you were still here.”

“Please shut the door again on your way out.”

Morgan’s voice was dry, his words clipped. There was no need to tell the searcher to leave. His intention was quite clear from his tone.

“Sorry, Doctor,” the man apologized again and withdrew. Kenzie waited to hear the catch snick back into place again.

Neither of them moved or said anything at first. Then Morgan rolled his chair back again.

“It is safe.”

Kenzie hesitated to crawl back into the open, where she was so vulnerable, but she steeled herself and extricated herself as gracefully as possible from the cramped quarters.

"I'm... thank you so much," she told him.

Words seemed inadequate. And so did any questions. There was no point in asking Morgan if he was really on her side. He had just demonstrated that. Though she feared that when she stood up and faced him, he would be pointing a gun at her.

It was just that kind of day.

Morgan didn't smile. He gave her a nod. "Are you all right?"

"Yes." Kenzie breathed out slowly. Her heart was still beating fast and probably would be for some time. The adrenaline was pumping through her veins, speeding up her thoughts and reaction time. Ready for another attack from any direction. "Thank you."

He slid a cell phone across the desk toward her and made no comment.

Kenzie picked it up. "You can get a signal in here?"

Morgan nodded. “Barely. This office is right on the edge of the shielding.”

She could call Campbell. Probably should call him to update him on the situation so that he could coordinate the joint operation with the state police who were gathering outside. Campbell himself would still be half an hour to forty-five minutes away, even with his pedal to the metal.

Instead, she called Zachary.

He answered almost immediately, though he could not have known who was calling.

“Goldman Investigations.”

He sounded out of breath as if he had been running. But Kenzie knew he wasn’t. He would be in a car headed toward her. Maybe in his own car, maybe with Campbell or Edwards.

“It’s Kenzie.”

Her voice broke, and for a while, she couldn't get anything else out, just breathing and trying to find her voice again.

"It's Kenzie," Zachary repeated to someone else. "I'm putting you on speaker, Kenz. With Sergeant Campbell. Are you okay? Are you safe?"

"I'm okay," Kenzie told him, once she managed to get her voice under control. It was still high and strained. "I'm safe and staying here until the police get here. The door is locked and they don't realize I am here."

"Can you talk?" Zachary asked.

"Umm… a bit. I'm with Dr. Tucker. He is… he helped me."

"Are you on speaker?"

"No."

"I thought he was one of the leaders on the project."

"He is. I… don't ask me to explain. I can't."

"Okay." He gave a little laugh. "Tell me again that you're okay."

"I'm okay," Kenzie repeated, chuckling as well. She was giddy with relief.

She could hear Campbell talking into his phone or radio in the background, giving the state police an update and letting them know that she was safe and they didn't have to rush in to find her. They could secure all of the exits and enter cautiously, watching for the men who were still searching for Kenzie. They might be armed.

"We should let your parents know you're okay," Zachary said. "Do you want me to call them?"

"My parents?" A lump grew in Kenzie's throat. Had Zachary told them she had been abducted? It was probably the right thing to do, but she hated to think they had been suffering, wondering whether she would be okay too.

“The Russians called them,” Zachary said apologetically. “On Lisa’s private landline.”

“Oh. How did they get that number?” Kenzie thought uneasily about how carefully Lisa had guarded that number. One of her friends knew someone. One of her friends had given it to the wrong person. How much else did they know? If they were close enough to get that information, were they close enough to figure out that Walter hadn’t really had a stroke? As far as Kenzie knew, her parents had told no one their secret. But it was possible that Lisa had confided in one or two trusted friends.

The kind of friends she would have given her private number to.

“Umm. I don’t think I can talk to them right now. And I don’t know how soon I’ll have to deal with the police and everything here, so I should get off the phone.”

“Okay. What room are you in?”

"On the second floor, in unit B. It is labeled 'Office.'" Kenzie looked at Morgan. "Does it have a number? I didn't notice one."

"There is no number on the door. Room 225 if they are looking at blueprints."

Kenzie relayed this information to Zachary so it could be given to the police. Kenzie said goodbye and ended the call. She placed the phone back down on the desk.

"Thank you so much. I'm... I'm glad you did not approve of... what the Russians were doing," Kenzie said carefully.

"Funding is vital," Morgan said tersely. "Donors like your family foundation are essential. Removing that funding creates a vacuum that must be filled, often without warning, and people panic and make poor decisions. You can't just take any funding that is offered. You can't sell your soul to the devil."

"So it wasn't your idea."

"Of course not. I was firmly opposed to having anything to do with the Russians. Which, of course, brands me as racist and reactionary." He grimaced and mocked his coworker's words. "'There is amazing research being advanced by the Russians. We need to remain apolitical in our decisions and not be swayed by rumors and gossip.'"

He shook his head, brows drawn down.

"You see where that has gotten us. Who knows how long it will take us to recover from this debacle. If ever."

Kenzie could sympathize with him. Out of all of the scientists, researchers, and doctors she had talked to, Morgan Tucker had been the most ardent about their work. Kenzie suspected that for him, the scientific advances were more enthralling than the opportunity for huge profits.

CHAPTER 68

They could hear the police coming. Heavy shoes on the tiles, doors opening and closing, and the cops calling out to each other as they cleared each room. There was a knock on the door with the call "Police!" rather than the door handle turning or the door being kicked down. Kenzie unlocked and opened it, then stepped back with her hands up to allow the police to enter and clear the room.

"This is Dr. Tucker," she told them as they leveled weapons at the doctor sitting at his desk. "He helped me. Rescued me from the kidnappers."

They checked the rest of the room, including checking under the desk, then nodded and allowed Kenzie and Morgan to lower their hands.

"Do you need any medical care?" one of the cops asked Kenzie.

She hadn't stopped to consider her own condition before that. She hadn't sustained anything more than some bruises or pulled muscles fighting back against her abductors. It had all happened too fast for her to do anything more than struggle ineffectually after it was over.

But she still had her injury from the attack by Dana Pratt to deal with. She touched the back of her head to make sure that it was not bleeding and that she had not popped her stitches with all of the physical activity. Dr. Wiltshire's neat stitches had held, and there was nothing to worry about but a throbbing headache. Her wrist was sore from pulling against the handcuff, but other than that, she couldn't identify any particular concerns.

"No... I think I'm okay."

"If we could get you both to come outside, we want to completely clear the building before proceeding. And Miss Kirsch, you will need to identify anyone you are aware was involved in your abduction. We don't want to let anyone leave the site without a proper review and identification."

Kenzie nodded. "Okay. Yes. Of course."

She hoped none of them had gotten away before the police had shown up, but there had been an interval between Kenzie's abduction and the police arriving. There was no guarantee that everyone involved in the plot was still there—or had been, to begin with. She doubted if the Oligarch himself was anywhere close by. He would not be running his enterprise out of a small-town clinic.

They escorted Kenzie back out the door she had initially exited through to find herself face-to-face with the fake security guard. This time, there was no one smoking near the door or discussing how to find her and get her out of there before the police arrived. The police had rounded up all of the employees and had them assembled in rows on their knees, with their hands behind their heads. Most of them looked baffled, terrified, or excited. Bright floodlights lit the area. There were tears on some faces.

But the men who had been hunting her were different. Their faces were expressionless as they stared off into the distance. The police guards recognized this and watched them with particular attention.

Kenzie took a deep breath and walked through the assembled detainees with two of the cops, Frankyl and Angelo, one on either side of her, and quietly pointed out the various men she knew were in on the abduction. Angelo took video footage as Kenzie identified each conspirator. She wondered about all of the people who had ignored Kenzie's arrival with the kidnappers, escorted into a secure room at gunpoint.

They had to know that wasn't normal. They must have been somewhat aware of what was going on, not to react at that sight. Kenzie murmured these comments to her escorts as well.

After circulating through the assembled employees, Kenzie looked around at them again to see if she had missed a section.

“What is it?” Frankyl asked.

“Dr. Hayes. He’s an older man, balding, with a white fringe... where is he? He was still in the building when I pulled the alarm, and he couldn’t get away until they released him... but where...?”

They all looked around, scanning for someone who met Kenzie’s description.

Kenzie’s eyes went to the gurneys populated with patients. They all had blankets over them, some of them pulled right up over their heads. Kenzie motioned to them without saying anything.

The cops nodded and walked with her over to the gurneys, where they started pulling down all of the blankets to reveal the bed's occupants.

When Dr. Hayes was revealed, he sat up, unsure what to do. He looked at Kenzie, the cops, and the video camera pointed at him.

"What's going on? I've been on shift for eighteen hours. I needed to get some rest. Is it all over, then? Can we go home now?"

Kenzie glared at him. He acted as if he did not see her.

"He was the one," Kenzie said. "He's the mastermind of all of this. Don't let his act fool you."

Hayes raised his brows innocently. "Mastermind? Of what? Miss... Doe here was brought to us as a violent, paranoid patient in need of care. Is she the one who set off the alarm? That doesn't surprise me. I was told she was a troublemaker at the previous facility where she was a patient. Actually talked one of the security guards into believing that she'd been kidnapped and was the victim of a conspiracy."

The cops gave Kenzie a look and then shook their heads. The story of who she was and what had happened to her had come from their superiors and the Roxboro police, not from Kenzie herself. They knew it was not just a delusion on her part.

"You know who I am," Kenzie told Hayes levelly. "Give up the act."

He shook his head innocently. "Really, I have no idea what you're talking about. I was told you were a Jane Doe brought here for treatment."

Kenzie opened her mouth to argue, then closed it. It didn't matter what he said. They would prove that he had been the one to lead the conspiracy. There would be records. Other men who had been involved at a lower level would roll over on him to get themselves out of a long prison sentence. She just shook her head. "I know he was involved," she told the cops. "Don't believe anything he says. He is dangerous."

"Get down from there," Angelo ordered, pulling his taser out and pointing it at Hayes. "Get your hands up. Do you have any weapons on you?"

Looking surprised and sad, Hayes allowed them to pat him down and handcuff him. He was moved away from the legitimate patients, and Kenzie and the police checked each one of the other beds to ensure that they were all patients awaiting or recovering from surgery, not other mobsters or doctors.

"Dr. Kirsch!"

Kenzie looked around to see who was calling her. Sergeant Campbell was making his way through the parking lot to talk to her. She looked for Zachary, surprised not to see him.

"He can't come inside the tape," Campbell advised when he reached her, interpreting her expression. "You can go see him in a few minutes. I'm sorry we're monopolizing your time. But... another matter requires your attention, if you are able."

"I was just working with these officers to identify the men I know were involved," Kenzie indicated them.

"Are you finished with that?"

Kenzie nodded, looking at them to make sure they agreed. Both cops nodded. Angelo had already turned off his camera and lowered it to his side.

Campbell nodded and looked gravely at Kenzie. "I need to know... how able you are to assist us. Have you been given any substances today?"

"No. They didn't drug me."

"You previously injured your head. How is that?"

"It's fine," Kenzie said, touching it again. "I just have a headache."

“Do you need a break? Need to lie down or go home?”

“What’s going on, sergeant?”

“And your frame of mind? You were violently abducted. I don’t want to assume you are in any state to assist with a job right now. If you are... foggy or tired or excessively anxious...?”

“I’m actually pretty focused right now. Which is why I’m wondering what’s going on. What do you need me to do?”

He studied her face for a moment, searching for anything that might suggest she was not capable of functioning at the moment.

“I’m fine,” Kenzie insisted. “What is it?”

“We have a body.”

"Oh!" Kenzie gave a little laugh. "Yes, I can do a quick review and scene survey with you. I'm not too traumatized to do my job."

"We are still within your jurisdiction. So if you are feeling up to it, I don't have to call Dr. Wiltshire out or get someone in from Burlington, when it isn't actually their territory."

"I'm fine. No problem. No need to get someone else out. I don't have my kit with me, so I might need... gloves, booties, evidence bags, reference tags, a notebook and pen. You, with your camera," she told Angelo. "I guess if there is anything else, this is a medical clinic and they'll probably have something I can use."

She looked at Campbell and still saw reservation in his eyes. Something was still holding him back. Did she look that rough after her abduction? Maybe it was just her altered appearance. She took off the reading glasses and Campbell's face came into better focus.

"It's Dana Pratt," he told her finally.

"Dana? Oh, no." Kenzie shook her head and sighed. "Why didn't she just go home?"

"I am concerned about conflict of interest," Campbell said. "She did attack you."

"Yeah…"

Kenzie considered. She didn't want to screw things up by getting involved in a case she shouldn't have anything to do with. She rubbed the bridge of her nose and thought. "Here is what we are going to do. When Dr. Wiltshire is unable to get to a scene in person, he will video chat with the LEOs, look around at anything he wants to see, get a video tour of the scene. So that's what we're going to do. I will be here only as an observer and to make suggestions. Dr. Wiltshire will be the attending medical examiner. I will not touch the body or anything at the scene. If something needs to be moved into another position to show it to Dr. Wiltshire, you will do it.

Everything will be recorded at the same time as it is being broadcast to Dr. Wiltshire so there is a full record of what happened. If any evidence needs to be collected, you or the techs will gather and submit it."

"Okay." Campbell nodded, looking relieved. Neither of them wanted any evidence to be excluded because Kenzie was conflicted out. But they also didn't want to call Dr. Wiltshire in from Roxboro and wait an hour or two for him when Kenzie was already there in person.

CHAPTER 69

Kenzie spotted Zachary waiting outside the tape as they returned to the building. She waved and blew him a kiss. He seemed to be holding up okay.

"How is he?" she asked Campbell, since they had driven in together.

"Like he is when he's working," Campbell assured her. "Focused, quick-thinking, that brain of his processing everything at once and making the connections."

"Emotionally?"

"Holding it together. I wouldn't be surprised if he crashes later. But he didn't panic. No meltdown."

Kenzie nodded. Hopefully, he would sleep tonight. For a long time.

They entered the building, and Campbell led her to a bathroom. It featured a shower area with no lip, making it accessible for a wheelchair or walker. There was also a large steel tub with a mechanical lift beside it, so hospital staff didn't have to be strong enough to lower an obese patient into the water or lift them out again.

The large tub was full, and Dana's body lay mostly beneath the surface, with just her nose and forehead above the waterline.

This was obviously not an accident or natural causes.

"Uh, can we use your phone?" Kenzie asked. "I... lost mine."

"Sure. I will get the good doctor on the phone. Zachary found yours, by the way. Careless of you to drop it out of the car. It will need the screen replaced."

Kenzie chuckled. She pulled on her gloves as Campbell called Dr. Wiltshire. He outlined the procedure they wanted to follow, and Dr. Wiltshire agreed. Campbell hung up and reconnected using video chat on an iPad.

"We'll need a sample of the water before we drain the tub," Kenzie advised. "We'll match it to the water in her lungs. Make sure she was drowned here and not drowned somewhere else and then staged here."

Frankyl and Angelo took a sample of the water. Angelo filmed as Campbell handled the iPad with the live link to Dr. Wiltshire. They did a video tour of the room, starting and ending with the body in the tub. Kenzie looked around for anything else important and then nodded. "Let's drain the tub."

"How do we get to the drain with her in it?" Frankyl tried to look under the body and figure out how to access it.

"Just press that button." Kenzie pointed to the drain release next to the faucets.

"Oh." The cop blushed. "Yeah, of course." He punched the button, and they watched the water start to drain.

"That will just take a few minutes. Then, we'll examine her as well as we can before taking her out. We can use the lift."

When the water had drained, they continued.

"Check for skin temperature, consistency, and rigor," Kenzie advised.

"How do I do that?" Frankyl looked around for special equipment.

"See whether she is warm or cold to the touch. Whether she feels waxy. Whether it is easy or hard to move her fingers, arms, and eyelids."

He had clearly been hoping to avoid touching the corpse. He was wearing gloves, so Kenzie encouraged him until he was finally able to touch it and report back on the conditions Kenzie requested. Campbell chuckled at the young cop's reluctance. "You'll have to do much worse than this one day," he laughed. “Wait until you find one ripening in a dumpster. This one is fresh and clean.”

Frankyl made a disgusted face. “This isn’t what I expected to be doing as a cop. I didn’t sign up to be a medical examiner.”

“You signed up to do a lot more than this.”

Frankyl shook his head. “I don’t like dead bodies.”

“He doesn’t like dead bodies,” Campbell repeated to Kenzie, teasing.

“It’s not going to be your last, officer,” Kenzie chuckled.

“I know, but I don’t have to like it.”

“No, you don’t have to like it,” Kenzie agreed.

As they moved the body around to be able to fit the strap of the lift behind it, Kenzie stopped them and had Angelo take video footage of Dana's shoulders and collar bones, which were darkening with bruises.

"Restraint bruises. She was held under the water. She wasn't unconscious when she went in."

There were no jokes about this. Angelo recorded the video grimly.

After using the lift to pull her out of the tub and position her body in the waiting body bags waiting on a nearby gurney, Angelo peered into the tub and panned over it with his camera. "Her phone is in here."

"Well, that's not going to be great for it," Campbell grumbled.

Frankyl retrieved it with a gloved hand. He examined it. "Actually, I think this is a waterproof case." He moved to wipe it dry.

"Let it air dry," Kenzie ordered sharply. "There might be prints."

"Oh." Frankyl was blushing again. "Sorry."

"More experienced cops than you have made that mistake," Kenzie allowed. "You just have to think everything through. What evidence might be on each object or surface at the scene. What can be done to preserve it?"

Eventually, they finished processing the scene. Kenzie checked in with Dr. Wiltshire to see if there was anything else he wanted them to see or do, and he signed off.

Chapter 70

"And now, doctor, I think it is time to reunite you with your partner and take you off the clock. You've done more than enough today. A full day of work, dealing with an assault, a kidnapping, and a call-out. You're finished."

Kenzie could feel the strain now that she hadn't felt immediately after being rescued, when the adrenaline had still been running high.

Now she could feel how tired she was and knew that once she let herself relax, she was going to crash. Her body was sore and bruised. Her head was throbbing.

"Yeah, I think I'm beat," she admitted.

The next question was how they were going to get home. Kenzie had not come in her car, and Zachary had not come in his. They were going to have to hitch a ride back to Roxboro. Maybe she could go in the medical examiner's van.

Few people were left in the parking lot and grounds surrounding the building. Kenzie wondered whether they had all been interviewed. Not just those involved in the scheme, but also the patients, who might have some insight into which medical professionals had been in the know. They might also manage to find out how much people had been paying for the procedures. They were missing a lot of financial information that Markov should have included with the files on her locket. Maybe she had intended to but had not been able to compile everything before she had been killed. Or perhaps they were in the files they still hadn't been able to decrypt.

Zachary looked up from his phone before Kenzie had a chance to call out to him. He jammed it into his pocket and opened his arms in an invitation. Kenzie walked up and embraced him. It was at that point that it really hit her: She could have been killed by the kidnappers, and this reunion would never have happened. She could have lost everything. Zachary could have lost her forever. How would that have affected him?

Zachary hugged her tightly. "Never do that again," he whispered fiercely.

Kenzie swallowed the lump in her throat. “Okay,” she agreed. She didn’t know where the flood of tears suddenly streaming down her face had come from. She really was crashing. Zachary rocked slightly, swaying her back and forth. Kenzie could have stayed in that position all night, only her legs started to feel like jelly and she wanted to sit down. Zachary kissed her.

“We’re going to drive back with Hal. Just over there.”

Kenzie followed his gaze to Hal, standing beside his car under a streetlight, waiting for them.

“Okay. I can make it that far.”

Zachary wrapped her arm around his neck and his around her waist as if she had sprained her ankle and he supported her all the way to the car, just in case.

“You want to ride in front?” he offered.

Kenzie shook her head. “No way. You can keep Hal company and pretend you’re the one driving, and I’m going to stretch out in the back seat and have a nap.”

Zachary opened the back door for her and shut it once she climbed in and got comfortable. Hal slid into the driver's seat. "Are you okay, Dr. Kirsch?"

"I told you to call me Kenzie," she told him, her eyes already closed. "I'm okay." She had to turn to avoid lying on the bump on the back of her head that she'd gotten from Dana. "How about you? I was afraid they hurt you when we got separated."

"I shouldn't have left you alone."

"You didn't. You left me with a security guard."

"But he wasn't really a security guard."

"You couldn't know that. I should have. I didn't know his face; I should have realized he didn't belong, but I thought he was just new."

Hal might have said something else, but Kenzie didn't hear it. She didn't hear another thing all the way home.

* * *

Zachary didn't want to wake Kenzie, but he and Hal couldn't figure out how to get her from the car to the house without waking her up, even if Hal tried to carry her. So eventually, Zachary shook Kenzie's arm gently and explained that they were home and it was time to go inside.

It was strange to go in through the front door without Zachary's car at the curb. Kenzie yawned. "I guess we'll have to bring your car back tomorrow. You can come in to work with me and get it."

"You're not working tomorrow. You need at least a day off. Maybe a week or two."

"I'm tired, but I'm not that tired. Sooner or later, I will want to get up and go to work."

"After everything you went through today, you need some recovery time."

"You'll get tired of having me home. I'll be fine. I don't want to make a big thing of this."

"It is a big thing. I know how it affected you last time when you tried to just go on like nothing happened and not tell anyone."

“I don’t imagine that will be a possibility this time.” There had been TV cameras outside the clinic when she had been outside pointing out each of her captors. They probably had footage of her calling out each one of them. Walter and Lisa would be watching it on TV. Dr. B would know the details. Zachary already did. There was no way she could hide it this time, and maybe that was better than trying to pretend it hadn’t happened.

Zachary opened the door and disarmed the burglar alarm. “Do you want to go straight to bed?”

“Not without my ice cream.”

“Ice cream it is,” he grinned his approval.

Hal, it appeared, was going to stay one more night. He would need to drive them to get their cars in the morning, so Kenzie supposed that made sense. Kenzie and Hal sat at the table and let Zachary get out the bowls, ice cream, and toppings. Kenzie overdid it on everything, knowing she couldn’t eat it all. But she was building a pleasant memory with Zachary, not just an ice cream sundae. They would remember the enormous pile of ice cream, syrup, and candy whenever the subject of the kidnapping came up, giving them a sweet recollection to laugh about instead of just the horror of the day. And besides, after how much she had been through during the day, she must have burned a thousand calories, and she hadn't eaten since lunchtime. Had she even eaten lunch? She thought she might have missed that too.

An alert came up on Zachary's phone while they were eating and Kenzie was complaining about how cold she was getting from eating the pile of ice cream. He looked at it and then at Kenzie.

"Your phone broke," he told her, though she already knew this detail. "I'll get it fixed for you."

"Uh-huh."

He nudged his phone toward her. "It's for you."

Kenzie looked down at the screen. A message from Detective Edwards.

Got a message from the forensic techs that a video was received on Markov's phone today.

Kenzie frowned. She looked at Zachary, brows drawn down. Who would have sent Markov a video so long after she had died? Everybody knew by now that she was dead. Then she sucked in her breath, knowing the answer.

Dana? she texted back.

Bingo, Edwards confirmed.

Can you send it to me?

There was a delay, during which Kenzie figured he was typing an answer, explaining that it was too disturbing or that she was off the case because of her kidnapping. But eventually, the front cover of the video appeared on the screen. Dana's bleak face looked back at Kenzie from beyond the veil.

Kenzie ignored the dread in her stomach and tapped the triangular play icon. Dana spoke into the camera, not to Kenzie but to Mariya Markov's ghost.

> I'm sorry. I never meant to be part of anything like this. I didn't know what they were going to do to you. Even after it happened, I didn't realize that... that I

> had just been his puppet and that he had only ever intended it to turn out one way.
>
> I put the beta-blocker in your drink because Dr. Hayes told me to. He said it would loosen you up so that you would tell him where to find all the information you had copied. And then... they would clean it up, delete it, and revoke your username so you couldn't access the server again.
>
> But I was there. I saw what he did.

Dana's voice broke. She put her hands over her eyes for a moment before continuing.

> I saw him put his hands around your neck and try to squeeze it out of you when you wouldn't tell him. You kept it close to your heart, you told him. He was so angry. I screamed and screamed and told him to let you go, and he did. He went through your purse and threw it down on the floor, too. I picked everything

up. There was no USB drive. No key to a secret locker or safety deposit box. Nothing.

He said you would tell me. If I just waited, you would decide that someone who loved you enough to stop him could be trusted.

I made sure that you got back to the party okay. That you got your key and made it out to your car safely. I watched Mr. Smythe see you on your way, just like I asked him to. I didn't know... that they were going to go after you. That they would force you to have an accident. I swear, I didn't know. I thought I had saved you.

I'm sorry, Mariya. I'm so sorry. I didn't know. I thought I saved you. But I just sent you to your death.

Dana wiped her red-rimmed eyes.

I love you, Mariya. I'm sorry.

Zachary looked as grim as Kenzie felt. But Dana had named Dr. Hayes. Her last action in life had been to name Markov's killer. And probably her own.

Hayes hadn't had wet jacket cuffs when he had come to talk to Kenzie at the clinic. Had he taken his jacket off to hold Dana under the water? Or had someone else done his dirty work? He had confessed that he didn't have the strength of the younger generations.

With a lump in her throat, Kenzie called Dr. Wiltshire on speaker.

"Hello?" He answered cautiously, not sure who it was. Zachary sometimes left his caller ID turned off, and Kenzie hadn't checked it.

"It's Kenzie."

"Oh, Kenzie." He sounded relieved. "How are you feeling?"

"Tired. Stuffed. But there's something else..."

"Yes, what can I do for you?"

"The phone that we got from the Pratt murder site

today…"

"Yes?"

"There is a video on it from Dana Pratt to Mariya Markov —"

"Do you know the date?"

"Today. Probably the last thing she did before she was killed."

"Mmm. No, not today."

"It was just sent to Markov today," Kenzie insisted. "I just watched it. Detective Edwards sent me a copy of what was received by Markov's phone."

"Well then, Miss Pratt deleted it from her phone after sending it. The tech guys made me a copy of the data on the phone. There weren't any calls or texts logged today."

"See if there is a video saved on the camera roll."

Dr. Wiltshire didn't answer. Kenzie suddenly realized how late it was. "Oh, I'm sorry. You're at home. I wasn't thinking. We can look at it together tomorrow. I didn't mean to disturb you at home."

"Actually, I'm still at the office. I wanted to get this evidence processed now so I can do the postmortem tomorrow. Just give me a minute. I'm checking to see if there is anything on the camera roll from today."

Kenzie waited. She realized Dr. Wiltshire expected to have to do the postmortem by himself tomorrow. Figuring she would stay home after her exhausting and traumatic day.

Even if she went in, Kenzie would probably be barred from being able to participate in Dana's postmortem because of the conflict of interest. She sighed.

"There is nothing on the camera roll from today," Dr. Wiltshire said. "Either she recorded it some time ago and just sent it today, then deleted it, or it came from somewhere else. Maybe there is a different phone. A second one. Or a cloud service set to deliver it at a certain time."

"Had she sent anything to Markov before? It sounded from the video like they were pretty close. She said before that Dr. Markov was her best friend."

"Yes. There were a number of messages over time. Let

me just look at it again." Dr. Wiltshire paused while he switched back to the messaging app. "It looks like mostly they shared jokes and memes," he observed. "Friendly, but not intimate. Last thing they exchanged was a funny cat video."

Kenzie got goosebumps. "Wait—a cat video?"

"Yes."

"From Markov or to her?"

"From Markov."

"A link or an attachment?"

"An attachment."

Alina's encryption key had only decrypted some of the files on the locket. Markov hadn't entrusted just one person with the key necessary to decrypt the files.

"Tell the electronic forensic guys upstairs that the video encryption key for the locket files is probably embedded in that video."

"I will do that," Wiltshire agreed. "Anything else?"

"Go home. Get a good night's sleep or you'll fall asleep in

the middle of the postmortem tomorrow," Kenzie teased.

"Yes, you're right. And you take tomorrow off. Take all the time you need. I can muddle along until you've finished your little vacation."

"Okay." Kenzie sighed. "You won't let me assist with Pratt's postmortem anyway, will you?"

"No. We can't allow any hint of conflict of interest. And I want you to get the help you need. You and Zachary have a therapist, don't you?"

He knew very well that they had couple's therapy every other Thursday.

"Yeah."

"Maybe tomorrow would be a good day to see her."

Kenzie rubbed her eyes, nodding. "Maybe it would."

CHAPTER 71

Kenzie had managed to schedule an emergency session with Dr. Boyle, since it was not their usual therapy day. And since the happenings at the clinic had been all over TV by the time Zachary and Kenzie finished—or didn't finish—eating their ice cream sundaes, Dr. B already knew the broad strokes of what had happened to Kenzie and made the time for her.

"Tell me how you're feeling, Kenzie," she encouraged. "I imagine you are having a lot of different emotions about this right now."

Kenzie nodded. "Yeah... it's all been kind of overwhelming. Yesterday, I thought I could just tough it out and get right back to work as usual. But today, it has started to hit me. It wasn't the same as before. I'm not sure why. Maybe because last time, the only person who knew about it was my dad, and he wanted it kept quiet. Neither of us wanted the police involved, it wasn't on the news, and Mom and Zachary didn't know. So it was easier to pretend it didn't happen and bury myself in work."

"And not deal with it."

"Yeah. This time... everybody knows. And I was pissed. I don't know why, but last time, I was terrified, and this time, I was furious. It was a totally different reaction. I'm still mad about it. I went through a lot more this time, fighting back, escaping, running away, and getting help. But instead of feeling more traumatized by it... I don't know. Maybe it's just because I'm talking about it right away, but I feel like it is manageable."

"Maybe you felt like you were more in control of your own fate, being able to escape like you did. Instead of being rescued by your father."

"Maybe."

"And you know that the people involved have been arrested. You know they can't come back after you again. It must feel good to have been able to do something about it."

Kenzie looked at Zachary for an instant, then nodded confirmation to Dr. Boyle. "Maybe that's it. Knowing that most of them are behind bars."

Dr. Boyle cocked her head. "Most of them? I thought that they got everyone who was at the hospital."

"Yeah. Everyone I could point out as being involved. But that isn't everyone. There are still staff members at Birch Valley who might have been involved, but weren't there. And the Russians... the police are trying to connect the head of the organization to the kidnapping and the other stuff that happened."

They had managed to decrypt the remainder of the files, and they were hoping to build a RICO case against the Oligarch.

"But they aren't able to?" Dr. B suggested.

"Cases like this can take months or years to build. It's a start, but even if they have enough information, they're not going to go out and arrest him today. He is still free. And he's not going to be stopped just because we got in his way or because the feds are trying to build a case against him. He's got a big network, and he's going to keep going until they stop him. Then, if they do get a bulletproof case against him… he'll probably flee the country before they arrest him."

With a mole somewhere in the police department, the oligarch would probably know about the state of the investigation before a warrant was issued for his arrest.

"So you don't have much hope that he'll be stopped."

"No," Kenzie admitted. "Probably not. And if he is… even if we manage to get him behind bars or he flees the country… someone else will just move in. Maybe someone from his organization. Maybe a rival. But we'll never be able to get rid of organized crime. People will always be willing to sell their souls for money or power."

Dr. Boyle looked at Kenzie steadily. “And how does that make you feel?”

There were many competing emotions. Fear and anxiety for herself and her parents. Frustration. Anger. Helplessness. Resignation.

But there was something else, too, something else that rose up against all of those other emotions.

“There might always be organized crime. People taking advantage of others through violence and corruption. But there will always be people who fight back, too. Even when they know that they can’t overcome the machine. I’m not going to stop.”

She looked at Zachary and took his hand.

“Zachary and my parents aren’t going to stop. We’ll do what we can to protect ourselves, but we won’t go quietly. The Oligarch may have money and men and resources, but he’ll never be able to overcome all resistance.”

She took a deep breath.

“Good people will never stop fighting for what is right.”

ABOUT THE AUTHOR

Award-winning Canadian author P.D. Workman has written over a hundred addictive page-turners featuring diverse and divergent sleuths, high-stakes investigations, and stories that linger long after the last page. Her books dive deep into characters' minds while exploring timely social issues through fast-paced, emotionally charged plots. Readers praise her work for its powerful emotional truth combined with unputdownable suspense.

Shunning sleep, when Workman is not writing, formatting, or marketing, she's probably running, reading, or spending time with her family.

P. D. Workman, does not shy from probing the deep psychological scars of childhood trauma, mental illness, and addiction. Also characteristic of this author, these extremely sensitive issues are explored with extensive empathy, described with incredible clarity, and portrayed with profound insight.

Kim, Goodreads reviewer

Some of Workman's titles have been translated into Spanish, French, Portuguese, German, and Italian.

Workman began writing at an early age and is a prolific reader as well as writer. She is also passionate about teaching and learning, expresses her creativity through art and cooking, and loves exploring the Calgary parks and green spaces where the Parks Pat Mysteries are set. She was a legal assistant for many years and has done extensive charitable work.

Workman was born and raised in Alberta, Canada, and is married with one adult son.

* * *

Check out her catalogue at pdworkman.com to start your next page-turner and sign up for news and special deals.

www.ingramcontent.com/pod-product-compliance
Lightning Source LLC
Chambersburg PA
CBHW081133300726
48982CB00005B/950
* 9 7 8 1 7 7 4 6 8 8 0 9 0 *